# Praise for Montecito

"Cox sensitively and intelligently explores Hollis' vulnerabilities, and out of that perceptive psychological profile spins a gripping crime drama. This is an engrossing story, both thoughtful and exciting. A marvelously entertaining suspense tale. OUR VERDICT: GET IT."

**—*Kirkus Reviews* (Critical Recommendation)**

"A compelling narrator and equally fascinating setting serve as a vehicle for this riveting tale. There's no rush to the storytelling on these pages. Both characters and situations expand little by little until the reader can finally see the whole situation. It's an immensely satisfying way to read. Montecito is like an exquisite little machine where all the moving parts slot impeccably together … Anyone interested in a compelling character-driven mystery will devour this story. It's unlike any crime novel I've read before but is no less gripping for it. This is an author I'll definitely be looking out for again."

**—Independent Book Review**

"Alive with realistic details, from the lifestyles of the mega-rich down to the business of stocks and free-trade zones, Montecito nudges readers to feel its protagonist's predicament—and dream along with Hollis of what it'd be like to have the billionaire lifestyle. But Cox spurs readers throughout to wonder at the cost of it all, especially as Hollis admits that there's "no ointment, gauze, or bandage that could shelter the devastation in my soul." To Hollis's credit, the answers aren't straightforward."

**—BookLife Reviews**

"With the beautiful backdrop set in Montecito, readers will love reading this story about a regular family making ends meet in a wealthy community. With forty-three-dollar coffee bills, ornate pizza ovens in backyards, freely pouring wine, and the beach a stone's throw from their doorstep, the people of Montecito are living large. Montecito will appeal to readers who enjoy a fantastic, nail-biting entrepreneurial scandal with twists and turns at every corner."

**—San Francisco Book Review (4.5 out of 5 stars)**

"Michael Cox showcases the immense promise of this smooth, professional, and highly competent writer. Readers are fully immersed in life most can only imagine, experiencing unimaginable highs and hellish lows. The realistic details, down to the most mundane yet hypnotic minutiae, bring this world beyond the fast lane to life in a truly gripping way."

**—Midwest Book Review**

# MONTECITO

*A Novel*

## Michael Cox

Printed in the United States of America

ISBN: 979-8-9879602-2-6 (paperback)

ISBN: 979-8-9879602-3-3 (E-book)

Cover Design by Karen Folsom Illustrations: https://kgfolsart.com/

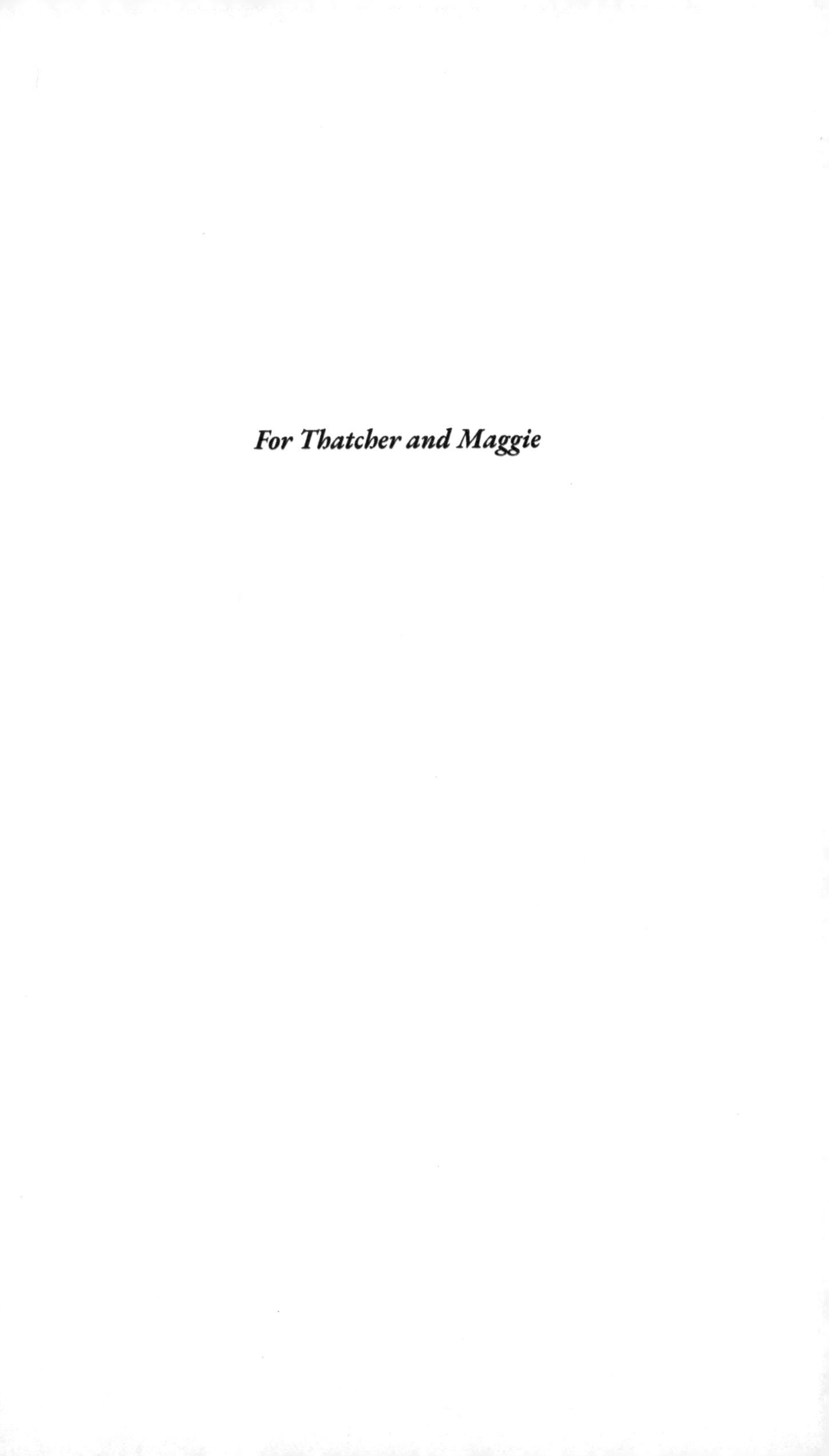

*For Thatcher and Maggie*

# MONTECITO

# CHAPTER ONE

As the knickknacks and novelties that formerly adorned my office rattled unhappily in the trunk of my car, I wondered how different my life would be if I had been born with the slightest understanding of when to keep my mouth shut. Nothing extraordinary, mind you, just enough good sense to recognize when my opinion was not needed, when a point had been made, when to nod and smile instead of argue. Considering that this was the third time in the last seven years I had been told to clean out my office, it certainly couldn't have hurt.

Fueled by frustration and self-pity, I took one of Highway 192's tight curves with the gas pedal mashed toward the floor. My endorphin rush evaporated the moment my rearview mirror flashed the sight of my cardboard box of trinkets flying from one trunk sidewall to the other. The ensuing sound of breaking glass reverberated like a well-earned *I told you so.* I thought of the one family photo I had proudly displayed on my former desk: my daughter, Isabel, in braces, squinting into the sun; my son, Trip, in a Stephen Curry jersey that hung to his knees; my wife Cricket's sun-kissed arms draped over them both. The bright, optimistic eyes of my family begging me for an explanation through a spiderweb of cracks.

While indignation partially explained my lead foot, I also had a practical reason for driving too fast. I was late for my kids' elementary school recital: the Spring Sing. I had already missed the beginning of the recital, but I could make it there for the finale. I had texted Cricket before I started the car: *Running late, but I will be there. Don't save my seat. Sorry.* The rest of my disappointing news could wait.

My serpentine route from downtown Santa Barbara to the Montecito Union Elementary School was not for the faint of heart. Alternately known as Foothill, Mountain, Mission Ridge, Stanwood, Sycamore Canyon, or East Valley Road—depending on where you merged—Highway 192 was a quintessentially local road. Its twists, double backs, sudden stop signs, and random name changes had no explanation. It was a road you learned only by getting lost, making it a perfect metaphor for my rattled state of mind.

Twenty-five minutes later, I put my Subaru Outback in park and walked past a rainbow of Teslas, Range Rovers, and BMWs, through the school's arched breezeway, and into the auditorium lobby, where all the other shamefully late parents crowded the doorway, craning their necks to see and be seen.

All except one, that is. Standing in the corner of the lobby, with a cell phone pressed to his ear, was a dapperly suited man I had never seen before. He stood at least six foot four and paced a triangle while conducting an orchestra with his free hand—a hand that even from my distant vantage appeared disproportionately large. I could not hear his voice for the sound of the elementary singers, but it was safe to call his conversation animated.

I returned my attention to the performance, hoping to find the eyes of my people. Cricket would be sitting where she always sat: center section, fifth row, just behind the parents and grandparents who had purchased multi-thousand-dollar reserved seats at the school's annual gala. I teetered on my tippy-toes and found the back of her head, her glistening chestnut hair reflecting the sunlight streaming from the auditorium's windows. The chair next to her was still empty; I cringed. Cricket had left her job on time, arrived early, secured the seats, and likely fended off inquiries from multiple parents. *Sorry! It's for Hollis,* she would have said, defending the territory for my feckless honor. While the fallout from my most recent rendezvous with unemployment was only beginning to blossom, this smaller failing stung immediately like a cold slap.

In the gaggle of performers, I first spotted Isabel, our fifth grader. She was stage left, middle row, and appeared to be singing through giggles. Next I caught sight of my son Trip's right arm, waving at me from the top row of the stage-right first graders. Judging by the way his body swayed, he too was on his tippy-toes, hoping to find *his* people in the mass of parents. Found me he had, there among the truants.

Just as I raised my arm to return Trip's wave, a gargantuan hand landed on my shoulder. "What have I missed?" I heard the hand's owner say as the unexpected weight of his appendage toppled me sideways. My elbow came down on the head of the woman beside me, sending her iPhone clattering to the floor.

"What the hell, Hollis?" The woman groaned, both hands clasping the top of her head.

"I am so sorry," I groveled. I did not know my victim's name, but she knew me, adding to my shame. "I..." I looked back at the man whose massive hand had caused me to fall and recognized him as the same man who had been having the spirited phone conversation in the corner of the lobby minutes earlier. He looked at me wide-eyed, his hand hovering in the air like a satellite; I resisted the urge to lay blame. "I lost my balance," I explained.

"Fine," she grumbled, reaching through a sea of legs for her phone, currently videoing the nothingness of the tile floor.

I turned back toward the singers, pretending that I hadn't just executed a professional wrestler's flying elbow on a fellow parent. My victim, and the gawkers surrounding us, followed suit, allowing the awkwardness to dissipate. When the coast was clear, the owner of the giant hand bent down to my height and repeated his whisper: "So, what have I missed?"

I took the stranger in for the second time that afternoon. On a good day the man had four inches on me; today it felt more like a foot. With his wavy blue-black hair, mocha skin, and impossibly white teeth, it was hard not to stare. His nose was Roman, his accent British with a pinch of Middle Eastern, his long fingers—now intertwined at his waist—were skeletal, like those of the Dementors in Harry Potter's nightmares. "Not much," I said, suspecting that he was not interested in a serious recounting of the recital's milestones, though I was not sure; I was never sure.

"Cyrus. Cyrus Wimby," he said, extending his tentacled hand.

"Nice to meet you," I said.

"And you are?"

"Oh, sorry," I said. "Hollis Crawford."

"Shhhh!" said the woman I had cracked in the head seconds earlier.

I shrank at her admonition, cutting my eyes to Cyrus. He raised his eyebrows and shrugged. "You have a child performing today, my friend?" he whispered.

"Yes, two," I whispered back. "A fifth grader and a first grader." I began to point, then realized the futility. "You?"

"I have a first grader as well," he said. "What is your child's name?"

"His name is Trip," I answered.

"How ironic!" Cyrus said, putting all thirty-two sterling teeth on display. "My daughter's name is Priscilla; our children are in the same class."

"Huh," I said, wondering whether I sounded aloof or clueless. Remembering names was not one of my strengths. I knew none of Trip's classmates' names and *almost* none of Isabel's, even though she had been a student at Montecito Union for six, going on seven, years. Certainly I'd heard plenty of stories involving a disproportionate number of kids named Sophia, Jackson, Dylan, and Riley, but the individuals themselves remained faceless.

"I'm almost certain of it," he said. "I never forget a name."

"That makes one of us," I said, which made him laugh.

"Tell me, Hollis," he said. "Do you golf?"

"No."

"Are you a horseman?"

I contemplated cracking a joke about not being a *horse*-man but a *hu*-man—a joke I was certain would have killed it—but I paused. *Maybe just play it straight for once, Hollis,* my inner voice —which sounded a lot like Cricket's—counseled. "No. I don't ride horses," I answered.

He shook his head. "Okay then. Do you like wine?"

I pursed my lips, considering the question. I did enjoy a glass of wine, but in Santa Barbara County, *liking* wine sometimes carried a deeper meaning. People in Montecito and Santa Barbara did not just *like* wine; they *owned* wineries. Santa Ynez and Los Olivos—made famous by the book and movie *Sideways*—were a half hour away, and wine-tasting rooms dotted State Street, the Funk Zone, and Coast Village Road. Wine, horses, boats, golfing, and surfing: These were not the mere pastimes of Santa Barbara County, but its passions. And since I could not surf, did not enjoy riding horses, got seasick on boats, and possessed a golf game best suited to a mini-golf course, I defaulted to *liking* wine with just enough zeal to retain my local-in-good-standing badge. "Yes. I like wine," I answered with an enthusiastic nod.

"Fabulous," he said as the children finished their finale and the crowd rose for a standing ovation. "Bravo!" Cyrus hollered over the heads of the rest of us in the lobby, then put two pipe-sized fingers in his mouth for an earsplitting whistle.

"Wine it is, then," he said, placing his palm back on my shoulder, his fingers reaching past my scapula. "Let us put a date on the calendar to get together for a glass."

"Oh," I muttered. "Okay." Was I progressing to a man date with this stranger, or was he just being friendly? I needed Cricket by my side to interpret these hieroglyphic social cues. That was how our marriage partnership worked: Cricket was my high-EQ social butterfly, translating the signals that were so obvious to everyone else. When it came to reading people, I was *in the fog*, as Cricket kindly put it.

Cyrus removed his hand from my shoulder and thrust it back toward my chest. I reflexively extended mine only to see it swallowed in a two-handed sandwich. "Now, I must be off to find my wife in that crowd. She will not be happy that I abandoned her during Priscilla's first school recital."

"You and me both," I said, surprised by the easy camaraderie I felt with this stranger. Unfortunately, his comment also reminded me of the 99 percent of my day preceding this moment and the painful conversations that still lay in front of me.

"Genevieve," Cyrus hollered through cupped hands over the heads of the crowd now pushing toward us. "Gather Priscilla, and I'll meet you in the courtyard."

Again, he turned to me. "See you soon, Hollis Crawford," he said, and in two giant strides he was gone.

# Chapter Two

To her credit, Cricket took the news of my latest failure with remarkable grace. If I had shown a tenth as much decorum in the face of disappointing news, I might still be employed. Nevertheless, I could tell she was frustrated with me. For months, she had listened to my growing complaints about CryptoWallet—my former employer—*cutting corners, lowering standards,* and her favorite, *destroying product integrity.* With a gentle smile, she warned me that she had seen this movie several times before and that it did not have a happy ending. When I would get particularly animated, she would remind me that sometimes in life, one needed to *go along to get along.* I nodded in acquiescence, though I had no idea what the hell that meant.

Cricket's trite suggestions were not recycled mom-speak. They were the cold truths of corporate survival. Iron laws that she had mastered, while I—theoretical head of the family—stomped on the business end of a rake like a cartoon fool. This was the ironic twist to my professional narrative: I had tremendous skills, but Cricket was the far better entrepreneur, employee, and executive. She was quite literally my better half.

Desperate to be of some use to the family, I vowed to take over the role of getting the kids to school and picking them up until I found another paying gig. This modest offer would allow Cricket to rejoin the Masters swimming program at Los Baños Del Mar, where she could pound water for seventy-five minutes before her workday began. Swimming was Cricket's private passion; she had been an All-American at the University of California, Santa Barbara, adding *better athlete* to her list of marital superlatives.

My first day as the kids' unpaid valet was a Friday, but not just any Friday. It was Flag Day at Montecito Union, affectionately known by the locals as MUS. On Flag Day, instead of reporting to their classrooms, the kids would gather in the school's central courtyard, sing the school song, hear announcements and perhaps a special presentation, then be off to start their day—all under the watchful eye of a surprisingly large group of parents who had nowhere else to be and plenty of time to get there.

"Sounds good," I said to Cricket as she reminded me of this on her way out the door with her heavy swim bag over one shoulder and steely determination in her eyes.

Correctly decoding the *why are you telling me this* look on my face, she added, "Parents are encouraged to stay for Flag Day."

I stared back blankly.

"I want you there," she clarified.

"Oh," I said. "Right. You bet." I forced a smile as she pulled the door closed, then slumped in chauvinistic shame as my mind played a black-and-while movie reel from the 1950s. There I was, center screen, standing in a crowd of clapping mommies while the mighty men of valor charged into the fields, armed with bows and arrows to gather the day's kill. As dated and mistaken as this mental image was, I was no less mortified.

At breakfast, Trip presented me with a permission slip for the following week's off-campus field trip. "What are you kids doing?" I asked.

"Horseback riding," he answered.

"Horseback who?" I replied incredulously, imagining ambulance-chasing lawyers licking their lips at the prospect of first-grade heirs to millionaire fortunes bouncing along the narrow trails in the Los Padres National Forest.

"Priscilla got a horse for her birthday," Trip explained, "and her dad rented out the stable so we can all go riding!"

"Priscilla?" I asked, recognizing the name as vaguely familiar.

"Priscilla Wimby," Isabel chimed in, balancing a cereal bowl, a spoon, and a gallon of milk atop a sideways-turned Cheerios box. "They're, like, super-rich."

*Wimby.* That was the name of the man with the obscenely long fingers who seemingly tried to make friends with me during the Spring Sing. Rare as they were, I did not forget people who tried to befriend me. Funny that I had never seen nor heard of Cyrus Wimby before yesterday, and now I had a two-day streak going.

"Do you *want* to ride a horse?" I asked.

"Shuh, Dad," he said, repeating a new phrase of his sister's.

"Then ride you shall," I said, signing the permission slip with a flourish. Trip said, "Thank you," while Isabel rolled her eyes at my dramatic flair.

The kids finished their breakfast, brushed their teeth, announced they were ready to go, and then disappeared. I wandered the house calling their names to no answer. Then I walked out the front door and found them sitting in my Subaru. "Let's go, Dad," Trip called.

"We're not driving. Out!" I demanded, waving them from the car like a traffic cop. "We live a mile from school; it's sunny out. We're walking."

"The valet line is really easy, Dad," Trip protested, reluctantly disembarking and securing his backpack.

"Valet?" I repeated, my face a scowl.

"Yeah," Isabel said. "All you have to do is pull up. The assistant principal and three teachers swarm the car, open the doors, unbuckle the little kids, and pull them out. It takes, like, ten seconds, and you don't have to move a muscle. Easy peasy."

"Yeah, Dad," Trip added, "it's like one of those race cars getting new tires."

My inner grumpy old man petitioned for a chance to speak. He wanted to lecture the kids about walking to school in snow, about yellow buses with no seat belts controlled by seat-hoarding gangs. But I told the old man to put his hand down. The kids had heard his stories before, and I did not want to invite more eye-rolling from Isabel.

After twenty minutes of grunts and monosyllabic replies, we arrived to find MUS bustling for its monthly celebration. This was not my first rodeo, yet I always managed to banish the memory of MUS in its all-hands-on-deck glory as if it were a dream. Laughably, this was because—when I was still employed at CryptoWallet—I spent my days on the relative mean streets of Santa Barbara, Montecito's larger, better-known northwestern neighbor. Despite the proximity, Montecito was a cocoon unto itself, and MUS—one of the premier elementary schools in the state of California—was its centerpiece. The school's average class size was fifteen students with two full-time teachers per classroom. The second graders got violins; fourth graders got cellos; personal computers were doled out like No. 2 pencils—all of it made possible by the enormous property taxes paid by Oprah Winfrey, Ellen DeGeneres, Rob Lowe, Ty Warner, and the countless other millionaires who called Montecito home.

Though we dreamed of owning a house in this paradise, the truth was, Cricket and I could not yet afford Montecito. With ambitious plans and small pocketbooks, we put off our goal of home ownership and rented a tiny, overpriced place in the MUS school district—our version of fake it till you make it. A tactical, long-game choice based on the assumption that my career was in its ascendancy.

It was a reasonable plan with one unavoidable flaw: me.

Isabel and Trip joined their classmates, sitting crisscross applesauce in the courtyard, while the parents stood, surrounding them like an amphitheater audience. A quick scan of the crowd revealed my premonition about the *mommies* to be ignorant nonsense—there were more fathers in attendance than mothers. Feeling shameful jealousy and resentment, I watched my fellow parents sip their soy lattes and cold-pressed celery juices as they shared upcoming weekend plans and talked of last night's Lumineers concert at the Santa Barbara Bowl. A mental health therapist would have taken one look at my state of mind and cleared their calendar for a month.

Flag Day began with the Pledge of Allegiance followed by the school song, a beautiful tune written by Montecito resident Kenny Loggins of "Footloose" and "Danger Zone" fame. Only the best for Montecito.

MUS's principal took the microphone, making announcements about the upcoming sixth-grade play and new iPad Pros for the kindergartners before turning the microphone over to the president of the school's PTA.

"The deadline for participating in our Annual Fund is only a week away," Mr. PTA president began. "As you all know, the expected contribution is one thousand dollars per family. Of course, you are welcome to give more." He paused for a few rolled-eye chuckles. "This year, I am proud to say that we already have ninety-two percent participation at or above the expected contribution level!"

The parents and students clapped as expected, but I cowered. Cricket had been hounding me to write our check for the Annual Fund for weeks. Every time she mentioned it, I swore I would take care of it. I even had the gall to act like she was being a nag.

Needless to say, I had *not* taken care of it. I was one of the 8 percent of the school that had not met the *expected contribution* level, and worse, I had given nothing. I am sure some of my fellow scofflaws had given what they could, but how many had done zippo like me? Fair or not, I had to write that check. I would not feel comfortable on this campus ever again unless I did. But oh, how badly would that $1,000-drain feel now that I was unemployed.

Panic gurgled in my stomach. As great as this school was, as beautiful as this town was, as happy as my wife and children were here, I was failing.

I reflexively took a step back from the swarm of children as the school's computer science teacher announced that two new 3D printers and one new laser cutter machine would be fully operational in time for the upcoming science fair.

Another step back. I wanted to disappear; I needed to flee.

Another step back.

I crossed my arms over my chest and tucked my chin, shrinking from the crowd.

Another step back and then a yelp.

"Whoa there" came the voice of the man whose toe I had just stepped on.

I turned, embarrassment lighting my face on fire. "I'm so sorry," I muttered.

"It is no problem, my friend," the man said, patting me gently on the shoulder with a hand the size of a palmetto frond. It was Cyrus Wimby.

I glanced down at his foot—size 16, at least. I felt slightly better about my mistake; he was practically wearing skis. As yesterday, Cyrus was dressed like a man who had business to attend to: wool slacks, polished cap toes, French-cuffed shirt with an English spread collar. By description, it was general business casual. But even a fashion dolt like me could tell that his clothes were elegant. He had accepted the tieless norm of a coastal California businessman, but that did not mean he had to look like a slouch.

I nodded—a normal shade of pasty returning to my face as I repeated my "sorry"—and turned back toward the sea of children.

"Yesterday it was that poor lady's head," Cyrus whispered in my ear. "Today it is my foot. You're a dangerous man, Hollis Crawford."

Another cringe; the expression was becoming my default. Though I suspected Cyrus was joking, I wanted to crawl under a rock. "That was, uh, nice of you to invite the class to go horse riding at your, uh, stable," I stammered, hoping to change the subject.

"Oh." He shook his head. "We only have four horses. It is hardly a stable."

Four horses seemed like a lot of horses to a horseless man, but I accepted his attempt at humility. "Well—still—thank you," I whispered, making sure not to draw the ire of the art teacher, who was excitedly informing the crowd of parents about the school's new ceramics kiln.

"You are so welcome, my friend." Each time I thought Cyrus's grin could get no larger, his lips spread further. Was it possible that he had extra teeth? "We are new to town," he continued. "It is hard on Priscilla to drag her from place to place. We thought this might help her make new friends."

"Where did you move from?" I asked.

"Most recently, we were back in my native Saudi Arabia. Before that, we bounced between Shanghai and Beijing for my work. Before that, Paris, where I met my darling Genevieve." He paused to pull a drawn-to-perfection creature from the crowd. "Sweetest," he said, "this is Hollis Crawford."

"Bonjour! Enchanté," Genevieve said, brushing past my outstretched hand to kiss my cheek. "So wonderful to meet you."

I blushed as if there were something intimate about a cheek-kiss greeting.

Genevieve was at least a foot shorter than Cyrus, but—thanks to a pair of ankle-breaking wedge espadrilles—she managed to cut the gap by almost one-third. Unlike most of the moms attending Flag Day, she was not dressed for Pilates; she looked plucked from the pages of *ELLE*. Her large, wide-set eyes were steel gray flecked with green, like emeralds mined from granite. She wore a perfume of star jasmine so perfectly scented that my eyes darted left and right in search of a flowering vine. Whereas Cyrus was roughly forty years old, Genevieve could not have been a day over thirty, but she tried to mask her youth with makeup. It gave the effect of a teenager playing grown-up and left me with a slight dirty-old-man feeling.

Her French was as pitch-perfect as her English, the sort of mastery that suggested she might have other languages and accents in her tool belt as well. And while she was as thin as a runway model, nothing about her seemed frail. In fact, despite her warm smile and gracious greeting, I was instinctively intimidated. As several of my prior bosses would attest, this was a unique feeling for me. I tended to be too unaware to recognize when I should have been intimidated and thus deferential. I almost laughed. Of all the people to trigger such a response, there was no reason it should accrue to a young, just over five-foot-tall stunner like Genevieve. The metaphorical *fog* Cricket said I walked in was downright soupy that morning.

"Nice to meet you, too," I said, finally dropping my gaze. Genevieve possessed the kind of beauty that was hard to look at for too long without feeling like you were gawking.

The crowd of children erupted in applause. Without my noticing, Flag Day was over.

"This is the man I met yesterday," Cyrus said to Genevieve as the crowd around us broke up and dispersed. "His son, Trip, is in Priscilla's class. He and I were having such an enjoyable conversation that I lost track of time and missed out on the end of the recital." Cyrus turned his head back toward me and gave me a nearly imperceptible wink.

Even from the *fog*, I understood the meaning of his wink.

"How lovely," Genevieve said. "Priscilla raves about Trip."

"I said the same thing, my dear," Cyrus added.

"Who is your wife, Hollis?" Genevieve asked. "Do I know her?"

"Well, probably," I answered. "Her name is Cricket, and—"

"Oh my, Cyrus!" Genevieve said, grabbing her husband by the elbow. "Cricket! She's the one I was telling you about. The adorable room mother for Priscilla's class. Oh, Hollis"—she turned her eyes back to me—"I have been dying to get to know your wife. Do you have plans for this Sunday afternoon? We are hosting a dinner party, and we would love the pleasure of your family's company."

"Oh," I said, my eyes wide. Cricket managed our social lives, briefing me only when necessary. This was efficiency at its finest, as I almost never made plans for anything. "I'm...I'm not sure," I stammered, turning my eyes back to Cyrus, pleading for man-to-man help.

"Your wife is named Cricket?" he asked, ignoring my SOS. "Is that her given name?"

"Stop it right this instant, Cyrus!" Genevieve said, slapping him with the back of her hand. "I won't have that rudeness."

Cyrus put his hands to his heart, feigning a wound. "My deepest apologies, Hollis."

"No offense taken," I said, "at least, not by me. Cricket is indeed her given name, and she wears it well."

Genevieve grabbed both of my hands as if we were about to do-si-do. "So, you'll come on Sunday? Really, you must."

I did not enjoy being touched by strangers, and between the kiss hello and the hand-holding, I was distinctly uncomfortable. Despite this, I managed to smile and nod affirmatively, hoping Cricket would be pleased by my foray into social planning.

Cyrus's phone rang. He whipped it from his pocket. "Apologies, I have to answer this. It's after midnight in Shanghai, so this call must be urgent." He pushed the Accept button, then placed the phone to his chest, hooking Genevieve's arm to leave. "It's settled then. Our place at five p.m. on Sunday." He returned the phone to his ear and gently tugged Genevieve's arm as the pair disappeared into the crowd.

# CHAPTER THREE

Even as Cricket, Trip, Isabel, and I were en route to the Wimbys' home for dinner, Cricket still couldn't quite believe that I had managed to—as she put it—"make a plan." Perhaps I should have been offended, but I wasn't. In thirteen years of marriage, I couldn't remember doing it once; her shock was justified. And my claim of having made plans with the Wimbys sounded even more dubious when Cricket initially asked me what I knew about Cyrus Wimby, and I racked my brain to come up with this mind-blowing insight: "He has very long fingers."

She shook her head. "What about Genevieve?"

To this question, more potential answers presented themselves. Should I mention the swimsuit-model curves? The kiss hello that made me blush? The nearly waist-length blond hair parted in the middle with the precision of a sculptor; straight at first and then erupting into a cascade of waves. "She has very short fingers," I decided to divulge. "So ironic."

As we piled into the Subaru for the short drive to the Wimbys' home, Cricket—as was her custom before any social occasion— reminded me what I was expected to know about the people I was soon to drink and dine with. The Wimbys had come to Montecito by way of Paris, Riyadh, Shanghai, and Beijing. Cyrus's father was a Kiwi, his mother a member of the Saudi royal family. They skied in Zermatt—where Genevieve's parents owned a home—and summered in Fiji—where Cyrus was becoming quite the surfer. Genevieve was once a chef, schooled at the Sorbonne. In fact, Cyrus met her in a restaurant in Paris after telling the waiter that he had to personally deliver his compliments to the kitchen. They had only one child, Priscilla; Genevieve had lost two others by miscarriage. Once Cyrus's new business was launched, they planned to adopt several more children from Africa.

"Why am I expected to know all of that?" I challenged. "Cyrus told me maybe five percent of that information. Why would I know the rest? It feels...invasive."

Cricket laughed as I made a left from Hot Springs Road onto the Wimbys' street, Riven Rock. "What can I say, Hollis? The Wimbys are an open book."

I pulled up to the Wimbys' security gate and took a nervous breath. There was another reason Cricket might have been trying so hard to make sure I was well informed about tonight's dinner hosts: the prospect of gainful employment for me. Further to the rumor mill, Cyrus Wimby was a business tycoon set to launch his next venture from the shores of Montecito. "Maybe he needs someone?" Cricket suggested the previous evening. "Maybe he needs you?"

She did not need to say anything else. We both understood that our family's survival on the Montecito treadmill required an economic contribution from me. Without one, our family's life was in for a major shakeup.

As I reached for the Wimbys' security gate call button with a slightly shaky finger, the realization that I wasn't just an attendee at a dinner party—itself cause for anxiety—but potentially auditioning for a job, gave me a sudden urge to throw the car into reverse and flee like a bank robber. I closed my eyes and took a deep breath, steeling my nerves. Perhaps this was one of those miraculous right-place-right-time moments? I had already survived mashing the guy's toes, right?

The security gates slowly parted, temporarily replacing my anxiety with anticipation. Like nearly all Montecito homes, the Wimbys lived behind a ten-foot hedge with a security gate designed to repel marauding hordes. From the street, one could only assume what was on the other side. Surprisingly, sometimes the homes behind the hedges were modest. Other times, the yawning gates revealed a nirvana of gardens and pools with a home stolen from the Mediterranean coast. Because you never knew what you would see when the gates opened, there was always a feeling of Christmas morning as you were buzzed into a new enclave for the first time. I felt a twinge of pity for Cyrus and Genevieve; thanks to the gossipy rumor mill, our collective expectations were unfairly high.

But as the maw of the gates fully opened, I saw that my pity was misplaced. The Wimbys' brilliant white home rambled, doing its best to downplay dimensions, but there was no hiding its glory. A one-hundred-foot reflecting pond with lily pads, croaking frogs, and massive koi ran from the home's front door like a giant tongue lapping its visitors inside. The crushed-stone driveway meandered forever as I crept along, taking in the scenery and looking for a place to park. Two Range Rovers and a fleet of sparkling white Porsches—911 Carrera, Turbo Cayenne, and Macan S (the nanny's loaner, I was to learn)—were parked just outside a garage that was bigger than our house.

Quickly, I considered my Subaru—which had not been washed in more than a month—and kept driving. Farther down, I found a turnaround shaded by pin oaks and parked my car. "You could park in Fresno if that would make you feel better," Cricket said, opening her door. Her ability to be comfortable, no matter the status or wealth of the crowd, amazed me. I was too self-conscious, calculating differentials and concluding my inferiority. She was unabashed, confident she belonged no matter the setting. I was not even confident that I belonged with her.

Isabel and Trip brought their bathing suits as instructed. We had not yet seen the pool, but the kids took off running instinctively like turtle hatchlings to the sea. I took Cricket's hand, and we retraced the driveway to the front door.

What I missed when I drove by the entrance the first time—distracted by the reflecting pond—was the front door's greeter, holding a silver tray of wineglasses. She was young, petite, with short-cropped black hair and an eager smile—a quintessential girl next door. "Welcome. Would you care for some Entre Nous wine? We're showcasing the Pinot Noir, Sauvignon Blanc, and the just-released rosé."

Cricket took the rosé; I took the pinot. "Entre Nous?" I asked.

"It's Mr. Wimby's new label," the greeter told me with an excited smile. "We're debuting it today."

I arched my eyebrows at Cricket, but she was too busy taking in the home. It looked like a slightly shrunken five-star resort with designer touches that I could not name but no less respected. There were no Lego bricks, no Nerf bullets, and no framed pictures of I-Love-You-Mom drawings. "What do you call this style?" I asked Cricket.

"Rich," she said over her shoulder.

A short stroll from the grandest of the Wimbys' three living rooms, we found the pool, where the rest of the party—five other adults and eight children—was already settled in. Isabel and Trip were lined up for the diving board; yes, there was an honest-to-God, spring-loaded diving board, one that lawyers and insurance companies had apparently missed in their mission to eradicate backyard fun. Cyrus and Genevieve were seated on pristine white outdoor couches with the other guests but rose to greet us as we approached. Again, I tried to shake hands with Genevieve, and again, my hand was brushed aside for a cheek kiss.

"You own a winery?" I blurted, instantly aware that everything about my tone and question was uncouth. Ironically, it could have been worse: My initial thought was to ask how they kept these couches so white.

Cyrus laughed. "You know what they say. A winery is an efficient way to make a small fortune ..."

"...out of a big fortune," Genevieve chimed in, completing the line they had no doubt delivered to other tone-deaf fools who had not known better than to ask.

"The rosé is lovely," Cricket said. "Cheers, and thank you for having us."

Genevieve clinked glasses, then whisked Cricket away to a secluded gathering of wives, her star jasmine perfume lingering in her wake.

Cricket's departure left me alone in the company of Cyrus and his male guests, who instantly assumed that I was a fellow Alpha; a predator taking leave from the hunt to socialize and count pelts. I stood taller, puffed out my meager chest, and attempted to stand in for the role. Meanwhile, Cricket circled with the wives, posing as a lady who lunches. Neither of us would have traded circles, but we were both miscast.

"Hollis, do you know Barton?" Cyrus asked. "He lives just off Channel Drive and has two daughters at Cate."

I did not know Barton, but I was grateful that he was a handshaker. Cate was a prestigious, international boarding school, more expensive than most private colleges and located five miles away in Carpinteria. "Nice to meet you," I said.

"And this here is my good friend, longtime business partner, and current houseguest, Landon," Cyrus said, tipping his wineglass toward a sour-looking man with alabaster skin, pale green eyes, and hair so red it was unmistakably orange. "Landon is visiting us from Palm Springs, here to put the finishing touches on the launch of our next and biggest venture yet."

My pulse quickened. The rumor that Cyrus had another gem up his sleeve was true.

"We'll see about that," Landon said, slamming several ounces of wine in one swallow, then raising his empty glass to catch the attention of one of Cyrus's staff.

I wanted to leap at this first pitch opportunity to unpack Cyrus and Landon's venture. What was it? How big would it be? And most importantly, did they have any use for a thrice-fired technology wiz? But prior to our arrival, Cricket had cautioned me not to appear too eager. Instead, she advised that I *stay chill*, which I then asked her to define. Definition in hand, I decided that launching into a barrage of questions ninety seconds after being introduced might qualify as the opposite of staying *chill*.

"Barton, how do you and Cyrus know each other?" I asked instead.

"We don't really," Barton said, chuckling. "My wife met Genevieve last week, and already it seems they are BFFs. I think I am just along for the ride. No offense, Cyrus."

"None taken," Cyrus said, nodding at Barton and then turning back to me. "Barton's wife, Evelyn, is on the board of trustees for Lotusland. Genevieve reached out about a corporate donation from my new company, and...well...the rest is history." Cyrus again rerouted his gaze back to Barton. "I'm sure we will fill in the gaps and catch up to the ladies soon enough."

I knew Lotusland, though I had never been. It was a botanical garden of exotic plants, walking trails, and manicured ponds, occupying forty acres of Montecito's gilded hillsides. This was not your typical public park, however. I investigated purchasing tickets to take the family one weekend, but balked when I realized it would cost $150 for the four of us to take a self-guided tour through Lotusland's curated trails. I did not like plants *that* much.

"How are you enjoying your visit to Montecito, Landon?" I asked.

Landon shrugged. "It's fine," he said. "I take off tomorrow. Going to take in a sunrise surf and then head back to Palm Springs."

"We'll see about that too," Cyrus said with narrowed eyes and an insistent grin. "You and I still have business to finalize, Landon, and you don't know how to surf."

Landon shook his head. "Our business *is* finalized, Cyrus. And, as to the surfing, I can figure it out. It isn't rocket science."

Cyrus rolled his eyes. "Well," he said, shifting gears and saving me from the feeling of having wandered into an uncomfortable family squabble. "Now that Hollis is here, let's take the tour." He stood, gathered his wineglass, and motioned for us to join him. "Come."

We dutifully followed, walking past the pool and its expansive patio to find a pizza oven housed in what looked like an igloo for a family of fifty Eskimos. A six-feet-tall, ten-feet-wide stack of almond firewood sat astride, waiting to supply the required five hundred degrees of heat. A short, stout Latino man in white apron and cartoonish chef's hat was minding the oven and adding logs.

"Holy cow," I said.

"Impressive," Barton said.

Landon chugged more wine.

"Indeed, my friends. Wait until you sample Genevieve's pizzas. You will never look at the humble pie the same way again."

I drank my wine faster than usual—though not nearly as fast as Landon—summoning liquid courage to broach the topic of Cyrus's business ventures in a manner Cricket would designate as *chill.* "So, is Entre Nous your new business enterprise?" I asked.

Cyrus looked hurt. "No, no, my friend. Wine is a hobby, not a business."

"Oh," I said, flummoxed by this delicate dance. Subtlety was not my strength, and moreover, it was inefficient. Why couldn't I just ask the question whose answer I sought?

Our group continued past the pizza oven, along a pea-gravel path that wound through a rose and herb garden and then crested a small ridge depositing us beside a putting green that was bigger than my front yard.

"Gentlemen, grab a stick," Cyrus said, pointing to a teak

cabinet filled with expensive-looking putters of various sizes and configurations. "Drive for show, putt for dough."

*It's just manicured mini golf,* my inner voice calmed. I picked out a putter, grabbed a ball, and headed away from the others to a hole centered in the flattest part of the green.

"Landon," Cyrus continued, "why don't you fill Hollis in on our latest gambit?"

"Not *our*," Landon said, sailing a twenty-foot putt past his target and into the sand trap beyond. "*Your* latest gambit."

"Now, now, Landon," Cyrus said, calmly sinking a twelve-footer into the same hole Landon had missed. "No one knows this story better than you." He waited for Landon to finish raking his ball out of the sand trap, then locked eyes on him until Landon returned his gaze. "Please, Landon. Humor me."

Landon broke the tractor beam of Cyrus's stare and nudged his golf ball to the green's fringe with the toe of his shoe. "It's pretty simple really," he said, bending over his ball, taking a practice swing, and adjusting his stance. "The company has acquired an extraordinarily rare asset that will allow it to single-handedly change the face of global trade." He took another practice swing, this one a little less aggressive. "The asset is a Free Trade Zone License issued by the Chinese government," he continued. "We are the first company outside of mainland China and Hong Kong to receive such a license, and the Chinese government has assured us that we have an exclusive right to use the license for the next twenty years."

"What do you do with this license?" Barton asked Landon, leaning raptly on his putter.

Landon looked up from his ball; Cyrus returned his gaze with a sly wink. "Tell him."

Landon again focused on his ball, brought the putter back in a steady parabola, swung with a far defter touch than his practice swings suggested, and sent his ball delicately scooting thirty feet of the green's terrain before bull's-eyeing the cup.

"Nice putt," I said; no one else commented.

"What do we do with the license?" Landon repeated. "We level the playing field."

"How so?" Barton asked, his arms crossed and his putter propped against his leg.

Landon cocked his head and grinned, beginning a slow walk to retrieve his ball. "Through our company, international retailers from Levi Strauss to Ralph Lauren—from Miami to Milan—can sell their goods to more than one billion Chinese nationals free and clear of the taxes and duties that would normally either kill their margins or make their products too expensive. We level the playing field. We enable global commerce."

Cyrus smiled like a proud papa. "I notice you said both *our* and *we* there, Landon."

Landon shook his head. "Slip of the tongue."

"Wow," Barton said, ignoring their insider squabble. "Are you looking for investors? Because I think a lot of folks around here would be interested in this story."

Cyrus shrugged. "Not really, Barton. No." He bent over a putt of his own. "I could see allowing someone to invest as a favor, but we don't need any additional capital."

"I hear you," Barton said. "I hear you. Well, if you're in the mood to hand out favors, count me as a gracious recipient. I would love to have you over to the Birnam Wood Club to introduce you to some of my friends. They like favors, too."

Cyrus shrugged again. "Sure. Why not?"

I could feel the focus shift toward investors with millions of disposable dollars and away from employees in need of paychecks, so I jumped in—*chill* or not. "Why don't you want to be part of this, Landon?" I asked. "It sounds exciting."

My question brought all eyes back to Landon, but he focused only on Cyrus. "It will be exciting," he said. "That's for certain."

I waited as seconds of silence ticked by, hoping for elaboration.

"I guess," Landon finally provided, "it's because Cyrus and I disagree about the value I bring to the equation. And unless my value is fully realized, I've got better things to do."

I nodded, again trying to wait for my open door. "I see, well..." I said, gingerly approaching the point of no return. "Cyrus, if you want to add another member to your team, it just so happens that I am thinking of"—*of what?* my inner voice challenged—"of a career change myself. Maybe we should talk about joining forces?"

In my head, this was an elegant, artful offer. *Chill* in every sense of my newfound understanding. But judging by Landon's snort, Barton's diverted glance, and Cyrus's furrowed brow, I was clearly wrong.

"As an *employee*?" Cyrus asked, sending Landon's snort into a snicker.

"Well...yes," I answered. "I founded my own company back in the day, and I have been a C-suite executive at several others; I was thinking I might be—I don't know—useful? It was...it was just an idea." I wanted to crawl into the sand trap and bury myself alive.

"Oh...certainly...well...I see," Cyrus stammered. "It's very impressive that you founded your own company, Hollis." He looked to Landon for support but found none—Landon was lining up another putt, his shoulders still bouncing at the resolution of his chuckle. "Regretfully, I think we're set for executives at the moment," Cyrus continued, "but let me noodle on the idea."

Landon lobbed his putt two feet from the hole and sauntered forward to finish it out, cutting his eyes discretely at Cyrus and shaking his head.

For his part, Cyrus looked embarrassed, but his expression only deepened my own shame. What had I been thinking? Tom Brady and Aaron Rodgers were proposing a game of backyard football, and I'd volunteered to be the all-time quarterback. *Idiot,* my inner voice chided.

"How did you get this license?" Barton asked, bringing the conversation back to the business and away from my asinine dreams. "There has got to be a story behind—"

"Cyrus? Landon?" a voice interrupted from beyond the sand trap. "Hollis? Barton? We are just about to serve the first course."

"Yes, my love," Cyrus called. "Coming!" He rushed to file his putter in the cabinet and shoo us all to follow suit. "A story?" Cyrus said, laughing mischievously as he waved us along. "If it weren't true, you would swear I was lying. Come on. I'll tell you all over dinner."

Barton and Landon followed Cyrus's lead, but I lagged, my limbs heavy with rejection.

Cyrus saw me trailing and paused. "Chop-chop, Hollis. You don't want to miss this."

I nodded, reluctantly picking up the pace. Cyrus might have had more money than God and the Midas touch for new business ideas, but he was wrong about one thing: I most definitely wanted to miss this.

# Chapter Four

I spent the rest of the evening in morose self-loathing. Cricket—ever the intuitive one—understood and left me alone to brood. It was a gift I did not deserve but appreciated.

The next morning—Monday morning—was no better. Isabel had to be at school at 7:30 a.m. for orchestra practice, and Trip was content to enjoy an extra hour on the jungle gym before classes began, so we wolfed our Cheerios and headed off into the day with the temperatures still chilly from the cloudless night.

While I had filled Friday's walk to school with questions and jibber jabber, I was not as loquacious this morning. The three of us trudged the mile toward school in relative silence until Isabel backhanded me with a question I should have seen coming and been ready to dodge.

"Is Mom going to have to go back to work?" she asked.

If cringing were sport, I would have been an Olympian. "Mom already works," I said, deflecting the real question.

"You know what I mean, Dad," Isabel said, stiff-arming my deflection.

Indeed, I did. Isabel's question had been preying on me and was reinforced when I caught Cricket sitting at the dining room table that morning—sporting her reading glasses and a pencil tucked behind one ear—poring over our bank statements and stabbing at her calculator.

It had not always been this way. During my senior year at Caltech—at the frothy height of the dot-com bubble—I founded a company named Gusher and ran it from a college flophouse in Pasadena. Gusher was based on compression algorithms I wrote to move massive data sets over the internet; it was novel at the time, but the technology was the precursor to today's streaming television services. With almost zero salesmanship or pitch skills, I was able to secure $2 million in funding for Gusher and was named to *Wired* magazine's "Top 20 under 20." Such were those insane days. When the bubble burst, the money dried up, and Gusher died the same predictable death as 98 percent of its wave-riding peers.

Thankfully, my dot-com failure was viewed by future employers as a sign of ambition, not incompetence. After two years manning the helm of a sinking ship, I toweled myself off and became the head of research and development at a steady-but-boring software company in Santa Barbara. It was a geographic move that introduced me to the woman who would better my life.

When Cricket and I first met, she was a rising star at a major national public relations firm. The year we got engaged, Cricket joined a few others and launched a boutique PR firm headquartered in Montecito. Cricket's ascent went from *rising* to *meteoric*. She opened art galleries, clothing stores, and interior design shops; she worked with reclusive celebrities and ambitious politicians. But like many jobs, her extraordinary talent did not match her internal passion.

Meanwhile, I shoved off from steady-but-boring shores to find the greater calling I knew was my destiny. Ports of call number one and number two on this subsequent journey had proven unfriendly, but CryptoWallet was on the horizon, and I was certain the third time was the charm.

So, Cricket and I made a pact. I would reboot myself as the chief operating officer of CryptoWallet, while Cricket would *retire* from public relations and follow her heart, becoming a full-time volunteer for a preschool focused on Santa Barbara's homeless children.

Even in retrospect, this pivot seemed reasonable. I was soon to be named to a fancy-titled position in a company with global aspirations. Sure, I had a $2 million failure under my belt and had been relieved of my duties at my prior two posts, but this was *different*. It would not be easy—being a single income, no-safety-net family in one of the most expensive communities in America never is—but it was doable. We could have made it; we should have made it.

But we had not, and, perhaps, it was time to pull the plug on this experiment. How many times did I need to test the hypothesis to prove it false? What is more, the family had a perfectly capable—nay, superior—replacement waiting in the wings in our very own Cricket. It was as if our family were a baseball team in desperate need of a hit, and instead of sending Ted Williams to the batter's box, we elected to cast our fortunes with Hollis Crawford, a man whose last solid contact came in T-ball.

"No, honey," I finally answered Isabel, determined to hide these honest questions behind a wall of false bravado. "I will work it out. Mom is good."

My hopeful answer did not lift Isabel's mood, leaving the three of us to complete the remainder of the walk in total silence.

We said our goodbyes on the sidewalk in front of Montecito Union, both kids giving me glum waves before ascending through the school's doors. I was initially grateful for the lack of a school assembly, but as I turned south to reverse the path home, I was struck by the intense melancholy of having absolutely nothing to do.

So, I walked.

With my hands stuffed deep into my pockets, my head hung low, and my sneakers kicking up a whisp of dust, I headed down San Ysidro Road toward Highway 101 and the Pacific Ocean beyond. I thought I just might perform a one-man rendition of the most hackneyed Hollywood scene I could imagine by moping down to the beach, finding a place to sit, and tossing pebbles into the lapping waves while an imagined soundtrack of Sade songs played in the background.

As I reconsidered the previous night's failure, it seemed obvious that I had allowed my hopes to outreach the bounds of reality. My meeting Cyrus the business tycoon at precisely the moment when I was most desperate for a second—scratch that—fourth chance was not the kismet that I dreamed it to be. I was now in exactly the same spot I had been in before I met Cyrus. The same hopes, prospects, and options—meager as they might have been—that I had when I drove too fast to the Spring Sing still existed. So why did I now feel so much worse?

Before I reached the intersection of San Ysidro and Highway 101, my depressing reverie was interrupted by the wail of sirens. I assumed at first that the emergency vehicles would pass under me as I crossed Highway 101 on the overpass, but to my surprise, the source of the sirens was the Montecito Fire Department's EMT truck, heading the same direction as me, straight toward the beach. Shortly after it passed, two Santa Barbara County cruisers joined the fray, all three vehicles headed toward the minuscule parking lot at the top of Miramar Beach.

I kept walking, curious but not alarmed, the vehicles now too far out of sight for me to understand the nature of the emergency.

I passed All Saints Episcopal Church, crossed the railroad tracks and the gated entrance to the exclusive homes of Bonnymede, passed the parked EMT truck and police cruisers, and made a right turn down the bougainvillea-covered path known as the Hammond's Trail. At the end of this path was my favorite Montecito beach: perfect for sad-faced pebble tossing.

Shortly down the trail, I was passed by two paramedics headed in the opposite direction, back to the parking lot. Their walkie-talkies buzzed, but the men were in no hurry. *Someone sprained an ankle and called an ambulance,* my uncharitable inner voice chirped.

The Hammond's Trail ended at a bridge crossing Montecito Creek, which was truly a creek for only three or four months a year. The rest of the time, it was a dry creek bed, occasionally backfilled with saltwater when the ocean tide was particularly high. I crossed the bridge, walked alongside a stunning beachfront home, and emerged onto Hammond's Beach.

There, one hundred yards west from the mouth of Montecito Creek, amid a gaggle of golden retrievers and labradoodles chasing tennis balls, were four police officers standing around a lifeless body.

This did not look like a sprained ankle.

More intriguing, something about the body exposed between the officers' legs looked familiar. A tractor beam of curiosity pulled me toward them, my skin tingling with anticipation. The body was that of a man, so drained of color he was faintly blue. He was shirtless, in board shorts with the neoprene and Velcro of a surfboard leash still strapped to his ankle and a surfboard lying beside him like a stretcher.

But that wasn't the familiar part. I took a few more tentative steps, growing more confident and more horrified with each footfall.

"Sir? Sir!" one of the police officers barked as I encroached on their circle. "I'm going to have to ask you to step back."

I raised both hands in a don't shoot pose. "I—I..." I stammered, slowly lowering one hand to point at the body. "I know that man."

# Chapter Five

The nearly naked body was so out of context that my mind wasn't prepared to acknowledge what I saw. It was like witnessing your kid's elementary school teacher dancing drunkenly on the bar at a honky-tonk.

The officer nearest to me turned, narrowing his eyes on me. "You know him?"

The officer's steely glare plus the guns, biceps, and crew cuts, made me rethink volunteering information. But it seemed a tad late to run away, so I feebly nodded yes.

The officer came closer. "Who is he?"

"Uh..." I began, taking in the dead man's alabaster skin and his shock of orange hair, my brain asking, *Are you sure?*

But there was no denying; I did know him. "I just met him last night," I said. "His name is Landon. He's visiting from Palm Springs. He's staying with a friend of mine up on Riven Rock."

"Who is the friend?" the officer asked, pulling out a small, spiral-bound notepad and pen.

"Umm..." My throat was dry as the creek bed I had just crossed. "Cyrus. Cyrus Wimby."

The officer scribbled the name, then raised his chin. "Can you contact Mr. Wimby? Get him down here for a corroborating ID?"

"Sure," I said, whipping out my phone. I thought about calling Cyrus, but I assumed he would screen his calls and not know my number. Instead of calling, I texted.

*Cyrus,* I wrote. *It's Hollis Crawford.*

I hit send and began composing my next line, but already the bubble of three dots was dancing on my phone's screen. *Hollis!* I received in return. *How wonderful to hear from you! Last night was grand. So glad you could make it!*

Cyrus's conviviality made what I'd already typed out sound too harsh. I edited my message to acknowledge his: *Yes, indeed.* I wrote. *Thank you for your tremendous hospitality.* I paused, feeling like I should say more about the wine, the food, the witty repartee. Then I remembered that I was writing to tell him his friend was dead and the police requested his presence. *For the love of God, call him, Hollis,* my inner voice chastised.

I dialed; Cyrus picked up before the second ring. "Hollis, my friend!" he said. "To what do I owe the pleasure?"

"Hi, Cyrus," I said. "Sorry for intruding on your day, but—"

"Oh," he interrupted, "'tis no intrusion to hear from a friend. Wasn't last night wonderful?"

I was already shaking my head, not because I disagreed, but because I was not going to get sidetracked yet again. "It was terrific, Cyrus. Look, I'm sorry to be the one to have to deliver this horrible news, but I am down at the beach and—"

"The beach?" Cyrus interrupted again. "Fabulous. Genevieve and I were about to head there ourselves. I was just waiting for Landon to get back from his morning surf before we headed out. Where are you? We'll join you."

Ugh, this was a lot harder than I expected, mostly because Cyrus seemed so damn happy. I did not want to be the one to tell him that his decades-long friend and business partner was stiffening at my feet, but it seemed I had no choice. "Landon is not coming back," I said.

"What do you mean?" he said, his voice suddenly serious.

"I mean, that is why I am calling. I'm at Hammond's right now, and I'm standing with a group of police officers and paramedics and…Well, there's no other way to say it: Landon is dead."

On the other end of the line was only silence for what felt like minutes.

"Hollis," Cyrus said firmly, "we don't know each other well, and I have been forewarned that Americans sometimes have"—he paused, searching for a word—"*odd* senses of humor. But even taking that into consideration, I find this joke entirely distasteful."

Again, I found myself shaking my head. "I'm sorry, Cyrus. I wish I were telling an off-color joke, but I'm afraid the truth is even more distasteful. I don't know what happened, but I am looking at Landon's body as I speak. He is dressed in navy board shorts, no wet suit or rash guard. He has an eight-foot lime-green surfboard strapped to his right ankle—"

I paused at the sound of a gasp. "That's my board!" Cyrus said. "Landon took it this morning!"

I squeezed my eyes shut. "I'm really sorry, Cyrus."

"Genevieve!" I heard Cyrus holler even though his phone was slightly muffled. "We must go! There's been an accident." Cyrus returned the phone to his ear. "Hammond's, you say?"

"Yes," I answered. "Just west of the mouth of the creek."

"We're on our way," Cyrus said. "Wait there for us, will you, Hollis?"

"Sure," I said, though I felt I had added as much value to the situation as I possibly could. "I'll wait."

I hung up and turned back to the circle of officers, which now included the fire department paramedics on standby to carry Landon away. "Cyrus is on his way here now," I announced. "Should be here inside of ten minutes."

"Thanks," the officer said, checking his watch.

Now that I'd proven myself helpful, the officers seemed content to let me hang near to their circle as their walkie-talkies beeped and buzzed and they spoke back in numbers and codes.

"Hunh," I said to the officer whom I had adopted as my liaison. "No wet suit?" The water temperature was in the low sixties that day. Admittedly, I was a wimp, but I would have needed full-body neoprene to jump in that water.

"Yeah," he said. "Who knows. From the looks of it, this guy didn't know what he was doing."

"What do you think happened?" I asked.

He shrugged. "Drowned, most likely," he said. "Though, judging from the bloom at his right temple, he took a header off his board first."

I pointed at the buried reef extending a few hundred yards off the shoreline—the reef that created the right break that brought surfers to this spot. "Did he hit the rocks, you think?"

Another shrug. "That's what it looks like," he said. "The waves are shot today, which is why no one is here. You'd have to be really unlucky to get up enough momentum to knock yourself out on a day like today. But it happens. That's why you're not supposed to surf alone."

I nodded, and the officer turned back to his fellow badge wearers. Judging by his tanned arms and his easy understanding of the ocean, I suspected the officer was a surfer himself. This was no big leap; most of Montecito's residents surfed or claimed to surf. But more, it was the officer's casual indifference to the dead man at his feet that convinced me he was likely a surfer. Perhaps because I was an outsider to their passion, surfers had always struck me as an insular crowd. Sure, there were plenty of folks in the surfing *business* who encouraged newbies, vacationers, hacks, and first timers to join in the fun. But I had always harbored the view that, to the indoctrinated surfers, the news of the death of a surfing virgin who hadn't followed their code was secretly seen as a blessing. It kept the sport smaller; it kept it theirs.

As the shock of seeing a dead body faded, I grew bolder. Landon's left hand caught my eye, and I squatted to validate what I thought I saw: his left ring finger was missing.

"Officer," I said, still in my catcher's squat, pointing at

Landon's missing appendage. "Did you notice his finger? It's gone."

My new pal sighed and half turned back to me. "Yeah," he said. "We know."

"But...that's odd, don't you think?" I challenged. "I met this man yesterday. He had all ten fingers then."

"It's not odd," the officer said. "That's probably how he drowned."

*He drowned because of a missing finger?* I thought. The officer read my face and turned to face me directly. "Look, I can't be sure, but here's what likely happened. Your man here took a dive off his board and cracked his head on the reef. While falling, he reached out to brace himself." The officer demonstrated outstretched arms. "His hands hit the reef same time as his head, and that missing finger gets caught in the rocks. Wouldn't have been a big deal except that his head also hit, so he's now unconscious. Absent the caught finger, he probably would have floated to the surface and maybe even lived. But as he is unconscious, he can't free his finger, which traps him below the surface, where he ultimately drowns. Eventually, a powerful swell comes through, and *pop*"—another demonstration, this time of a finger taking flight—"off comes the digit."

"Wow," I said.

He nodded.

"You've seen this before?"

"Nah," he said, "but I've seen plenty else."

The officer turned back to his compadres, leaving me to contemplate his theoretical synopsis. It made perfect sense, though I was surprised at how cleanly the missing finger had been removed. I would have pictured something jagged, but admittedly, my source for that bias was the faded memory of too many horror movies watched through the cracks between my fingers.

A few minutes later, I spotted Cyrus and Genevieve running down the last stretch of the Hammond's Trail, headed straight for me and the now shrouded body of Landon. Suddenly, I felt as if I shouldn't be there, that I was invading a private, intimate moment. I backed away as Genevieve flew past and threw herself on her knees beside Landon's body, weeping.

Cyrus stopped beside me, breathing hard, his eyes welled with tears. He put a massive palm on my shoulder and shook his head, his eyes taking in the scene. "Thank you, Hollis," he choked out.

I shook my head. "No, I—"

But before I could complete the thought, Cyrus wrapped both arms around me, pulling me into a mummifying embrace.

My entire body stiffened. Kisses hello, do-si-dos, and now man hugs. This was far too much touching for my taste. But as I felt Cyrus's massive body shudder, I knew there was only one thing to do. Slowly, I raised my hands and patted his back.

# Chapter Six

The *Santa Barbara Independent* called to ask me for a quote for their article on Landon's death. I declined. News Channel KEYT asked if I would speak on camera. I declined that, too. It felt strange that my accidental stumbling upon an already discovered dead body somehow made me a minor celebrity. I wanted nothing to do with any of that.

For a few days, the local news reran old stories reminding locals and visitors alike of the common safety procedures for a happy, successful—and most importantly, survived—surf adventure. Then the story was gone.

As the hubbub died down, my impending personal financial disaster reemerged on my front burner; I still had no plan. By my math and logic, my one month's severance from CryptoWallet bought me two weeks to formulate said plan. Already I was halfway through my grace period, and I had nothing to show for it.

For several days, Cricket and I danced around, but not with, the eight-hundred-pound gorilla that followed me around the house. But as the first week of my unemployment bled into the second with nary an update to be had, Cricket offered to help me conduct a postmortem on my time at CryptoWallet to see if there was anything to be gleamed from this latest failure.

I wanted to cross my arms and pout a petulant no. I knew exactly why I had been fired. I had known it even before my best friend and fellow CryptoWallet executive, Paul—the man who had helped me land the job to begin with—reluctantly delivered the death blow, explaining that I was being "released to pursue other opportunities."

"For what it's worth, I think you were right," Paul had admitted, referring to the most recent executive squabble I had found myself embroiled in—the one that was the final straw and secured me a sturdy new cardboard box. "But being *right* is overrated," Paul had continued. "I know this is hard for you to hear, Hollis, but sometimes you have got to back off. Sometimes you have got to let things go."

This was not new news. Indeed, I could not let things go. I was argumentative. I missed cues as to the emotional state of others. I needed to prove that I was correct even at the cost of bruised feelings. I had an outsized passion for justice; even the slightest of wrongs required righting. In past employment exit interviews, I had been told I was *tone deaf*, *stubborn*, *rigid*, *tedious*, and generally lacked empathy. Unfortunately, these were all-too-accurate descriptions. I had also been described as *weird*, a *freak*, and a *jerk*. These descriptions lacked the necessary call to improvement; I could attempt to develop empathy, but I could not unweird myself.

All of these were telltale signs of my substandard emotional intelligence, also known as *Low EQ*. Once, perhaps after the first or second firing, I self-deprecatingly referred to myself as *on the spectrum*. Cricket was quick to explain to me that *the spectrum* was an overused term that insensitively combined a host of legitimate, discrete disorders into a singular, amorphous one. Once again, there I was inadvertently offending. As an alternative, Cricket proposed we coin the phrase *in the fog* to describe all the unique joys of knowing, loving, and dealing with me, Hollis Crawford. The phrase was perfect: When it came to reading others, I was definitively *in the fog*.

So, even though I had a firm grasp on my deficiencies, I knew I had no alternative but to recite them again with Cricket, seeing if there were any silver linings under all the dark clouds.

"I'm not giving up on you," Cricket concluded, "but I can't tell where your head is."

I began to raise a finger to point at my skull; Cricket shook her head, no. It was not the time for a joke, apparently.

"Do you want me to go back to public relations?" she asked more pointedly.

"No," I said.

"Then what is your plan?"

"I don't know."

"Fine," Cricket said, shaking her head. "You want more time? I'll give you more time." She stood from the kitchen table, signifying the end of our pep talk. "But I won't hesitate to blow the whistle on your time if I have to," she continued. "There's too much on the line here. I've got a job. Two of them, in fact. And I love both my jobs. All I'm asking you to do is try. Put yourself out there. Make calls. Network. Join LinkedIn."

I puckered my face; she ignored me.

"Who knows where it will lead," Cricket continued. "But one thing is for sure: You're not going to land a job pretending to be *Mr. Mom*."

She was right on all fronts, and still I had no plan.

That evening, as I emptied the dishwasher and folded laundry, my cell phone pinged the sound of an incoming text message.

*Hollis, my friend,* the message read. *Thank you so much for your assistance with the tragedy that befell our dear friend Landon. It has been a very trying week both personally and professionally.*

*I can only imagine,* I texted back.

*Indeed,* he added. *With that in mind, I find myself in need of some help, and the only person I could imagine turning to was you.*

I stared at my phone as if it had just grown a leg. I had no idea what to write in reply. Thankfully, Cyrus rescued me.

*Could we meet tomorrow for coffee to discuss?*

*Of course,* I replied. *Starbucks?*

*Surely not!* He shot back. *Merci. 10am?*

*See you there, then.* I wrote.

# Chapter Seven

To avoid getting her hopes up, I did not mention the backstory when I told Cricket of my pending coffee date with Cyrus. For all I knew, Cyrus was going on vacation and wanted me to gather mail and water plants in his absence. I wasn't going to put Cricket through another game of rope-a-dope just because I had allowed a green shoot of hope in my barren garden. Besides, it seemed a little morbid to be dancing on Landon's freshly dug grave.

Nestled in the heart of Montecito's Country Mart, Merci was abuzz when I arrived at ten minutes before ten. I hovered awkwardly just outside the small stone wall that delineated Merci's outdoor tables from those of the coffee shop next door and the grocery directly opposite. I grew hungry watching staff bring out petit fours and scones along with coffees of every size, shape, and hue. Just before 10:00 a.m., a table for two opened up, and I pounced indiscreetly. At ten after ten, I ordered an Americano, no cream no sugar; the waitress seemed disappointed with my lack of creativity. Join the club, I thought.

At fifteen after ten, I pulled out my phone for the fiftieth time, turning the cell signal on and off, checking to make sure I didn't have the phone on silent, and refreshing my email inbox.

None of it changed the truth that I had received no messages of any kind.

At twenty after ten, Cyrus arrived, cell phone pressed to his ear, speaking in an Arabic tongue. When he finally ended the call, I stuck out my hand for a shake and arched my eyebrows for an explanation.

"So very sorry, Hollis," he said. "I've been sitting in the parking lot for nearly a half hour talking with my mother. She was devastated at the news of Landon's passing, and I could not get off the phone until she had calmed down." He swallowed my offered hand between two of his, his flexible-straw fingers stretching well past my wrist and up my arm.

Embarrassment surged through my system. I was expecting an apology and now felt like I needed to offer one. "No problem, Cyrus," I said, trying to reverse my judgmental eyebrows. "Does your mother live here?"

"No, no," he said. "She is in Riyadh. It is her home; she would never leave."

"You have other family there?"

"Oh, yes," he said. "All of my family; I am the only one who left. Mother turns ninety-two next week, and more than two hundred people will attend her birthday celebration."

Impressive, I thought. If I were to have a birthday party, I was certain it would take a cash bribe to get two hundred people to attend. As it stood, I typically tried to avoid acknowledging my birthday, and any celebration would happen only if Cricket was in the mood to host a subset of her best friends whose husbands also happened to get along with me.

A waitress passed nearby; Cyrus politely waved her over. He complimented her hair, asked about her afternoon plans for this glorious Montecito day, and placed an if-I-could-trouble-you order for a cappuccino, maple scone, and Greek yogurt with honey.

I tried to think of some equally flattering comments, but my mind was blank. "Do you offer refills?" I asked her sheepishly, holding up my empty mug.

"I'm happy to get you a refill," she answered, "but we do charge for them."

"Never mind. I'm overcaffeinated as it is," I said, pretending I wasn't just being cheap.

"No such thing, my friend," Cyrus said with a laugh.

As we waited for Cyrus's coffee to arrive, my pulse leveled up. I wanted to hear what Cyrus's big favor was, but he seemed content with chitchat, asking my opinion of his Entre Nous wines and, conversely, describing Landon's poignant memorial ceremony in Palm Springs.

I was willing to endure the small talk because I had already learned so much at the previous week's dinner party. The company was called ExOh Holdings and had been named by Priscilla in a cheeky take on "XO," shorthand for "hugs and kisses." At this revelation, I had only been able to shake my head. In my family, the kids name the hamster. If they're lucky, they get to name the dog. But in the Wimby family, the kid got to name a future billion-dollar company.

The origin story of ExOh's chief asset—its Free Trade Zone License that would level the playing field of global trade—was as jaw dropping as it was predictable: It came by bribe. At the time, Cyrus was working as the chief negotiator for the sale of Saudi Arabian crude oil to the Chinese government. In exchange for favorable terms, Cyrus was gifted the license on which ExOh's business model was based. It was gross, it was dirty, and it did not shine a favorable light on Cyrus.

But it was also perfectly tailored to confirm how most Americans assumed business in China was *really* conducted. With the audience's preconceived worldview validated, no more questions were asked; Cyrus's backstory was swallowed hook, line, and sinker. In hindsight, I recognize this as lesson one in Cyrus's masterclass on psychology and communication. But I didn't see it then, and I wasn't alone.

Back at Merci, with Cyrus's cappuccino finished, his scone half-eaten, and his granola recently delivered, I decided I could safely push the conversation forward without violating Cricket's imperative to *stay chill*.

"So," I began, "last night, you were texting that you needed some help?"

"Indeed, I do," he said, taking a deep breath. "Let me ask you a question, Hollis. Have you ever lived abroad?"

I was flummoxed. Had we taken a U-turn back to chitchat, or were we moving on? I decided to play along. "Well, Cricket and I spent three weeks in—"

"No," Cyrus interrupted. "Not an extended vacation. *Lived.*"

"Oh, right. Well, then no."

He nodded. "It's a thorny affair." He dabbed the corners of his mouth with a napkin, then folded his hands under his chin. "I find myself in a bit of a quandary. I'm the chairman of a US corporation. I purchased a lovely little home in your country..."

*Little?* I thought.

"...I pay my share of local taxes, just like everyone else. But, for example, I cannot secure a US bank account. There are certain forms, documents, and attestations that require a signature and a Social Security number, which I do not have. It's beyond frustrating."

"I can imagine."

"The role I was negotiating with Landon—dear Landon— was that of the company's CEO. He was to be my US proxy. But with his passing..."

Cyrus took a sip of coffee as if waiting for me to respond. I did not. This was not a negotiating strategy; I didn't know what to say.

"The other night, at our dinner party," Cyrus finally continued, "you mentioned your interest in joining my team. You said that you had previous experience founding a startup and had worked as a C-suite executive at multiple companies..."

I nodded, my hopes rising.

"At the time, I was confident I would eventually work things out with Landon," Cyrus continued, "and—under that assumption—felt that we did not need another executive. But now, given Landon's passing"—he paused to sigh—"that assumption is turned on its head. Now I am quite literally on the hunt for an experienced executive to fill Landon's shoes, and I couldn't help but think of you."

My mouth involuntarily fell open. "As CEO? You want me—"

"I looked you up," Cyrus interrupted, anticipating my surprise. "Hollis Crawford. *Wired* magazine's 'Top 20 under 20' for 1999. You raised two million dollars."

I closed my eyes and shook my head. "Yeah, but the business failed."

"Please," Cyrus said, waving away my caveat. "You raised two million dollars. The only failure is that you didn't raise twenty-two, or fifty-two, or one hundred and two million dollars."

I chuckled, grateful for the ego boost.

"So. What do you think?" Cyrus asked. "Are you open to leaving your current job to work for ExOh?"

My *current job*? Only then did I realize that Cyrus had no idea I was unemployed. On the evening of his dinner party, I only told him I was "thinking of a career change." Was I obligated to spill the beans, or could I keep my disclosure vague? Within my perpetual *fog*, white lies blended into the mist. As a result, I was truthful to a fault, often earning professional demerits for being brutally honest with my coworkers. But what was the virtue of all that honesty if it did nothing but cost me?

"I'm open to it," I said, even as my insides knotted in disapproval.

"Outstanding!" Cyrus said, smacking the iron tabletop, sending the dishware clattering. "This isn't the Fortune 500," he continued. "At least, not yet. I need someone who is flexible, comfortable with ambiguity, and keeps their eyes on the big picture. Does that describe you?"

No. It did not describe me. It described the opposite of me, or at least the opposite of the me I had always been. "One hundred percent," I lied, realizing quickly how slippery the slope of falsehood was.

"Then let's do this," he said, lightly pounding his fist on the table. "I want to offer you the position of chief executive officer of ExOh under the same terms I ironed out with Landon. The ideal of ExOh is to be lean and mean. Corporate headquarters are here in Montecito, but our operations will be in Shanghai. When you get settled and our corporate footing is solidified, I want you in Shanghai once a month to make sure everyone knows who is in charge..."

I couldn't help but shake my head at the thought of it. What would Cricket, Isabel, and Trip think of dear old dad off to Shanghai on business? They would be prouder of me than they had ever been before, that was for sure.

"...I am looking for the right Montecito office space, but for the time being, we'll be remote. I work from the fifth bedroom of my home and host meetings at the house or at restaurants around town. I assume you have a home office like everyone else in Montecito?"

I pictured the twelve hundred square feet that comprised our overcrowded home. I was not bunking the kids into a single bedroom just so that I could feel better about myself. That left the well-worn tradition of working from the garage—so common in broader Santa Barbara that they had a term for it: a gar-office. Our garage was a single-car affair with more cobwebs than windows, but it would work. "Yes," I said.

"Very good. On to compensation and the agreement Landon and I struck." He smiled. "I think you're going to be really excited by this. My comp plan is leveraged to maximize upside. Everyone on the team works for stock, not cash..."

*Oh no,* I thought, swallowing hard, picturing our already dwindling bank account.

"In lieu of cash—which would immediately be halved by taxes

and other such inefficiencies—I am very, and I mean *very*, generous with stock grants. As I agreed with Landon, I will issue you one million dollars' worth of ExOh's restricted stock at today's heavily discounted price. At each one-year anniversary of your tenure, you'll receive an additional one million dollars in stock at the same price." He paused to lean in and whisper, "This is a gold mine, my friend. Conservatively speaking, your initial allocation will be worth in excess of ten million dollars by this time next year."

*Ten million dollars!?!* my inner voice screamed. How in the world could I go from unemployed to ten million dollars? It was a sum I could not imagine, delivered over a timeframe I could not fathom.

And, unfortunately, it was probably moot. How could I accept a job without a penny of cash coming in? My Crypto-Wallet pay had barely covered our expenses, and my previous bouts of unemployment had seriously dented our savings. All I had left was retirement plan money, and breaking the seal on that was a no-no. There would be taxes, fees, penalties, and probably some sort of public notice in the *Montecito Journal*. Most important: What would Cricket say?

I shook my head. "It is an exciting offer, Cyrus. Let me discuss it with Cricket."

"I wouldn't respect a man who didn't consult the wisdom of his better half," Cyrus said. "But please do remember, Hollis: I need you. I cannot help but feel that our meeting at this crossroads of time, place, and opportunity is heaven sent—for you and me both."

I nodded; my head filled with many of the same cosmic what-ifs.

Cyrus waved down the server and asked for our check, which was already tucked into the pocket of her apron. He looked it over, then touched the breast pocket of his coat. "Oh, this is embarrassing," he said. "I've left my wallet at home. Let me run back and get it."

"I've got it," I said, motioning him to sit back down. Though if I had known I would end up paying $46 for a cup of coffee, I might have splurged for the refill.

He stood to leave; we shook hands. "I know it's last minute, but Genevieve wanted me to ask if you and Cricket would come to dinner tonight?"

"Again?"

Cyrus laughed. "Yes: again. Genevieve loves to host dinner parties, and we both enjoy meeting all the fine people of Montecito. Besides, Genevieve is making her key lime pie tonight. This, you must try."

# Chapter Eight

After hosting her book club the previous night and going to a friend's birthday dinner at the Lark the night prior, Cricket had her heart set on burgers from Tinker's and a family movie. But when I revealed that my coffee date with Cyrus had yielded a potential opportunity—avoiding the unsavory specifics of his offer—Cricket eagerly jumped on board for a return visit to the Wimby estate.

Just like the first time, Entre Nous wine flowed freely, and artisanal pizza slices were consumed as quickly as they were plated. The kids swam, then retired to the television room—which was more *private theater* than *room*—leaving the adults to luxuriate by the firepit.

Two other couples were in attendance that evening—both invited by Genevieve, who met them at events where the rich and successful congregated. I did not know either couple personally, but I knew them by name and reputation. John Colton's family founded Miramar Bank and Trust, now a billion-dollar bank, and he sat on every nonprofit board in Santa Barbara. And Susan Workner ran *the* residential real estate firm in Montecito—one that only dealt with properties with price tags over $5 million and served champagne at open houses.

The conversation was effortless and elegant; Cyrus and Genevieve were master hosts. Cricket kept everyone laughing as each conversation topic zoomed from one tangent to the next, while the enormous firepit lit everyone's faces. We did not speak of Landon, who neither John and his wife, nor Susan and her husband, knew. Even for Cricket and me, Landon's coming and going now felt like something we might have imagined. Only Cyrus and Genevieve had truly known Landon, and they seemed to be processing their grief well.

I slipped into a state of easy motion that almost felt comfortable; it was a surreal notion to a man who rarely felt comfortable outside his house. Then the inevitable happened.

"So, Hollis," Susan Workner said, "what do you do?"

Her intentions were almost certainly honest. I was the quiet one; she was trying to bring me into the conversation. But I felt the blood drain from my face as all eyes turned to me. "Well, I..." I began, then stuttered silent, my gaze hopping from one dinner party guest to the next, as if they knew the answer to my existential question and might clue me in. Predictably, all I received in return were expectant smiles, waning as the anxious seconds ticked by.

"If I may?" Cyrus said, interrupting the awkward silence, his eyes fixed on mine.

Unsure where Cyrus would turn the conversation, but grateful nonetheless, I nodded.

"Hollis works with me," he said, a toothy smile growing over his face.

Cricket grabbed my knee, but my now bulging eyes were glued to Cyrus.

"Hollis," Cyrus continued, undeterred by my frantic expression, "is ExOh Holdings' brand-new chief executive officer."

Cricket's hand turned into a vise, but my thoughts were too scrambled to decode her intent. I had not said *yes*. More pressing: Cricket was in the dark. I had told her nothing material about Cyrus's job offer of a highfalutin title, vague responsibilities, and no paycheck. It was the most intriguing offer in my otherwise empty hopper, but still, I hadn't decided to accept it.

Had Cyrus saved me or cornered me? A whisper of paranoia begged me to raise a finger and object, but my hand refused to respond. This wasn't a trap; it was a blessing. How could it be anything else? My untimely firing, my happenstance introduction to Cyrus at Montecito Union, Landon's surfing accident—this was the Fates throwing me a much-needed bone.

And besides, with the toothpaste now out of the tube, what choice did I have but *yes*?

"That's terrific! Congratulations, Hollis," Susan said, raising her glass to me with a quick nod. "Pardon the dumb question, Cyrus, but what is this ExOh Holdings?"

Cyrus began to spin his tale, describing with glee the massive retail opportunity in China and how the Amazons and Alibabas of the world were structurally segregated from it. I listened for a minute before Cricket's repeated squeezing of my knee finally registered. I turned to look at her and saw her admiration. It was a look I had not seen in some time. When our eyes met, she squeezed my knee even harder, leaning in and whispering, "*This* happened over coffee?"

I arched my eyebrows. "Kind of," I whispered back.

"When were you planning to tell me?"

I shook my head. "Surprise?"

Her smile said it all: pride, a little bit of shock, and a lot of relief. "Wow!" she whispered.

Wow indeed. My emotional pendulum swung from uncertainty to fear to gratitude. The look on Cricket's face made it clear I could not back out now. I still didn't know how I would explain the no-cash-compensation scheme to Cricket, nor how I would *survive* the no-cash-compensation scheme. The smile faded from my face as these weightier thoughts took hold. Cricket must have sensed my anxiety because she removed the hand from my knee and threw it around my waist, pulling me in for a sideways hug.

"And what will you do, Hollis?" John Colton asked me as Cyrus finished his soliloquy.

Heads began to turn my way before Cyrus wrestled them back under the command of his voice. "What will Hollis do?" Cyrus began. "What *won't* he do? You probably don't know this, but Hollis was a dot-com superstar, the founder of a company that had the potential to be a juggernaut. If not for the vagaries of timing, we might have been dining with a humble Elon Musk tonight..."

My face scrunched like a dubious pug's even as Cricket patted my knee in support.

"But I digress," Cyrus continued. "Hollis brings to ExOh a wealth of knowledge from his days as a CEO: founding and running a startup, raising money from investors, and deftly managing people. His expertise was the missing piece of our puzzle. With Hollis in the fold, there is no limit to ExOh's future success."

Cautiously, the eyes of Cyrus's guests turned again to me, the unwitting savant in their midst. I wanted to object to Cyrus's overly rosy characterization of my expertise and talents, but Cricket threw her arm around my shoulder and suddenly, at least for one night, the truth didn't seem so important.

"Well, John," I began, "Cyrus and I just came to an agreement on working together this morning." I nodded at Cyrus to bring him in on my acceptance of his ramrodding; he raised his glass and winked in acknowledgment. "I am going to be Cyrus's right-hand man in getting ExOh's stock trading again," I continued. "I am going to get the company's global operations coordinated and efficient. And I am going to pick up Cyrus's dry cleaning and get his car washed. Whatever it takes."

The last line drew a chorus of hoots and another silent toast from Cyrus. I didn't know what I was doing, but the moment was alive with possibility. I had plenty of questions—chief among them, how to finance this *possibility*—but Cyrus believed in me. Somehow, some way, this was meant to be.

"Well, on that glorious note, let's have dessert," Genevieve announced.

The group moved from the firepit back to the dining table, which had been reset for dessert in our absence. With a nod of Genevieve's head, the pie was presented unsliced; Genevieve liked to do the slicing herself, Cyrus told us, divvying out bigger slices to her favorite guests.

We passed our plates over one at a time and received our shares. The pie had a buttery graham cracker crust with the faintest hint of mint. Sandwiched between the lime and the crust was a thick layer of dark chocolate. On top, homemade whipped cream squeezed from a pastry bag with a petal piping tip. It was worthy of a photo—an observation not lost on Genevieve. She positioned her plate in front of a few candles with a glass of Entre Nous in the background and snapped several pictures for Instagram. Then we dug in.

Magnificent was not an adequate descriptor. I have never tasted anything like it. The lime and chocolate paired perfectly with the pinot noir. Each bite and sip combination sent my taste buds swooning. I finished my slice and looked longingly at Cricket's. When she was done—she was blessed with the ability to know when she was full and the wisdom to listen to that voice—I implored her to share the remnants with me. I then finished hers too.

"This is unreal, Genevieve," I said.

"I am so glad you like it," she said, clapping her hands together.

"Almost professional," John Colton added with a grin. "If your man ever gets in a pinch, you could probably pay the rent with this pie."

Genevieve's eyes narrowed to the size of gunnery slits in a World War II pillbox. "I *was* a professional, Mr. Colton. And I can more than pay the rent with my talents."

Even I—a decorated veteran of the foot-in-mouth faux pas— recognized that John Colton had struck a nerve. This was the moment when I usually groveled an apology, but Colton took a less contrite path. "Oh, I'm sure you could," he said, his grin broadening into a can't-you-take-a-joke smile. "But thankfully, you don't need to."

Genevieve returned his toothy smile with a forced one of her own.

"You know," I said after several beats of silence that seemed to make everyone else uncomfortable, "I love to bake. This is probably beyond my pay grade, but I would like to give it a try. Can you share the recipe with me, Genevieve?"

Genevieve put down her wineglass, her forced smile morphing into pursed lips. "I'm sorry, Hollis," she said, shaking her head.

I waited for her to elaborate, but she added nothing. "Don't worry," I offered. "You won't catch me selling pies. I cook for an audience of four—that's it."

The corners of her pursed lips edged up slightly. "It's nothing like that, Hollis," she said. "Cyrus assures me that you are a man who can be trusted..."

My eyes shifted to Cyrus; he nodded in acknowledgment.

"But this recipe is a family secret," Genevieve continued. "One I'll never share."

# Chapter Nine

Cyrus arranged a global video teleconference so that I could meet the rest of his ExOh team. To accommodate all time zones in an equally painful manner, the call was held at 10:00 p.m. Montecito time.

I was nervous all day. To satiate those fears, I read anything I could find about global finance, Chinese trade barriers, Asian import tariffs, trade wars, and how those who have managed to set up profitable Chinese retail operations accomplished it. Research had always been my blankie, and at no time had I felt more in need of new knowledge than now.

While making dinner that night, Cricket pressed me for the terms of my new employment. I knew we would come to this topic eventually, but I had been avoiding it; this was where her flood of enthusiasm would meet its wall of resistance.

"If you're not being paid, you're not being valued," she correctly argued.

"It was a nonnegotiable issue, Cricket. No one on the executive team is getting paid in cash," I said. "It's take it or leave it."

"Hmmm," she said, then went back to preparing the meal, turning the options over in her head, comparing the crushing weight of the rock to the unyielding exterior of the hard place.

I was desperate for her validation. So much so that I briefly considered voicing a supporting argument based on the economic theory of comparative advantage—desperate times indeed. Comparative advantage is a theory that argues for free trade based on the surprising conclusion that every country should specialize in its *relative* advantages, even if those relative advantages are *actual* deficiencies. Marriages are like this, I planned to argue. Yes, Cricket was a better breadwinner than me. She was also a better CEO of the Crawford household and a better nonprofit volunteer. Unfortunately, she could not wear every hat in the house unless she planned on adding a neck brace.

So, what to do with inept Hollis? CEO of the Crawford household? Child Protective Services would be on premises within a week. Nonprofit volunteer? I wouldn't survive a day. Breadwinner? By process of elimination, it remained the only option where my success was conceivable.

I cracked a slight smile at the logic of this argument. The smile lasted for a millisecond before I grasped the pitiful emasculation of it all.

I sat, watching her cook, waiting for the white smoke signifying that her papal conclave had reached a conclusion.

"You really believe in this?" she finally asked.

I swallowed. "I do. I really do." And I did. I really did. I believed Cyrus's story about ExOh becoming the next Amazon, and every time the practical reality of not getting paid crept to the front of my consciousness, I thought about $1 million worth in stock on the way to becoming ten million in cash. I was not going to get an offer like this anywhere else.

She nodded. "How will we get by? I can't exactly ask for a raise," she said. "Two times zero is still zero."

"I have a plan," I said. The plan was the unthinkable sin of cashing in my retirement money early. I had run the numbers in anticipation of Cricket potentially giving me the go-ahead. If I set up an automatic withdrawal program on my individual retirement account, the after-tax, after-penalty value of my account divided into twelve equal installments would match a decent take home salary for a start-up business executive. By the time my retirement funds ran out, my ExOh stock would be fully vested and worth millions, and this little speed bump would become a fun piece of Crawford family lore.

Cricket nodded along. "I hate that plan."

"Me too," I said. "But it's the best one I've got."

More cooking; more silence.

"You *really* believe in this?" she repeated.

"I *really* do," I repeated.

She stirred a pot of boiling water as her mind stirred the possibilities. "I told my parents about ExOh," she said.

I closed my eyes tight. Cricket's parents were fantastic and had supported me through all my stumbles. But the thought of the three of them speaking *about* me made me incredibly uncomfortable. "What did they think?"

"They were excited," she said. "Dad thinks he might want to invest."

Cricket's dad loved to unwind from a long day of teaching physics at UC Santa Barbara by watching CNBC's aftermarket shout-fests. They were cotton candy to his intellect. "That's really kind of him," I said, "but not yet."

"They want you to see that they believe in you," she said.

I cringed at what I was about to say next. "Well, Cyrus has set some kind of minimum investment size, and I think it is pretty big."

"Oh," she said. Cricket's parents had done just fine, but they weren't sitting on piles of cash. "Well, it's the thought that counts, right?"

"Right," I agreed, grateful that I wasn't adding the responsibility for Cricket's parents' retirement savings to the draining of my own. "So, we have a plan?" I asked. "An approved plan?"

"Since when do you need my approval?"

"Since always."

She smiled. "Yes, we have a plan."

# Chapter Ten

By 10:00 p.m., with nervous anticipation burning through my stores of energy, I was wiped out. I needed sleep, but I settled for coffee. This was a bad move, but I figured it was better to deal with the repercussions of late-night overcaffeination than to yawn my way through my initial meeting with the rest of the ExOh team. With my heart rate chemically jacked into cardio territory, I booted my laptop, plugged in my headphones, and clicked the meeting link.

Five one-dimensional faces were already online and engaged. I checked my watch; had I screwed up the time zones?

"Hollis!" Cyrus said. "Great to have you."

"I'm really sorry, Cyrus," I said. "I can't believe I got the time wrong on my very first team meeting."

"No, no," Cyrus said. "You did nothing of the sort. I started a little early with the rest of the team to give them some background on you and to suss out some other issues..."

Cyrus was the only one smiling. I couldn't tell if the other blank faces were expressing stress, concern, or mere professionalism. Oh, to have Cricket whispering in my ear.

"Let me introduce you to the rest of the team," Cyrus continued. "Umed is based in Tel Aviv. He oversees technology and is neck-deep in our website relaunch right now."

"Nice to meet you, Umed," I said, waving awkwardly at the passport-sized photo on my laptop screen. This immediately felt sophomoric; I recalled my hand. Should I volunteer my own tech background? No, that might come off as competitive or territorial. Sixty seconds in, and I was already a mess of contradictory impulses.

"Noah, based in Sydney, is head of sales. Kai, based in Hong Kong, is head of finance."

"Noah. Kai," I said, nodding at their pixelized heads—a more adult approach, I hoped.

"And finally: Reuben, based in London," Cyrus said. "Reuben is head of legal."

I nodded at Reuben as well but could not make out his image for the cigarette smoke circling him like Pig-Pen's dust cloud.

"Okay," I began. "It's great to meet everyone." I nearly waved again, but thankfully caught myself. "Maybe we could, uh," I stammered, "go through a quick status report on the main initiatives under way? I've been a member of the team for about twenty-four hours, so I'm still trying to get up to speed."

"Indeed, indeed," Cyrus said. "Gentlemen?"

One by one, Noah, Kai, and Umed gave me high-level overviews of in-process work and upcoming milestones. Noah was principally focused on major branded retailers looking to establish Chinese beachheads. Kai was working with several Hong Kong banks to create factoring programs to minimize working capital expenditures. And Umed was rebooting our corporate website and creating a client portal to autotrack shipments and provide English translations of Mandarin status updates.

It was as if the team had been working together on this initiative for decades, not months. Their polished delivery was on point, comprehensive, and confidence inspiring, even to someone just beginning to grasp the basics of the business.

Then it was Reuben's turn to speak from within his veil of

smoke. "Impressive, no?" he said, his voice thick with a BBC accent. "Try not to bugger it up, will you?"

I flinched at the sudden one-eighty. One minute we were team building; next, I was dropped mid-scene into an episode of *Succession.*

"Reuben," Cyrus interjected. "We've been through this, and—"

"And I'm still not satisfied," Reuben interrupted. "We could have any executive in the world running this venture, Cyrus. Instead, you've chosen someone you met pushing a pram in the park."

"It was an elementary school recital," I corrected before realizing that Reuben was being facetious to prove his point.

"Your objections are noted," Cyrus said, ignoring the foot in my mouth. "My choice to place Hollis in this role was not happenstance or knee-jerk."

"Perhaps not," Reuben quipped, "but that doesn't make it wise."

Cyrus shook his head, disappointment oozing from his Zoom square. I sat frozen, not sure what aspect of my qualifications needed defending. Was it my inexperience as CEO? Was it my lack of familiarity with global trade? Was it the fact that I had never been to China before? On second thought, what defense could I possibly offer? If I were Reuben, I would have been angry too.

"Hollis accomplished more before the age of twenty than any of us," Cyrus declared, the fingertips of each of his massive hands planted on his desk, giving the impression of two octopi. "Can you—can any of you—lay claim to doing something as audacious as starting a company at the age of nineteen and securing millions in investor fundraising?"

"No, but—" Reuben attempted.

"No, indeed," Cyrus said, cutting Reuben off. "As CEO, Hollis is not being tasked with the reinvention of the wheel. Noah, Umed, Kai, myself, and even you—Reuben, my doubting friend—are world class in their roles. ExOh's flight path is preprogrammed. All Hollis has to do is sit in the pilot's chair and take the credit. He is a man of immense talents, tasked with immediate responsibilities that are, quite honestly, beneath him. But I have no doubt he will tackle them with gusto and make us all proud."

At this point, I was red with embarrassment. Never had any boss gone to bat as hard for me as Cyrus—a man I still barely knew—was presently doing.

"You're betting the company on him," Reuben said as Noah, Kai, and Umed sat mutely watching the volleys, taking no sides, offering no opinions. I wondered why they remained silent. Then a personal recollection from two jobs prior leapt to mind, explaining their reluctance. In this painful memory, I had been a senior vice president in a disagreement with the company's chief technology officer about the most efficient way to encrypt our server-to-mobile messages. The CTO was fifty years old—ancient, I thought at the time—and did not understand the latest specs I had been churning out. Per always, when he did not understand something, he rejected it, labeling it *unnecessary*. Instead of backing down, I bet him one dollar that I could prove that his method was four times slower and half as effective as mine. Everyone else in the room took a metaphorical step back, recognizing my mistake. The CTO had no choice; he accepted my bet. When I won, he handed me the dollar bill, and thirty minutes later, he handed me my first cardboard box.

Unlike me, Noah, Kai, and Umed were too smart to stick their necks out on either side of this debate. Silent they remained.

"Bottom line, Reuben—and for that matter, Noah, Kai, and Umed as well," Cyrus said, his eyes narrowed. "Do you trust me?"

Without pausing, all four ExOh executives nodded.

"Thank you," Cyrus continued. "And I, you. So with that mutual trust established, I am asking each of you to extend your faith in me to my handpicked CEO, Hollis Crawford. I am confident that Hollis is up to the challenge. Isn't that right, Hollis?"

All spotlights were now on me, awaiting my acceptance of Cyrus's seemingly bottomless trust. Not since my mother had assured me—incorrectly, I might add—that I could do anything I put my mind to, had I felt such unearned faith. It was like being wrapped in a warm blanket. Without any supporting evidence, I embraced Cyrus's view of me as a fait accompli, leaving only one possible answer to his question: "One hundred percent."

## Chapter Eleven

Cricket was asleep when I crawled into bed, giving me more time to complete my mental tallying while the thoughts were fresh. Despite the late hour and artificial caffeine effects, I felt reborn, my mind spinning on ways to live up to Cyrus's advanced billing. At one point in the darkness, I turned on the bedside lamp to scribble notes: ideas for Umed's website reboot project, client recommendations for Noah, and a deep dive with Kai on finance software vendors.

I retreated to the darkness, my initial satisfaction at penning a list of to-do's fading fast. That list I had scribbled on the bedside notepad was a vestige of the old me: sticking my nose where it doesn't belong, airing my judgments as if I'd been asked, demanding everyone else follow my lead. These were what had cost me previous chances to succeed. Cyrus had designed a lean organization of experts that he entrusted to do their jobs. Why would I interfere with that? Well intended as my suggestions might have been, this behavior was a wash, rinse, repeat of my prior workplace failures. I could not—I would not—do that.

The first thing I did the next morning was crumple that list of notes and bury it in the bathroom trash can, deep under used dental floss and Q-tips, assuring that I would never attempt to retrieve it. The crumple weighed mere grams, but I felt pounds lighter.

With a free day in front of me and no concrete understanding of what my job entailed, I took the kids to school and let Cricket swim with the Masters. I hoped this might be my new life: a better family man, around more, available more, happier.

The kids groaned when they found out Dad was taking them to school, but once we started walking, they warmed into far more engaging versions of the monosyllabic kids who joined me on our previous walks.

There was no Flag Day ceremony this day, but I was still shocked by the number of parents who lingered around the school—sipping coffee and chatting—long after dropping off their children. Just as my insecurity was about to rear its jealous head, a series of rational counter-thoughts emerged. For all I knew, these parents might have the sort of ill-defined, chunky jobs that I had just signed onto. Perhaps they too worked for little to no cash and only the promise of future upside. I knew nothing about my fellow parents, just as I was still learning about the realities of my own fresh-faced adventure.

True or not, these thoughts filled me with a sense of kinship for my fellow MUS parents that I had never felt before. Perhaps, in some way, I belonged here after all.

With my free day, I decided to tackle my gar-office, readying it for whatever my work was to be. The garage was a single-car shed with a manually operated sectional door. Built in the 1920s, it was completely impractical for parking an actual car—we tried once with Cricket's twenty-three-year-old Toyota Land Cruiser, and it looked like a baby trying to reenter the birth canal—so we used the garage solely for storage.

Inside, with the sectional door shut, it felt like a tomb, sending shivers up my spine. I quickly decided that mine would be an open-air gar-office.

Like it or not, I would be sharing this space with the junk we had been storing here since moving in, so step one was to move everything out, culling where possible. By the time I had separated the keeps from the tosses, I had a nice collection for donation to the thrift store.

Step two was to wage war on the spiders. I donned my straw lifeguards' hat from Santa Barbara Surf Shop, a pair of Cricket's swim goggles I had borrowed without permission, and gardening gloves, then grabbed a broom, steeling myself for the heebie-jeebies. When I reemerged from the garage after a spirited bout of jousting, I looked like Indiana Jones in the iconic opening scene of *Raiders of the Lost Ark.*

The webs were defeated, but were there spider babies in the crevices waiting to reclaim their homeland? After four cans of Raid Max Spider Killer, I had filled every joint and crack in the garage and inhaled enough fumes to take years off my life. I stumbled from the garage, took off my battle gear, and lay in the grass until my consciousness fully returned.

With the air clear, I commenced step three: actual cleaning. A second round of sweeping the rafters brought down the dust like rain. At lower levels, I used Cricket's organic, no bad ingredients, you-can-drink-it-if-you-want spray cleaner—comical after all the spider toxicant I had already inhaled—and roll after roll of paper towels. By the time I was finished, I was unrecognizably dirty, but the garage looked decent.

Step four: I reorganized the remaining storage items along the most scarred of the garage's walls and modified two shower curtain rods and several sheets to create a barrier between my professional self and the family's toys. It was the garage equivalent of a mullet: business in the front, party in the back.

Several of the items in our storage were fortuitous: a rectangular folding table and two old metal filing cabinets. The folding table was too wobbly on its own, but when mounted on top of the filing cabinets, it formed an excellent desk. A cheap floor lamp with a one-hundred-fifty-watt bulb lit the gar-office adequately, but woe unto anyone who stared directly into the lamp's core. For a chair, I stole from the dining room; who needs dinner guests anyway? And finally, I installed a Wi-Fi extender to up the wireless signal strength in the garage.

With my laptop booted and working, I sat in the makeshift office chair and stared at my new gar-office surroundings. It would do, I concluded, but God help me and my back if this situation persisted for more than a year.

The next morning, I took the kids to school again while Cricket swam before her work, then went to meet Cyrus at Merci. As with our first coffee date, I arrived early, and Cyrus arrived late. Our orders were repeated—though I did allow myself a refill this time—and our conversation easy. This time there was no confusion over my desires and his objectives; I was here to receive my marching orders.

Cyrus came prepared too. "So, here is the crux of my challenge," he said, sliding a pile of papers across the bistro table. "Thanks to—well, there's no other way to say it—xenophobic tensions between the United States and the Middle East, I was not awarded the visa I needed to run ExOh properly. I mean"—he threw his hands in the air—"it's laughable. The US government should be begging me to set up shop here, and instead, they are treating me like a tourist..."

I nodded sympathetically, though I was over my skis on this issue. Like most people, I did not have a solid understanding of the US government's available visa programs or their requirements. My knowledge was strictly limited to news stories about illegal border crossings and migrant workers.

"As CEO," Cyrus continued, "you will largely be performing executive tasks that my visa status restricts me from completing. You are, in effect, my proxy."

He licked his fingers, peeled off the first document from his stack, and presented it to me for my signature.

"This document registers ExOh Holdings Incorporated as a

California corporation and reassigns the company's tax ID number," he said as I dutifully signed.

"This appoints you to the board of directors," he said, sliding a second document under my pen. I had not served on a board of directors since my days at Gusher at the age of nineteen. A pleasant tingle tickled my spine as my pen slid across the page.

"This is ExOh's bank account application with Miramar Bank and Trust."

"Miramar Bank and Trust?" I asked, signing the third document.

"You remember John Colton from dinner?"

I nodded.

"Miramar Bank and Trust was founded by his family," Cyrus said. "John is making a sizable investment in ExOh and practically begged me to open this account. Between you and me, I think John wants a seat on our board." Cyrus winked. "I plan to make him work for it."

I shook my head, wondering how I'd been so lucky to fall into Cyrus's magnetic obit. An orbit where generational millionaires are made to *work for it*.

"This new Miramar account will receive ExOh's investor funds," Cyrus explained. "Our operating account is at Citibank in Hong Kong. Once the new account is established, we'll be open to receiving the investments John, Barton, and many others have pledged." Cyrus paused, leaning in conspiratorially. "I must tell you, the reception from your fellow Montecito residents has been through the roof. It's truly humbling." He put a hand to his heart and shook his head.

I nodded, grateful for the validation of local bigwigs. People tend to romanticize the trope of lone wolf success while they crave the confirmation of crowds, and I was no different. "Great to hear," I said. "What else?"

"We're just getting started," Cyrus said. "I'll need you to coordinate the handoff between Kai and our external accountants..."

I scribbled notes as Cyrus ticked off my to-dos, my sloppy

handwriting looking more like Egyptian hieroglyphics than cursive English.

"...and our third-party legal counsel..."

My automatic pencil finished one stick of lead, requiring about twenty clicks to get the next piece loaded. Cyrus kept talking.

"...and, of course, we'll need to get the company's new ticker registered with the OTC, our company profile completed, and you will need to submit a Live Scan to the Department of Justice..."

I broke the lead. More clicking.

"Did you get all of that?" he asked.

"Yeeeessss," I said, stretching out my answer as I scribbled the final instructions to myself. "Did you say OTC?"

"Yes, OTC," he explained. "It stands for over the counter. It's a stock exchange for newer companies like ExOh. It's just a stopgap: By this time next year, we will be trading on the NASDAQ."

"Okay," I said, writing, *stopgap* in the margin of my notebook, the word staring back at me accusingly. Why was the stock trading on an exchange I had never heard of? Why was a stopgap necessary? What would it take to make this jump to the NASDAQ?

My inner grumpy old man raised his cane to these ask questions, but I grabbed his arm. I needed to do some research, that's all. There was no need to bother Cyrus with a bunch of questions that only underscored my ignorance.

"That is it, my friend," Cyrus said. "Can you handle it?"

I looked at the stack of papers and my scribbles, my head aching with the realization of my knowledge gap. I had so much to learn, but once I understood, I was sure I could handle it. More to the point, I *had* to handle it. My family was counting on me. "No problem," I declared.

"Terrific," Cyrus said, beaming just as his jacket pocket vibrated with an incoming call. His face turned surprised, then serious when he saw the caller ID. "Apologies, Hollis, but I must take this," he said, standing so abruptly that his chair nearly toppled backward. He hit the receive button, wedged the phone between his ear and shoulder, and scooped up his remaining papers. "Vlad, my friend," I heard him say as he walked away. "I was just about to call you."

It was not until he'd driven off that I realized he had once again left me with the bill.

# Chapter Twelve

Eager to prove my worth, I attacked the administrative tasks before me like a vulture to roadkill. It was far from intellectual work, but I imagined my new position was like one of those management grooming programs at a large company, where hopeful trainees are ushered hither and yon to learn about every aspect of the company's empire. This was my stint in *administration*, I reasoned, and it was revelatory if not stimulating.

I opened the new bank account, filed forms with the California Secretary of State, and updated the company's registration with the OTC Exchange. For each of these tasks, I signed my name on the literal and figurative dotted lines. Coincidentally, my new professional role stirred some sort of gastrointestinal issue that I had never experienced before. Gluten insensitivity? Lactose intolerance? Too many carbs; not enough carbs? I bought a tub of extra-strength Rolaids.

With the ExOh bank account now open, investor funds began flowing in the form of checks and wires for amounts from fifty thousand to a half-million dollars. I recognized all the names as Montecito and Santa Barbara residents. Within two weeks, our funding account had received three million five hundred thousand dollars.

Cyrus and Genevieve continued to host Montecito's wealthiest at weekly dinner parties. Cricket and I were now assumed attendees, while Isabel and Trip were always invited. In addition, both of my kids were riding horses with Priscilla Wimby on a weekly basis. It was as if the Crawfords had been adopted by a wealthy benefactor, and my whole family was finally getting the life I'd wished I could provide them; though, in truth, I had never imagined I could provide them with any of this.

The wood-fired pizza oven was far more versatile than its name implied. Roasted chickens, salt-domed fish, steaks; as I should have understood from the beginning, it was simply a fancy, large outdoor oven. Desserts varied too: homemade ice cream, cookies, crème brûlée, rhubarb tart, and of course, key lime pie. I asked for the recipe each time. "Family secret," she repeated, denying my requests.

There was nothing about Cyrus and Genevieve that Montecito did not already have. I saw Julia-Louis Dreyfus at the Montecito Village Grocery. I saw Ellen DeGeneres and Portia de Rossi walking on Padaro Beach. I saw Oprah Winfrey at a candlelight vigil after the Montecito mudslides. I passed Jack Johnson carrying his surfboard down the Hammond's Trail. I saw Prince Harry riding his bicycle. I saw Kevin Costner at Oliver's vegan restaurant. I saw Rob Lowe at Rincon. I saw one of the Baldwin brothers—I could never remember which one—so often that I caught myself saying hello as if we were friends. In a town of ten thousand people, it took two hands to count the residential real estate listings priced at more than $50 million. Anonymous people with wealth measured in multiples of nine figures walked up and down the sidewalks of Coast Village Road daily.

Within that backdrop, the Wimbys were a classic Montecito power couple. Cyrus, the indomitable business tycoon turning all he touched to gold. Genevieve, the trophy wife with Michelin-starred hosting and culinary prowess. In another sufficiently enlightened marriage, Genevieve might have been the muscle behind the family's fortunes. Alas, she married a man whose success rendered commercializing her skills moot; oh, to have such problems. Together, they were the stereotype that proved why stereotypes exist.

Yet, despite these familiar notes, the Wimbys brought something that the Montecito community lapped like a hungry cat. It was not their wealth, although they had plenty. It was not their diversity, although that was one thing lily-white Montecito did lack. It was not their interests; horses, wine, and gastronomic delights were par for the course in Santa Barbara County.

When I look back on it now, I think that *something* was the Wimbys' ravenous desire to share. Everyone in Montecito needed some degree of privacy, hence the ubiquitous towering hedges. But not the Wimbys. They were in a race to reveal it all—to meet, to learn, to cultivate. Everything they had was available for the asking, as if they had gotten it all for free.

# Chapter Thirteen

The first time Cyrus instructed me to move money from the ExOh bank account, the request was for $49,000 by wire transfer to a Citibank account in Hong Kong. He called me three times that morning to verify it had been sent, then waited on the phone as I clicked refresh repeatedly until the confirmation code appeared. The transaction took a total of fifteen minutes from send to receipt; no complications.

The next day, he instructed me to move $99,000.

The next day, $149,000.

The next day, two wire transfers of $249,000 each.

The next day, $500,000 even.

There were no complications or alarms with any of the transactions: Miramar Bank sent the money, and Citibank Hong Kong received the money. Just over $1.5 million remained in ExOh's Miramar Bank account.

"Splendid," Cyrus declared. "Fantastic work, Hollis."

"What were those transfers for?" I asked.

"Checking the plumbing," he said. "Sometimes banks have difficulty talking to each other. Sometimes their wiring policies are different than promised. You always need to make sure that you understand exactly how the money moves long before you *need* the money to move. By then it's too late."

While this was new to me, the explanation made sense. "So, the transferred money will fund growth of ExOh, right?"

"Exactly," Cyrus said. "Kai will use the money to pay ExOh's Chinese employees and operating partners. Effectively, the US division of ExOh just loaned money to the Hong Kong division. The right hand sharing with the left. It's all within the ExOh umbrella."

As Cyrus explained this to me, I kicked myself for not getting an MBA at some point on my bumpy road. Surely some graduate business school would have made these concepts familiar. Instead, I was constantly behind and persistently asking for explanations. Cyrus was gracious in supplying answers, but I would have preferred not needing his crutch. Maybe an executive MBA or a night program was in my future? Either way, as uncomfortable as the vulnerability was, it was thrilling to be stretching my boundaries for the first time in many years.

With a few of these new concepts feeling less foreign, it was time to see if I could put them on display for a friendly audience of two. That night, we were meeting Paul—my best friend and former CryptoWallet partner—and his wife, Jenny, for a bonfire and s'mores at Hammond's Beach. I was looking forward to the chance to catch up with Paul and toot my own horn a little. This is shameful to admit—Paul was my friend and he wished me well —but my fragile ego needed a chance to strut.

I had prepared for this evening the only way I knew how. Paul and Jenny were likely to ask softball questions, but what if they didn't? It didn't matter; eventually I would need to become an expert on ExOh in the same way I was an expert in C++ and binary algorithms. While Cyrus had shown himself to be a patient teacher, I needed to prove I could learn on my own. Google could not help. Amazon was useless. The Chinese websites were written in Mandarin. The only thing left for me to do was wear out my library card in a way I had not since college.

The first time I visited the Montecito branch of the Santa Barbara County Library, I walked in and out, thinking I must have the wrong address. It was like a dollhouse model of a library, not the real thing. However, what it lacked in size, it more than made up for in service. If a book existed on the shelves anywhere in the county library system, I could request it, and request it I did. Within three days, every book in the county that might possibly shed light on Chinese trade was delivered to the Montecito branch for my leisurely pick up. When I imagined the great wheels of action required to deliver me these books for free, I felt guilty and vowed to make a donation to the library just as soon as a few of my ExOh shares hit the jackpot.

I learned many things during this library research. Most importantly, I learned what a black hole ExOh and its investors were stepping into. I could not find a single document—academic, governmental, memoir, trade rag—that informed me how China's import laws worked. Not that I doubted Cyrus's tale of rules and special rules—*All animals are equal, but some animals are more equal than others*—but I wanted to understand it independently of his explanation. Unfortunately, I could not confirm his account, nor could I disprove it.

This information void made me uncomfortable even as I understood why it existed. China—a communist country notorious for double standards—would have nothing to gain by creating a handbook documenting its duplicitous rules. But if I could not verify the rules of the game, neither could anyone else, including the wealthy investors wiring ExOh tens of thousands of dollars daily and introducing Cyrus to their friends to further the money-gathering machine. The old Russian proverb cautions to *Trust but verify.* All we had was trust.

Trust was not good enough for the old Hollis Crawford; he demanded proof. But the new me refused to give in to the dream-killing nitpicking that the old me could not resist. As my family prepared for a celebration with friends, I put a thumbtack in my remaining concerns, vowing to revisit them in the future. For the rest of this day, I would bask in the rarefied glow of professional success.

Our destination, Hammond's Beach, was accessible only at low tide or by the same unmarked, bougainvillea-draped path that I had walked the day I stumbled upon Landon's body: the Hammond's Trail. While only a quarter mile in length, the sum value of the real estate backing up to the trail would easily top a half billion dollars. A few steps down the beach from the trail's terminus—just inland from where Landon was found—was the three-acre Shalawa Meadow, an ancient burial ground of the Chumash, the first nation of the central coast of California. The beachfront meadow was largely unmarked, save for a small circle of stones and a single inscribed marker. To out-of-towners, the meadow might appear to be the aesthetic choice of property developers, providing a gracious oceanfront lawn in front of the small neighborhood's seven- and eight-figure homes. That presumption could not have been farther from the truth. It took decades of vicious fighting from the Chumash, environmentalists, and local preservationists to keep the meadow as a monument to those who lived on this land for at least ten thousand years before the white man barged in.

For the locals, the beach's offshore reef made it a favorite with surfers looking for a nice right-hand break that delivered consistent waves with the slightest of swells. Its relative remoteness also made it the least crowded of Montecito's beaches and the least patrolled by park rangers. Thus, it was the perfect spot for a bonfire.

Paul brought shovels and starter logs; no need for traditional firewood, as driftwood was easy to find along the ungroomed beach. Cricket brought her s'more-making paraphernalia: two dozen wood-handled roasting sticks and a s'mores assembly line process worthy of a patent. Jenny brought pre-dessert snacks and plastic wine tumblers, and—thanks to Cyrus's generosity—I brought a few bottles of Entre Nous wine. The kids—eight in total once friends were included—played in the waves and tossed a football, while Cricket and Jenny set up a home base of blankets and food, popping the cork on a few bottles of wine. Paul and I dug the fire pits, taking care to line the edge of the holes with heavy rocks, and prepared the stacks of driftwood for the bonfire that was to come.

With the work done, Paul and I helped ourselves to some of Cyrus's wine and joined Jenny and Cricket on the blankets. They were laughing hysterically over something we probably were not meant to understand, so neither of us bothered to request an explanation. A smile overtook my face as the sun crept toward the horizon. I felt alive, embracing the world in a way wholly foreign to my memory.

"Wait! Finally," Jenny said, stifling her laughter. "Tell us, tell us. What's with this new mysterious job?"

Cricket leaned back on her elbows, giving me a sly wink. As much as she was the spark, launching our family to fun and adventure, she was quick to remind me that I was the family's emotional compass. When I was struggling, it brought everyone else down. There was only so much she could do to swim against my riptide. But lately I could see my budding hopefulness reflected in her. We were closer. Touching more, laughing more, talking of our future without weighty caveats and provisos.

"I don't want to bore you," I said, waving her off.

"Please! I want to know," Jenny begged.

"Careful, Jenny," Paul said. "When Hollis thinks something might be boring, you should heed his warning."

I proceeded with my own version of Cyrus's spiel about the trading licenses, the lack of competition, the massive market opportunity, and my evolving role.

"How big is your team?" Paul asked.

"Small but growing," I answered, intentionally vague.

"Will you be traveling to China very often?" Jenny asked.

"Yes," I confirmed. "I'm looking forward to taking the whole family once things get off the ground." My stomach tweaked at this comment; I dug a Tums from my pocket and popped it with a sip of Pinot.

"What do you think about all this, Cricket?" Paul asked.

She rose from her elbows and hugged her knees tightly. "I'm really proud of him," she said.

"Me too," Paul said, lifting his glass.

"Me three," Jenny echoed.

I raised my glass, acknowledging the toast. I am sure my face burned crimson, but with the sun racing to close the day, it was easy to hide. "We should start the bonfires," I said.

Paul and I lit the starter logs and watched the wood take the flame, as proud as if we had invented the concept of fire. With the lap of the flames visible, the kids ran in from the water, shivering and begging for warm towels and hoodies.

Cricket and Jenny manned the graham crackers and Hershey bars while Paul and I threaded marshmallows onto the sticks. Trip dropped three into the fire and began to cry—exhaustion and low blood sugar doing their dirty work—before I stepped in and helped him complete his first successful s'more.

Once the kids had their fill, they ran back to play, leaving us adults to enjoy the fires by ourselves. Eventually, with the sun long gone and the creep of chilly air battling the warmth of the flames, we put out the fires and packed up, heading back down the Hammond's Trail with lighter loads, fuller stomachs, and lifted hearts.

# Chapter Fourteen

THE NEXT MORNING, I received a group message from Cyrus to me, Umed, Kai, Noah, and Reuben on the mobile app named BatSignal, Cyrus's preferred encrypted messaging program. Cyrus liked its security, he said, and Umed, Kai, Noah, and Reuben seemed to agree. Our group communiqué listed all participants with first names only and each person was identified by random objects, avatars, and inanimate photos. All except Cyrus and me, of course; he in French cuffs and an accompanying pocket square, me in my best navy blazar.

*Website is up. Looking sharp. Thank you, Umed,* Cyrus messaged.

The previous version of our website had been thin on details; it was more of a *coming soon* site than a true company profile. True to my pledge, I had resisted the urge to offer my services to Umed, letting him handle the task on his own. With the website finished, I felt relief. The same solace someone on a diet feels, making it to bed without diving into the ice cream carton in the back of the freezer.

And when I saw the work Umed had completed, I was proud that I had kept my nose out of it. The site looked terrific. Plenty of eye candy, graphic slides, and menus that performed intuitively.

I was thrilled to see that Umed was up to the task. Cyrus had promised a team of experts, and if the website were any indication, I could take him at his word.

Under *Investor Relations* were several PowerPoint presentations that I had developed under Cyrus's direction. He was a verbal communicator, not a written one, so it took time to re-create his magic two-dimensionally. The presentations were packed with statistics, declarations, and promises that unfortunately bore no footnotes; Cyrus's knowledge was the only flashlight in this dark forest. At the end of each presentation there were brief bios of the core executive team, written by me with details provided by Cyrus.

Despite the dozens of Zoom calls and my own authorship of each team member's bio, I was anxious to click the website's *Team* link, with its tantalizing promise of putting clear faces and complete backgrounds to all our names.

At the top left was the company's patriarch, Cyrus Wimby, in French cuffs and blazer, his electric smile burning pixels off my laptop. Clicking on his picture lead to a bio, mentioning his distinguished career working for the Saudi royal family and declaring him a graduate of the University of Oxford.

Wait? Cyrus told me he graduated from Cambridge. I made a note to let Umed know of the error.

To Cyrus's right was me. The picture looked like me. The bio read of me.

On the next row down came the other four members of the executive team. Wow, these guys cleaned up nicely. Almost unrecognizably so. In our Zoom calls, everyone had scruffy beards and sleepy eyes. In these pictures, the rest of the team was clean shaven, freshly coifed, and dressed for business. The difference was stark. Noah's photo in particular left me scratching my head. Acknowledging that Zoom calls using grainy computer video cameras could be hit or miss, I would have bet money that Noah's eyes were brown. But the Noah on our website had electric-blue eyes. Strange, I thought. Though, for all I knew, Noah wore tinted blue contacts or liked to Photoshop himself for dating and hookup apps.

A few other biographical differences caught my eye. Website Noah had previously worked for Yahoo! but investor presentation Noah had worked at Google. Website Kai's hobbies included triathlons, but investor presentation Kai competed in marathons. Website Reuben had been a solicitor for thirty years while investor presentation Reuben had only been practicing for twenty-five years. And according to the website, Umed had a PhD from the Technical University of Munich—a fact missing entirely from the presentations I had prepared.

I took a deep breath, reminding myself that this was a just-released beta version of a website. There had been no committee meetings to debate the content or verify its accuracy. Mistakes were bound to happen. In short, *stay chill, Hollis*; these were easy corrections.

Below the executive team were at least one hundred smiling faces and names that I had never met before, organized by city—Shanghai or Beijing—and function. All the names were Chinese; all the schools and experiences were unfamiliar to my Anglo eyes.

I felt a familiar pang of inadequacy that I was the chief executive officer of this company, and yet I was only now visualizing the human size and scope of our operations. I chastised myself; this was not the kind of executive I wanted to be. I needed to visit our China operations. I needed to see our people and facilities myself. I could not be the man who simply sat on his Montecito perch and approved financial statements.

I rejoined the BatSignal discussion and echoed Cyrus's praise for Umed's work on the website. *Nice work, Umed,* I tapped out. *The website looks fantastic.*

*Hear, hear,* Cyrus replied.

*One thing,* I typed. *There are a few discrepancies between the bios of the investor presentations and those in the Team section of the website.*

*Ah,* Umed wrote. *I will fix.*

Initially, this felt sufficient, before the obvious question occurred to me: How did he know which set of facts was correct? I typed and backspaced over a few different follow-up questions, fearing with each draft that I sounded like a hall pass monitor. The old Hollis would not have been so considerate. I recalled an exit interview from a prior job when I was criticized for not forgiving my coworkers of their mistakes. "You can't treat someone like they are an idiot forever just because they got something wrong once," I was told. On its face, this seemed like valuable feedback, but truth be told, that particular *someone* was in fact a certified idiot.

*I did not know you had a PhD, Umed,* I finally wrote, settling on an indirect approach. *That's impressive. Sorry I left that out of the presentation.*

*Yes,* he wrote back without elaboration.

*Easy enough to fix, Umed,* Cyrus chimed in. *Thanks for the eagle eyes, Hollis!*

*Stop being you,* I chastised myself. I took a few deep breaths. *No problem, guys,* I wrote, in the language of the new me. *Once Umed is done with the website corrections, I will update the presentations.*

*Fantastic resolution, team,* Cyrus replied. *Nice work, everyone.*

I nodded even as my gastrointestinal discomfort leveled up. Rolaids and Tums were like sugar pills; I had now graduated to Prevacid. I popped one and waited for relief, noticing that one of my eyelids was twitching while an unfamiliar trapezoidal tension roped my back.

What was my problem? ExOh had a beautiful website. The small errors were fixed. Everyone had been humble and apologetic. Mistakes happen. Why was my body revolting?

Part of me wanted to talk to Cricket about this tiny thing that had spooked me. Another part recognized that—professionally speaking—I was the boy who cried wolf. How many times had I come to her complaining of small inconsistencies and discrepancies built into sandcastles of worry? Further, what was she going to do? My complaining would only transfer my anxiety to her; she deserved better.

This internal pep talk worked. My anxiety declined. My fingers stopped shaking. My stomach relaxed. My old demons retreated.

I synchronized the presentations and sent them to Umed for uploading.

*Updated presentations received and posted,* Umed wrote. *Thanks for your help.*

Nanoseconds later, Cyrus again chimed in supportively. *Good work, everyone.*

I chuckled to myself. Overreacting was one element of my *fog.* Thankfully, this time I had managed to keep from revealing my lunacy to the rest of the team. This was good; this was progress. Maybe the new me was finally starting to gain the upper hand on the old me.

Before the old me had a chance to strike back, I pressed my newfound advantage. I opened my LinkedIn profile and penned a post, announcing the new website and business relaunch. My network boasted a total of 341 connections—rural billboards collect more eyeballs on a Sunday—but for me, this was an important statement of ownership and a further blow to my demons of doubt.

The move felt so good, I typed an email to Cricket's parents, cc'ing her. *Wanted to share an update on ExOh Holdings,* I wrote in the subject line. In the body, I pasted a link to the redesigned website prefaced with *Thank you for believing in me.* Within minutes, Cricket's father replied: *Proud of you, Hollis. Let me know when I can invest!* Cricket wrote back privately with a series of applauding GIFs and the three words that matter most: *I love you.*

# Chapter Fifteen

I successfully shifted my morning meetings with Cyrus from the Country Mart's Merci to his home. More often than not, I ended up paying the Merci bill and—as great as the coffee and setting were—I could not afford it.

Our meeting venue was now the Wimbys' library room with a set time of 10:00 a.m. I was physically incapable of arriving late, but Cyrus lived by more flexible constraints. To while away the time, I brought books from the public library on trade policy and macroeconomics, still searching for the how-to that would shed independent light on ExOh's China advantage.

At thirty minutes after ten, the Wimbys' nanny—whose job transitioned to maid when Priscilla was at camp or school—notified me that Cyrus requested my presence in his bedroom.

"Hollis!" he hollered as I entered uneasily. Even if nothing was on display, other people's bedrooms made me uncomfortable. Unfortunately, Cyrus was packing a suitcase, meaning I was confronted with stacks of his underwear and socks. My discomfort amplified.

"Where are you headed?" I asked, my eyes steering clear of Cyrus's undergarments.

"Fundraising trip," he said. "Demand is high; need to strike while the iron is hot. We are headed to La Jolla, Laguna Beach, Newport Beach, Huntington Palisades, Malibu, Pebble Beach, and Carmel-by-the-Sea."

*We?* He had not mentioned it before this moment, and—surprise—I didn't appreciate sudden schedule changes. But a fundraising trip? What an exciting experience. "That's a lot of driving," I said casually, biding my time for all of three seconds. "Uh, when you say *we*, do you mean—"

"Sorry," Cyrus said, shaking his head. "John Colton and I," he clarified. "These are his connections, his friends. It is just the two of us. Well, us and his Gulfstream." Cyrus smiled. "I don't like to drive."

John Colton, current patriarch of Miramar Bank and Trust, was now both a significant investor in ExOh and a member of the company's three-strong board of directors. The connection to the bank and John was paying off: John seemed to know everyone of significance in California and was now arranging private investor meetings. I presumed the meetings and the Gulfstream were the proof of desire Cyrus had envisioned when he told me he wanted to see John Colton *work for it.*

My jealousy aside, the prospect of more money coming in was tremendous news. If it was good for ExOh, it was good for me.

"When I return in ten days, I will be dragging a treasure chest behind me," Cyrus declared. "You worry about getting the stock relisted. Speaking of, do you have a status report on that?"

Indeed I did, and I was excited to deliver the news of my first genuine contribution to the team. "We're at the finish line, Cyrus," I said, whipping out my own set of paperwork for a change. "The accounting and legal teams have given us a thumbs-up. All that is left is a signature, and we can set a date for trading to resume."

Cyrus turned from his suitcase and embraced me with the mother of all bear hugs. Given the length of his arms, it was like being attacked by an anaconda. "I knew you could do it," he said, picking me up so that only my toes touched the ground.

When he finally let go, it took a second for me to regain my breath and shake off the discomfort of a lot more man-on-man contact than I was comfortable with. "I even brought my lucky pen," I said, waving a slightly chewed Bic ballpoint.

"Well, let's see you do it," he said.

I reached forward, presenting him with the papers and the pen; his forehead wrinkled. "For you," I clarified.

Cyrus squinted. "Not for *me*. For you."

I shook my head. "No, I insist. You've been working on this forever. I've been working on it for weeks. This is your moment in the sun."

"Be that as it may," he said. "I cannot sign. We've been over this."

"I understand, but—"

"You understand, do you?" he snapped, his eyes narrowing to slits. "Do you think I enjoy being in this position? ExOh is my company. It's my legacy. It's my life's work. And I can't even sign a simple record of our financial results."

My heart rate climbed the asymptotic curve toward panic. "But surely the authorities would want the person signing this to be the most knowledgeable person, wouldn't they?"

Cyrus interlaced his fingers behind his head and stared at the ceiling. "Do you want to hear the latest?" he asked, ignoring my question.

I recalled my outstretched hands and nodded.

"The State Department is refusing my visa because they believe I brokered a sale of embargoed Iranian oil. It's ridiculous!" he declared, waving his hands so wildly I thought I might catch a stray slap. "I made one phone call. One! That's an introduction and nothing more. The whole thing is a witch hunt."

"I'm really sorry," I said, assuming I was supposed to apologize on behalf of my native country.

He shook his head and waved away my apology. "I know it's

not your fault, but it's..." His angry eyes suddenly turned glassy with tears. "It's humiliating."

I knew the onset of Cyrus's waterworks meant that I was expected to show sympathy and lower my resolve. But I was facing my own storm of muddled feelings, and the fact remained that I did not feel comfortable attesting to financial results I could not verify. "I'm..." I paused, searching for the right words. "I'm a little in the dark here. I haven't seen the contracts and invoices that justify these financial statements."

"Get the contracts and invoices from Kai," Cyrus said, his demeanor again whipsawing, this time to dispassionate calm. "You're the CEO. Everything in this company is at your disposal. All you have to do is ask for it."

I shook my head reflexively. "I don't think that—" I began, stopping midsentence when Cyrus raised his giant hand like a traffic cop.

"Do you want to know why Reuben balked at my hiring you?"

I swallowed, recalling Reuben's angry protest over my appointment. "Why?"

"He said you weren't a leader; you were a critic. That your default position was to find imperfections and then harp on them. That you weren't interested in solutions, only problems."

I exhaled, not sure whether to be impressed or horrified. I didn't know where Reuben unearthed this critique, but it unfortunately dovetailed with the criticisms I had received from more than one boss who asked for the return of my employee ID. Had Reuben background checked me? My now persistent stomachache gurgled at the appearance of this Ghost of Christmas Past. I searched my pocket for more pills, but I had none.

"I stuck my neck out for you, Hollis," he continued. "I defended you against Reuben's attacks, and I stood by you even after I discovered that you lied to me."

The hits were coming fast and furious at this point, but the last blow caught me on my heels as my wrinkled forehead and pinched eyebrows revealed.

"Don't play dumb," Cyrus said. "When I first broached the idea of you joining ExOh, you told me that you were, quote, *open to leaving*, close quote, your current employer. We both know that was not accurate. You were not *open to leaving*. You had been unceremoniously fired."

The memory of that moment came back in a rush. Our first coffee meeting at Merci. Cyrus had not known I was unemployed. *What harm would it do?* I had thought. An innocuous lie, or so I believed. For someone who rarely lied, I had chosen a poor time to start a habit.

"I would have been well within my rights to show you the door once I learned of your lie, but I didn't," Cyrus continued. "I think there's a loyal team player within you, but I need you to prove me right."

I nodded sheepishly, my counterarguments exhausted.

"So, here we are," he said, spinning the diamond wedding band on his finger as if tightening a screw. "You came to me looking for an opportunity at ExOh. I put you in a prestigious position. I fought for you when members of my team doubted you. I revealed my vulnerabilities, and I trusted you to fill those gaps."

He stared at me until my eyes rose to meet his.

"This was always the job," he continued. "From the onset, I told you that I needed you to be my proxy. I could not have been clearer as to my needs and expectations."

I wrestled my embarrassed eyes away from his stare, focusing on his size-sixteen shoes instead. Cyrus was right; he had been clear. The disconnect was on me. I had not fully grasped the meaning of *be my proxy* when confronted with a blank dotted line.

"Whatever you need to do to educate yourself, do it," Cyrus declared. "Get the contracts and invoices from Kai. Create your own financial reports. Hire an accounting tutor. Pray for a sign from God. Whatever it takes. But make a decision and make it fast because, as of this moment, *your* discomfort has become *my* bottleneck."

He waited, letting these words marinate the room, knowing I would be unable to avoid his gaze for long.

"You have two choices," he finally said when my eyes returned to his force field. "Get on board or get gone."

# Chapter Sixteen

On the second night of Cyrus's fundraising trip, he messaged our team with some good news by BatSignal.

*Greetings, gentlemen,* his message began. *Great start in La Jolla; checks should be rolling in soon. We decamped in Laguna Beach tonight. Additionally, let us all congratulate Noah on landing three phenomenal clients for ExOh. We will be the exclusive importer of record for Selfridges, Bloomingdale's, and Galeries Lafayette for all sales into mainland China. Huge get! Well done, Noah!*

This was incredibly reassuring news. It is one thing convincing investors to back a company—in and of itself a massive challenge—but wholly different wooing customers. And these were not just customers; they were majors.

*Great work, Noah!* I replied, joining the chorus of congratulations.

*Hollis, we need a press release for our US investors,* Cyrus continued. *Noah, please supply Hollis with all the necessary details so he is comfortable.*

The subtlety of this jab was not lost on me. I debated my reply carefully given my thin ice and prior scolding. *To be safe, should the press release come from you, Cyrus?* I replied. *Most of our investors don't know me, and I don't want this great news ending up in their spam folders.*

*No time like the present,* Cyrus wrote. *Copy me. Everyone needs to start seeing you as the man responsible for driving the value of their investment.*

My stomach tweaked. I popped my fifth Prevacid, now well over the recommended daily dosing. *You got it,* I wrote.

Within seconds, Noah responded with an avalanche of Docusigned contracts, spreadsheets, and a draft press release prefilled with estimated revenues, quotes from senior executives, links to websites, and *About* sections for all four corporations composed. All I had to do was copy, paste, and email. The entire exercise should have taken me fifteen minutes.

But an hour later, I still had not pressed *Send* on the mail merge. Under the banner of "too much information," I had spent large chunks of this sixty-minute delay in the bathroom performing the rectal equivalent of dry heaving.

What was wrong with me? The press release was professional and elegantly written. The details were plentiful and informative; the quotes were pithy. I should have been impressed and grateful that the work had been done for me.

But I wasn't. My discomfort stemmed from seeing that all the quotes from ExOh were attributed to *me*. No mention of Cyrus or even Noah to be found. I didn't care that I hadn't said the words—I wasn't naive enough to assume that any executive's press release quote was an actual verbatim transcript of spoken words. But I did care that I, the least informed member of the ExOh team, was standing on the end of this plank alone.

I nervously searched for press releases from other companies, surveying how many corporate insiders are typically quoted within. The good news—or what should have felt like good news —was that most of the time, only one person from each company was quoted. Since I was the CEO of ExOh Holdings, who else should the quotes be attributed to?

Still, this realization did little to calm my internal rumble.

As I delayed, I recalled the unequivocal mandate issued at the conclusion of my previous conversation with Cyrus: *Get on board or get gone*. Serving as Cyrus's proxy had always been the job. I had no reason to doubt him or the rest of the team. And thanks to Cyrus's declaration that every ExOh contract, document, invoice, and spreadsheet was at my disposal, I was now drinking from a firehose of verifiable information. It was all there. It was all documented; it was all legitimate. What excuse justified my further delay?

*Hollis?* Cyrus wrote on BatSignal. *I'm sitting across the table from a VERY interested prospective investor who says he hasn't yet received the press release announcing our latest client wins. When will you be sending that out?*

I cursed my past corporate failures, my confidence, my trust issues, my unreliable gut, and—most emphatically—my perpetual and endless *fog*. If there was ever a moment to *go along to get along,* wasn't this it? What was I waiting for?

*Right now,* I replied, and I hit Send.

# CHAPTER SEVENTEEN

DAY five of Cyrus's Gulfstream *for*-profit fundraising tour paradoxically coincided with the annual *not*-for-profit fundraiser lunch at the Storyteller Children's Center—the charity where Cricket devoted every waking moment not already consumed by her family. It would have been nice if our family could have cut a big check, but we could not. Instead, Cricket focused on the time and talent portions of charitable giving, using her innate people skills to round up thirty guests who might have possessed a little less time or talent but plenty of treasure.

Naturally, Cricket invited Genevieve. It seemed like an obvious fit; in fact, Cricket had already penciled Genevieve in as one of the purchasers of an entire table for a donation of $10,000. I was present when Cricket made her pitch, which included the shockingly incongruous fact that Santa Barbara County had the third-highest children's poverty rate in the state of California.

But Genevieve declined. Not only did she decline the table, but she declined a seat. Instead, she offered to take Isabel and Trip horse riding with Priscilla while Cricket attended and worked the event. "It's the least I can do," I remember Genevieve saying. The accuracy of the statement left Cricket speechless; it was literally the least Genevieve could do.

With Cricket at the event, I dropped the kids off at the Wimbys' house. But instead of heading back home to work, I went to see my doctor. I think it's fair to call him *my* doctor because, like plenty of doctors in town, he had to be coerced into seeing new patients that had Obamacare insurance. The out-of-pocket annual fee allowing me to call him *my* doctor was $300, sick or not. I figured I might as well use him.

The Tums, Rolaids, Prevacid, and now Prilosec routine was getting me nowhere. My stomach ached constantly; the bloating, gassiness, and irritability were icing on the cake. In addition, I had an itchy skin rash that Benadryl cream could not cure. I was too young to be falling apart, but it felt like my inevitable end was already in motion.

My height was the same, staving off shrinkage for another day. I had lost seven pounds since he last saw me, but I assured him this had nothing to do with getting in better shape. The truth was that within fifteen minutes of putting any food in my mouth, the food wanted out. It rarely succeeded in gaining its immediate freedom, but I paid dearly for keeping it captive.

My blood pressure was a little high; my heart rate—typically abnormally low—was now slightly above normal. All slightly worse signs but not uniquely alarming. The doctor examined my skin rash and asked plenty of questions about off-path hiking, new pets, new plants, skin creams, diet changes: all dead ends.

"How's Cricket doing?" he asked.

"She's great," I said.

"The kids"—he checked his notes—"Isabel and Trip?"

"Also great."

"Work?"

I hesitated. "Uh, it's...going."

"Busy?" he asked.

"Yes and no."

"Are we going to play twenty questions, or are you going to explain what's going on?"

I proceeded through a sanitized version of my anxieties and

fears. But even to me, it sounded like I was projecting my personal issues onto an innocent corporation. It was a startup business. What startup business doesn't have quirks and idiosyncrasies? Voicing my fears only showed me to be the worrywart hall monitor I did not want to be. Why had I made this appointment? What a waste of everyone's time.

"Have you thought about talking to someone?" he suggested.

"I'm talking to you, and my copay is ninety dollars."

He laughed; I did not.

"I mean a psychiatrist," he clarified.

"I know what you mean. You're suggesting that the problem is in my head?"

"I have no idea what the problem is," he clarified. "But the skin rash is not consistent with any allergy pattern, infestation, or bug. Your vitals are normal. Your prostate is fine, your tonsils are fine, and your appendix is fine. Your lungs are clear; your heart is strong. I'm happy to order a colonoscopy and endoscopy, but you're young for those, and the fact pattern isn't suggestive of serious gastroenterological issues. You're no Olympic athlete, but as far as I can see, you are absolutely fine physically. Yet..." he trailed off.

"Yet..." I repeated.

"Your head," he said, thumping his temple with a forefinger, "is sending you signals. I don't know what they mean, and it sounds like you don't either. Maybe the best way to figure it out is to talk to someone."

I thanked him and took three business cards for recommended psychiatrists, then headed back to my gar-office. I never called any of them.

# Chapter Eighteen

Cyrus returned from his fundraising road trip with $6 million in commitment letters and an itch to throw a dinner party. Equally giddy was ExOh's new board member and provider of the private jet that escorted Cyrus on his victory tour, John Colton. John brought his wife and another prospective investor, Max Beauregard, who had a dead-fish handshake and said five words the entire evening. Cricket and I were no longer *invited* to these dinners in the sense of any optionality; we were simply told when to arrive.

Bottles of Entre Nous flowed like water, which, ironically, was not in ready supply. At one point early in the evening, I wound my way through the estate to retrieve more water and stumbled upon Genevieve, hard at work in the kitchen, stirring lobster risotto. I knew Genevieve had been a chef; I knew cooking was her passion. But I had suspected that, at this point in the Wimbys' empire gathering, she had become more of an *executive* chef—one who directs others but avoids the apron.

A timer went off, and she hustled from stirring the risotto to open the oven doors. Before I could see what was inside, I smelled it: key lime pie. The pie's union of sweet, sour, and mint replaced

Genevieve's star jasmine perfume as the dominant scent in the kitchen. She pulled the pie from the oven and stared at it like a mother at her infant.

"Smells fantastic," I said, interrupting the moment. "Is today the day you are going to bless me with the recipe?"

She smiled, placing the pie on a cooling rack. "I wish I could, Hollis, but no. As I said, it is a family secret."

"Okay," I said, nodding like a guy who had just repeated a tired old joke that he still found funny. "Can't blame me for trying."

"Actually," she said, her eyes lasering through my retinas, "I can."

My eyebrows stretched skyward, but I kept smiling as that unfamiliar feeling of intimidation rekindled in my gut. As before, it was a laughable reaction. Apparently tiny, beautiful women turned my *fog* into a whiteout.

"Uh..." I finally stammered, holding up empty glass water bottles, "just here to grab some more waters."

"The refrigerator in the pantry," she said, pointing behind me.

I grabbed two water bottles and returned to the larger group, rebuking myself for exhausting Genevieve's patience. Had Cricket been with me, she would have elbowed me before I asked about the key lime pie for the umpteenth time. I was not trying to annoy her. The truth was, I didn't have much to say to Genevieve. She was a creature from another planet. Key lime pie was my bridge to her world, so I traversed it. But apparently, I had done so one too many times.

We sat for dinner, and Cricket offered to make the toast. This was out of character for her, and my stomach immediately tweaked an anticipatory warning. "Here's to a better-than-expected round of fundraising," she said, to which everyone clinked glasses and sipped their wine. "With an unexpected topper," she added once the clinking had ceased. She set down her wineglass and pulled a folded check from her clutch. "I know fifty thousand won't change the fate of the company, Cyrus, but my father has been captivated by the story of ExOh Holdings. If you will accept it, he would like to become one of the company's investors." Cricket handed the check over to Cyrus.

I was too shocked to do anything other than watch; it was as if I were having an out-of-body experience. Hadn't I last told Cricket *not yet* when she asked about her parents investing? My stomach gurgled.

Cyrus's broad shoulders relaxed as he reached to accept the check. He turned to me, a glassy sheen in his eyes. "I am honored," he said, folding the check and placing it in his pocket. "With that touching gesture, why don't I turn the spotlight over to Hollis, who is handling the issue of returning ExOh's stock to active trading status. Hollis, do you mind giving everyone an update?" He smiled and picked up his fork.

He smiled because he already knew the update. After my freakout over signing the financial results, I followed Cyrus's orders and requested from Kai all the supporting information necessary to independently corroborate ExOh's financial results. What I received was more than six thousand pages of documents compressed into multiple zip files. I spent eighteen hours going through the trove to reconcile a single reported revenue number. At that rate, it would take me months to complete my review— months I did not have. What was the point anyway? If everyone in an organization was required to independently reconstruct everyone else's work, the entire business would grind to dust in the friction of repetition. The concept of *division of labor* was not just a cornerstone of efficiency; it was common sense.

Once I came to this realization, only one logical conclusion survived my decision tree. I signed the financial results, submitted the paperwork to the OTC, and set the date for the resumption of trading in the conveniently tickered EXOH.

"Absolutely, Cyrus," I began, still battling an uncomfortable pulse in my intestinal tract. "Our financial filings are complete, everything has been reviewed and approved by the OTC, and trading is set to start on Monday."

"Where will it open?" John Colton asked. He was curious because Cyrus had sold the new shares at $10 each, and no one wanted to see a loss on the first day, even if it was only on paper.

"It will open at ten dollars, John," I said. "Obviously, we can't control where it goes from there, but we are hopeful."

"I'm more than hopeful, John," Cyrus said, placing his fork down and folding his hands under his chin. "In fact, I'll bet you one dollar that the stock finishes up more than fifty percent on the day."

John smiled. "I'm beginning to think that I don't want to end up on the other side of any of your bets, Cyrus."

"Anyone, then?" Cyrus asked, turning to the table. "Max, how about you?"

Max, still mute, closed one eye in contemplation, then nodded.

"One dollar it is!" Cyrus said. "To be settled on Monday."

The meal proceeded with the easy banter of old friends. Cricket spoke about the Storyteller Children's Center's mission, the surprising level of poverty among children in Santa Barbara County, and the success of the fundraiser luncheon. While John and his wife had missed the luncheon, they pledged ten thousand dollars on the spot. Curiously, the Wimbys had not yet donated to Storytellers, but I suspected they would in time.

At some point, Genevieve excused herself, returning to the table with her pie, now decorated with flowers of piped whipped cream. Everyone took a slice, and silence ensued while the first bites were savored. My stomach was no better than it had been when I visited the doctor, so I picked my battles on the food front. The risotto, as delicious as it was, did not sit well, so I had been grateful for a speaking role during the entrées. But Genevieve's key lime pie was worth whatever pain ensued.

Cyrus cracked a few jokes, but the only memorable sound at

the table was the scratch of forks on china. Slowly, the plates were cleaned, or the eaters gave in, and Genevieve received her compliments. Even speechless Max Beauregard chimed in, regaling us with his only five spoken words of the evening: "My God, that was good!"

# CHAPTER NINETEEN

I MADE sure to be online at 6:30 a.m. California time when the retickered EXOH returned to the list of actively traded stocks. Much emphasis is placed on the first day's trading outcome, but I knew it was the long term that mattered. Still, optics were important; Cyrus's job would only get harder if the stock closed the day under its $10 offering price.

This potential complication became an afterthought within minutes. EXOH immediately zoomed from $10 to $15 and bounced between $15 and $20 for the remainder of the trading day. I was fixated, my eyes glued to the upticks and downticks like watching a riveting game of Pong. Each time the stock drifted to $15, a new buy order would arrive on the stage, buffering the downward trend.

When the trading day ended with our stock at $19.57, I called our lead broker at Humphrey Brothers to thank him for the market-making support.

"I didn't do a thing," he told me.

"What do you mean?" I asked, not sure if he was being literal or humble.

He laughed. "All the trading was offshore."

Once again, I was over my skis, embarrassed by what I did not know. "What do you mean?" I reluctantly repeated.

"I mean, nobody initiated an order through my desk. It was all offshore traders in the Caymans, BVI, Hong Kong, and Panama."

I had no idea what to say or what this meant, but I wasn't going to repeat the exact same question for a third time. "Is that unique in your experience?"

He exhaled. "Very. Stocks like this rarely attract the attention of the big boys on the first day, but your debut was different. I don't know the names of the buyers and sellers, but only the most sophisticated traders and hedge funds have offshore trading desks. This was not mom-and-pop." I could hear the surprise in his voice, and that made two of us. "Congratulations," he concluded. "You went from the backwater to the big leagues in one day."

It was my turn to exhale and once again chastise myself for the revelation of yet another blind spot. I thanked our lead broker—despite his insistence that he had been a bystander—and hung up.

I began to dial Cyrus next, but mid-dial, I received Cyrus's inbound call.

"What a day!" I said, eager to celebrate the near doubling of EXOH's price today.

"Yes," he said. "Hey, I—"

"That was thrilling," I interrupted. "I couldn't take my eyes off the screen."

"Yes," he repeated. "It was grand. Listen, I need an update on the balance of our Miramar bank account." He sounded rushed.

I logged into the account to check the balance. Cyrus's coastal fundraising trip had been far more successful than even he had anticipated. The $6 million in commitments turned into $7.5 million in cash and grew further when Max Beauregard followed up the morning after Cyrus's dinner with an investment of an even $1 million.

"We have eleven million, six hundred twenty-two thousand in the account as of today."

"Perfect," Cyrus said, pausing. "Wire five million to the Hong Kong bank account right away."

I swallowed; five million was the biggest wire yet. Just typing in the numbers made my fingers shake. "What should I put on the memo line?"

"What?" he said.

"The note you put into the system indicating what the wire is for," I explained.

"Oh, right," he said, talking even faster. "Uh, general expenses or intercompany loan. Just tell me when it's done."

I listed *intercompany loan* on the memo line and clicked submit. "It's on its way," I said. "Hey, it looks like you won that dinner party bet with Max Beau—"

"Great, thanks," he interrupted and hung up.

*Good talk, Rus,* I thought as I slid my phone across my desk in frustration.

That evening I barely ate dinner yet again as the rash on my hands crawled to my armpits. Even Trip commented that my scratching made me look like a monkey. I felt like a monkey too.

By bedtime—between the gastrointestinal discomfort, the itchy pits, and the strange vibe from Cyrus—I had reached an internal tipping point. I needed to talk to Cricket; I wanted to talk to her. But I feared that giving voice to my anxieties would make them real, and they could not be real. I was walking the tightrope with no net; looking down was not an option.

"I didn't want to bring it up in front of the kids," Cricket said as we were turning down the bed, "but I saw Genevieve's post on Instagram today. Holy cow, Hollis! That is amazing! The stock doubled!"

"Nearly doubled," I corrected, ever the stickler.

"Awww," she mocked. "Not good enough for you? Let me tell you, Dad is over the moon! He is planning to call into *Mad Money* tomorrow to get Cramer's take ... whoever Cramer is."

"That's terrific," I said, faking a smile.

"What's that face for?" she said, suggesting my fake smile was less than convincing. "Did you expect better?"

I crossed my arms over my chest and scratched my itchy pits, then buried the heels of my hands in my eye sockets. "I don't know, Cricket. I'm just not feeling well."

She smiled, but her forehead registered her concern. "What is it?"

"That's the thing," I groaned. "I don't know. I just...I don't feel good."

"Physically?"

"Yes."

"Anything else?"

"I...I don't know."

"Are we...? Are *we* good?" she asked.

"Oh God," I said. "Of course! *We* are the only thing I know for certain is good. It's nothing, really." I tried walking the conversation back. "I'm just—"

"You haven't been eating well," she suggested.

While this was true, my issues weren't driven by choices between nutritious food and junk. It wasn't what I was eating; it was how food was settling. I wanted to say this, but saying it would only open a door I wanted kept closed. "I know. That's probably it."

"And I can tell you're carrying a lot of stress. It looks like you've lost some weight."

"Seven pounds," I said, patting my tummy as if I were proud. I wanted to point out that bad nutrition and weight loss rarely go together, but that admission would invite further scrutiny. I no longer wanted to talk. I just wanted to go to sleep and wake up without the gnawing in my stomach. "But I'm sure it will come back when things settle down."

"Have you been sleeping well?" she asked. "Sleep is very important."

*Yes,* it was important, and, *no,* I was not sleeping well. "I'll work on it," I suggested.

She looked at me skeptically. "You have to take care of yourself, Hollis. You're too important to us."

This made me smile despite my upset stomach. "Thank you, Cricket."

We climbed into bed. "Is there anything I can do?" she asked. "Anything?"

My mind reeled in a desperate search for firm footing. I was drowning in uncertainty. Overthinking even as every day revealed a fresh blind spot. Worse, the whisper of a paranoid voice in the back of my brain was slowly invading my active consciousness. What if my inadequacies as CEO of ExOh were not obstacles for me to overcome? What if they were part of a plan?

I looked at my loving wife, her face imploring me to let her help. But there was nothing she could do. The truth was I no longer trusted myself. My instincts—man's survival sirens from the days when our ancestors were still cracking the code of fire—had proven wonky. I couldn't walk away from millions of dollars because I was *uncomfortable*. After all, I was in the *fog*, and from within, nothing was certain.

"No, Cricket," I said. "It's fine. It will all be just fine."

# Chapter Twenty

I'M sure I slept at some point, but I can't recall when. I checked the night-light on my Timex Ironman at least fifty times, and it always seemed to be twenty minutes from the last time I checked.

It pained me not to share my amorphous concerns with Cricket, but it would have hurt more to see the look in her eyes when she realized—once again—that I was failing. If I let her see the cracks, I feared she would lose what remained of her faith. It was nutrition, it was sleep, it was stress—it was anything but a return of my demons of professional destruction.

The next morning began without an obvious emotional hangover. Cricket inquired and I responded, "Much better, thank you."

Our once-new routine was now our everyday routine: Cricket to Los Baños for her Masters swim and me to MUS with the kids. Isabel and Trip no longer complained about the walk, and despite my defeated state of mind, I was grateful for the time with them.

Once home, I gathered my things from the gar-office and packed to meet Cyrus at his house to go over the state of ExOh and its plans. The fear and frustration I felt the prior evening was not gone, but I had to stop looking for what was wrong and find a way to make this work. ExOh's stock continued to hover near $20 per share, which meant that the shares Cyrus promised me for my sweat equity were now worth $2 million; all I had to do was keep my nose down and my mouth shut long enough to cash them in. There was nothing more to discuss. I was the chief provider for my family, and this was my job, plain and simple.

Our house had a single-car driveway, so I always parked my car on the street in front of our three-foot-tall row of bushes; our miniature version of a hedge. I walked in a haze that morning, replaying Cricket's questions and my evasive answers. I did not notice the black Mercedes S600 parked just across the street or the short, barrel-chested man leaning against its hood.

"You Hollis Crawford?" the man said just as I inserted the key into the driver-side door.

As lost as I was in my own head, I'm sure I jumped like a frightened rabbit. "Uh, yeah," I said, turning to eye this curious stranger. Sidewalks were nonexistent on Montecito's residential streets, and our nonvehicular traffic was limited to joggers and bikers. It was strange to see anyone standing on any street that was not within walking distance of the beach.

I turned my head left and right, looking for witnesses. The man had said all of three words, but I was leery. His accent was Eastern European, and his white-blond hair was slicked back, accentuating large slate-gray eyes. He wore a trench-length black leather coat, and though he was shorter than me—no taller than five foot six—I knew without needing to test the thesis that he would have whipped my tail in a fight. Even as I wanted to take a few steps backward and perhaps run into the safety of my home, I couldn't help but notice that the man was actually quite handsome. The trench coat, the deep accent, the cigarette dangling from the corner of his mouth, the cold stare: It was all purpose built to evoke fear. But underneath it was a man that likely made the ladies swoon.

He flicked the cigarette into the street and did not bother crushing it. I thought of explaining to him that Santa Barbara County remained in a drought and cigarette butts were a major fire risk. But the man met my eyes, and I saw a character straight from *Goodfellas*; I kept my mouth shut.

He approached me casually, hooking his left thumb into the waistband of his slacks to jack them up as his right hand tucked the butt end of his shirt in tight. "Very nice to meet you, Mr. Crawford," he said. "A lovely home you have here." He looked around me as if seeing my tiny home for the first time, then stuck out his hand.

I shook his hand, doubting that I had blinked since he said my name. "Uh, thank you," I said. "And you are?"

"My name is Vlad."

"Vlad what?"

"Just Vlad," he said, smiling. "That's all that is important."

I wanted to know his last name but not badly enough to argue with him. "Okay. Well, nice to meet you, Vlad. How do you know my name?"

"Ah," he said, "excellent question." He removed his pack of cigarettes and tapped one out, offering it to me. I declined. He took the cigarette for himself, then fished a Zippo from his jacket pocket, lit it, and took a drag deep enough to suck the lit end down one-half inch. "We have a common business partner."

A mixture of fear and confusion caused my brain to cramp. "Who?" I asked.

He smiled. "Cyrus Wimby, of course."

"Oh. Oh right, of course."

"Are you planning to see Cyrus today?" he asked.

"Uh, well, yes," I stumbled. "I was on my way to his place just now."

"Fantastic," he said. "I will drive you."

I shook my head. All I could think of was my mother warning me not to get into the cars of strange men, and if I had ever met a stranger man, I could not recall him. "I'm fine," I said.

"I insist," he said, grabbing my elbow tightly enough that I knew I was indeed coming with him.

I should have told him to follow me, but I didn't. Like a sheep to slaughter, I walked to his passenger door and got in his car. I can't recall how many times I've watched scary movies, wishing the character in distress would resist or run, anything but quietly acquiesce. Yet, in that moment, I did exactly as they had done, assuming—as those fictional idiots had—that if I were agreeable, I would not be hurt.

I fastened my seat belt—because God forbid I get in a car accident on the way to my murder—and waited.

"Directions, please," Vlad said.

"You don't know?" I asked.

"If I knew, why would I be bothering with you?" he said, smiling wide enough for me to see the flash of gold on a back molar.

I pointed him forward, directing a left turn here and right turn there. The drive was a hair longer than our walk to MUS and was completed in five minutes. He pulled up to the keypad that guarded the security gates. "Code?" he asked.

Without hesitation, I blurted the code, then admonished myself for being so quick to reveal secrets. I would not be the prisoner who bravely endured torture and confinement to safeguard what he knew, I concluded. I would be the one who asked for a pad and pen and drew my captors a map.

As the gates opened in response to the code, I surveyed the area, looking for security cameras. Surely Cyrus had them, and if he did, he would know it was not me driving this sparkling Mercedes. But I never saw a camera.

"Beautiful," Vlad said as he pulled through the gates. "Reminds me of the place he had in Tuscany."

I cocked my head. "Cyrus lived in Italy?" I asked. "He never mentioned that to me."

Vlad just laughed, inching closer to the area where the three gleaming Porsches were normally parked. Just one today: Cyrus's 911 Carrera. It appeared that Genevieve and the Wimbys' nanny were away, and I couldn't help but consider that a blessing.

Vlad pulled perpendicular to the back end of the 911,

forming a T that hemmed the car in. I could open the passenger side door only a foot wide, barely enough to squeeze through. "Could you give me a little more room?" I asked.

"You'll manage," Vlad said, hopping out of his side.

As always, Cyrus did not rush out to greet me. Vlad and I walked unaccompanied from the garage as if we lived there. As was Cyrus's and my routine, I simply let myself in the front door —an extra-wide stable door whose top half was open to ease my entry—and waited for Cyrus in the library room.

Also part of the routine: Cyrus kept me waiting. I sat on the sofa, nervously perched on the edge of a cushion, tapping my foot and checking my watch. Three, five, ten minutes rolled by. Vlad walked around the room, pulling volumes from the shelves, occasionally cracking the spines to inspect their interiors.

"You think he's read any of these?" Vlad asked.

"I...I assume so," I stuttered.

He chuckled, then went back to inspecting.

Up until that moment, I had operated on autopilot, but as we waited, rational thoughts and questions returned to my brain. What the hell were we doing here? What was going to happen when Cyrus finally showed up to his own meeting in his own home? I was nervous, but should I be *scared*?

I heard the click-clack of Cyrus's leather-soled shoes on Spanish tile and knew the answers would be coming soon. I shifted myself even farther to the edge of the sofa cushion in anticipation.

Cyrus entered with his head down, flipping pages of a stapled document as he walked toward one of the cane armchairs opposite the sofa. Vlad quietly turned, clasping his hands in front of his genitalia, cocking his head to wait for recognition.

Just before sitting, Cyrus tossed the document on the coffee table and finally looked up, sweeping his view from bug-eyed me on the couch to sinister-looking Vlad in the leather trench coat.

"My friend!" Cyrus said, throwing his arms wide and moving quickly to embrace Vlad.

One corner of Vlad's mouth rose subtly, but otherwise he did not move.

Cyrus grabbed Vlad's shoulders and kissed both cheeks. "It has been far too long, my friend. Come, come." He motioned toward the sofa. "Join us."

Vlad broke from his pose, moving slowly to the cane armchair opposite Cyrus; the three of us now formed an equilateral triangle. "You're a hard man to find," Vlad said.

"Nonsense," Cyrus said. "Here I am."

Vlad shook his head. "I started with Landon, only to learn that he is no longer with this world."

Cyrus nodded, his expression serious. "Yes. Landon died in a surfing accident. Tragic mishap, really."

Vlad smirked. "If you say so."

I leaned forward, waiting for Cyrus to object, ready to do it myself if he did not. I'd seen Landon's body, after all; he died in the surf. But Cyrus said nothing, and in the face of his silence, I could not summon my own voice.

"It did not matter," Vlad continued. "I moved on, tracking down your old friend Abdullah."

Cyrus swallowed but said nothing.

"Abdullah was rather reluctant to divulge your location," Vlad said. "It took a little"—he paused and smiled—"*persuading*, before he told me you were in Montecito. Even still I had to stalk this man here"—Vlad pointed to me—"to find you in the flesh."

I had no idea who Abdullah was, and judging by the slightly pale expression on Cyrus's face, I decided it was not a good time to ask.

"Well, I wasn't intending to be hard to find," Cyrus said, turning to look at me. "And I'm glad my right-hand man, Hollis here, could lead you straight to me." He smiled as affectionally as ever, but I felt frigid under his gaze.

"We have business to discuss," Vlad declared, leaning forward, elbows perched on knees.

"Indeed, we do," Cyrus said. "Tea? Coffee?"

"No," Vlad said; Cyrus did not appear to be offering any to me, so I stayed silent, hoping to be forgotten.

Cyrus pinched his chin with those skeletal fingers and let his eyes drift into space. "On second thought," he said, "I do not think we need Hollis for this discussion."

Vlad smiled. "That is your choice."

Cyrus would get no argument from me; I wanted out of there like a rat wants out of a python's terrarium, but there was one slight problem. "I, uh, rode here with Vlad," I squeaked.

Cyrus forced a smile. "I will call you an Uber, my friend." He picked up his phone and punched away.

Vlad leaned back in his chair. I caught his eye, and he gave me a slight wink.

"On its way," Cyrus declared. "If you do not mind, wait beyond the gates. I'll buzz you out now."

I did not mind in the least. Without further delay, I leapt to my feet. "Nice to meet you, Vlad," I said, offering a quick bow. "Cyrus, we'll talk later."

"Tomorrow," Cyrus said. "Here. Same time."

I nodded, stepping aggressively past the coffee table at the price of an inch of skin from my shin. I did not acknowledge the pain or pause to inspect the wound. I was in motion, and I would not stop until I was beyond Cyrus's gates, waiting for the Uber to take me home.

# Chapter Twenty-One

With over-the-counter medicines useless in treating my gastrointestinal issues, I resorted to sucking on hard ginger candies and drinking green tea mixed with a delicious-sounding powder named slippery elm bark, recommended by the sympathetic folks at Montecito Natural Foods. For good measure, I bought a case of inexpensive sparkling water from Smart & Final; a good burp always seemed to help.

Just as with everything else, I wanted to tell Cricket about Vlad abducting me and the odd subsequent meeting with Cyrus, but I was still trying to decide if I was insane or not. Maybe this was yet another instance of my *fog* playing tricks on me. I didn't know yet, and I didn't want to alarm her until I knew.

My hands shook most of the day as I busied myself with superficial work tasks and waited to hear from Cyrus. Clearly, I had felt physically threatened by Vlad, but had Cyrus? If so, he had not shown it.

Maybe—as usual—the problem was me and my *fog*. Just because Vlad looked and spoke like someone from a mobster movie did not make him a killer. Moreover, Vlad said he and Cyrus were business partners, and Cyrus certainly treated him as such. I chastised myself for succumbing to cultural stereotypes of Vlad as the Eastern European hit man.

Try as I did, these thoughts did little to calm my mind or my GI tract. I picked up the kids from school at 3:00 p.m. and lingered, hoping to catch sight of Priscilla, Genevieve, or Cyrus, but came up empty. The BatSignal app was quiet, and I had received no emails. I settled into our family's evening routine resigned to the fact that I would not learn more until I met Cyrus face-to-face the following morning.

I woke to a BatSignal message the next day that delayed my learning further: *Need to postpone our meeting until Monday,* he wrote. *Headed to Napa to talk to my vintner. Be on the lookout for more good news on the client front from Noah. In the meantime, I hope you and your family have a terrific weekend!"*

I was dumbstruck; both relieved that Cyrus had not been murdered and mystified by his carefree indifference. Perhaps the whole thing was a manifestation of my *fog* after all? Regardless, it was Thursday, so now I would have to let my mind run on concocted theories and explanations for four more days before I would get some sort of explanation for who Vlad was, why he was looking for Cyrus, why he accused Cyrus of being hard to track down, and so many other questions. If I was not already crazy, I might be soon.

# Chapter Twenty-Two

By Monday morning, I was wound like a jack-in-the-box. I had heard nothing from Cyrus over the prior four days—since meeting Vlad at the end of my driveway—and nothing from Noah or anyone else at ExOh. I made the kids leave early for school and then speed-walked them, both infractions earning Isabel's ire. As soon as I got home from MUS, I hopped in the Subaru and took off.

When I got to Cyrus's, the code to the security gate had been changed. I pressed the call button, and he answered. I had not spotted a camera the last time I was here, but this time it was unmistakable, blinking red daggers at me from its perch behind and above the keypad.

Cyrus opened the gates, and I parked in my normal spot, beyond the garage, under the pin oaks. I rushed in, certain I would find Cyrus waiting for me in the library. But he wasn't there. He wasn't there ten, or fifteen, or twenty minutes later either. I began to pace the room. Had I made the whole thing up? Was it a figment of my imagination? A sign that the *fog* was sending me over a cliff of insanity?

Thirty-five minutes after I arrived, Cyrus entered his own library punching away on his iPhone. He navigated to the cane armchair without looking up; I dutifully took my seat on the couch. After he typed away for another minute, his phone made the whooshing sound of a sent message and he put it down on the coffee table. "Did you have a nice weekend?" he asked.

The verdict was in: crazy. I stared back blankly. "Uh, sure. And you?"

"Lovely," he said. "Genevieve checked Priscilla out of school early on Friday and met me at Auberge du Soleil for a wonderful Napa weekend."

I nodded. I would probably find the straitjackets and padded rooms of the asylum comforting, I thought. If my interpretation of the events with Vlad had been accurate, there was no way they could have affected me so deeply and Cyrus so marginally. I spent much of my weekend in a mental fetal position while Cyrus and family had gone off to a breezy vacation in Napa. I thought of those psychiatrist business cards my doctor had given me—the ones I had tossed like trash. I needed to retrieve them and set up appointments immediately.

But Vlad was not going to excuse himself from my head voluntarily. Crazy or not, I had to discuss this with Cyrus. I took a deep breath and dove in. "So," I began, inserting a light chuckle just to emphasize that I was not *overreacting* or *freaking out*, "tell me about Vlad. He's quite a character."

Cyrus smiled, leaned back in the armchair, crossed his legs, and interlaced fingers behind his head. "Indeed, he is," Cyrus said, shaking his head as if he had so many delightful stories to tell and he was struggling to find the perfect one. "I've known Vlad for ages. Great friend; good man. Salt of the earth, as you Americans like to say."

I nodded, trying hard to keep my forehead from wrinkling.

"He's a drama queen, though," Cyrus continued. "Loves to give people the impression that he's a tough guy. You probably picked up on that."

*You probably picked up on that?* Even a man *in the fog* could recognize Vlad as a mob movie body double. "Yes, a little," I said. "He was...intense."

"Yes, well, he was all teddy bear after you left. Broke out his phone to share photos of his youngest girl and his new puppy, a miniature chihuahua."

Cyrus riffled through some papers, seemingly content to call the Vlad portion of our conversation over.

"What was he here to see you about?" I pressed.

Cyrus looked up, surprise mixed with a pinch of irritation on his face. "Same as everyone," he said casually. "He wanted to get an update on ExOh."

"Oh," I said. "Is he an investor?" I hadn't seen his name on any wires or checks.

Cyrus's breezy manner grew a little stiffer. "He contributed his interest in a prior deal, so yes, he is an investor."

I nodded—enthusiastically, I hoped. "Was he excited by what he learned?" I continued.

Cyrus's expression shifted again, this time toward impatience. "Of course."

"Great to hear," I said, faking my biggest smile. I was letting the old, skeptical, *prove it* Hollis have a little run of rope, and he was enjoying the moment.

Cyrus took my smile as a sign that we were finally done and again shuffled papers.

"Why do you think he had such a hard time finding where you lived?" I asked, ignoring Cyrus's signals.

Cyrus looked full-on pissed off now; even from inside the *fog,* I understood that. "How should I know, Hollis?"

I recognized that I was on shaky ground, but I could not stop; old Hollis had the microphone and would not give it back. "And your friend Abdullah?" I asked. "Good thing Vlad found him, right?"

Cyrus pursed his lips, again fidgeting with his papers, though this time it felt more like stalling. "Abdullah is great," he finally said. "He's a good man." Cyrus straightened his papers, knocking them on the table three time like a gavel. "Shall we move on?"

Though I wasn't satisfied, I couldn't think of any more questions, and—taking advantage of the pause—new Hollis retook control. "Of course."

Cyrus tossed one subset of his papers across the coffee table to me. "I have good news," he said. "I have an agreement in place to open an Entre Nous tasting room at the Montecito Country Mart. Those"—he pointed to the papers—"are the architectural renderings of the space."

I dutifully picked up the papers and examined them one by one, though I wasn't sure why this was good news for me or for ExOh. Entre Nous was Cyrus's self-described hobby, not mine. "This looks terrific," I said, sliding the papers back across the table when I felt I had given them the appropriate amount of ogling.

"Doesn't it?" Cyrus said proudly. "So, we have a little work to do around this in order to make the deal final."

My eyes opened wide.

"It's time to bring ExOh into this wine deal so we can really expand operations." He slid a second set of papers across the table to me. "I'm going to have ExOh purchase a fifty-one percent stake in Entre Nous. I have valued the wine operations at two million dollars—a steal for sure, but there is no reason for me to be greedy as I sit on both sides of this fence."

I squinted. "You want to sell a piece of your winery to ExOh?"

He shook his head, looking slightly peeved. "I don't *want* to sell a piece of my winery; I *am selling* a piece of my winery. The agreement is right here." He slid a third set of papers my way. "Already signed by me and John Colton, so we need your signature to finalize."

I glanced quickly and saw Cyrus's signature in blue ink and John Colton's electronic, Docusign signature. Questions stacked in my head like a Jenga puzzle. What makes Entre Nous worth $2 million? Who determined that valuation? Why isn't John Colton's signature in fresh ink like Cyrus's? I knew I couldn't ask them all, so I settled on one. "What does your winery have to do with ExOh's Free Trade Zone License?"

"Allow me to bring you under the hood," he said patronizingly. "I see ExOh as a retail trade conglomerate. Both an ecommerce enabler through our Free Trade Zone License and an owner —curator really—of the world's finest brands. I would not suggest that LVMH or Richemont need to be shaking in their Cartier watches just yet, but we are coming for them. Oh yes"— he laughed—"we are coming for them."

I realized I had just received a trial run of Cyrus's latest investor pitch. High on vision, low on details, this was standard course for entrepreneurs of all stripes. "Okay," I said. "So, you need me to sign?"

"Yes," Cyrus said. "That document is the board of directors' resolution authorizing the purchase of Entre Nous."

I signed.

"And this," Cyrus said, sending a fourth set of documents my way, "is the lease on the tasting room at the Montecito Country Mart."

I closed my eyes and nodded. A headache was blooming. One signature was leading to the next, and each turn was catching me on my heels. Attempting to avoid more questions of disloyalty, I had agreed to value Cyrus's wine hobby at $2 million, to pay him $1 million in cash, and to pay for a lease on a tasting room. Was all this even legal? I didn't know, and I'd forfeited my time to research; the ink was already dry. "Of course," I said, forcing a smile.

He returned my smile. Two smiling men, neither actually appearing happy.

"As to the payment of one million dollars?" I asked.

"Right," Cyrus said, handing me a slip of paper. "Wire the money to that account this morning."

I looked at the slip. The account was at the Bank of Bermuda in the name of VIP Partners LLC. "VIP Partners?" I asked.

"Yes?" Cyrus said impatiently.

"That's you?" I asked.

His eyes narrowed. "Obviously."

"Of course," I said, shaking my head dismissively. "The, uh, Miramar Bank and Trust account has about four million dollars in it. Still a lot of money, but—"

"Don't worry, Hollis," Cyrus interrupted. "I'm a keynote speaker at the Central California Economic Summit next week. More money will be coming in soon."

I nodded uneasily.

"The look on your face troubles me, Hollis."

My eyes opened wide, trying to hide what I knew he had already seen.

"This isn't about money. I assure you," he said. "A million dollars does not move the needle for me."

I nodded, aggressively this time, willing my face to appear enthusiastic and empathetic—two unfamiliar emotions. "I understand."

"No, you don't *understand*, Hollis." He stood, circling behind the cane armchair, leaning his weight on the chair's back. "Ugh," he grunted, giving the chair a shake, his hauntingly long fingers draping down the woven backing like icicles off a roof. "I don't *need* this aggravation. I don't *need* to build another multi-billion-dollar business. God knows I have plenty already."

He pushed off the chair and crossed his arms over his chest. "I'm sick of those skeptical eyes, my friend. Have you checked our stock price lately?"

I had, of course. It was hovering at around thirty dollars. "Yes," I said.

"You have three million dollars' worth of stock, am I correct?"

I nodded.

"So why am I constantly having to reassure you?"

"You're not," I objected, hoping to sell something neither of us was buying. "I'm just being cautious."

"This is getting old," he said.

# Chapter Twenty-Three

Cyrus may have been certain that a flood of investor money was on the horizon, but I was suddenly an anxious bean counter. It felt like the company's obligations were soon to outstrip its assets. If Cyrus were to be proven right, the tap would turn at the Central California Economic Summit.

The Summit was an annual three-day boondoggle snuggled next to the Fourth of July, organized to bring hundreds of bankers, investors, and economists to America's Riviera for our version of summer. In contrast to most of the country, Santa Barbara's summertime temperatures settled into the low-to-mid seventies, even with the sun in full blaze. This year-round pleasantness seeded the *we live in paradise* snobbery that civic planners were anxious to perpetuate.

The Summit's keynote dinner was held at Montecito's famous Coral Casino. The Coral, as the locals call it, was a luxurious beach club tangential to the Four Seasons Biltmore. The Coral's glamour was in its bygone day's simplicity. In cahoots, Cyrus had chosen to dress for the business-casual event in a tuxedo. And not just any tuxedo, but the sort that Frank Sinatra and Sammy Davis Jr. would have approved. In an elegant, throwback tux, he looked like he needed a cigar and a champagne coupe.

Set on a perch overlooking Butterfly Beach, the centerpiece of the Coral was an Olympic-sized swimming pool around which Montecito's and Santa Barbara's grandest have luxuriated for decades. Olympic swimming pools—fifty-meter pools—are rarities to begin with; they are incredibly expensive to build and maintain and, let's face it, unnecessary; most people are too lazy to swim half that distance. But planting one of these glorious pools right next to the Pacific Ocean—effectively *on* the beach—feels almost obscene. And in keeping with the obscenity, the initiation fee for new members of the Coral was nearly a quarter-million dollars.

As the story goes, the Coral's pool is technically fifty meters plus one foot. Why? When the club was under construction, some inaugural members got themselves wound up over the idea of turning the Coral into a commercial venture, one that could host swimming competitions, inviting the sport of swimming's great unwashed inside. To quash that dream, another member— one with his finger in the construction—secretly changed the blueprints for the pool, adding an extra foot. The switcheroo was not discovered until construction was complete and irrevocable. With the pool's length beyond regulation, there would be no public swimming events at the Coral. Welcome to Montecito; loitering is prohibited.

Guests entered the Coral's ballroom through a glass-lined courtyard staring down at the Pacific and Butterfly Beach. People tended to congregate at this wall, standing slack-jawed while one of their party drew the short straw and trudged off to retrieve cocktails for the group. It was here, holding court, that I found Cyrus. I had not watched him operate a large audience before, but he was just as magnetic as he was in small groups. Towering over most in attendance with his brown skin, electric smile, and a laugh amped higher than normal, Cyrus drew the crowd's eyes to him no matter where else they were meant to focus.

I, meanwhile, ventured from one corner of the ballroom to another, doing my best to appear purposeful in my movements so my aloneness would not draw attention. For someone who is a tad uncomfortable around other humans, humans in crowds made me want to lock myself in a closet. This is where I felt my *fog* issues most acutely. I was confident that I had absolutely nothing interesting or exciting to say to any of these people; it was a well-earned confidence.

The bar was one of the stops on my 'round-the-ballroom circuit. I was drinking soda water and lime in a whiskey tumbler, making it look like a vodka soda. By that measure, I should have been falling down drunk as I was on my fifth. The bar was, of course, offering Entre Nous wine exclusively. While I had my uncertainties, I was also wowed by Cyrus. He lured and seduced in ways I could not have conceived.

The Summit had chosen Cyrus because he and ExOh were a local economic novelty. The county touted tourism and real estate as its two biggest industries. Gaining momentum behind these grand-daddies, software and technology startups were sprouting, spurred on by the amazing engineering department at the University of California, Santa Barbara. Cyrus—with his New Zealand and Saudi Arabian roots and background in the oil industry—and ExOh—with its focus on the old-as-Magellan business of global trade—were a rainbow unicorn. The Summit simply had to hear from him.

Of course, as my social opposite, Cyrus loved the stage. I had offered to translate the notes of my PowerPoint presentation into a draft speech; this sent him into a roiling belly laugh. Genevieve would write his speech, he assured me, and it would be fantastic.

The speech was to be delivered between the salad and entrée courses. Much of it was familiar to me or to anyone who had been invited to enjoy dinner at the Wimby house. But he was so smooth onstage that previously spoken words held greater gravitas: ExOh was not just facilitating trade; it was freeing the world.

As the CEO of ExOh, I was anxious for Cyrus to set his hat on the stage and start dancing for money. The wire to VIP Partners—aka Cyrus—and another $3 million wire to Hong Kong had the Miramar bank account below $1 million for the first time since fundraising began.

"This may be the biggest financial opportunity since Bill Gates decided to license the C prompt," Cyrus said, bringing his speech to a rousing conclusion. "A backdoor to one-point-five billion shoppers who do not know what it is like to easily purchase something made in the US of A. I wake up each day pinching myself."

Heads wagged around the room. He had them right where he wanted them.

"And the best part is the scalability of the business. It is and was cash-flow positive from the first day. I have already raised every penny of equity I will ever need..."

I leaned so far forward that my head nearly clanked my water glass. *What is he saying?* I wanted to stand and wave my white napkin in protest.

"Many of you are already shareholders. Congratulations to you! Our stock restarted trading just over two months ago and, already, it has nearly quadrupled. As wonderful as that is, it is just the beginning of our ascent. ExOh's business plan is now fully funded and ready to take on Amazon and Alibaba..."

*No, no, no! We need more money!* I dropped my forehead into my hands, massaging both temples.

"In fact, we at ExOh are already considering our legacy; a legacy that begins today." He moved from the podium to the center of the stage, advancing his slide show beyond what seemed to be its finale. The next slide read, *The ExOh Global Relief Charities.*

My title might have been chief executive officer of ExOh, but I was a pure observer at this point.

"Ladies and gentlemen, the ExOh Global Relief Charities will provide monetary support to counteract human atrocities around the world. Initially, we will focus on the plight of Syrian refugees..."

I looked around the room; not a single person was on their phone.

"ExOh Holdings Incorporated will match all donations to the ExOh Global Relief Charities five-to-one! Our goal today is to raise two hundred thousand dollars from the Summit and match that with one million dollars from ExOh. Who is with me?"

There was a rousing round of applause that made me cringe. I was not a veteran of the fundraiser circuit, but I was uncomfortably familiar with the mechanism Cyrus was about to launch: the paddle-raise auction. Montecito Union Elementary school's annual fundraiser ended in much the same way: an auction that begins with, *Who here today is willing to commit fifty thousand dollars to this worthy cause?* and painstakingly descends to a version of, *If you haven't raised your hand at this point, just give us one hundred dollars so you can show your face at Pierre Lafond.*

Within ten excruciating minutes of cajoling, clapping, and paddle raising, Cyrus had raised $225,000 from this generous crowd.

"I am blown away by your spirit of giving," he said. "I want to introduce you all to ExOh's chief executive officer, Hollis Crawford; Hollis will you stand, please?"

I reluctantly stood, and a spotlight found me. I squinted and shaded my face.

"Hollis and I will be oceanside after dessert to get your contact information and accept your generosity on behalf of ExOh Global Relief Charities."

Cyrus took his seat at the table front and center of the stage, and the Coral's waitstaff promptly delivered plates of what can be best described as above-average conference food to everyone. I pushed mine around—my stomach was practicing its contortionist's routine—gnawing only on the dinner roll, which was too bland to cause issues. For dessert, a pale version of Genevieve's key lime pie mocked me. I took a small taste, hoping for a bit of the old magic. It was good but not transcendent; I pushed it away as well.

As soon as the first Summit attendee stood from dessert, I hopped into the oceanside lobby, hoping to get Cyrus's ear before any of the ExOh Global Relief Charities donors showed up. But that didn't happen. Cyrus mingled in the ballroom as a circle grew around me.

A large man with a boisterous Texas accent, cowboy hat, and bolero nominated himself as the group's spokesperson and cut to the chase: "Who do we make the checks out to?" he asked.

"Excellent question," I said.

# Chapter Twenty-Four

At the conclusion of the Summit event at the Coral, a group of wealthy investors cornered Cyrus and Genevieve, demanding a chance to squeeze their way into ExOh's apparently closed capital raise. *No, no*, he demurred. *Yes, yes*, they insisted. After his arm was sufficiently twisted, Genevieve stepped in, offering to host the group of anxious investors for a Fourth of July party at their home the following night. Her offer was greeted with hoots of celebration, as if she were a mother who had finally relented to her children's pleas for ice cream.

*Terrific*, I thought, standing on the outside of Cyrus's circle as the impromptu Independence Day celebration was planned. I'd been so distracted of late that it hadn't occurred to me that one of my favorite holidays was just around the corner. Hearing of Cyrus's party made me nostalgic for the Crawfords' own Fourth of July tradition. We would spend our day in and out of the waves at Miramar Beach, then hop on our bicycles and head to a second beach, East Beach (beach *shopping* is an important aspect of life in Montecito). There, we would spread out on blankets, eat to-go from Mony's Tacos, and watch the fireworks launched from boats off Stearns Wharf. Occasionally it was *freezing cold*—near sixty degrees in Montecito speak—or foggy, but that didn't matter.

Even when the fireworks looked more like cloud-to-cloud light-ning than fireflies, it was a day to savor.

I was still smiling at the thought when Cyrus began to list what he would need from me in order to host the party. My smile faded. "If you don't mind," I said, "we have a Fourth of July family tradition of our own. I'm not going to be able to make your party."

Cyrus nodded, threw a paternal arm over my shoulders, and whispered, "I'm not asking."

To salve the wounds of our upset family plans, he volunteered Genevieve to take Cricket, Isabel, and Trip horse riding with her and Priscilla that morning. While the rest of my family was excited for the opportunity to ride, I stewed in disappointment. It was one more interruption of the sacred traditions that bind blood relatives into the long narrative of family.

As the sun broke on the Fourth, and my family departed for their equestrian adventures, I filled the day with the mundane. I got my Subaru washed at the Chevron on Coast Village Road so it would feel less self-conscious in the crowd of Range Rovers and Porsches at the Wimby house. I bought three mature tomato plants from La Sumida Nursery and planted them in our back-yard. Knowing that my evening picnic at East Beach wouldn't happen, I treated myself to an adobada burrito from Mony's and ate every last bite, stomach pain be damned.

When we arrived at the Wimby home, the driveway gates were yawning. Instead of winding back to find my own parking spot, red-vested valets were waiting to whisk my thankfully clean car away. The greeter who had worked every prior Wimby party—the one every parent would have loved as a babysitter—had been replaced with a blonde in a black dress so short it might have fit her when she was twelve years old. She looked stolen straight from Hugh Hefner's grotto.

Cricket took a glass and said her thanks, but when she turned to me, there was curiosity in her eyes. It wasn't the buxom blonde; Cricket was always pointing out pretty women to me, admiring some facet of their beauty. She wasn't intimidated or bothered by any sense of competition. It was the upped ante that she recognized and the meaning behind it that she questioned. The Wimbys' parties were always big; this was exponentially bigger. Why? We continued into the party with the observation unvoiced.

As at the Summit, Cyrus was surrounded by a gaggle of out-of-towners with money to burn. I recognized the Texan—same hat, new bolero—and several of the others, but I decided not to invade the circle. There was nothing I could add to Cyrus's spiel.

Instead, I walked the party, hand in hand with Cricket. She paused to say hello several times, but she too seemed content to be with me alone. In a month, she would compete in the Dwight Crum Pier-to-Pier, a two-mile open-ocean swim from Hermosa Beach to Manhattan Beach. The endless training had turned her always-fit body into a loaded spring. She had eyes on her personal best time, recorded during her All American, senior year of college. If she failed to break that old mark, it would not be for lack of effort.

I, on the other hand, was beginning to look like the disappearing man. I had by this point lost eleven pounds since I began working for Cyrus and ExOh, and the dark gar-office was draining the remaining color from my skin. Increasingly, we looked like a May-December marriage, even though I was technically the younger spouse by three months.

But that did not matter this night. I was so proud to be holding her hand, to call her mine. If I had to suffer with my own demons of discomfort to finally do good by my family, so be it. I would have gladly paid a higher price if asked.

Genevieve, too, was holding court. When she spotted Cricket, she waved her over, but Cricket gave my hand an extra squeeze and stayed by my side. Genevieve was not willing to give up; she broke from her circle, gave Cricket a two-kiss hello, and forcibly pulled her from my grip.

She could steal the flesh but not the memory.

This evening, the pizza oven was churning out massive skillets of paella, individualized into miniature Chinese food containers. I cannot count how many bottles of Entre Nous were consumed, but the cash raised from recycling the empties would have fed a homeless man for a month.

Reluctantly, I made my way back to Cyrus's assemblage, which now filled the library room. Huff Monroe, the Texan who was standing shoulder to shoulder with Cyrus, was jovially sloshing wine as he listened to Cyrus's stories that had journeyed beyond ExOh to other global conquests. Several times, Cyrus made a show of saying, "Genevieve isn't here, is she?" scanning the room for his gorgeous wife, then tucking in to tell a quieter story to which most of the room was not privy. It didn't matter to me, but I could tell others on the outer rings desperately wanted to be closer, to be the ear into which those salacious details were delivered. Everyone seemed to want a piece of Cyrus.

Several more times, I heard Cyrus publicly declare ExOh's fundraising closed. More quietly, I heard him say that he would only accept more cash if the investors had the ability to "move the needle," a phrase equivalent to, *make me an offer I cannot refuse.*

As before, I was superfluous. Perhaps this should have bothered me, but it didn't. I knew my strengths, and salesmanship was not on the list.

At some point, the servers switched from paella to muffin-sized pecan pies. They smelled wonderful; I passed.

The light dimmed, and I finally found Cricket again, this time separate from Genevieve, though still in the hub of several conversations. I gave her elbow a slight pinch; she turned and gave me a kiss.

"Let's sneak out of here and rescue the kids," I whispered.

"Can we?" she whispered back.

I looked over my shoulder at Cyrus, still regaling the crowd. "I think he can handle it."

"You're on," she said. "Besides...we need to talk."

I cocked my head curiously as we moved to leave. She was too busy waving, nodding, and smiling to notice.

The valets were sitting on their hands when we came out the front door. My Subaru was easy to find—it was the only one at the party—and we were quickly on our way.

"So—" I began, halting at her raised hand.

"First, your wallet," she said with a hand-it-over wag of her fingers. "I need cash for the babysitter. Quick. What's four times fourteen?"

I fished out my wallet and tossed it into her lap, laughing. My wife was whip-smart, but she didn't fill her brain with rote math facts. Instead, she disguised her questions as quizzes for me. "Fifty-six," I answered.

She counted out the bills while I drove, both curious and anxious to learn what we needed to discuss.

"That was over the top, don't you think?" she finally said, the money folded discretely into her palm as if she were planning to grease a bouncer.

"What was over the top?"

"That display."

"The party?"

"Yes, Hollis"—she sighed—"the party."

"It was like all the others," I said, "maybe a little bit...*more.*"

She guffawed. "Everything about the Wimbys is *more.* This was *gratuitous* more."

"It's the Fourth of July," I argued, my spine stiffening. Even as I pushed back, I knew: Cricket had picked up the scent of the same inconsistencies plaguing me.

She shook her head dismissively. "No," she said. "Something was different."

I squinched my face. "Come on," I said. "I think it was pretty much in line with all—"

"Why do they try so hard, Hollis?" she interrupted. "Why do two people *that* beautiful and *that* rich work so hard to win friends and backers? It doesn't make sense."

"Well," I stammered. As usual—possessing only half the information—Cricket was two steps ahead of me, distilling the randomness into its underlying essence. I decided to attempt feeding her the excuses I had chewed myself. "Technically, they're still new to Montecito," I began. "And Cyrus is raising money for ExOh, so he has to be in sell mode all the time. And..." I stopped at the resumption of her declining head shakes.

"That's not it," she said. "To be fair, I thought those same things the first half-dozen times we went to their house, but not this time. There was..." Her voice trailed off as I turned onto our street, only a quarter mile from home. "It seems crazy to say this, because—I mean—look at them. They have everything. But tonight, there was a sense of..."

I knew what she was going to say, and I closed my eyes in dread; admittedly, an ill-advised move while driving a car.

"... desperation," she concluded.

I nudged my Subaru next to the diminutive hedge fronting our house and shut off the engine. While I did not trust myself, I leaned on Cricket like a flashlight in a dark cave. Yet even as she gave voice to my private concerns, I didn't want to hear them. The moment I acknowledged these doubts as legitimate, our ExOh lottery ticket—currently worth $4 million—would disappear. Did I really want to be that guy? The one who walked away from millions over a couple of inconsistencies and a *hunch*?

I had to face it: The hand I now held was the best one I was going to get. I could not bear to repeat the mistake I'd made with CryptoWallet. It was going to be a success, and I had managed to get kicked out of the band just before the first album went gold. This one had to—it just had to—work.

I placed a gentle hand on Cricket's knee and employed the time-honored words of centuries' worth of stalling husbands: "Can we talk about this later?"

"Fireworks?" She frowned with arched eyebrows.

"I hear there might be some," I said, unbuckling my seat belt and hopping from the car before she could object.

We burst through the front door just as both kids emerged from their respective showers ready for bed. Judging by their wide eyes, you would have thought we were springing them from jail. We paid the babysitter and hustled the pajama-clad kids into the car for a final sprint to the beach.

Luckily, it was a fog-free night, meaning we didn't need to make it all the way to East Beach to guarantee a view of the show. With that in mind, we found street parking on Hill Road, just behind the Four Seasons Biltmore, and dashed over its grounds and through its lobby—Isabel riding on my back, Trip riding on Cricket's. With seconds to spare, we found two spots on the elevated concrete wall looming over Butterfly Beach and wedged our kids in. Trip turned to me—his dog-headed security blanket clutched in his hands—and said, "I can't believe we made it, Dad," just as the first salvo of fireworks burst above the Santa Barbara Harbor.

# Chapter Twenty-Five

"Where were you last night?" Cyrus demanded, arriving only fifteen minutes late for our meeting the next morning—practically on time.

I looked around the room as if he might be talking to someone else. "I was here," I protested.

"No, you weren't," Cyrus said. "At least you weren't here when the fireworks went off."

My face pinked. "I'm sorry, Cyrus. I...We have a family tradition of taking the kids to the beach to watch the show, and I didn't want to break it. It seemed like you had everything—"

"I wasn't talking about *those* fireworks," he said, his tentacle-like fingers pantomiming explosions overhead. "I was talking about these." He thwacked a stack of freshly inked papers onto the couch beside me.

"What is...?" I began, thumbing the papers, each identical in form. "Are these new investor agreements?"

"I told you not to worry."

I flipped the pages, tallying the amounts as I went, my heart racing. "Eleven million dollars?"

"Only eleven?" Cyrus said. He flipped through his own papers. "I forgot one."

He sent one more document my way, this one signed by Huff Monroe, he of the bolero collection. It was for an additional nine million dollars. "You raised twenty million dollars last night?" I said, my voice suddenly raspy. After the bizarre Central California Economic Summit event, where he told the crowd he was done raising capital, I felt as disconnected from his business plan as ever. ExOh's bank account at Miramar Bank and Trust was in freefall, buffered only by the $225,000 received from those who had given to the new, and still baffling, ExOh Global Relief Charities.

Cyrus looked back at me matter-of-factly. "I told you I would take care of it," he said. "At this point, Hollis, I would expect to see a little less shock and a little more gratitude on your face. Have I failed to deliver on any promise made thus far?"

I raised my hands involuntarily. "No, Cyrus." I shook my head. "Not at all. I'm...I'm sorry. I didn't mean to give you the impression that—"

"You know, in most companies," he interrupted, "the CEO oversees raising the money. Why don't I let you steer this boat for a little bit? See how you like being the one responsible for everything?"

Certainly, I was no stranger to frustrated bosses, but this time I felt more incompetent than self-righteous. The truth was that I couldn't do what Cyrus was doing. I couldn't schmooze. I couldn't host. I couldn't regale, wow, or inspire. I might be struggling with a few questions, but judging by the enthusiasm of ExOh's investors, those doubts put me in a crowd of one. If I was not quick to heal Cyrus's growing annoyance with me, I might find myself cast to the side at precisely the moment when the tide seemed to be turning in the company's favor. *No, no, no, NO!*

"I apologize, Cyrus," I began, prepared to grovel and flatter until he smiled. "I promise, I have your back. If you sense surprise, it's only because I'm in awe of you. You've done an amazing job putting ExOh in position to succeed."

I could see his face soften a little; I hoped that meant I was on the right track.

"I realize I have a lot to learn," I continued, "and I'm working hard to build the skills I need so I can take things off your plate. I promise you; you have my full faith and support."

A slight grin returned to Cyrus's face. I counted that as a victory.

"Very good, my friend," he said, retaking his seat. "The wires for the new investments should start coming in today. We have plenty of bills to pay in Asia, so I'll need those funds transferred to Hong Kong immediately."

I swallowed. "All of it?"

"All of it."

Moving money always made me nervous, especially when the moved amount had seven zeros in it and left the Miramar bank account with pennies. But I wasn't about to let Cyrus see that concern on my face. "Absolutely."

Cyrus's full smile returned; that was the answer he wanted to hear, I guess. "Good," he said. "We'll need a press release about the capital raise ASAP. Also, have you talked to Noah?"

*Have I talked to Noah?* I had not *spoken* with Kai, Reuben, Umed, or Noah outside of our first Zoom call and had only exchanged written messages with them via the BatSignal app. Increasingly, Cyrus would send out group messages that were never responded to by anyone. It was the strangest executive arrangement I'd ever witnessed. "No," I said. "Was I supposed to?"

Cyrus whipped out his phone, tapping and swiping with his right hand. "Three new clients," he said. "Burberry, Zara, and São Paulo Alpargatas. Noah estimates annual revenues of"—a few more swipes—"eighteen million dollars from these customers."

"That is fantastic news, Cyrus," I said. "When did Noah—"

"Put out one press release about the capital raise," Cyrus interrupted with a raised hand, "and a separate press release about the new clients and projected revenues. As before, Noah will provide the details."

Per usual, it was seventy-two degrees and sunny in Montecito, but I nevertheless shuddered. "Of course."

"Excellent. Get me those press releases to review this afternoon. I want both pieces to hit the Associated Press newswire before the market opens tomorrow." He closed his eyes, cracking his neck side to side. "Next week, we'll be—"

"Cyrus!" a voice bellowed from the hinterlands of the Wimbys' sprawling house. "What the fuck did I say about my luggage?" The voice continued, growing louder as it approached, the speaker's high heels echoing off the hardwood floors. "Do I *literally* have to do everything for you?" It was Genevieve, only in a tone I had never heard from her before. "Man the helm? You want to man the helm? You can barely keep—Hollis!" she said, coming to a full stop when she saw me sitting wide-eyed on her couch.

"Yes, dear," Cyrus said, with an exaggerated sense of calm. "We were just having our morning executive meeting. Just like always at about this time." His pseudo-smile conveyed a hidden message. Genevieve's eyes were locked on his, quickly softening from devilish glare to gracious host.

"What was I thinking?" she said, taking the final three steps into the sunken living room. "Hollis, please excuse my interruption."

I stood, and she approached, dismissing once again my futile attempts at shaking her hand and moving in straight for a kiss hello. The room's tension was tar thick, but it was a reprieve for me. I had just barely escaped yet another groveling at Cyrus's feet, and now he seemed distracted by whatever was going on with Genevieve. I hadn't known her long, but she didn't strike me as the kind of person who dropped f-bombs casually. And what to make of her *man the helm* utterance? Every couple has their insider references, I reasoned, but nautical-themed ones were new to me. Regardless, even though the substance of the argument was over my head, I was grateful for the interference.

"We are getting ready to visit our home in Fiji," Genevieve said, eyeing me and turning a cold shoulder to Cyrus, "and, well, it wouldn't be a vacation without a little chaos." She smiled, clasped her hands together, and turned her body to Cyrus. "Sweetie," she began, though it still didn't sound sweet, "I found my Louis Vuitton luggage stuffed haphazardly into the closet of the guest bedroom. Several pieces are scratched, and I cannot find the keys to the locks. I believe I put you in charge of storing these things after we returned from Oman, no?"

Cyrus bit his lower lip and scratched his chin. I wasn't astute at reading the room, but even a dolt like me could recognize that both Wimbys wished I were not here.

"Let me finish up with Hollis, *dear*, and then I'll find those keys and sort out your luggage situation, okay?" He smiled, but there was no covering his frustration.

"Of course, *sweetheart*," she said, matching his concealed frustration with her own veiled fury. She turned and marched away, stomping the floor even louder than on her arrival.

Cyrus turned his eyes back to me, suddenly looking very tired. "Where were we?"

"Uh," I stammered, "I think you were advising me about the incoming investor funds."

"Right," Cyrus said, still distracted. "Right. So, I want you moving that money to Hong Kong the instant it clears our Miramar account."

"Yes. Absolutely. You got it," I said, as enthusiastically as possible; I was nodding like a bobblehead and nearly gave him a thumbs-up. All of this was procrastination. I had one more thing to discuss, and I dreaded broaching it. Cyrus's Syrian refugee fundraising drive had come from left field the night of his Summit address, and I was unsure how to handle the next steps. It was a reasonable query, but I sensed that it was old news to him and might chafe our newly healed scab. "And, uh, one last thing," I stuttered. "How do you want me to handle those donations to the ExOh Global Relief Charities?"

"What?"

The irritated look on his face was exactly what I feared. "The, uh, ExOh Global Relief Charities?" I squeaked.

"I heard you the first time," he said. "What about it?"

"Well," I said, my stomach knotting. I had just clambered to solid ground, but my grip was slipping. "We need to send charitable donation receipts."

Cyrus rolled his eyes. "So, send them."

I swallowed. "But this is sort of an official process. It's for tax purposes. So, we actually need to—you know—donate the money to a charity."

He shook his head. "Fine. Give it to the United Way."

Every fiber of my being wanted to just say, *sure,* and be done with pushing the issue further, but I couldn't stop my mouth from moving. "Is the United Way doing charity work in Syria? Because I know that was the cause that you highlighted when—"

"I do not give a flying fuck what the United Way is doing!" Cyrus yelled. "Give it to the Red Cross. Give it to UNICEF. I do not care. Just donate the money to someone doing something in Syria and send the fucking receipts!"

Three f-bombs in five minutes; I was on a roll. "Okay, I can definitely do that," I said, back in bobblehead mode. "And then, do you want the matching money from ExOh to go to the same charity?"

"What?" he repeated.

I wasn't going to make the same mistake in questioning his auditory capabilities, so I tried rephrasing my question. "You—I mean, *we*—pledged to match the contributions from donors five-to-one. So, ExOh needs to make its own charitable donation of" —I paused, pretending I needed to do the math in my head— "one-point-one-two-five million to the same Syrian relief charity."

He scowled at me, ready to explode. Several seconds ticked by, his face slowly relaxing into a grimace of mild irritation. "Of course," he said. "But Kai will make the matching donation out of the Hong Kong account. You just pass the money along, and I'll take care of the rest."

The distant sound of a train whistle echoed as I processed his words and formulated my follow-up questions. Why wouldn't I just send ExOh's matching donation at the same time I sent the contributions from everyone else? The back-and-forth made no sense. The old me wanted to object. But, as previously noted, my intuition had a spotty track record; if it were a restaurant, I would give it a one-star Yelp review. More important: Challenging Cyrus on this issue would be a direct affront to his honesty.

My brain tried to square its circle. I wasn't doing anything wrong, I attempted to reason. I'd be transferring money and following a direct order. If Cyrus Wimby—majority shareholder of ExOh Holdings—said he would handle the matching charitable donation from a bank account I didn't control, I had every reason to believe he would, didn't I?

But what if he didn't follow through? Wouldn't the outcome still be positive? UNICEF or the Red Cross or the United Way or some other equally worthwhile charity would be receiving money inspired by Cyrus's efforts, even if his efforts were rooted in a falsehood. That counted for something, didn't it? And what good would come from me pitching myself onto the train tracks? Who would that serve?

In the nanoseconds that I contemplated these questions, Cyrus's eyes narrowed. *What's it going to be?* those eyes said.

Two quotes from my inglorious professional past leapt to the fore of my brain, *Hollis cares more about being right than moving forward*: an exit interview truism I had received along with a carboard box. And once again, *Go along to get along*: the unfortunate reality of professional survival Cricket had schooled into me. Was I ever going to learn from these past mistakes? Was I going to sabotage every opportunity in front of me if it didn't fit perfectly into the preconceived notion in my head?

ExOh's stock price had touched $42 that morning, making my on-paper position now worth $4.2 million. Life-changing money, even in Montecito. I wasn't going to screw this up by listening to any voice coming from inside my *fog*.

"Will do," I finally said.

# Chapter Twenty-Six

With Cyrus and family off to Fiji, I opened my eyes to Montecito for the first time in months. Thank God I did; it—at least temporarily—saved my sanity. The ratcheting tension with Cyrus had worn me to a nub; I was in desperate need of some mental R and R. Increasingly, I felt I could do no right in his eyes, especially when sitting in his library as he listed new demands and shook his head at my annoying questions. I'd hoped that by the time the Wimbys returned from their three-week adventure, Cyrus would find me fresh-faced and amenable—a return to the early days of our working together when he seemed to value my inputs, and the demons of my skepticism were dormant. After all, it was summer in Montecito. If I couldn't rediscover a sense of joy and optimism now, it would be hard to imagine where and when I might find it.

For a town always wearing its *Paradise* badge proudly, it was summer when Montecito's claim seemed the most legitimate. Montecito summers were rainfall free—not even a sprinkle—from the end of May through the end of October. While the rest of the country dealt with thunderstorms, tornadoes, oppressive heat and humidity, and—by the end of summer—hurricanes, the only real question in Montecito was whether there would be morning fog and how long it might last.

Perhaps there was an argument that winter was Montecito's golden season. Yes, it rained occasionally, but the grand total winter precipitation typically amounted to no more than fourteen inches. If the overnight low broke forty degrees, it would be the talk of the town, with Montecito's ladies breaking out their Moncler ski puffers. Most winter days, it would still be sunny, and in that sun, Montecitans would bask in their shared paradise, trying hard to remember what month it was. And certainly, winter was the time of year when New Yorkers and Chicagoans most gazed upon our hamlet with envy.

But for me, it was all about summer. Sunny summer afternoons brought Montecito to the beach, and perhaps the beach was where Montecito was at its most egalitarian. Aside from the Coral Casino, the beach was no one's and everyone's. Butterfly Beach—in front of the Four Seasons Biltmore—and Miramar Beach—in front of the brand-new, nineteen-years-in-the-making Rosewood Hotel—were the main beaches, with secretive Hammond's tucked between. At low tide, one could walk all three beaches, end to end. A visit to Miramar or Butterfly would find clumps of sunbathers, empty towels vacated by surfers in the water, and lots and lots of walkers, often accompanied by four-legged friends who were unofficially welcomed to gallivant off leash.

Free of Cyrus, I front-loaded my workdays to join the rest of Montecito in these afternoon pilgrimages to the sand. There, Isabel would circle with a gaggle of girlfriends, Trip would boogie board and build drip sandcastles, and Cricket would swim out and back to the buoys staked two hundred yards offshore, then wander from pod to pod saying hello and catching up with friends.

With me in tow, Cricket was thrown off her game. She invited me to join her on the out-and-back swims. *Too cold*, I would say. She invited me to join her in the friendly catchups, but—who was

I kidding—we both knew I was conversational deadweight. *No, thank you,* I would say. After a few afternoons of my tagging along, I was beginning to wonder why my family let me; what a giant pain in the ass I was!

To make up for my faults, I brought a large shovel, enticing Trip and Isabel into elaborate sandcastle building. Sandcastles became dolphins, became whales, became sand igloos, became underground bunkers. By the end of the first week, muscles that I had not seen in years sprouted from my shoulders and back, and a healthy glow returned to my skin. Thanks to my continued gastrointestinal issues—diet related, I was now convinced—I had lost fourteen pounds since signing on to ExOh. This was the wrong way to lose weight, but with my new shoulder muscles and slight tan, I looked as good as I was going to look. Almost passable as Cricket's husband.

When my digging was done and my family tired of me, I would just sit, staring offshore at the oil platforms. Ah, the oil platforms—a reminder that even Eden had its apples and serpents. Below the surface of the twenty-five-mile-wide channel separating Montecito from Santa Cruz Island lay one of the largest naturally seeping oil fields in the world. As early as the eighteenth century, mariners in the Santa Barbara Channel noted the sheen on the water and the tar balls occasionally accumulating on the sand. Offshore oil drilling began here in 1898 and thrived—despite perpetual objection from the locals—until a disastrous spill in 1969 coated thirty-five miles of Santa Barbara County beaches in oil and dead birds. Thus, the boom came to an ignominious end and ushered in a new environmental consciousness, beginning with the first Earth Day in 1970.

Nineteen offshore oil platforms remained in the Santa Barbara Channel, seven of them visible from Montecito's beaches. During the holiday season, the platforms were dressed as blinking red and green Christmas trees, attempting to soften their image as weapons of environmental destruction. The display was pretty but ineffective. It was an abusive father trying to win back his estranged children with birthday gifts.

To remind us that we can't escape our nature, the tar balls still came and went at unpredictable intervals. Most locals dedicated a pair of flip-flops as *beach-only* and kept a rag and baby oil handy as insurance. Curiously, the Montecito Chamber of Commerce didn't note any of this in its brochures.

Uncharacteristic of me, I never took my phone to the beach. BatSignal had been quiet since Cyrus left, and for that I was grateful. I knew the entire business was not on vacation, and that—as the company's CEO—I should demand to be kept in the loop, but I didn't want to levy that demand. I wanted a break. I wanted to pretend that I was like much of the rest of Montecito: of working age, but hardly working. To do so, I latched on to Cyrus's trip like a barnacle on a boat and made his three-week *va*cation my own ten-day *stay*cation. It wasn't part of my nonexistent employment agreement, but that didn't stop me from taking it.

And, for once, I let the inconsistency slide.

# Chapter Twenty-Seven

As the final days of Cyrus's vacation—and my staycation—wound down, our family packed up and headed south to Hermosa Beach in support of Cricket and her entry in the Dwight Crum Pier-to-Pier. With Jenny, Paul, and their children in tow, we caravanned from Montecito at sunrise, stopping first at the Aquarium of the Pacific in Long Beach—for the girls—and then at the Battleship USS *Iowa*—for the boys. By the time we sat down to a pre-race pasta feast at 7:00 p.m. in Hermosa, Cricket was ready to send us all back home so she could get to bed. But once everyone settled into our room at the Beach House Hotel, she changed her tune and thanked us all for the support.

Cricket had been training for this brutal swimming challenge for months, with an eye to breaking her personal best record in this, her fortieth year on planet earth. It wasn't unusual for a forty-year-old to achieve new athletic feats, but it was quite another thing when the athletic feat in question was a mark set during a year in which said forty-year-old had been an All American collegiate swimmer. To beat her best, she would have to swim the grueling two-mile, open-ocean course in under forty-three minutes. Considering that I would barely get wet in the chilly Pacific Ocean and that I still had not mastered a swimming pool flip turn—I lost all sense of direction the moment my feet went over my head, typically thrusting one useless leg toward the sky while the other slapped the pool deck—this feat was beyond my comprehension.

The morning of the race, we nonparticipants loaded up on pancakes and bagels—as if we needed more carbs—while Cricket sipped English breakfast tea and ate four almonds and two tangerines. I could sense her excitement, but more, her nerves. Turning forty years old had morphed this athletic goal into an act of defiance against the gods. She would not go gently into that good night. As I poured more syrup on my pancakes and opened a pat of aluminum-wrapped butter—my stomach enjoying a rare reprieve—I was grateful that at least one of us would be around to hold our grandchildren.

With breakfast complete, we moved to the sand and said our goodbyes and good lucks to Cricket as she made her way through the pod of silicone-capped, goggled competitors. If she achieved her goal, she would likely finish in the top ten overall. For that reason, she needed to elbow her way to the front of the line, making sure she got a clean start on the sprint from sand to water.

If anyone was more nervous than Cricket, it was Isabel, who idolized her mother in a way every girl should but few do. Cricket was lining up with the men, many of whom looked like Michael Phelps imitators, and she was about to whip most of their asses. This knowledge swelled our Isabel with pride. It was not just any woman; it was her mother.

Trip had long ago lost any semblance of male chauvinism. He loved and respected me, for sure, but he instinctively recognized his mother as our family's superhero. On some level this should have made me jealous or resentful, but I felt none of it. Trip and Isabel were correct. Cricket inspired me daily. I wasn't sure why I had the good fortune to be her partner, but I counted that gift as the greatest of my life.

Paul, Jenny, and their children joined us in the crowd of onlookers, shouting whoops and good luck wishes to all. Finally, with the crack of the starter's pistol, Cricket's open swim division launched into a sprint, elbows flying and legs pumping. I was surprised by the brutality at the front of the pack, but Cricket was giving as good as she got, lowering her shoulders as the group approached the tide line. At *only* five foot seven, Cricket deftly avoided a few sharp elbows whiffing over her head, leaving me to wonder if her position in the front lines might have been tactical brilliance. With the synchronicity of ballet dancers, she and her fellow frontliners dove over an incoming wave, pierced the ocean, and took off in a sea of arms churning saltwater into foam.

The first leg of the swim was to the end of the Hermosa Beach Pier, then north to the Manhattan Beach Pier, finishing with a short run in the sand. Two miles in total. As I watched Cricket battle the men and make the turn north, I realized that my lower lip had been hanging like a limp flag, and I was about to drool on my own T-shirt. A tugging on my pocket from Trip brought me back to the moment; already the rest of our crew was walking north, and I was at risk of being left behind.

As I brought up the rear—Isabel running on the sand, screaming encouragement that Cricket would never hear—my cell phone vibrated. I reached into my pocket and thumbed the ignore button. Five seconds later, it rang again. Again, I stilled the vibration. On the third call, I decided to check, assuming it was one of those annoying robocalls that pretend to be dialing from a number nearly identical to your own, hoping to trick you into answering out of curiosity.

It was not a robocall. It was Cyrus, who had not spoken to me in sixteen days—since he left for his vacation home in Fiji—and had not BatSignaled me in more than a week.

"Hi, Cyrus. How is Fiji?" I said, walking the Strand, stores and restaurants to my right, sand and water to my left.

"Fiji is as it always is, Hollis: perfect," he said in a tone that can be best described as curt. "I need you to go to my house," he continued.

"What's going on?" I said, expecting that he might need me to pick up his mail or check to make sure the lights were off; you know, typical CEO-of-a-public-company tasks.

"I'll explain when you get there," he said.

"Well," I said cautiously, "I'm not in Montecito at the moment. I'm in Hermosa. Cricket is—"

"This is urgent, Hollis. I'm sorry to interrupt your weekend plans, but I need you at my house ASAP."

I was still walking north along the Strand, shaking my head. I was adding up the numbers, trying to calculate the minimum amount of time it would take me to get home. Cricket would be swimming for another forty-plus minutes. There would be some sort of awards ceremony, right? Maybe an hour for that. Then we would all walk back to our hotel, from which we had thankfully already checked out. The walk would take another half hour at a minimum, and then we needed to drive home. It was only one hundred miles, but in Sunday traffic on the notorious parking lot known as the 405, conservatively, that would take two and a half hours. Then I would need to drop everyone off and drive to Cyrus's house. I added it up. "I can be at your place inside of five hours," I said.

"I said ASAP, Hollis!" he hollered. "Is that phrase lost in translation? In what country is five hours considered *soon*?"

"I..." I stammered, still walking north. Isabel had given up on her cheering and joined me on the Strand. Out of nowhere, she reached out to hold my hand and smiled at me in a way I had not seen in some time. "I'm sorry, Cyrus, I'm with my family in Hermosa, and I can't get back to Montecito for five hours."

I heard a fist hit something solid. "That's just grand," he seethed. "In five hours, I will have the business cards of your successor printed."

"That is not fair, Cyrus. It's a Sunday and..." I didn't want to go into a full explanation of where I was and what I was doing. "And this is important."

"So is your job, I presume," he said. "It's your call."

The line went dead, and the pancakes in my stomach lurched.

"Is everything okay, Dad?" Isabel asked.

I swallowed, sandwiching her hand in mine. "Yes, sweetie. Everything is fine."

I began to walk faster, still clutching Isabel's hand. Paul and Jenny were ahead of me, but I could see their heads bobbing. Would they help? Of course they would help. They would understand, or at least Paul would. What choice did I have? Even without knowing that I had cashed in my retirement savings and was pretending to receive a paycheck, Paul would explain to everyone that when the boss yells *Jump*, the only question is, *How high*? I wasn't the first to have a family weekend ruined by the demands of work, and I wouldn't be the last. Right? *Right*?

As my stride increased from casual to speed walker—and Isabel lagged from beside me to behind me—I said these things to myself, justifying a decision that didn't feel like a choice. I didn't see how I could possibly walk away from ExOh at this moment. If the cost of this steadfastness disappointed my family today, I would make up for it when I sold my ExOh stock and the Crawfords stopped being Montecito's reigning paupers.

"Paul, Jenny," I said when I'd finally caught them.

"Isn't this amazing?" Jenny said, smiling similarly to how Isabel had only a few moments earlier.

"Yeah, it's fantastic," I said distractedly. "Look, I need your help."

Paul cocked his head but didn't stop walking; he knew as well as the rest of us that Cricket would beat us to the finish line if we didn't hustle. "What's up?"

"I..." I stammered, slightly out of breath. "I need to go in to work."

"Now?" Jenny said, stopping cold on the Strand, her eyes wide.

I nodded, unable to get the word out.

"*Now?*" she repeated.

"Yes," I finally said. "I'm sorry—believe me—but...but, yes."

"Okay," Paul said, placing a hand on my shoulder as if to keep me from falling. "Okay, what do you need us to do? Do you want us to bring everyone home? We can do that, can't we, honey?" He said, turning to Jenny.

"Uh," she said, her eyes toward the sky like she was solving a complicated trigonometry problem. "Uh, yeah. We can put the third-row seats down and put a few bags in the footwells, and—if we put the boys in the back row—then yeah, I...I think we can."

"You're leaving, Dad?" Isabel said, catching up just in time to hear my pathetic cries for help.

"I'm sorry, sweetie," I said, barely able to make eye contact for my shame, "but I have to."

Isabel nodded, but her eyes glistened, signaling burgeoning tears.

"I can't believe this," Jenny said.

"I..." I started to say, then stopped. What words would have made this any better?

"Don't worry," Paul interjected, his hand still on my shoulder. "We'll get everyone home, safe and sound. These things happen."

I guessed that these things did indeed happen, but in that moment, I could not have felt more impotent. I could picture Cricket, three hundred yards from where I stood, churning the sea in the hopes of breaking through a barrier of achievement, while I—ostensible family protector—abandoned them all. "Thank you, Paul," I said. "Thank you, Jenny." He nodded and patted my shoulder; she just stared at me.

"Get going," Paul said. "I have a feeling you'll be paying a price for this for a while to come; might as well make it count."

I nodded, kissed Isabel on the cheek, ruffled Trip's hair, and took off at a sprint.

# Chapter Twenty-Eight

I called Cyrus as soon as I had navigated onto Interstate 405 and was officially en route. "I'll be there in two hours," I told him, feeling confident that this answer would satisfy him.

"Go straight to my house," he barked. "Call me when you get to the gate."

I drove recklessly, weaving in and out, crossing three lanes at a time, hitting ninety miles per hour for stretches. I hadn't driven like that since before Isabel was born—since before I had something to lose. By the time I cleared the tri-cities of Camarillo, Oxnard, and Ventura, I knew I would beat the herculean two hours I had estimated for the drive. In a perverted manner, my heart was pumping as if I had accomplished something. Something like swimming two miles in the open ocean? What a joke.

I pulled up to the Wimbys' twelve-foot gate and grabbed my phone. But in a rare moment of keeping my priorities straight, I texted Paul: *Hey Paul. Are you guys good?*

*Hey Hollis,* he wrote. *We are good. She did it!! Forty-two, thirty-one!! Top female finisher and sixth place overall!!*

Joy and shame overwhelmed me. Cricket had done it. She had set her mind to a phenomenal feat and achieved it. Meanwhile, I had deserted her at her moment of triumph. Tears welled in my eyes as my Subaru's engine ran and my bladder pleaded for relief. What was I doing? God help me, Cyrus's sudden emergency had better be worth what I had sacrificed.

*Amazing,* I wrote back. *Please give her a hug from me.*

*I will,* he replied. *I hope the work emergency gets resolved.*

He didn't say any more, and he didn't need to. We both knew that I was in a boatload of domestic trouble. *Thank you. Drive safe,* I typed, then opened my phone app and dialed Cyrus again.

"You there?" he answered.

"Yes."

He gave me the new gate code; ever since Vlad's surprise visit, I had been buzzed onto the estate without being privy to the access code. I parked my car while he stayed on the line. "How do I get into the house?"

"There's a hide-a-key in the garden behind the pizza oven," he said. "Looks like a pile of dog shit."

Fitting, I thought, trudging to the back of the house. I found the fake pile of poop and extricated the key. "Got it."

"Go to the door closest to the pool," he said. "It is also the closest to the security system. As soon as you enter, go straight to the pantry beside the kitchen. There is a touchscreen in there that will be flashing. I'll give you the codes when you're in front of it."

I did as instructed but felt queasy as *INTRUDER ALERT!* flashed on the touchpad, even though I knew exactly who the intruder was. "I'm here."

He gave me one set of codes, which I entered. On completion, a second screen flashed, requiring more codes. Then a third. A countdown timer blinked in the upper corner the entire time, making me feel like I was diffusing a bomb. "It's off," I said when the final code was received, and the touchscreen returned to a soothing color of blue.

"Go to my office," he said.

Again, I followed instructions as my heart raced. It took a minute to wind through the estate, reaching his walnut-paneled office with its views of the swimming pool and a distant glimpse of the putting green. "I'm at your desk," I said, slightly out of breath.

"Go to the weeping fig in the corner of the room," he said. "Just behind the trunk, there is a set of three keys. Grab them."

Three soiled keys in hand, I said, "Done."

"The gold one goes to the lower left drawer of my desk. Open it."

I moved to his desk, nestled my cell between my shoulder and ear, and opened the drawer.

"Stop wedging the phone to your ear and put it on speaker, Hollis."

I pressed the speaker button and held the phone in front of my face, looking at it as if it had sprouted horns. How did Cyrus know *how* I was holding my phone?

As if reading my mind, Cyrus said, "Yes. I'm watching you."

My head swiveled until I saw the blinking red light from the corner behind the weeping fig.

"Found me," Cyrus said.

My spine tingled.

"In the back of the drawer, behind the file folders, there are seven—" He stopped cold, the sound of muffled angry voices, one of which was his. "Fine," he grunted, returning to the phone. "Eight—not seven—eight RemoteToken fobs. Do you see them?"

I did indeed see them. RemoteToken fobs looked like keyless entry car "keys," with small screens that displayed six-digit numbers. The numbers were like exploding passwords, considered by many to be the most secure passwords outside of fingerprints.

These fobs were also ancient technology, replaced by actual fingerprints, face recognition, and two-factor authentication. I knew of them because I was a tech geek, but my kids would never see one of these fobs in their lifetime. For Cyrus to have one fob was unique; to have seven—scratch that—eight of them was downright bizarre.

I picked up the tokens one by one, counting out all eight.

Each was marked distinctly with either colored tape or fingernail polish. "I've got them," I declared.

"Find the one with the red tape—"

"No, you fucking idiot!" I heard in the background; the *idiot* part barely muffled as Cyrus again tried to smother his phone, this time less successfully. Without question, the screamer was Genevieve.

After a few more seconds of heated exchange, Cyrus returned, faking calm. "The one with the yellow fingernail polish, I should have said, not the one with red tape."

"It's right here," I said, holding it up to the weeping fig as proof.

"Good," he said. "It's got a countdown indicator on the screen. Beside the numbers are six little bars, each one representing five seconds. Let me know when all six bars are showing."

I didn't stop him from explaining how the RemoteToken worked, but I already knew. I knew more about RemoteTokens than Cyrus knew about China and Free Trade Zones and Saudi Arabian oil, but something cautioned me to hold my tongue for the moment. "Almost there," I said, waiting ten more seconds, then, "Okay, all six bars are showing."

"Read me the number," he said.

I did.

I could hear the clicking of his keyboard.

"Okay, I'm in," he said to me, then repeated, "I'm in," louder, but directed away from his phone, presumably toward Genevieve. She said something in reply. I couldn't make it out, but it didn't sound nice.

"Are we good?" I asked. "Is that all you needed?" *Please say no,* I prayed. Surely Cyrus didn't demand that I desert my family, hours from home, breaking every California Highway Patrol code to get to his house *ASAP* to read six digits off a RemoteToken fob. And for what? Why was this so *ASAP* important? Why did he desperately need access to whatever server or system or bank or...*bank*?

I heard light keyboard clicking on the other end of the line. "Is that all you needed?" I repeated. *Please say no; please say no.*

"That's it."

I set the fob down on his desk and buried my head in my hands.

"I'm still watching," he said through my phone's speaker.

I sat up like a scolded child.

"There is one more thing," he said. "I am about to BatSignal you our address in Fiji. I want you to take those eight RemoteTokens and FedEx them to me. In the same drawer where you found the fobs, I have FedEx envelopes and shipping forms that already have my billing info entered. Fill in our address and take the envelope directly to FedEx. Do not pass go. Do not collect two hundred dollars. Go straight to the FedEx store, and—"

"It's Sunday, Cyrus. The FedEx store is closed on Sunday."

"Don't interrupt me, Hollis! If the store is closed, there is a drop box on Coast Village Road, just past Jeannine's Bakery. I want you to take your phone and make a little movie of yourself dropping those fobs into the addressed envelope and feeding it into the drop box. I want that video delivered to me by BatSignal in fifteen minutes. Do you understand?"

I turned to look at the weeping fig, my face wrinkled in shock.

"Do you understand?" he repeated.

I nodded but said nothing.

"Good," he said. "Fifteen minutes. Arm the security system on your way out."

I returned to the forehead-in-palms pose, still sitting in Cyrus's desk chair.

"You should get going," my phone cracked. "And don't forget; I'll be watching."

With that eerie warning, he hung up.

# Chapter Twenty-Nine

With the understanding of a saint, Cricket forgave my bailing on her in her moment of triumph. At least her mouth said it; her eyes begged to differ. They were the eyes of a gagged hostage, filled with rage, fear, and bewilderment. Each time I tried to discuss the situation—Cyrus's call, his demands, the cost of saying no—she cut me off before I could explain. "It's okay. I understand," she would repeat, and then walk away.

This graciousness was the opposite of what I wanted. I wanted her to yell at me. I wanted tears and spittle. I wanted her to unleash hell on me. I deserved it in so many ways. For missing her pier-to-pier triumph. For sidestepping her attempts to discuss the Wimbys. For sinking so low professionally that the phrase *bet the farm* had literal application. And perhaps worse of all, for hiding my discovery of Cyrus's RemoteTokens.

With regard to this latest crime against my better half, the truth was I didn't yet know what the RemoteTokens meant or signified. Until I did, I wanted to keep their existence a secret. As demanded, I had sent the fobs along to Fiji in a Bubble Wrap mailer. Physically they were gone, but I'd retained their electronic footprints. And with them, I was certain I could figure out exactly what I was doing with Cyrus Wimby. Was I building a business?

Was I handling critical tasks? Was I furthering legitimate ends? Or...was I not?

No more unfounded hope, no more wishful thinking, no more blind adherence to—or rejection of—whatever I saw from inside the fog. I needed answers, and to get them, I would use the best of my legitimate talents. Once I understood what was going on, I would tell Cricket everything. We would either laugh about the silly misunderstandings or plot our family's next pivot—a pivot that could well involve shoehorning all of us into the spare bedroom of Cricket's parents' house.

To formally apologize for my Hermosa Beach desertion—and in celebration of Cricket's personal record—Paul and Jenny's family joined ours for a backyard barbecue. It was my idea, and I was solely responsible for pulling it off. Normally, Cricket would take some of the load off, but she seemed fine letting me perform this small act of contrition without her helping hand.

The meal was my poor impersonation of Ina Garten, my go-to muse whenever I was the family chef. That night I was grilling Ina's Asian salmon and baking her roasted broccoli. I still had a few bottles of complementary Entre Nous—was I going to receive a W-2 for wine as wages?—and I opened them all. With some accompanying coconut-infused rice, this was my cannot miss meal; even Isabel, my picky eater, always cleaned her plate on the nights of this lineup.

Upon entry, the kids ran off to play, leaving the four adults to pretend there was no eight-hundred-pound gorilla defecating in the kitchen corner. I poured everyone a glass of wine and raised a toast to Cricket. With a few sips of lubrication, the gorilla shrunk to six hundred pounds.

As men are wont to do, Paul followed me onto the patio to watch me grill the salmon. I was a stickler for grilling the *right* way: over charcoal in an original Weber grill. As a technology geek, I was a leading-edge adopter of gadgets and form factors that promised efficiency. But when it came to grilling, I was a card-carrying caveman.

This time alone with Paul also gave me a chance to properly congratulate him on what amounted to a massive—but not unexpected—gut punch for me. The front page of the *Santa Barbara Independent* had relayed the news that morning: "Local Startup CryptoWallet Raises Fifty Million." I had known, from the day I packed my cardboard box, that CryptoWallet was destined for success, but reading about Clyde Bostich—the man who fired me because I complained too much—and his metaphorical victory lap ripped the scab right off my wound. That said, Paul was still my friend—one of few—and I was genuinely happy for him, even if I was jealous as hell.

"Congratulations on the equity raise," I said to Paul as I lifted the charcoal chimney. "Wow. Fifty million dollars."

He cringed. "I'm sorry, man."

"Sorry? Cut it out!" I said. "I can't be your friend if you're going to pity me."

"Not pity," he said. "It just felt like talking about it was rubbing salt in the wound."

I slid the grill grate in place and closed the lid. "Not at all," I said. "I'm happy for you and happy for the company. Maybe not so much happy for Clyde, but—hey—two out of three isn't bad."

Paul seemed relieved that I wasn't jealous, or at least camouflaging it well. This wasn't easy for me, as I was generally an open book with my emotions. Time and again, this had gotten me in trouble. I couldn't hide disgust, disappointment, or disdain, and any attempts to backtrack were fruitless. But if I was ever going to have a poker face, this was the moment.

"So, what's the plan for the fifty million?" I asked.

Paul smiled. "The usual. New office furniture. A bigger marketing budget. Expanding the sales team. Raises..."

I nodded, willing away judgment from my face. "That's terrific," I said. "Just curious, but what about the security stuff? Has Clyde earmarked any of the money toward tightening up?"

Paul shook his head. "What can I say? It's not at the top of Clyde's to-do list at the moment."

"Understood," I said. "Clearly he and I didn't see eye to eye on that."

"Now, there's an understatement." Paul laughed.

I joined Paul's laugh, trying to keep the mood featherweight. "Even the issue with the tokens?" I pressed. "He didn't deem that one a priority?"

"Tokens? The fob thingies?" Paul asked.

"Yeah," I said. "You know, the random-number generators for those old-school bank accounts." My heart was thumping in my ears as my blood pressure skyrocketed. I was a down-on-his-luck pirate who had stumbled on a treasure map. Before I trudged off into the jungle, I needed to understand whether the local tribesmen were friendly or cannibals.

"Right," Paul said. "Nah, we haven't dealt with that yet. I think we only have a handful of those on the system."

"Sure," I said, nodding. "Makes sense."

"Nobody knows about it but you, anyway," Paul said, slapping me on the back as I lifted the lid to place the salmon filets down for three minutes of intense heat.

My heart bounded into cardio territory at his words; it was exactly what I needed to hear. CryptoWallet had washed their hands of me and done nothing to fix the problems I had been fired for complaining about. *Deep breaths,* I told myself. I chuckled nervously and threw myself under the bus as cover. "That's me," I said. "Chief of Worry. Head of Nonissues."

At one point, Paul asked about ExOh, and I replied only that I was keeping *busy,* then let it drop. There was no need to elaborate.

I flipped the salmon filets once, and after another three minutes, moved them to the outer edges of the grill's surface, keeping the lid off. In another nine minutes, they would be done and set aside to rest under a final coat of marinade. The kitchen beeper went off, and I rescued the broccoli from the oven, tossing it with lemon juice, lemon zest, toasted pine nuts, and Parmesan: perfect. I poured myself another glass of wine and threw away the first bottle empty, feeling a purposeful tingle.

I don't know if the gorilla had shrunk all the way down to a spider monkey, or if I just got tipsy enough to believe that everyone was having a wonderful, carefree evening. I do know that the plates were licked and that by the time everyone had their ice cream—Montecito's very own Rori's—and berries, I heard several groans suggesting overconsumption. As far as I was concerned, those groans signaled success.

When we said our goodbyes, Jenny gave me a hug—another good sign. In my experience, the forgiveness of a wife's best friend is often the hardest to win.

Cricket tried to help with the dishes, but I thanked her and sent her away.

I tasked Isabel with Trip duty, and she welcomed the assignment. She'd been suggesting that she'd like to start babysitting for neighbors next year, so Trip served as both a guinea pig and an audition. She did well, helping Trip brush his teeth and dress for bed, then completing her daily reading requirement with a chapter of *Percy Jackson and the Olympians: The Lightning Thief*, read to Trip as he snuggled with Charlie, his dog-headed security blanket.

Meanwhile, I stuffed the dishwasher and handwashed what remained. With soap suds up to my elbows, I haphazardly scrubbed and rinsed, considering what Paul had said and how I would use it. His words—*nobody knows about it but you, anyway*—repeating in my head like the refrain to a lullaby.

# CHAPTER THIRTY

THE WIMBYS RETURNED from Fiji just in time for the grand opening of the Entre Nous tasting room. In a mismatch for the ages, Cyrus had left me to herd the construction and interior design crews in his stead, and it was this work that filled most of my time while they were away. Each time I visited the site, I walked past Merci, where Cyrus and I met for our first coffee and where this entire journey began.

In contrast to the broader Country Mart—with its shades of brown and blends of Mission, Spanish, and retro-modern styles—the tasting room was done in blinding white. So much of it, in such a similar shade, that a coffee table staged in a small living room set claimed more than one damaged shin during the grand opening party. The only thing preventing more injuries was the size of the crowd: body to body. The people formed a negative image of the furniture, indirectly illuminating the safe zones.

To commemorate the event, Cyrus debuted a Vintner's Reserve Cabernet Sauvignon called Priscilla and a new red blend —Cabernet, Grenache, Syrah, Mourvèdre—called Rosaland, the name of Priscilla's horse. The invitation-only guest list had been chosen by the Wimbys; my only contribution was Paul and Jenny.

It was a who's who of Montecito, including all of ExOh's local investors and the inner circle of Miramar Bank's John Colton.

Cricket knew most everyone there, including a celebrity couple she had worked for back in her public relations days. The couple cornered her and begged her to ditch the Storytellers Children's Center—at least temporarily—to help them turn their divorce into a PR bonanza; she graciously declined. While she seemed to be having fun, I felt extraneous as usual. My palate was not refined enough to appreciate great wine from good wine, and I was naturally suspicious of subtle, unverifiable claims. Priscilla and Rosaland were being sold for $90 a bottle—a price Cyrus assured everyone was a steal. Plenty of tasters nodded in agreement, but I could barely tell the difference between these penthouse wines and their basement-dwelling cousins.

Thanks to Cyrus, all attendees were automatically enrolled as executive members of the Entre Nous wine club, earning free tastings for life. They probably didn't care, given their income tax brackets, but this membership came with minimum quarterly purchase of $200 that would be automatically charged to the credit card they casually swiped to complete their wine club enrollment.

I guess this should have made me happy. I was the CEO of the company owning fifty-one percent of a money-printing machine. But I was a physical wreck, having now lost eighteen pounds since joining ExOh, all of them the wrong way. Perhaps that is why the wine didn't taste unique or special. In those days, little that passed my lips was rewarding.

"Bula bula," Genevieve whispered into my ear from behind, giving me a head-to-toe shiver.

I turned and traded cheek kisses. "Bula what?" I asked.

"Bula bula," she repeated. "Fijian for hello."

"I learn something new every day," I said, clinking my wineglass against hers. Our eyes met, as good fortune mandates, then drifted toward Cyrus. He was behind the pourer's bar in the middle of an animated story while a semicircle of onlookers listened raptly.

"Look at him," Genevieve said. "In his element."

I nodded. "Cyrus excels at this. He is a natural-born—"

"He likes to talk," Genevieve interrupted.

I nodded again, less certain that my acknowledgment was appropriate. "He certainly does."

"But you and I know that success isn't achieved by talking, right, Hollis?"

Another, even weaker nod.

She laughed, seemingly to herself. "You can talk about the rib eye or the porterhouse or the filet mignon till you're blue in the face. You can describe the lovely pasture in which the herd grazed. You can brag about the aging. You can paint the picture of exquisite marbling and fork-tender preparation. You can recite the flavor profile of your mesquite charcoal, and you can hint at the inclusion of a secret dry rub that harkens back to the East India Trading Company..."

Genevieve turned her eyes from Cyrus back to me and finished her wine in one gulp. "But no one is eating steak," she continued, "until someone slits that cow's throat."

I swallowed, fighting the urge to cover my Adam's apple with my free hand.

"Where is Cricket?" Genevieve said, saving me from the awkwardness of having no reply.

I scanned the room but couldn't find her. "I don't know."

Genevieve narrowed her eyes. "Well, the last I heard, this was a work event." She raised her empty wineglass, indicating the need for a refill. "See if you can round her up, Hollis. I'd like to catch up with her."

*Good luck with that,* I laughed internally. If Genevieve thought Cricket was going to hop-to at the snap of some fingers, she was sadly mistaken. I have never met a more independent spirit in my life than Cricket. She never shied away from a challenge, and she would not be outworked, but she also never submitted to subjugation. "I'll see if I can track her down."

"Do," Genevieve said before moving on to another pod of far more important people.

I had expected Genevieve to return from Fiji in the afterglow of vacation bliss, but I sensed no such thing. Beginning with the prevacation blow-up over the care of her luggage, continuing through her scathing background commentary when Cyrus sent me to retrieve his fobs, to now, she seemed stressed. Anxious. Even, perhaps, angry.

I set my glass down on the white marble tasting bar and shimmied through the room to the exit, ostensibly to find Cricket.

Once outside the tasting room, the fresh air of freedom filled my lungs. I decided a few laps around the Country Mart would not hurt anyone. With my hands in my pockets and my gait set to stroll, I passed the barbershop and the toy store, lingered in front of an apothecary and a pizzeria under renovation, then turned a corner to find Cricket and Jenny sitting against a rock wall with plastic spoons, cups of Rori's ice cream, and guilty smiles.

"Whoops," Cricket said.

"Don't worry." I laughed, "I'm not the hall monitor." I took a few steps closer, eyeing their ice creams. "But I do accept bribes."

She handed me her spoon, and I took a tiny bite of her favorite flavor: salted caramel. It was fantastic and did not, thankfully, result in more stomach queasiness for yours truly.

I leaned against the wall beside them. "The wine not doing it for you?"

"Meh," Jenny said, shrugging.

"Ditto," Cricket said. "Maybe I'm just over it."

I nodded. There was no reason to argue, and I didn't disagree. I thought of mentioning Genevieve's *request* that Cricket return to the party, but I quickly shelved that notion. If anyone was required to genuflect for the Wimbys it was me, not Cricket.

"Do you mind if we go?" Cricket asked. "I think I've had enough Wimby extravagance for the week."

"No." I shook my head. "That's fine."

"Send Paul out," Jenny said. "He has the keys. We'll take Cricket home."

I kissed Cricket on the cheek and said my goodbyes. Paul was easy to find on my return; he was sharing tasting notes with John Colton, who—in addition to being the head of Miramar Bank and Trust and an ExOh board member—was also an investor in CryptoWallet.

"Tobacco, really?" John Colton said as I invaded their circle.

"Notes of it," Paul insisted. "I'm also getting"—he stuck his nose in the glass of Vintner's Reserve Cabernet—"nutmeg."

"Interesting," John said.

"Pardon me, gentlemen," I said, "Paul, can I steal you away for a moment?"

He shook John's hand and followed me toward the room's open doors. "What's up?"

"The girls want to leave," I said. "They're at Rori's."

"No sweat," Paul said. "I was just about to blow my cover anyway."

"What? No tobacco? No notes of nutmeg?"

Paul shook his head. "All I can taste is the essence of fermented grapes. And between you and me, pretty average ones."

"So, I'll put you down for a case," I said.

Paul patted me on the arm. "See you soon."

With Paul's exit, any semblance of a safe zone was gone too. I didn't want any more wine, but I asked the pourer for a quarter-glass of Pinot Noir so I could safely appear to be participating. Glass in hand, I spotted Cyrus and decided to make my way over, taking my place among his disciples.

"Hollis," Cyrus said as soon as he spotted me, "how much was it that we raised for the Syrian refugees? It was five hundred thousand, right?"

My stomach twisted as Cyrus's eyes narrowed on me. I could feel the eyes of the others in his circle zeroing in for confirmation.

"Just about," I choked out, knowing the more accurate answer was *Just about half of that*.

He nodded. "Okay. *Just about* five hundred thousand," he repeated, "and then my company, ExOh, matched that with one and a half million. So, all together, we donated two million dollars to help alleviate one of the greatest human rights travesties of our time. Isn't that right, Hollis?"

Cyrus's eyes again found me. *Say it!* they demanded. In truth, I had split the actual donation of $225,000 between two charities with Syrian refuge relief efforts: CARE and Direct Relief, the latter a group headquartered in Santa Barbara that Cricket and her mother had been volunteering with for decades. As to ExOh's matching donation, I had no idea. I had moved every penny of the rest of the recent equity raise to the company's Hong Kong bank account, just as Cyrus had insisted. From that windfall, Cyrus pledged that he would pay himself the $1 million that ExOh owed him for the company's stake in Entre Nous and make the matching donations to charity. I had no doubt that Cyrus had paid himself, but the charities? Only Cyrus knew if he'd actually pushed the button on those donations. Nevertheless, I squeamishly answered, "Exactly," just as I knew I was obligated to do.

Cyrus nodded. "For those of you who do not know, Hollis Crawford here is ExOh's chief executive officer. Hollis, be sure to give these guys your card in case they want to learn more about ExOh, the next Amazon.com."

I shook hands, smiled, and passed out my business card. With roughly one-quarter of Cyrus's charisma, I was not the crowd pleaser he was. Soon, I found myself alone yet again.

Even though every fiber of my being wanted to leave, I vowed to stay to the end. After being criticized for departing the Fourth of July party early, I wouldn't repeat that mistake. I carried my prop of wine from pod to pod, faking genuine conversation; had I been wearing a step counter, I would have gotten a good day's exercise circling the room. When the crowd finally drew down to a handful, I felt like I had accomplished something, though I was saddened by how compromised my sense of accomplishment had become.

I tried to invade the final pod of nine by edging in next to Cyrus. It's possible that I was being oversensitive, but I could have sworn he saw me and refused to expand the circle. Eventually, John Colton edged over to allow me in, just as Cyrus said, "Shall we?" and everyone began to gather their jackets and purses, heading for the exit. I took up the rear, clueless as to where we were headed. As if noticing me for the first time, Cyrus laid his gargantuan paw on my shoulder. "We're going to Lucky's," he said, naming the venerable steak house at the end of Coast Village Road next to the Montecito Inn. "Would you help the pourers do inventory and then lock up?"

"I don't have the keys to—" I began to say before he jangled a set of shiny silver keys in my face.

"Thanks, Hollis," he said, turning to leave.

"Thanks, Hollis," I heard from Genevieve in the distance.

And just like that, they were gone.

# Chapter Thirty-One

Being treated like a servant would have hurt much more if I were a sensitive guy. Thankfully, I am not. The Wimbys walked off to their celebratory dinner at Lucky's, and I locked up the tasting room and went home, grateful that I wouldn't have to fake another smile that night.

My life was already far more complicated and duplicitous than I preferred. Like Clark Kent, whiling away his time at the *Daily Planet*, I continued to do Cyrus's bidding while leading a second life on the side. That life centered on unraveling the mystery of the RemoteToken fobs, which now strikes me as a bad title for an episode of *Scooby-Doo*.

On the day I discovered the fobs in Cyrus's desk drawer, I FedExed them to Fiji, just as Cyrus had demanded. Before sending them, I took photos of each fob's serial number. Under normal circumstances, and in normal hands, the serial numbers would be useless. But nothing about this was normal.

Back in the halcyon days of my collecting an actual paycheck as the chief operating officer of CryptoWallet, my specialty was knotty challenges. CryptoWallet's business plan was theoretically simple: seamlessly consolidate all of a person's bank accounts, credit cards, and—ta-da!—crypto currencies into one hub. The

CryptoWallet wallet meshed these disparate accounts and currencies into one, greatly simplifying a complex financial existence. It was a cool idea.

Like most cool ideas, it was easier to say than to do. Banks are like paranoid neighbors who barricade themselves behind walls, fences, shrubbery, and *No Trespassing* signs. The last thing they want is for some other company to come between them and their customer. So, the coding necessary to accomplish CryptoWallet's *simple* idea was beastly. When a customer logged into their CryptoWallet, the system had to simultaneously log into every individual account the customer maintained, pulling and consolidating the latest bits and bytes of information, then combining and reformatting it all into a single view.

As Isabel might say—so long as I was out of earshot—*thanks for the history lesson, boomer.* But this trip down memory lane has actual relevance: The thorniest bank accounts for CryptoWallet to log into were those guarded by RemoteToken fobs. Yes, Cyrus's fobs.

As described previously, RemoteToken fobs generate random six-digit numbers that explode every thirty seconds to be replaced by new numbers. These numbers serve as ever-changing passwords. The customer does not have to memorize anything; they just have to possess the fob. CryptoWallet didn't have many customers with bank accounts guarded by RemoteToken fobs, but the company had designs on global dominance. To achieve that, they needed a RemoteToken solution. Needless to say, this was precisely the kind of knotty project that had my name all over it.

The challenge was that the underlying account password—the six-digit number—was always changing; storing it was useless. So I worked with the programmers at RemoteToken to create code whereby our customer would enter the serial number on their fob and the current password the first time they linked the account. My code would then look inside the RemoteToken server to verify both the serial number and the code. If both numbers matched, the link was approved by RemoteToken in perpetuity.

To coax RemoteToken into accepting this work-around, I gave them several assurances. I promised that I would isolate the code that accessed their system on a separate server located in a galaxy far, far away from CryptoWallet's actual business servers. If that wasn't good enough, I also promised that my code would act as a black box, receiving the serial number and exploding password, checking those numbers against RemoteToken, and returning only a *True* or *False* answer to CryptoWallet. At no time would anyone at CryptoWallet ever be able to *see inside* the RemoteToken servers.

If CryptoWallet had followed through on my promises, the RemoteToken server would have been as impenetrable as ever. Despite my arguing, flailing, complaining, crying, and general petulance, CryptoWallet did *not* follow through. Instead of spending its money on security, as I had promised, the company spent it on a splashy debut at the Las Vegas Consumer Electronics Show and sent me packing in cardboard box number three.

As all this gobbledygook suggests, the serial numbers in my possession *should* have been useless. But CryptoWallet took a security shortcut, betting that no one would figure out its secret. Certainly, they would not have suspected innocent-to-a-fault me, a man riding so tall on his high horse that they had to cut him loose.

They were wrong. With the serial numbers in hand and the hacking chops to exploit them, I set off in search of the answer to a question that had been nagging me since the first day Cyrus Wimby asked me to open a bank account and start transferring millions of dollars: What the hell was in that Hong Kong bank account?

# Chapter Thirty-Two

After untold hours stolen from workdays, evenings, and weekends, my hack was nearly finished, and by all indications, completely undetected. In the movies, hackers sit down at a keyboard, let their fingers fly like Mozart, and seconds later, uncover a motherlode of data, often streaming across the screen like a tidal wave. Maybe some hacker somewhere works like this—there is no best-practices handbook or annual convention, after all—but not me. I like to think of hacking as an untimed laser maze escape room. If you go fast, you'll make a mistake. If you take time out of the equation, there is no challenge you cannot solve.

Complicating my progress, professional hacker was not my primary or even secondary profession. I was still chief executive officer of ExOh—though more and more I felt like a traitor—and more important, I was a parent!

As August threatened to become September, the pesky job of parenting screamed for its share of my shrinking availability. This would be Isabel's sixth-grade year—her final year at MUS—and Trip's second-grade year.

The move from first to second grade scared Trip for reasons that scared me. He had learned from his sister that the quantity of reading would triple and that, while technically there was no homework, he would be expected to read for thirty minutes at home every night. This distinction made no sense to him; what was homework but work at home? I must admit, he had a point.

Cricket and I were anxious to see how second grade agreed with Trip, fearing that something might be off. He excelled in any subject that involved touching things; science and art were his favorites. But when it was time to crack a book, his confidence dissolved. Worse, our sweet, curious boy became defiant: hiding, running, shaking his head with closed lips as if I were trying to force-feed him English peas. And while first and second graders are not known for penmanship, Trip's was uncomfortably bad. He gripped the pencil like he was trying to choke it and scratched the page angrily. This was the same kid who drew masterful airplanes, boats, and dragons; why were *e*'s, *m*'s, and *q*'s such a challenge?

Of course, as the head-in-the-sand father, I was convinced all that was needed was more effort. What in this world had ever been accomplished without persistence in the face of obstacles? Cricket, on the other hand, believed the root cause might have nothing to do with effort; she thought Trip was dyslexic.

I didn't want to consider this hypothesis. Dyslexia was considered a disability. Trip was not *disabled*, at least not in the way that term implied weakness. He was good at some things, less good at others. Why did we need to slap a label on him? Cricket listened to my appeal, patted me on the shoulder, and handed me her copy of Sally Shaywitz's book, *Overcoming Dyslexia*, knowing that I was powerless against science.

As Cricket and I walked Trip and Isabel to school on the first day, my heart was heavy with the realization that Trip—and we, as his support network—had a long battle on our hands. It was not just dumb old Dad who had to be won over, but teachers, administrators, and—most crucially—Trip himself. Hard work lay ahead, and no one could do it for him.

Two hundred yards from school, Isabel gave Cricket a kiss on the cheek and me a wave, then took off. She was too old to be escorted in by her parents. Trip, meanwhile, squeezed my hand tighter. We knew he had a fantastic teacher and a class of fourteen children, including—as had been the case in first grade—Priscilla Wimby. With only four second-grade classrooms, the two of them in the same class had been a 25 percent probability, but Cricket had learned that Genevieve made a special request for the two kids to be together. Whether by chance or by choice, that wish had been granted.

I was disappointed but didn't want to let anyone see it. Cricket seemed fine but far from excited. She had her own list of concerns about the Wimbys based solely on her intuitive people skills. I still hadn't mentioned Vlad or the RemoteTokens. Ever the perfectionist, I was waiting to complete my investigation before I voiced its conclusions; the outcome had the ability to throw our lives into turmoil once again.

By the final bell announcing the start of the school day, Trip's classroom was filled beyond the fire marshal's guidelines with fourteen children, the teacher, the teacher's aide, and thirty-four parents. For the mathematically inclined, that might seem like too many parents, but you would be forgetting the compounding effect of divorce. Six of the lucky fourteen children had more than two parents attending the first-day festivities, which entailed awkwardly watching their second grader check out the room's mascot (a frog), complaining about their seating assignment, making a mess of the arts and crafts cabinet, and—in the case of two children—crying as if they were being tortured. After nervously squeezing my hand the length of the walk to school, Trip now seemed excited and was happily recapping his summer with a few friends. He was seated in the same pod as Priscilla, an irony that gave further credence to the idea that their union had been requested by the Wimbys.

My uncertainty aside, Trip was thrilled by this. He called Priscilla his *girlfriend*, though he meant the term literally: a girl who was his friend. Apparently, the new moniker was paying off. Three minutes into the new school year, Priscilla presented Trip with a baby-blue and red Rainbow Loom friendship bracelet with white Perler beads intricately woven among the bands.

"Did you make this, Priscilla?" I asked, certain that I couldn't make such an object with a week of practice.

"Yep," she said. "It's just like mine."

Trip and Priscilla held their wrists side by side for our examination.

"Impressive," I said.

"Can Trip come riding horses with me this weekend?" Priscilla asked Cricket; even the eight-year-old knew who was in charge.

"Please, Mommy, please!" Trip cried.

Cricket hesitated, looking to me. She didn't usually consult me on such matters; why was she in this case? Maybe it was just to see if any part of me flinched. For reasons I'll never truly understand—but will forever regret—I simply shrugged.

"I don't see why not," Cricket said.

"Yeah!" both kids cheered in unison.

As room mother for the third year running, Cricket greeted the teacher, Ms. Johnson, and moved us to the opposite side of the room. She knew she would have Ms. Johnson's ear plenty and felt it was important to allow others this chance. Shortly after us came Cyrus and Genevieve, only they planted themselves beside Ms. Johnson, forcing all subsequent parents to interrupt them to make their own introductions. It was an odd attention grab for two people who otherwise seemed to trust that they were the center of the universe.

There was a definite frostiness in the Wimbys' attitude toward us as well. When I saw Cyrus, I reflexively stuck out my hand. He responded with a quick head nod, ignoring my attempt at a handshake. No kiss from Genevieve, although she did wave. Cricket noticed it too. "Did you do something?" she asked, watching the Wimbys avoid eye contact while boxing out the other parents.

"They're pissed at you for leaving the wine tasting early," I said.

She laughed, then stopped abruptly. "You're kidding, right?"

"Yes, I'm kidding," I said. "If it is anything, I'm sure I did it."

Ms. Johnson gave a couple of quick remarks, then told the parents that it was time to leave. Second graders were big kids, we were told. The two crying kids were peeled from their parents' legs and handed over to Ms. Johnson. The rest of us filed out with our heads down, a little embarrassed that we had made such a show of the *first day of school* and a little upset that we had been ushered out unceremoniously. Sometimes the kids grow up faster than the parents.

I held Cricket's hand as we exited, pleased we had survived another first day without incident. As the last to file out, I expected that the socialization was over, but as usual, I was wrong. I made a turn to walk home and Cricket elbowed me. "Coffee hour," she said.

"Oh, of course," I said, reminding myself that no one in Montecito was on the clock. Even I now had a reasonable expectation of workday flexibility—unless, of course, I was in Hermosa Beach on a Sunday with my family.

We ambled over to the coffee and croissants provided by Renaud's Patisserie, then joined the mingling. I heard Cricket's name called a few times and knew she was in good company. I, on the other hand, felt the creep of the old familiar panic attack combined with the urge to get back to my work—and by work, I mean hacking.

When I finished my coffee and said hello to Cricket's first pod of friends, I whispered into her ear, "Would you mind if I headed home?"

She patted my arm and gave me a thumbs-up without turning her head from a friend who was busy describing their family's twelve-week summer in Sun Valley.

Freed, I pivoted to leave and promptly bumped into Cyrus, once again stepping on his big toe.

"Watch it, Hollis," he said, holding his coffee wide so that the sloshing liquid wouldn't land on his crisply pressed shirt. Oh, what a difference time makes. The first time I stepped on Cyrus's toe, he invited me to dinner. This time he sounded like he wanted to punch me.

"Damn, I'm a klutz," I said. "Very sorry, Cyrus."

He took a deep breath. "It's fine, my friend," he said. "You are leaving?"

"Yes, I uh..." I paused. "I need to get back to work." A plausible excuse, but I feared he could see right through me. Dishonesty was not my strength, and further, seeing Cyrus's face made me feel guilty for my treachery. I told myself that the point of my hack was to prove that Cyrus Wimby and ExOh Holdings were *legitimate*, not because I was hung up on becoming a crime fighter. But with every line of code stretching micrometers closer to the truth, I think I subconsciously knew I was not going to exonerate Cyrus.

"Good," he said, not seeming to notice the subtleties of my countenance. In fact, he wasn't really looking *at* me; he was looking *over* me. "I'm riding with Genevieve the rest of today," he continued. "But we need to catch up. How is tomorrow morning?"

"Riding horses?" I asked.

"No, Hollis. Just riding around in the car."

My forehead furrowed.

"Yes, Hollis. Horses."

"Oh, sorry," I apologized again. "A little slow on the uptake today." This was true; I had been up till 3:00 a.m. working on my hack, and my body was not as resilient as it used to be. That said, I probably should have been able to figure out he meant *riding horses* without asking. "Trip told us Priscilla invited him to join on a ride this weekend. Thank you. He's excited."

"She did?" Cyrus said, shaking his head. "She did not have permission to make that invitation."

"Oh," I said. "Well, I'm sure he'll understand if you need to—"

"No," Cyrus sighed. "We'll make do."

"Okay," I said cautiously. "Uh...thank you. That's very generous." I smiled through my frustration. I didn't really care if Trip went horse riding or not. Truthfully, the whole thing made me feel like a charity case, and I wished Trip didn't like riding so that we could cut the conversation off with a gracious *no, thank you.*

"It's fine," he said, waving away my thank-you like a magnanimous king. "For tomorrow, I want you to brief me on what it would take to get ExOh's stock upgraded to the NASDAQ exchange. We have some investor interest. Could mean big money."

"Sure," I said, as my brain recalibrated how I had planned to spend the remainder of the day. I had at least ten more hours of hacking in front of me and now this topic to research from scratch. But it wasn't like I could say, *Could you give me an extra day? I have something far more interesting on my plate.* "You got it," I assured him.

"Cyrus?" Genevieve said, at his elbow. "Oh, hello, Hollis,"

"Hi, Gen—"

"Cyrus, come with me," Genevieve said, cutting me off. "There's someone I want you to meet."

Without a goodbye, the two of them turned, but this time—before they could leave me—I was the one who was already gone.

# CHAPTER THIRTY-THREE

As I delicately unwound the final strands of the RemoteToken's security web, my heart thrummed at the rate of a marathoner cruising to victory. This was my happy place, my fortress of solitude, my man cave, and my comfy slippers all wrapped into one. The computer made sense to me in ways other people never have. It was logical; it was consistent. It didn't expect me to protect its feelings or tell it white lies. It registered commands and delivered results. The computer and I knew that when something went wrong, it was my fault, even if I didn't know *why* it was my fault. There was no interpretation; there was only input and output.

When I communed with my computer, time ceased to follow its normal rules. Hours and minutes crawled and sprinted interchangeably. All bodily functions became optional. I couldn't tell you how many times I thought to myself, *If I don't pee now, I will wet my pants*, only to fidget for another few hours before yielding to nature's desperate plea.

I hadn't had this feeling in a very long time. If the Remote-Token security web was Yosemite's El Capitan, the CryptoWallet server was a playground jungle gym. I had to pause several times to make notes of the unexpected laxness in their protocols, which would one day come back to haunt them. One night, I even dreamed of presenting my findings to CryptoWallet's founder, Clyde Bostich, and him being so overwhelmed with gratitude that he offered me my old job back. It was one of the best dreams I can recall.

Of course, when I woke to my non-paying job reality at 4:30 the next morning, I was overwhelmed with sadness for what I had lost and why. I had been a talented worker with noble intentions. I had also behaved like a querulous child when things had not gone my way. In the end, I got what I deserved.

Now I was working at a job I didn't understand, for a man I increasingly didn't trust, and paying myself out of my own retirement savings. Meanwhile, CryptoWallet's security weaknesses remained and, if not fixed, could spell the downfall of the company. My lack of diplomacy had resulted in a net loss for everyone.

And in some respects, here I was again, sticking my nose where it didn't belong. I was certainly—as Trip's teachers sometimes reported—*off task*, but my goal was to diffuse, not detonate. The mystery of ExOh's finances and how Cyrus was running the business from this siloed Hong Kong bank account had been undermining my faith in him for months now. I needed to satiate my desire to understand so I could go back to doing my job without that nagging voice in my head warning me that something was wrong. I just needed a look, a peek, really. That would be enough.

Losing CryptoWallet and gaining ExOh had burned one other thing into my DNA: I no longer desired titles, public accolades, prestige, or any of the other trappings of *greatness*. If it had ever been in the cards, I was now over it. Doing great work filled me with pride; unearned titles filled me with dread and paranoia. I longed to stay in the present moment: at one with my computer, on a mission of discovery. This I could do and do well, to mutual and universal satisfaction. I did not want or need to be CEO of anything.

And suddenly, without fanfare or fireworks, the escape room and all its lasers were behind me. I was inside the RemoteToken server by way of CryptoWallet. I had previously set up an ExOh account on CryptoWallet, and now—with a bug inside Remote-Token—I could link Cyrus's Hong Kong bank account and understand what had been withheld from me since I signed on to ExOh.

What was I expecting? To paraphrase US Supreme Court Justice Potter Stewart, I would know it when I saw it. The transactions should be those of a business: revenues received, bills paid, the occasional influx transferred by me. I wasn't a forensic accountant, and I wasn't interested in becoming one. I just needed to see receipts from Bloomingdale's, Selfridges, Galeries Lafayette, Burberry, Zara, and São Paulo Alpargatas and outflows to the litany of technology and sales consultants listed under me on ExOh's homepage. That would be enough to satisfy the swirling hydra of acid in my stomach, which no medicine or home remedy could slay.

With the final keystrokes, ExOh's CryptoWallet began to fill with transactions. In the movie version of this scene, I would be sitting in a dark room (check, it was 1:00 a.m. and I was in my gar-office) and my glasses (sorry, I don't wear glasses) would reflect my screen's flashing pixels to a camera positioned behind my computer to capture the torrent of data and the look of discovery on my face. In real life, I figured this might take a while, so I stepped out of the gar-office to relieve myself in the garden while the data flowed. As usual, I'd been withholding my own torrent for at least an hour.

When I came back, my computer screen was oddly still. I suspected that my internet might have gone snoozing, as these wee hours were prime time for system upgrades. But no, I was at full strength. So I took my seat and scrolled.

Page down, down, down, up. Control-home. Control-end. Control-home. Page down, down, down, up. Control-home.

*That cannot be.* I rubbed my eyes, suddenly feeling the exhaustion of twelve hours of sleep over three nights. Again, I paged up and down, top to bottom. This was the correct account—I recognized the transfers I had originated—but I couldn't make sense of what else unfurled on the screen before me.

There were no revenues.

There were no expenses.

Most importantly, there was no money; the account was empty.

# CHAPTER THIRTY-FOUR

I REPORTED to Cyrus's library room that morning as instructed. I brought a travel mug of black coffee, but there was no risk of me nodding off. My nerves were frayed, my right eyelid twitching painfully from the cocktail of sleep-deprivation and caffeine overdose. I arrived a few minutes early as always, even though I knew I would be kept waiting. It was okay. More than ever, I needed time to think.

I remained in a cloud of shock. There had to be an explanation, but how could I ask for one without revealing how and why I was asking?

One thing was for certain: There was no abandoning this quest. My glitchy stomach assured me that any relief was conditional upon answers, and right now I had none. I hung my head, letting my neck crack, temporarily relieving the pain radiating in my temples.

Cyrus strode in whistling—a first. "How are things today, my friend?"

I cleared my throat. "Good, Cyrus. And you?"

"Whoa, my friend!" he said as he took his seat. "You look like hell. Have you caught a bug of some sort?"

I shook my head, trying to blink away my red-rimmed eyes. "No. I mean, yes," I stammered. "Seasonal allergies, I think. Having a tough time sleeping."

"Indeed," Cyrus said. "Get yourself some Benadryl or Zyrtec or something. You shouldn't be out in public like this."

I smiled sheepishly and nodded. "I'll get it taken care of."

"So," he said, putting two feet on the coffee table and clasping his hands behind his head. "Tell me: How can we get ExOh upgraded to the NASDAQ exchange?"

"Well..." I said, then yawned. I'd done the research as Cyrus demanded, finishing in time to get a grand total of ninety minutes of beauty rest. The simple answer was that ExOh currently traded on an exchange that housed the lowest tier of publicly traded companies: stalled startups, shell companies, former bankruptcies, community banks, and a whole lot of businesses safely described as *other*—it was the land of misfit toys. The NASDAQ was for *real* public companies. To go from the sandlot to Yankee Stadium, the company would need to go through an audit, produce registration statements at a higher standard, upgrade nearly every aspect of its compliance. In short, ExOh would need to behave like a responsible adult. After my previous night's discovery, I wasn't sure this was even possible. "Sorry," I said when my yawn subsided. "It's a pretty straightforward process with several different routes by which—"

"Which route would we use?" Cyrus interrupted, indicating he wanted the answer, not the backstory.

"Right." I yawned again. "We would only qualify for the market capitalization and assets route, which requires—"

"Brilliant," he interrupted again. "So, is it just paperwork?"

"Well," I said, concealing a third yawn, "it's a lot of paper-work, but—"

"No problem—"

"BUT," I shouted, interrupting him this time. "We would need a full audit."

He took his feet off the coffee table and sat up, elbows on knees. "Why?"

"I don't know, Cyrus," I said, leaning my elbows on my knees as well. "I guess they figure that some folks can't be trusted."

He turned his eyes to his bookshelves. "Well, fine. Find us an auditor here in town. Preferably one who wants to hitch their wagon to our star."

"That won't work," I said. "ExOh would be required to use a specific kind of auditor. One that specializes in public companies. It's called a PCAOB auditor, and—"

"Fine," he interrupted. "Get us one of those, then."

I nodded, holding his gaze, contemplating how far to push this. "They are going to demand to see the bank statements, you know. No local audits this time. No promises. No pinkie swears. It's all or nothing."

"How do you know that?"

"Because I interviewed three of them yesterday," I said. "They each sent me checklists, and all their checklists listed the same items." This was a lie that I had no trouble voicing. The truth was I had not called anyone, but I suspected I was right, and I knew Cyrus had not done his own research.

Cyrus looked angry but not flustered. He leaned back again, relacing his long fingers behind his head, staring at the ceiling. "Here's the thing," he began. "Huff Monroe has another four million dollars lined up for us, but he tells me he can get us *thirty* million if we move the stock to the NASDAQ."

I nodded excitedly. This was it. The fear versus greed pendulum in all its swinging glory. I didn't yet fully understand the game Cyrus was playing, but Huff Monroe was giving him thirty million reasons to open his kimono. If Cyrus's reticence was purely paranoia, $30 million might inspire him to take a Xanax and accept the disinfecting benefits of sunlight. I could only hope.

"The company could certainly use thirty million dollars," I

began cautiously. "Why don't we engage a proper auditor, turn over the bank statements, and get this—"

"Here's what I want you to do," Cyrus interrupted for the umpteenth time. "Send Huff an email. Tell him that you are working on getting the listing upgraded. Tell him that if he invests ten million now—before the NASDAQ listing—we will write him an option to purchase twenty million more at the same price *after* the NASDAQ listing."

I shook my head. "I don't think I can say that in good faith unless you are really willing to disclose—"

"You can and you will, Hollis," he said.

"But, Cyrus, I don't—"

"I am assigning you to *work on it*, Hollis! You are the CEO of the company; this is your job. Phone an auditor every day between now and New Year's until you find one that can handle our audit and its unique requirements. *Work on it* until you have exhausted every feasible option. Then—and only then—will you no longer be *working on it*," he said. "Are my instructions clear?"

I nodded; his instructions were indeed clear.

"Terrific. Then do whatever you need to do to feel confident that you are *working on it* as instructed. Understand?"

I dropped my head. "Okay," I whispered. I wasn't ready to call his bluff yet. I needed to understand whether I had discovered a minor discrepancy or a massive fraud. Telling Cyrus that I was onto him before I was truly ready would destroy my ability to discover the full and complete truth. At that time, I naively thought that nothing was more important than this truth. The unfolding of future events would teach me how wrong I was.

"Excellent," Cyrus said, standing to signal that my presence was no longer required. I gathered my papers and coffee mug and made my way to the front door only to be stopped by the click-clacking of Genevieve's heels.

"Hollis!" she said, hurrying down the hallway. "Oh good, I was afraid I would miss you."

"Hi, Genevieve," I said, raising my coffee mug without

moving in for a more formal hello. I was anxious to get back home, to be free of Cyrus's gaze.

"Would you ask Cricket and Isabel to join us for horse riding on Saturday?"

"Oh, I ..." I looked at Cyrus, who had made a big deal of acting as if including Trip in the jaunt had ruined his family weekend. "I thought you guys were having a family ride?"

"Not anymore," Cyrus said.

"Cyrus is playing golf," Genevieve said, rolling her eyes.

"Not just golf. I've been invited to play the Valley Club," he said, miming a golf stroke. "John Colton is sponsoring me for membership."

I had heard of the Valley Club but had never seen the club's entrance, nor did I know where in Montecito the club resided. In that sense, I *knew* of the Valley Club in the same way I *knew* of ménage à trois.

"Please. Will you ask Cricket and Isabel to join us?" Genevieve said, clasping her hands together in prayer. "It will be such fun. I haven't caught up with Cricket in ages."

I looked at the two Wimbys, nearly side by side, and felt the need to question all my assumptions about Genevieve. Did she have any idea what her husband was up to? Did she know anything other than that he was a *business tycoon* who clearly took care of her every need and desire? I recalled prior moments when it seemed Genevieve was more than just a kept woman. She stood up to John Colton, condescendingly suggesting she could "pay the rent" with her cooking. She gave me that eerie speech at the Entre Nous opening—the one that concluded with a reminder that no one gets to steak without a dead cow. Those sparks seemed distant memories now, as she stood with pleadingly clasped hands, talking of horses.

Genevieve was not Cricket, I concluded. Where my wife was not so secretly our family's chairman, CEO and commander in chief, Genevieve was simply a passenger in Cyrus's first-class ride. Perhaps the life she led was too grand for penetrating questions.

Or perhaps, standing at the edge of true knowledge, she instinctively backed away.

I felt sorry for Genevieve, though I respected her dilemma. Even with those we know best, we are blind to what we don't want to see.

"I'll ask Cricket," I said.

# Chapter Thirty-Five

It took me more than an hour to craft the five sentences of my email to Huff Monroe. Surely he would sense my hedged, cautious words. Surely an investor with enough money to casually discuss tens of millions of dollars would intuitively step back at the first flash of warning. Surely I would be saved from having to receive and transfer his money.

Surely not. The next day, ten million arrived in our Miramar account from Huff's personal account in Texas. A wave of nausea came and went, but I powered through, recognizing the perverse silver lining. I knew once I moved the money, I would have a chance to watch the distributive aftermath via CryptoWallet. It was like my very own ant farm.

As I expected, I moved the money from the US to Hong Kong, then phoned Cyrus; thirty minutes later it disappeared. Just like our US account, the Hong Kong account seemed to be nothing more than a pass-through. Every penny I transferred in was subsequently pushed to an HSBC bank account in Sydney, Australia. Was *this* the company's operating account that I longed to see, and if so, could I access it?

I opened the pictures folder on my laptop and found the eight images of RemoteToken fobs, seven still with mysterious lineage.

What were the chances that the HSBC account was attached to one of these remaining fobs? Fairly good, it seemed to me. While this should have made my stomach knot further, I felt relief. My body wanted to know the truth.

Ninety minutes later, I had the HSBC account added to the CryptoWallet. This time there were several large payments made to generically named limited liability corporations located in the Cayman Islands, but still no sign of the lifeblood of a business: revenues. Nothing from Bloomingdale's, Selfridges, et al, and no signs of paychecks, bills, consulting fees, or anything paid to anyone with a heartbeat. After each inflow from Hong Kong, the Cayman LLCs each took their share. The balance was then wired to yet another ExOh account in yet another country: ICICI Bank in Mumbai. It was like watching the digestive tract of an animal that ate money.

The sun set, the gar-office grew chilly, and I kept working. By process of elimination, I found the RemoteToken fob tied to the ICICI Bank account. In just under an hour—I was getting good at this—I had this latest account ready to be added to my CryptoWallet.

What-ifs and maybes sprinted through my mind as my cursor hovered over the *Link Account* button. I had been certain Hong Kong would fill the information gap. Then confident that Sydney would do it. Now I was hopeful that Mumbai would hold the missing key. With each step down the ladder, my surety slacked. Was it possible that—

A hand landed softly on my shoulder, sending me screaming like a petrified child.

"Jesus, Hollis!" Cricket said. "You're going to wake up Oprah."

My heart was in my throat. "Oh my Goodness, Cricket. I'm so sorry. I don't..." I shook my head, struggling for words. "What... what time is it?"

"It's after midnight, Hollis. You skipped dinner again. I know you've got a lot going on at work, but this is getting ridiculous."

My stomach growled, confirming her timeline. "I'm sorry."

"Come to bed, Hollis. Whatever it is, it can wait."

I dutifully followed, stopping in the kitchen to swallow a handful of Cheerios and drink directly from the milk gallon. Cricket shook her head at me. "It's like I have three kids now, and you're the worst of the group."

I apologized again and fell into bed as if I had been drugged.

That night I dreamed that I had been only one bank account away from discovering exactly what I sought: that the layers of bank accounts were simple financial engineering, conveniences for paying taxes and making local transactions; that it was all there, and business was booming. ExOh was making money hand over fist. Our investors were soon to look like mini Warren Buffetts. That it was all just a big misunderstanding.

The first sound I heard the following morning was that of a fork scraping a pancake through a puddle of syrup. It was 8:30 a.m. on a Saturday, and Cricket had filled in for me as chief of Saturday-morning breakfast. I groaned, sitting up in bed to a sleep-deprivation headache. Much like a hangover, there was no cure but time.

"There's Mr. Sleepyhead," Trip proclaimed as I trudged into the kitchen for a cup of coffee. Cricket kissed my cheek, while Isabel scrolled through Instagram on Cricket's phone. We had not yet given into peer pressure and purchased Isabel a phone, but her twelfth birthday was in December, and that was the agreed-upon compromise date. To be honest, Cricket was looking forward to it; she would regain full custody of her own phone.

There were extra pancakes, so I tried a short stack on for size. They agreed with my stomach, so I helped myself to seconds. Even though my hacking mission might end disastrously, at least in terms of my employment, my gastrointestinal tract seemed to enjoy the hunt. Of course, my biorhythms were completely distorted by my lack of sleep and nutritionally deficient diet, but for the first time in months, I wasn't suffering from stomach cramps. On the pendulum of trade-offs, this was a win.

"What's on the docket today?" I asked Cricket.

"You forgot?"

"I guess it goes without saying."

She rolled her eyes. "We're all riding horses with Genevieve and Priscilla today."

I nodded. "Right, right, right, right," I said. "Wait, I didn't think you wanted to go?"

She squished her face, a signal that I had said something I wasn't supposed to say. She came in closer to me, whispering, "I didn't want to. Trip doesn't care because he will be with Priscilla, but Isabel said she would only go if I went, and that she really, really, really wanted to go. So, I'm going. What are you going to do with your day off?"

I squished my face, a signal that I didn't understand the meaning of the phrase *day off*.

"You know," she said slowly, "Saturday? A day of rest and recuperation? A day to let the mind heal and the heart play?"

"Right," I said. "I'll be working."

"What am I going to do with you, Hollis?"

I kissed her on the cheek and began to clean up the kitchen from the breakfast festivities; cleanup was my default job around the house. Already I was excited about the day in front of me. It just might prove to be enough time to reach the end of the RemoteToken thread, and—please, please, please—prove that all of this was just one big misunderstanding, fueled by my ignorance and paranoia. As much as I loved the hack-twenty-four-seven ethos, I was too old for this. I needed some sleep.

I drove the rest of the family the seven miles south to the stables in Carpinteria, where Genevieve and Priscilla were waiting. A polo match was about to begin on a beautiful carpet of green, and everywhere I looked were white pants and riding boots. Except, of course, for my family; Trip and Cricket were wearing blue jeans, while Isabel had found a pair of khaki-colored pants that looked like a darn good alternate uniform for horse riding.

With the family set for the day, I took off for home. The fog of sleeplessness and the drive to discover the truth blinded me to everything else in my life. In retrospect, I must have believed my previous night's dream: that my hacking quest was one sure to end in the discovery of an amusing misunderstanding. Why else would I have just dropped the three people I love most in the world with someone I didn't trust?

Back in the gar-office, I linked the ICICI account from Mumbai, hopeful that this would be the honeypot. I was quickly absolved of my optimism. Like the Sydney account, Mumbai connected to a host of ambiguously named accounts—these in the Isle of Man, a place I'd never heard of before—but revealed no revenues. After Mumbai's Isle of Man leeches consumed their share of each inflow, the balance was passed to an account in Amsterdam.

I had five RemoteToken fobs remaining.

Amsterdam distributed funds to a handful of accounts in Monaco, then dropped the balance to an account in Helsinki, Finland.

Four RemoteToken fobs remaining.

Finland distributed funds to accounts in Panama, then passed the remainder to an account in Vienna, Austria.

Three RemoteToken fobs remaining.

Vienna made payments to accounts in Liechtenstein, then passed the rest along to Brussels, Belgium.

Two RemoteToken fobs remaining.

Brussels paid accounts in Bermuda, then spit out the balance to an account in Zurich, Switzerland.

I buried my head in my arms, bleary from four hours of playing Whac-A-Mole without a hit. I had hacked into seven bank accounts in seven countries, each time hoping that my worst fears would be resolved and each time feeling like a naive fool. All the accounts were empty. The thrill of the hunt—an endorphin-laced high that had sustained me to this point—was eviscerated. In its place was pure dread.

Why had Cyrus done this? Why string together seven bank

accounts that existed only as conduits? It seemed that the primary purpose was to keep the money in motion. I'd read about such schemes before, orchestrated by covert drug cartels. These bandits knew that the banks and regulators were too slow to catch the action in real time and quick to give up once the money left their borders. That pattern would certainly fit what I found here—swift, back-to-back-to-back transactions, each bank transfer a flight from one country to the next. My thoughts were venturing well off the fantasy grid at this point, and at each turn, the conclusions made me want to retrace my steps, close the doors behind me, and pretend I'd seen nothing.

There was still this one final Zurich bank account. If only this account contained the verifying financial records I sought, all of the rest could be dismissed as needless drama manufactured by yours truly's wild imagination. I wanted to be wrong; I needed to be wrong. Sure, the odds that this final Zurich bank account was *the one* were infinitesimally small, yet there remained a sliver of hope. I knew if I opened this final door, hoping to find that sliver, I'd never be able to go back to a world in which I didn't know the truth.

I picked my head off my arms and dove back into the Remote-Token server one final time. Any illusions that I had an escape hatch were as empty as the seven bank accounts I had already examined.

The first hack took hours; this one took minutes. I was as familiar with the laser room as a blind man in his kitchen. With a mirror of the fob's passcode in hand, I went back to CryptoWallet and input the necessary information to link the accounts. Without thinking, I clicked the button to link them and watched as my screen filled with the Zurich account's historical record.

My phone rang as my virtual wallet filled with new transactions. I rarely got phone calls, and even when I did, I usually ignored them. My few friends knew this. That meant calls were almost always telemarketers, political pollsters, and kind people who just knew I needed reduced interest rates. Because of this,

Cricket insisted I have a special ringtone just for her calls so that I would know when I needed to answer. So as information showered my screen, the acoustic intro riff of Damien Rice's "Coconut Skins" echoed from my phone's tinny speakers.

I pushed the answer icon, expecting to say hello and hear about the day riding horses, or options for dinner, or a vacation idea, or a just-arrived invitation, or simply, *I love you*. Instead, I was bombarded by the sound of ambulance sirens. I looked at the phone; the caller ID still read Cricket. "What's going on?" I yelled, combating the cacophony.

"Hollis? Hollis? Can you hear me?" Cricket yelled back.

"Yes, I hear you. What's happening?" Somehow amid all the background noise, I could hear Isabel's muffled crying. I pictured her face buried into Cricket's shirt.

"Hollis, I need you to meet us at Cottage Hospital right away," Cricket said to me, followed by, "It's going to be okay, baby. It's going to be okay," directed at our sobbing daughter.

I stood from my desk, sending my chair toppling backward, and patted my empty pants pockets for my keys. I had just dropped the family at the stables; where were my goddamn keys? I knew nothing, but I was terrified, jumping straight through concerned and alarmed to DEFCON 1. "What is it, Cricket? Who's hurt?"

I wish I could tell you that I would have been equally worried had the answer been Genevieve or Priscilla, but that would be a lie. In the nanosecond between my question and Cricket's answer, I prayed the most selfish prayer of my life: Let it be anyone else.

"Oh, Hollis," she moaned. "It's Trip."

# Chapter Thirty-Six

I DROVE to Cottage Hospital as if I planned to be a patient, not a visitor. By the grace of the Fates, I arrived without accident. I parked on Junipero, a short sprint from the hospital's emergency room entrance. As soon as I shifted my Subaru into park, my emotional dam broke. Nickel-sized tears pelted my pant legs; my airways clogged with snot. My forehead fell to the steering wheel as I sobbed. It was a thirty-second burst of unrestrained fear, the controlled exercise of a pressure valve to keep the pipe itself from exploding.

As quickly as it began, it—at least temporarily—ended. I slapped myself three times to reinitiate dominance, much as a dog owner grabs his pup's muzzle. There would be plenty of time for crying, but I couldn't let Cricket see me broken before the battle even began. With the interior of my elbow, I mopped my face and exited the car.

As the automatic doors parted, memories of past hospital visits came roaring back. After all, there's no such thing as a color-less trip to a hospital; each has its own line in an earnest poem.

"Trip Crawford?" I asked the frazzled crew of nurses at the reception desk. "I'm his father."

Several heads turned to me at once, a few perplexed expressions suggesting that they might not have every hospital patient's name committed to memory. But the intake nurse nodded, then asked a colleague to take over so she could escort me to the intensive care unit. I had so many questions, but at that moment, I just wanted to see my family. I traversed the endless walk in a fog; if the nurse had quizzed me on the escape route, I could not have begun to answer. Finally, she delivered me to the doors of the ICU waiting room. She paused with her hand on the door and met my eyes with a flash of sympathy. "In here," she said, pulling the door open.

There were several pods of people in the room, all experiencing their own flavor of anguish. In the far corner, I spotted Isabel sitting next to Cricket, their heads folded together. Cricket's eyes were fixated on the carpet in front of her feet, and she had a wad of Kleenex in her hand. Isabel spotted me first, but she said nothing. Her face simply balled itself into a look of agony as she stood and ran to me, throwing her arms around my waist and planting her teary cheeks against my midsection. Cricket followed, her head bowed, her legs moving slowly. She picked up speed as she got closer, and eventually the three of us formed a Crawford family huddle of tears.

I massaged the backs of both of their heads, pulling them in tighter, grateful for their clothes-soaking tears. I'm not sure how long we stood like that, but it took a tap on the shoulder from an operating room nurse to break our embrace apart.

"Dr. Johnson wanted me to tell you that we'll be in surgery for the next few hours, but he'll come find you when he has an update," she said. "For now, try to make yourselves as comfortable as possible. Move around. Go for a walk. Get a drink in the cafeteria. Just remember to leave a cell phone contact number at the reception desk, and we'll track you down as soon as there's something to report."

We all nodded in unison. She reached out and put a hand on Cricket's shoulder. "Think good thoughts," she said, forcing a smile.

I followed Cricket and Isabel back to their seats, already tagged as the domain of the Crawford family. In my experience, ICU waiting rooms operated like tent cities. Families intuitively staked their territories, separated—if they are lucky—by a few chairs, so that one group's quiet conversation didn't interfere with another's silent contemplation. Even when empty, the seats somehow let it be known they were saved. Eventually a family would disappear, their loved one coming through or losing their fight. Those who remained behind would watch as a new family and its new tragedy took the old one's place.

"What happened?" I asked when I finally felt the cloak of privacy.

Cricket shook her head. "We don't know."

"Something spooked Trip's horse," Isabel said in a hush.

"But these are trained horses, right?" I asked. "They don't just take off at the sight of a mouse, do they?"

"We weren't with them when it happened, Dad," Isabel said, staring at her shoes. "Me and Mom and Genevieve were way behind. Priscilla and Trip had gone ahead of us."

"So, then what?" I asked. "They were ahead of you, and then what?"

"I don't know what it was, Dad," Isabel said. "But Priscilla just...she just—"

"She just screamed," Cricket interrupted. "One of those bloodcurdling, high-pitched wails straight out of the movies."

I tried to calibrate this cryptic information. Was the scream the cause or was it the effect? Was Priscilla's scream remarkable in an absolute sense—you would have heard it if standing next to a concrete mixer—or only notable relative to the silence of the surrounding mountain trail. So many questions. I settled on the simplest: "Why did she scream?"

"We don't know, Dad," Isabel repeated. "When we got to her, she was crying so hard. She was trying to say something, but I couldn't understand her."

Cricket cleared her throat. "We had to focus on Trip." She hung her head. "He was...uh, he needed our full attention."

As usual, Cricket was right. I was trying to understand the *why*; she was dealing with the *what*. "Of course," I said. "Of course. Did the paramedics tell you anything?"

Cricket closed her eyes. "They were very kind," she said, "but no. They didn't really say much. It was, uh...other than the obvious things, it was hard to tell how bad the damage was."

I buried my head in my hands. "What were...?" I cleared my throat and dropped my voice to a whisper, the words feeling obscene. "What were the injuries you could see?"

"His leg was broken," Isabel said.

I felt a flood of relief. Broken bones healed. A little time, maybe surgery? At worst, the insertion of a metal pin. He would get a cool cast his friends at school could scribble on. Just a broken leg; this was good news! Isabel and Cricket were probably overreacting, still suffering from shock.

"Not broken," Cricket clarified, "more like shattered."

There goes that theory, I thought, erasing my brief spout of optimism. I closed my eyes. "Upper leg or lower leg?"

"Both," Isabel said. "It was..." She shuddered without completing the sentence.

"And then, there was so much blood around his head," Cricket continued. "I think that's the hardest part. I just couldn't tell. There was just so much...blood."

"I think he hurt his ear," Isabel said. "Did you see that, Mom?"

"Yes, dear," Cricket said, her eyes squeezed shut as if trying to *unsee* it.

"Was he...?" I paused, unsure if I had the stomach to hear the answer to my next question. "Was he in pain?"

"No," Cricket said, sitting up a little straighter and taking a deep breath. "No. He was unconscious."

"He moaned a little when they put him on the stretcher," Isabel added, "but he didn't wake up."

"But his pulse?" I asked. "He never lost his pulse, did he?"

"It was weak," Cricket confirmed, "but no. Even in the ambulance. He never..."

She did not need to complete that sentence. I knew what she was unable to say: *He never died.* I sat back in the uncomfortable waiting room chair, my mind wandering from the *what* back to the *why* of it all. "Do you think Priscilla's scream spooked Trip's horse?" I asked.

Cricket shrugged. "It might have been her scream, or it might have been whatever *caused* her to scream," Cricket said. "I don't know, Hollis. We're in the dark here, too."

"Do you—"

"I don't know, Hollis," Cricket said, placing a hand on my knee. "I don't know."

We sat in silence for what felt like a long time. No one pulled out a phone. No one grabbed a magazine. We just sat, lost in the maze of our thoughts. We would hear from the doctor soon, but until then we had only our imaginations. These moments are a good test of one's internal optimism barometer. Without the burden of actual knowledge, my brain tried to discount what Isabel and Cricket had reported of Trip's physical injuries. It was as if I'd heard a rumor from an untrustworthy gossip; I needed proof before I could believe.

But if I was an optimist when it came to *what*, I was fighting lunacy when it came to *why*. I had gone too deep down the Cyrus Wimby rabbit hole by this point; my head was full of borderline insane conspiracy theories. *This was an accident,* I kept trying to tell myself. *It has nothing to do with Cyrus.* This optimistic mantra did me no good; by the time Genevieve and Priscilla joined us in the waiting room, I was ready for my straitjacket fitting.

"Have you heard anything yet?" Genevieve asked breathlessly. Priscilla stood behind her mother, bleary eyed, her head bowed, squeezing Genevieve's waist like a life preserver.

Cricket shook her head. "It'll be a while, I'm afraid."

Genevieve took the seat catty-corner to Isabel, and Priscilla climbed into her lap, curling up like an infant. "I just don't know how this could happen," Genevieve said. "Trip was riding Flip-Flop. She is one of the gentlest horses in our stable. She barely trots."

We all nodded. A fog of blame hung over the room, searching for a place to settle. Genevieve wanted to make sure we weren't intent on blaming the horse. Believe me, Flip-Flop was nowhere near the top of my suspect list.

Priscilla curled up tighter into her mother's lap. "I'm sorry," she squeaked.

"Oh, honey," Cricket said. "This isn't your fault." She reached across and patted Priscilla's knee.

Again, I nodded, but something told me not to wave away this particular apology. In my experience, children do not say *I'm sorry* the way adults do. We use it ceaselessly as shorthand for I'm sorry *for you:* I'm sorry you got fired. I'm sorry your dog died. I'm sorry it rained on your birthday. These are not events we adults are trying to absorb blame for. But when kids say *I'm sorry*, they are genuinely apologizing. Fair or unfair, they feel responsible and are requesting absolution. I'm not saying that at that moment I thought Priscilla had shoved Trip from his horse, but she was expressing remorse for some set of actions that she felt played a role in Trip's injuries. This, in my opinion, demanded follow-up.

I waited. Cricket did not follow up. Genevieve did not follow up. Isabel did not follow up. This was almost certainly my clue that humans who reside *outside the fog* understood that now was not the time to pick Priscilla's wound open. I suspected that this collective belief was based on thousands of years of Homo sapiens interaction, evolving from grunts and howls to the words of William Cullen Bryant. Priscilla needed time to process and heal, it was determined; she would talk when she was ready.

This was a wise consensus, no doubt. And a man more sensitive and empathetic might have heeded this unspoken advice. But I was ready now, and as far as I was concerned, Priscilla's apology was my invitation to interrogate an eight-year-old.

"Priscilla, honey," I said, leaning forward on my knees. "Can you tell us what happened?"

As soon as the question was voiced, Genevieve tensed. As if registering her mom's anxiety, Priscilla shook her head side to side, saying nothing.

"Anything at all?" I pressed. "Do you know why Flip-Flop got excited?"

Priscilla looked up at Genevieve.

"I don't think she's ready to talk yet," Genevieve said.

I nodded, registering her subtle suggestion to stop, then ignored it. "I know this is hard, Priscilla, but you were the only one there when it happened. Do you remember what made you scream? Was there a loud noise? Was there a fallen tree limb? Did Rosaland get scared?"

Priscilla nodded.

"Oh," I said, tingling at this initial response. The adults wanted me to stop, but Priscilla wanted to talk; I just knew it. "So Rosaland got scared, too. And does Rosaland get scared very often?"

Priscilla shook her head. Genevieve sat up straighter; Cricket placed a hand on my thigh. More clues that my behavior was not within the social norms. On the plus side, I recognized them. On the minus, I ignored them.

"I see," I said. "So, something must have happened, right? Because if Rosaland doesn't get scared often, but she got scared today, something must have made her scared. Don't you think?"

Slowly, Priscilla nodded.

"I know you want answers, Hollis," Genevieve interjected, "but I really think it would be best if we all take some time and let our heads clear." She hugged Priscilla tightly.

I nodded at Genevieve without the slightest intent of stopping. I fully acknowledge this was mean, selfish, immature behavior, but if given the opportunity to rewind time, I would do it all over again just the same. "Priscilla, honey," I continued. "Did the thing that scared Flip-Flop and scared Rosaland also scare you?"

Priscilla nodded. Cricket squeezed my thigh. Genevieve hugged tighter.

"Wow," I said and meant it. With each small revelation, Priscilla peeled back another layer of opacity. "That must have been something really frightening, huh? Is that what made you scream?"

Again, she nodded.

"There are a lot of wild animals on those trails," Genevieve blurted.

A flash of rage filled my face. Why was Genevieve interfering? Couldn't she see that Priscilla was helping us understand what happened to Trip? *Calm down, Hollis*, I told myself. Genevieve was just protecting her daughter; it is a mother's instinct. I smiled. "Your mom is right," I said. "There are all kinds of animals up there. Some are kind of scary. Do you think it was an animal that scared everyone?"

Priscilla shook her head. Genevieve glared at Cricket with eyes that said, *Make him stop!*

But I wouldn't stop; I couldn't stop. "Okay," I said. "So, it wasn't an animal. That's really helpful. Thank you for being so helpful."

Priscilla looked up at her mom again, this time with an expression of relief.

But apparently Genevieve saw it differently: "Hollis, really. That is enough," she said. "I know you all need some space to focus on Trip and his injuries. We only dropped by to give you our best wishes and because Priscilla wanted to make sure you knew how sorry she was that this—"

"What do you think it was, Priscilla?" I interrupted. "What could have been so frightening that it scared Flip-Flop and it scared Rosaland and it scared you so badly that you screamed?"

"Hollis," Cricket interjected, joining the chorus of adults subtly denouncing me. "I think Genevieve is right. Why don't we—"

"What was it, Priscilla?" I asked.

Again, Priscilla looked at her mom. I could read her face clearly. She was not asking to be saved from the mean man asking all the intrusive questions. She wanted permission to speak.

"What was it, Priscilla?" I repeated.

"I think it's best if we—"

I moved to the edge of my seat, almost in a catcher's squat. "What was it?" I whispered.

Priscilla squeezed her eyes shut as if chasing away a vision. "It was a man," she said.

# CHAPTER THIRTY-SEVEN

CRICKET TOOK her hand off my thigh and joined me on the knife edge of her chair. "A man?" she said.

Genevieve shook her head in protest. "Sweetie," she said. "I think you are confused. There wasn't any man up there."

Priscilla tucked in her chin. "There was, Mommy."

"Tell me about the man," I said, and I meant it. I was not humoring Priscilla, asking her to describe her imaginary friend. I believed her. As crazy as it might have sounded, and as easy as it would be to dismiss her story as some sort of post-traumatic stress disorder, I was certain Priscilla was telling the truth. There was a man in those woods. "Was he really tall like your dad? Or was he short like Isabel?"

Priscilla stared at me, her eyes unfocused. "He was in the middle," she said.

"Sweetie," Genevieve said again, pulling Priscilla's chin out of its tuck so their eyes could meet. "We talked about this. There are no men up there. There are no roads up there. There are no homes up there. You did not see a man."

Priscilla retucked her chin once again. "But I did, Mommy."

My skin prickled. *Why is Genevieve trying so hard to silence Priscilla?* As a parent, I had certainly seen my fair share of wild imaginations and creative story telling. I didn't need Genevieve to referee the conversation to come to a reasonable conclusion. Who was she trying to convince that there had been no man, Priscilla or me? "What was the man wearing?" I asked, pressing forward.

Genevieve scowled at me.

Priscilla squinted, again rewinding her mind's eye. "Black," she said.

"And did the man do anything?" I asked. "Did he try to talk to you?"

She shook her head. "He tried to grab me."

Simultaneously, Cricket and I leaned so far forward that our heads nearly clunked.

"Priscilla? Come now," Genevieve said. "I've heard quite enough."

Priscilla buried her head in her mother's chest just as Cyrus came through the door of the ICU waiting room, fresh from his round of golf at the Valley Club.

"I came as soon as I heard," he said, rushing to Genevieve's side, kissing his wife. "Hollis. Cricket. Isabel. I am so sorry this happened to your poor sweet boy. I just don't know how—"

"Is that when you screamed, Priscilla?" I interrupted. Cyrus's arrival guaranteed that I was on countdown timer. Genevieve had suggested I stop; Cyrus would demand it. "Did you scream when the man tried to grab you?"

Priscilla nodded.

"What is this about?" Cyrus asked.

Now ignoring both of Priscilla's parents, I charged toward the finish line. "And is that what scared Flip-Flop?" I asked.

She nodded again.

"What are you talking about, Hollis?" Cyrus said. His spine straightened; his eyes narrowed. He was not used to his questions going unanswered.

"Priscilla thinks she saw a man on the riding trail," Genevieve said, encircling Priscilla in her arms as if to shield her from me.

"Even though that is impossible. Preposterous really. Tell them, Cyrus."

I found Priscilla's eyes through Genevieve's arms and locked on them. "When Flip-Flop started to run," I asked her, "what did the man do?"

"Flip-Flop knocked him down," Priscilla said, her voice muffled. "But then Rosaland got scared and…and…and I never saw the man again."

"Hollis, what are you doing?" Cyrus challenged. "I think it's pretty clear that Priscilla has been traumatized by today's events. This story makes absolutely no sense and—"

"Why do the two of you keep interrupting your daughter?" I said, standing to—at least temporarily—obtain a height advantage. "I'm just asking her what happened. She was there; you were not. Why can't she answer a few questions?"

Cricket reached for my arm to pull me back into my seat, but before she could, Cyrus stood as well; my height advantage evaporated.

"You've been through a lot today, Hollis," Cyrus said. "But this is inappropriate. Why don't we all take a deep breath and agree to discuss this again when Priscilla has gotten some sleep and had a chance to reflect."

This was the first time I had lain eyes on Cyrus since my discovery of his chain of undisclosed bank accounts with their zero balances. And then, of course, there was the end of that chain: the anchor. The Zurich bank account in a notorious zone of secrecy, Switzerland. I had only just linked that account to the CryptoWallet when the call came from Cricket. I had only just begun to see what that Zurich account held. But now that I had seen it, the Cyrus Wimby before me was unrecognizable. Nothing that I thought I understood was true.

Cyrus's face was stern but not angry—the converse of my own, I suspected. I'm sure an objective observer would testify that the tall, good-looking man with the impossibly long fingers was calm and rational, while the other guy sounded a little reckless, a little unhinged, a little pissed off. Guilty as charged.

As I suspected, my opportunity to question Priscilla was indeed over. That was, unless I was prepared to punch Cyrus and rip Priscilla from Genevieve's arms. The punching would have been a relief, but I was not yet ready to become a kidnapper. With every ounce of strength in my body, I summoned the courage to say, "I'm sorry, Cyrus. I don't know what I was thinking. You're right."

Cyrus's shoulders relaxed; a smile returned to his face. He placed a hand on my shoulder: "It is okay, my friend."

# CHAPTER THIRTY-EIGHT

After an awkward kiss-and-make-up, the Wimbys moved to depart the ICU waiting room. At the door, Priscilla broke from her mom's grasp and ran back to Isabel for another hug. This time Priscilla sobbed. Genevieve returned to retrieve her. "Now, now, Priscilla," she said. "Let's leave Isabel and her parents alone for a little while."

With the Wimbys gone, we Crawfords reconvened our silence. I had no idea what Isabel was thinking, but—judging by the vise-grip hold Cricket had on my knee—I suspected Cricket might want to unpack that conversation and its revelations further. I looked at her and she looked back. I opened my mouth to speak, but she cut her eyes at Isabel and shook her head. Eager to prove that I was not completely incapable of following instructions, I gave a quick acknowledging nod.

As we waited for news from Trip's doctors, I ruminated on Priscilla's man in the woods. Was he fact or fantasy? Reasonable people would no doubt draw varying conclusions, but I was feeling unreasonable.

The ICU reception desk roused us from our thoughts with a call for Cricket. All three of us approached the desk, no one wanting to be left out of whatever update we were to hear. Trip was in recovery, we were told. He would be transitioned to the ICU in another couple of hours. I inquired about an update from Dr. Johnson and was assured we would get one when he was free. Ah, the infinite waiting.

We settled back in our seats, and Isabel fell asleep. I could only imagine how taxing all this drama must be to an eleven-year-old mind. Again, I turned to Cricket, inviting further conversation; she shook her head. She was right, this was not a bomb to diffuse in public.

Finally, Dr. Johnson poked his head into the waiting room and invited us to follow him to the room within the ICU that would be Trip's home for who knew how long.

The room was empty. "Where is Trip?" I asked, feeling fooled. Was this the waiting room within the waiting room? The room was painted in soothing tones of dark gray. A few machines waited to work their magic, but more would arrive, I was sure. It felt spacious for the moment, but that moment was soon to pass. I wondered about the fate of the room's previous inhabitant. Had they graduated to life beyond the hospital or to the great beyond?

"He's on his way," Dr. Johnson said. "I wanted a chance to brief you before he arrived."

I instinctively crossed my arms over my chest, squeezing tight, preparing to be punched.

"So, we spent a lot of time with your young man in surgery today," Dr. Johnson began. "I know you have lots of questions. Many of the answers will come in time. But here's what we know as of now..."

I raised my hand like a student to his teacher; Cricket pulled my arm back to my side.

"Of greatest concern was the injury to his head. On that front, I have good news. Trip suffered a depressed skull fracture, just above his left ear. This is a dangerous type of fracture because the skull presses down into the brain cavity at the risk of causing an intercranial hematoma, intercranial swelling, and potential brain damage."

Isabel gasped; Cricket pulled her tight to her hip.

"During surgery, we were able to lift the depression, relieving the associated pressure on the brain. There was a slight hematoma, which we reduced by drawing blood. We are monitoring the intercranial pressure within his skull and, so far, we are encouraged."

"Will there be"—I cleared my throat to force out the next words—"brain damage?"

Dr. Johnson nodded. "Certainly that's an important question. Unfortunately, we won't know for sure until the intercranial pressure is normalized and he is resuscitated from the coma."

"He's in a coma!" Isabel blurted.

"Yes," Dr. Johnson acknowledged, his hands raised, "but it's for his own good. A medically induced coma is how the body focuses all its energies on the most essential tasks. It's a good thing, I promise."

Isabel hung her head, unconvinced.

"His leg?" Cricket blurted, unable to formulate a complete question, only its essence.

"Yes, his leg," Dr. Johnson continued. "Trip's left leg, as you know, was broken during his fall. We placed three pins in his femur and two each in his tibia and fibula. It is simply too early to prognosticate the degree of his recovery or its timeline. At this point, the most important thing is to keep his body infection free so that his bones will accept the foreign objects."

"But he *will* recover, right, Dr. Johnson?" I asked.

Dr. Johnson turned his earnest eyes to me. "If we can keep infection at bay, there is every reason to believe that he can recover use of the leg."

*Recover use of the leg?* That was not clear enough. I wanted my specifics. Would he be lucky to walk or able to run? Would he have a permanent limp? Would his legs grow at the same rate? I shook my head, trying to empty my brain of the endless string of questions.

"It's the least of our worries," Cricket interjected. "But what about his ear?"

Dr. Johnson shook his head side to side as if amazed. "I'm no accident scene expert," he began, "but given the size and shape of the wound's laceration, it's likely that what separated your son's ear from his head was a horse hoof. The injury could have been so much worse. A moving horse hoof is a deadly weapon and—in this case—that weapon was centimeters from your son's brain and spinal column. A few shades closer, and we would be having a vastly different conversation. He almost certainly would have lost an eye, the fracture would have been deeper, the hematoma would have hemorrhaged. Brain damage would have been certain. There's no guarantee he would have survived. So, as hard as it is to imagine in this moment, the partial loss of your son's ear is a sign of a great blessing."

Cricket put a hand over her mouth and closed her eyes.

"We were able to reattach the back of his left ear without complication," Dr. Johnson continued. "The upper third of the ear—the helix and fossa..." He paused, seeing our confused faces. "This part," he said, wagging the cartilage-filled upper lobe of his own ear, "was, unfortunately, severely compromised. We removed it, creating a clean suture above the antihelical fold. Down the road, you and Trip may choose to pursue plastic surgery options. But for now, the remaining tissue should heal without infection."

Cricket nodded. I pulled her close, connecting the three of us in an embrace.

From down the hall, the rumble of a gurney announced Trip's arrival. Isabel, Cricket, and I stood back, giving the nurses a wide berth as they maneuvered his bed back and forth into position among the awaiting monitors and machines. With expert deftness, plugs and cords were attached, lighting previously dormant electronics; the whir and bleats began.

Trip's head was mummified by gauze, leaving a single closed eye uncovered and a glimpse of his lips visible around the ventilator tube. His left leg was cast from hip to toe and held aloft by traction ropes. The cast, the tubes, the gauze, the machines: all surrounding our tiny eight-year-old boy who already looked shrunken by the trauma.

The nurses departed, but Dr. Johnson remained. "Here's the plan," he said. "We need to keep Trip here in the ICU until we see signs of the intercranial pressure decreasing into the desired range. Once that happens—and assuming his vital signs remain normal and there are no signs of infection—he'll be transferred from the ICU to a regular hospital room. Unfortunately, here in the ICU, you will be limited to visiting hours. But once he's transferred to his own room, you can be with him as much as you want."

*Alone? I have to leave him here alone?* I thought. My tears began to stream yet again.

"I'll leave you with Trip for now," Dr. Johnson said. "There's one more visiting hour this evening, and then you can come back tomorrow morning and see him again. If there are any developments, you'll be the first to know."

We nodded, still huddled together.

Once Dr. Johnson left, we each grabbed one of Trip's appendages—Cricket held his right hand, Isabel his left, me his right foot—and we sat. For the first time that day, I prayed that time would move more slowly.

The evening's final visiting hour was identical, save the visit from Dr. Johnson. Trip's nurses were all kind and encouraging, with absolutely nothing new to share. That was fine if unsatisfying; we were in the epitome of a no news is good news situation.

Isabel, Cricket, and I moved from room to room to room and ultimately to the car and home without much conversation. Exhaustion had overtaken us all, and there seemed to be nothing worth words. We silently ate our to-go burgers from Santa Barbara's own Habit, bused our plates, and readied for bed. Priscilla's man in the woods certainly loomed large in my head, but I was too tired to consider my next moves that night.

By the time I joined Cricket in bed, my mind had executed its own version of a coma; I was not thinking, only following the rote, presleep checklist. I climbed under the covers and turned off my light, joining Cricket in darkness. It was then that she finally spoke.

"Hollis," she said. "The story Priscilla told? About the man who tried to grab her?"

"Yes," I said.

"Do you believe she was telling the truth?"

I pride myself on applying a scientific approach to complex questions. As intuitive as an answer might appear, it was important to consider alternatives before reaching conclusions. In that vein, Genevieve and Cyrus had plenty of common sense on their side when they dismissed the idea that there would be a man on those trails under any normal circumstances. These were narrow mountain trails cut for horses, and there were no nearby roads or houses. Even if a man had scrambled trailside, it would take a lunatic to attack a girl on a one-thousand-pound horse.

A black bear was certainly a possibility. Though rare—especially in broad daylight—black bears are known to roam those hills. Maybe Priscilla's horse had gotten between a mama bear and her cub. And maybe the sight of a bear spooked Flip-Flop. It was a plausible tale.

Even more likely, whatever scared Priscilla was something small: a darting deer, a snake, an innocuous rustle in the underbrush. Perhaps Priscilla got scared, screamed, and inadvertently caused Flip-Flop to freak out. And now, with all the damage done, Priscilla would like to have a better justification for her calamity-inducing scream. A mysterious man in the woods would certainly suffice.

So, yes, there were many rational reasons to dismiss Priscilla's story as fantasy or confusion or both. But I knew too much. I had seen the falsified financial records. I'd uncovered the zero-balance bank accounts and all their siphoning corporations. I had found the Zurich bank account—the place where the buck literally stopped—all told, a blueprint for money laundering and thievery.

And perhaps most important, I had met Vlad, a man whose air of malice still haunted me.

"I do, Cricket. I think she's telling the truth."

Silence.

"Do you think this is tied to Cyrus Wimby?" Cricket asked.

"I do."

Silence.

"You've been carrying this around for some time now, haven't you?" she asked. "And you've been keeping it from me."

I cleared my throat. "I'm…I'm sorry," I said. "I've been trying to protect you from—"

"That is not the way marriage works, Hollis!" she interrupted. "We are *partners*. I do not need you protecting me from anything!"

"I…I know," I mumbled.

"I mean—let's be honest here—if either of us needs to be shielded from information so as to avoid overreactions, it's you!"

I nodded; there was no arguing that point.

"But I don't do that to you, do I?" she continued. "I treat you with respect. I treat you as an equal. I don't pretend you're too fragile to process potentially disturbing information!"

Again I nodded, this time with my head bowed like the scolded child I was.

"And now here we are. My boy…" Her voice cracked. "My boy is in the hospital. And you: Look at you. You're wasting away, Hollis. What have you lost now, like twenty pounds? And your hair; it's starting to fall out."

Indeed, I was one extended bout of erectile dysfunction away from full emasculation. "I know," I repeated.

More silence.

"So, what happens next?" she finally asked. "What are *we* going to do?"

"I have to prove what I suspect," I replied.

Cricket flipped on her bedside lamp, and I saw that she had been crying the whole time. "Tell me everything," she said.

# CHAPTER THIRTY-NINE

AFTER TEN DAYS of successfully battling swelling and infection in the ICU, Trip was resuscitated from the medically induced coma and removed from the ventilator. Medical philistine that I was, I assumed this status change would result in Trip sitting up in his bed and asking for ice cream. But no. He was no longer in a coma, but he was still unconscious, exhibiting occasional reflexive eye flutters, groans, and grimaces but nothing purposeful.

While this step in the recovery process did not register with Trip, it was monumental to me. Out of the coma and off the ventilator, Trip was relocated from the ICU to a hospital room: We could now be with him 24/7. Or, at least, one of us could. Cricket and I argued over who would stay at the hospital, but I prevailed and packed my bags for an indefinite sleepover. I won not because of any merit, but because we both knew I would be far less *present* for Isabel at home. I was not capable of compartmentalizing. I was an obsessed Labrador retriever: Once the tennis ball appeared, I could think of nothing else until it disappeared. Cricket was once again punished for her more evolved status.

Like most other things in *paradise*, Trip's new digs were plush by hospital standards. I was prepared for a cot but instead got a small built-in sofa that folded out to a reasonable-sized bed.

Certainly, I had slept in far less comfortable spots. Also, thanks to a recent renovation, Cottage Hospital had a stronger Wi-Fi signal than my gar-office. As I packed my laptop and power cord, preparing to finish my excavation of Cyrus Wimby's tunnels, it occurred to me that the most important decision of my life—or at least of the last year—had been electing to continue the Crypto-Wallet health insurance policy through COBRA. I'm not sure what we would have done without it.

On our first morning as roomies, I watched the nurse change the bandages on Trip's head. As much as I thought I hated the bandages, I hated what they covered more. As I should have expected, his head was clean shaven. The incisions over his left ear seemed to be healing well, but that didn't distract from the reality of the wound site. His poor ear looked as if it had been caught in the garbage disposal. The wounds were a healthy shade of pink, devoid of angry red streaks and other telltale signs of infection. The nurse carefully redressed each exposed area and recocooned his head in gauze. When done, she smiled at me and said, "Looking good."

I smiled back, but there was no ointment, gauze, or bandage that could shelter the devastation in my soul. This was all my fault.

If I had not gotten fired three times in seven years.

If I were not so self-righteous.

If I had not drained our savings to the point of desperation.

If I had not courted Cyrus Wimby for a job.

If I had listened to my instincts, which, for once, were correct.

If I had accepted that we were never going to compete with Montecito's metaphorical Joneses, that we were renters—of a home, of a school, of a life—and chosen not to let my feelings of inadequacy and jealousy push me into chasing a too-good-to-be-true home run.

If I had recognized Vlad as the canary in the coal mine that he was.

And even if I went back in time and repeated every one of

these other idiotic missteps, I still could have avoided this horrific accident if only I had exercised the common sense *not to* deposit my family at the doorstep of the man I suspected was perpetrating a global fraud. If I had only done just this one thing right, Trip would be fine. He would be sitting in his second-grade classroom trying to figure out how to get out of doing his reading or writing assignment instead of lying comatose at Cottage Hospital with a shattered leg, a fractured skull, and a partially missing ear.

It was all my fault.

I would carry my responsibility for Trip's injuries all my waking days and beyond; if there was such a thing as *beyond* and if *it* would host damaged goods like me. But as Trip lay comatose—and I pecked away at my computer, digging deeper into Cyrus's web of lies—I made myself a promise: Cyrus would shoulder his share of the responsibility too.

Cricket and Isabel visited us daily. They brought sunshine to our quiet room and were able to recognize signs of progress that I missed.

"His color is better today," Isabel would observe.

"His blood pressure is more normal today," Cricket would remark.

I was thankful for these missed observations, improvements I could not see for all my staring.

For many hours, I would just sit holding Trip's hand, talking to him, and making plans for our future. I read to him from the first Percy Jackson novel, which he had loved and, when it was finished, moved on to the second and then the third, fourth, and fifth. I imagined Trip waking from his coma, retelling vivid dreams of his adventures with Percy, Annabeth, and Grover. At least it would underscore that my vigil had mattered.

On the fifth day after Trip's relocation, Cyrus dropped in for a visit. I was expecting this. Not, of course, because Cyrus wanted to check on Trip, but because he wanted to check on *me*. I had turned on my *out of office* email notification and was having all my messages forwarded directly to Cyrus. Kindhearted soul that he was, he was forwarding them right back to me. I did a version of the same on BatSignal, fixing my status indefinitely at *Do Not Disturb.*

"My friend," Cyrus said, taking a guest chair, "how are you holding up?"

He had caught me in the middle of one of Percy's epic battles with evil; there are plenty of them to choose from, so imagine whichever one you would like. I had recently completed a map of every entity associated with the second of Cyrus's pass-through bank accounts and was about to begin the third but was relishing this break to commune with Trip. Thankfully, Cyrus caught me reading and not typing. I closed the book. "Doing okay."

"So very glad to see you here, instead of that dreary waiting room. Progress!"

I nodded. "Yes."

He smiled and returned my nod. His eyes shifted around the room; he tapped his heel. I sensed that he had come prepared with only a handful of icebreakers in his repertoire and was counting on me to add the commentary that would turn *how are you holding up* into a five-minute conversation. Then, once the niceties were exhausted, he could get down to the real reason he was here. Unfortunately for him, I was not playing my part.

"Have you gotten any recent updates from Trip's doctor?" he asked.

"Slow but steady," I said.

Again, he consulted the room for inspiration. "Flat-screen televisions," he said, noting the dormant screen. "Hospitals have come a long way."

"It's a nice room," I said.

He cracked his neck and moved farther down his preplanned list of discussion topics. "So, with a little time to reflect, Priscilla says she is now certain that it was a bear that caused her to scream."

"Okay," I said. There was absolutely no reason to argue this point, though I was sure he was either lying or Priscilla had been brainwashed into a revised telling of the story.

"I've alerted the County Sheriff's Office and the US Forest Service of the incident," he added. "They have a hotline. I'm not sure what they can do, but at least they are informed now."

"Thank you," I said.

I wasn't looking at him but at Trip, and from the corner of my eye, I saw Cyrus bow his head and massage his scalp. A devilish part of me enjoyed his discomfort.

"So," he said, his warm-up topics exhausted, "I recognize that you are in the middle of hell here and that timing could not be worse, but our second-quarter financial results are ready for release."

"Okay," I said.

"It was a blowout quarter," he added. "The market is going to flip."

I smiled; I knew the truth. No matter what that press release and schedule of financial results said, not one dollar of revenue had been recorded in the quarter. It was a complete fabrication. "That's great news," I said flatly.

He nodded. "Yes, it is. But uh"—he cleared his throat—"as the company's CEO, the release needs your signature in order to be posted to the Securities and Exchange Commission." He stood and handed me the release and a pen.

I flipped to the back page and signed without reading a word, then handed the papers and pen back. Should I have refused? Perhaps, but as the saying goes, there's no such thing as half pregnant; I was taking this baby to term.

Cyrus looked stunned at the ease with which I had signed but did his best to hide his surprise behind an appreciative nod. "We're likely to be taking in some fresh investments over the next few weeks. Can I count on you to watch the Miramar bank account for me?"

"Yes."

"And you'll transfer whatever comes in?"

"I will."

He stood, the look on his face almost giddy. That is until his eyes refocused on Trip and his feigned solemnity returned.

"I think he's looking much improved," Cyrus said, though he had no basis of comparison from which to make such a judgment.

"Better," I agreed.

Cyrus tapped the papers on his leg, counting—it seemed—the appropriate number of seconds before he could leave. "Well, I should get going," he said after ten taps. "It was very good to see you, my friend."

I nodded, my eyes never leaving Trip.

"Okay then. Until next time," he said, then departed.

I smiled at my boy. "That was an epic cold shoulder, Trip. Well done. You have the steely nerves of a hostage negotiator." I patted his hand, then opened our book and returned to Percy.

# Chapter Forty

Three days later, Trip's tracheotomy tube was removed. Another week, and his helmet of gauze was reduced to common bandages, revealing that his shaved head had begun to sprout its new carpet. With each passing day, he looked less like a victim and more like my boy.

As Cyrus had predicted, the market *flipped* over ExOh's second-quarter results. I read the release and numbers for the first time from my laptop. Upon reexamination of my missed BatSignal messages, it was clear that Noah had supplied the numbers—blindly blessed by our cut-rate CPA and high-dollar lawyer—and Kai had written the commentary. I was quoted heavily in the accompanying press release. For things I never did and never would say, they were great quotes. ExOh had recorded $43 million of fictitious sales in the second quarter and a pretend profit per share of just over $2. Additionally, in an act of uncharacteristic bravado, I had promised the world that ExOh's run rate revenues would top $200 million by year end. Wow, I was impressed by me. I sounded very much like a CEO.

ExOh's stock price jumped to $62 per share, prompting a round of virtual high-fives between Cyrus, Kai, Umed, Reuben, and Noah over BatSignal. They even threw some unwarranted praise my way. I nodded along mutely, aware that Cyrus was not just faking the financial results; he was faking the trading too.

You see, hacking skills are like muscles. It had been a while since I'd called on mine to lift heavy objects, but now, those once atrophied muscles were back to fighting shape. Thus, I was like a hammer looking for nails. In addition to hacking all of Cyrus's hidden bank accounts, I decided to worm my way into the OTC Markets' central server. From there, I could see the details for every trade of ExOh's shares, allowing me to finally solve that conundrum from ExOh's first day of trading: Why had virtually all the trades been between mysterious entities in the Cayman Islands and Hong Kong?

The answer, of course, was that these *mysterious* entities were no longer mysterious—at least, not to me. I recognized their names from the hidden bank accounts. They were all on the Cyrus Wimby dole, getting paid out every time Cyrus raised money from duped investors. In exchange, the Cayman Islands and Hong Kong boys played hot potato with ExOh's stock, trading shares back and forth as needed to keep the stock price moving higher and give the impression of a frothy market.

Like mosquitoes to a bug zapper, the rising stock price brought more investors to ExOh. Another $7 million was wired to the Miramar bank account from investors new and old who wanted more skin in Cyrus's game. I dutifully moved the money along to Hong Kong, then watched as the trail of parasitic accounts consumed their shares before the balance plopped into the Zurich account. If Zurich was Cyrus's personal piggy bank— as it appeared to be—he was keeping just over 80 percent of every dollar that entered the top of the funnel. Since I had joined on to ExOh, Cyrus had raised $65 million under false pretenses, and the Zurich account had swollen by $54 million.

I say *swollen* because, unlike the other bank accounts in this scam, the Zurich account had not started at zero, nor was it solely funded by ExOh. The Zurich account now held more than $217 million. That staggering sum begged the question, how many times had Cyrus used the ExOh scam playbook? And similarly, what other scams was Cyrus simultaneously running?

I was no longer keeping any of this from Cricket. Like watching a breaking news marathon on CNN, she and I would overanalyze each snippet, looking for new angles and theories. At first I think she harbored a bit of blame toward me; even from within the fog, how could I have missed all these warning signs? But as the depth and breadth of Cyrus's scamming came into focus, she began to appreciate that it was not all about my gullibility. Sometimes you have to tip your hat to the magician.

Despite all my digging, there was only so much I could discover on my own. ExOh was now revealed to be just one part of Cyrus's global mechanism for laundering money. Drugs? Gambling? Smuggling? Sex trafficking? The list of illicit pursuits at Cyrus Wimby's fingertips was long, but he had the financial infrastructure in place to chase them all down; Cyrus could be the Procter & Gamble of fraud.

Unfortunately, I knew that in signing my name to the financial release and transferring the money from the US to Hong Kong, I was adding to the list of Cyrus's victims. But it was too soon to blow my whistle. I wanted more evidence; I needed more time. I had one chance to get this right, and I had no idea what Cyrus would do when he realized I was on his tail. Would he run? Would he flip the script to paint me as the perpetrator? Or—thinking back to Landon's surfing accident, which seemed less accidental by the day—was he capable of violence?

The only thing I knew for certain was that it would be a lot harder to do anything if he was already in handcuffs.

# Chapter Forty-One

With the passage of yet another week, Trip consciously opened his eyes for the first time in thirty-two days. There was no accompanying soundtrack or dramatic aha reveal. He caught me tapping away on my laptop, putting together the final pieces of the Cyrus Wimby jigsaw puzzle. Shamefully, I didn't notice his purposeful movements until I heard his sweet voice scratch out a raspy, "Dad?"

Not that the cosmos was finally turning my way, but Trip's awakening could not have been better timed. With twenty-four days to pour my guilt, anxiety, and nervous energy into hacking and internet sleuthing, I had created a one-hundred-fourteen-page dossier on Cyrus Wimby, ExOh Holdings, and its string of money-laundering bank accounts. Perhaps in an alternate reality where Trip had not been injured, I would have chosen to simply *tell* the authorities of what I had learned instead of creating a dissertation on the subject. Who knows? To me, it felt like time well spent. The mission kept me focused; the focus kept me sane.

As I have experienced in previous hospital adventures, the word *soon*—as in *you will soon be processed for release*—has a different meaning when uttered by doctors and nurses. In their lexicon, it is solely a directional indicator. *Soon* only means *sooner* than you were thinking before you heard the word *soon*. We received our notice of impending release on a late-September afternoon but did not leave the hospital until the next morning.

With the assurance that we would eventually be going home, I finally asked Trip about the day he was injured. As I suspected, he could neither confirm nor deny the presence of a man or a bear in the woods that day. He saw *something* black leap from the side of the trail for Priscilla. He heard her scream; he felt Flip-Flop bolt. Then the world turned upside down and dark.

"I'm sorry, Dad," he said.

"Don't worry, Trip," I said. "I know everything I need to know."

Cricket and Isabel picked us up from the hospital in Cricket's Land Cruiser, windows covered with shoe polished words of encouragement and balloons tied to the bumper.

"You're not throwing a party, are you?" I asked.

"Of course not," Cricket said, then winked.

On our arrival home, the house was decorated with more balloons and *Welcome Home* signs. Paul, Jenny, and a few of Cricket's other close friends were waiting in the front yard, along with several of Trip's MUS classmates and their parents. Our Sonos speakers were outside, crooning Cricket's favorite playlist, titled appropriately, Who Wants to Have Fun. Old-fashioned metal wash bins were filled with ice and beverages for all ages.

Trip had always been shy like his father, but since his coma awakening, he seemed to possess more of Cricket's spunk. His wheelchair with straight-leg extension was a party foul waiting to happen with every turn, but he found great fun in embracing it all. Whenever someone would express an iota of sympathy, he would snap back that he was going to be just fine —better even—because with pins in his leg, he was just like Iron Man.

Trip's greatest challenges were on the horizon. In the surgeries to come over the next year and beyond, there would be many days with no crowd, no balloons, and no music. But for today, he was saying all the right things and giving me hope that the devastation I had wrought would indeed be overcome.

By early afternoon, Trip had passed out. We transferred him to his new bed—delivered by the hospital supply company that morning—and thanked all those who had come to share the joy. The Wimbys were not invited.

With the well-wishers dissipated and Trip finally back home, my thoughts returned to what lay in front of me. My takedown dossier on Cyrus Wimby and ExOh was all I hoped it would be. I had already given it to Cricket for her feedback, feeling much like a debut novelist delivering his first novel. She found plenty of typos and wrote margin notes like *punch this up* and *dumb this down,* but generally, she was my biggest backer. On the cover page, I assigned Cricket one question that continued to baffle me: *Does Genevieve know?*

Despite the natural suspicion that Genevieve—as Cyrus's wife—had to know *something,* I had found no evidence that she was a party to the frauds. Her name was nowhere in the documents. She had never provided directions or instructions to me. She had never met with investors in any capacity other than that of Cyrus's loving gourmand wife. She was the epitome of a 1950s housewife: She cooked, she entertained, she dressed for her man, she added to his sheen of accomplishment, she served as another trophy for his case.

Cricket, too, was adamant that Genevieve was in the dark. "She's in love with a bad man," Cricket said. "Love is not only blind, it's blind*ing.*"

"What about her dismissal of the man in the woods?" I challenged.

Cricket nodded. "Honestly, I think she just wanted you to leave Priscilla alone."

I accepted her answer without further argument. It seemed that Cyrus Wimby was the sole proprietor of his crimes.

As the day began to wind down, it struck me that it had been almost a month since I'd slept in my own bed. By 4:00 p.m., the accumulated exhaustion had crept up on me like a mountain lion to a wounded animal. I dozed on the couch, trying to clear my head of the buzzing thoughts, when a new one bit: *How* would I deliver my dissertation to the authorities? Was I supposed to drive to the FBI office in Los Angeles and knock on the front door? I'd reached for my laptop to google the question, when the doorbell rang.

It was quite rare to get a walk-up visitor in Montecito. The lack of sidewalks and the tall hedges were a deterrent to all but the Girl Scouts who could sell ice to Eskimos. Cricket did not move, so I got up to answer the door, feeling for my wallet just to make sure I had a few dollars on me.

But the three men at our front door were not Girl Scouts. Dressed in tailored navy suits and wearing aviator sunglasses, the three men looked like muscular male versions of nesting dolls, each one the same only taller than the next. My heart rate immediately leveled up. The shortest of the men—at the lower end of five feet tall—was wearing a wired earpiece. Though the earpiece made him look like a Secret Service agent, I doubted these visitors were here to inform me of a surprise visit from the president.

I took a deep breath. If I could have hidden from them—ducking into the kitchen and pretending not to be home—I would have. But our front door was framed by sidelight windows; our visitors could have watched the TV from their position outside. I was trapped, so I moved forward and opened the door.

"May I help you?" I asked.

"Hollis Crawford?" said the earpiece-clad man.

"Yes?"

"I'm Agent Daniel Andrews with the FBI," he said, reaching into his jacket and pulling out a bifold wallet displaying his credentials. "Would you mind if we asked you a few questions?"

# Chapter Forty-Two

MOMENTS prior to the arrival of Agent Daniel Andrews and colleagues, I felt in control of what, where, and how I would deliver my evidence against Cyrus Wimby. Now that the FBI stood on my doorstep, I was thrust into a nervous meltdown. Had I waited too long? Had Cyrus framed me? Was Agent Andrews going to waterboard me?

"Sure," I said to Agent Andrews, glancing over my shoulder to Cricket in the living room. "I'm headed to the gar-office, dear," I said, then quickly closed the door before she could question me.

"This way," I said, leading the three agents from the front door to my gar-office. I pulled open the garage's sectional door—extra dirty after four weeks of my absence—sending a plume of dust toward the well-dressed men.

"I just want to chat," Agent Andrews said, waving a hand in front of his face. "I don't want to buy your lawn mower."

"Sorry," I said. "It's just...well, this is my office."

Agent Andrews took off his aviators and narrowed his eyes on the dingy recesses of my office. Then he placed a hand to his earpiece and let his eyes fall to the gravel driveway. "Agent Green," he said after a few seconds' pause, "why don't you head back to the car. Agent Smith, stay with me."

As Agent Green headed down my driveway, I noticed, for the first time, the hulking matte black van across the street. It was a Mercedes Benz Sprinter, tricked out as if it were set to cameo in the twenty-eighth installment of the Mission Impossible movie series. Though its windows were heavily tinted, Montecito's bright sunshine backlit the van, highlighting shadows within. Thanks to those shadows, I perceived the outline of yet another member of the FBI team sitting in the front passenger seat. It was impossible to know for sure, but the outline of this person— juxtaposed to their seat—made them look small—like a teenager waiting for their parents to drive them to soccer practice. Regardless of their stature, the anonymous person made for at least four FBI agents at Casa de Crawford.

Agents Andrews and Smith joined me in the cavern of my gar-office. I flipped on a few lights and reflexively booted my laptop, now back at home in its docking station. Then I pulled out and dusted off two folding chairs for my guests. Agent Smith moved his chair back a few feet as if he were only an observer. He sat, crossing his arms over rock-hard pectorals.

Agent Andrews sat less confrontationally: his legs crossed at the knee, his hands folded in his lap. He didn't smile at me, but he didn't scowl either. As a team, these guys looked as if they were at a Hollywood audition for FBI agents, right down to the closely cropped hair and expressionless *I've seen it all before* faces. But of them, Agent Andrews was clearly the leading man, right down to his below-average height.

He was almost too attractive to be an FBI agent. I briefly wondered if distractingly good-looking agents might be part of an FBI interview tactic. As his large green eyes scanned my gar-office, the corner of his mouth turned up comically. "I must say, Mr. Crawford," he finally said, "I've executed terrorists in rooms more cheerful than this."

My eyes turned to saucers.

He nonchalantly adjusted his earpiece. "Relax, Mr. Crawford. I doubt anything like that will be necessary today."

I tried to smile at what might have been a perverse olive branch, but Agent Andrews did not reciprocate.

"We're here to ask you some questions about a business colleague of yours," Agent Andrews said. "A Mr. Cyrus Wimby. You know Mr. Wimby?"

"Yes, sir."

Agent Andrews nodded. "Mr. Wimby is not in any sort of trouble. We are just doing some field work. Filling out the file on a foreign national that we don't have that much information on."

"Certainly," I said, nodding nervously. I had no idea where to begin. Should I just vomit information at him? Drop to my knees and tell the entire pathetic story? Or wait to see what he was looking for? I wanted to tell him everything, but I decided to let Agent Andrews determine the pace. "How can I help?"

"Let's start with the professional, shall we?" he said, flipping his five-by-eight steno notebook to a page and pulling a pen from his coat jacket. "Mr. Wimby is an investor, is that correct?"

"Yes," I said. "That is how he describes himself."

Agent Smith cocked his head suspiciously; Agent Andrews stared at his notepad.

"Mr. Wimby is the majority shareholder of a company here in the US, is that correct?"—Agent Andrews flipped to a different page in his notebook—"ExOh Holdings?"

"That is correct," I said.

"And you are the chief executive officer of that company?"

"Yes, sir."

He flipped back a page in his steno pad. "And how long have you known Mr. Wimby?"

I let my eyes wander as I pretended to do the math. Agent Smith, still a few feet removed, watched me as my eyes danced. The way he stared made me feel like an intruder in my own gar-office. "Roughly six months," I finally said.

"Mr. Wimby is a wealthy man, is that correct?" Agent Andrews asked.

"It would certainly appear so," I said, chuckling.

Neither agent returned my chuckle. Agent Andrews paused again. "As you may or may not know," Agent Andrews finally continued, "Mr. Wimby is in the United States on a…a type of visa that…how shall I put this? That does not allow him to operate a US-based business. Would you say that Mr. Wimby is in compliance with that restriction? That he is—as they say—a *passive* investor in ExOh Holdings?"

Suddenly, my frothy anxiety was replaced by a surge of endorphins. This was my opening; this was my moment. I leaned forward, placing my elbows on my knees. "That is not correct. He is the opposite of a passive investor."

Agent Smith tightened the stranglehold on his own bulging pectorals; Agent Andrews scribbled. "I see," he said. "So, you claim that Mr. Wimby is playing an active role in the management of ExOh Holdings?"

I twitched in my seat, simultaneously desperate to reveal everything and nervous to speak. What was I waiting for? Thirty minutes prior I was online, googling how to meet with the FBI. Now—miraculously—they were here, sitting uncomfortably in my gar-office. It was as if the Fates had decided to favor me, saving me the inconvenience of a four-hour round-trip drive. *Let's go. Spit it out,* my internal drill sergeant hollered.

I took a deep breath and waited for Agent Andrews to look up from his notepad so that we were iris to iris. When he finally did, I opened the taps: "Cyrus Wimby couldn't be more active if he had a motor up his ass."

Agent Andrews pursed his lips. "That's a new one." A pregnant pause and a few more scribbles. "So, tell me about ExOh Holdings. What does the company do? What is Mr. Wimby's exact role?"

Again, I chuckled nervously. *What does the company do?* Such an innocent, obvious question. I spent months trying to craft a thorough, witty answer to that question, one I understood and could peel back to reveal layers of deeper nuance. The Free Trade Zone License. Chinese import law. Amazon and Alibaba.

It was a romantic tale of a budding global conquest, and it was all a lie.

"So," I began, "in order to sell a product in China, a company needs to—"

"Oh God," Agent Andrews interrupted. "Let me save you some oxygen." He shook his head as if I had annoyed him. "You see, Mr. Crawford. Sometimes I ask questions, not because I want to know the answers but because I already know the answers, and I want to hear what you will say in the face of known facts. But in this case, I can tell that you are about to take me through a painful history lesson on global trade, so let me stop you right there. I have a master's in economics from Cornell. I have been the head of the FBI's Global Trade Surveillance unit for more than a decade. I am a guest lecturer at both Harvard Business School and Harvard Law on the topic of international cartels and money laundering. I am well aware of Chinese Free Trade Zone Licenses and their rarity, and I have reviewed a handful of Power-Point presentations on ExOh Holdings authored—I believe—by you."

I nodded, my ribs vibrating with each rumble of my heart. "So, you know a little more about ExOh Holdings than you were letting on?"

"You catch on quick, Mr. Crawford. And given that prior knowledge, I don't need a refresher course on global trade," Agent Andrews continued. "Nor do I need an explanation of ExOh Holdings' *purported* business plan. I need to know what ExOh Holdings *actually does*. Can you help me with that?"

Again, I nodded, any remaining hesitation obliterated. "The company is a massive fraud," I began. "It is a variety of the classic Ponzi scheme. As far as I can tell, ExOh Holdings has never generated a single dollar of revenue. Its financial filings are fraudulent, its investor presentations are fantasy, and every investment dollar Cyrus Wimby raised for the company has been siphoned off to a network of bank accounts around the globe. The money has been stolen."

Agent Andrews cut his wide eyes to Agent Smith and then back to me. "Stolen, you say?"

"Gone," I said, nodding. "Well, almost gone, I should say. I know where he hid it."

Agent Andrews closed the cover on his steno pad, placed it in his lap, and joined Agent Smith in hugging his chest. "Tell me," he said. "How do you know all of this?"

I turned to my computer, pulled up my dissertation, and hit Control P, sending it to the printer; then I turned back to Agent Andrews. "Because, while I may be a lousy chief executive officer of ExOh Holdings—I am an excellent hacker. With a little inadvertent help from Cyrus, I infiltrated the bank accounts he was using to siphon off the money. He delivered ExOh shares to the investors, but he took the money for himself."

"Accounts, you say?" Agent Andrews asked. "As in plural? As in more than one?"

"Yes," I said. "Eight accounts in total." I counted them out, tallying them on my fingers. "Hong Kong, Sydney, Amsterdam, Mumbai, Helsinki, Liechtenstein, Brussels, and Zurich."

Agent Andrews sat still for several seconds looking like a DVD on pause. "Eight is certainly a lot of bank accounts," he finally said. "How did—"

"They're all linked," I interrupted. "Each account has a specific set of entities that it pays off; then the balance moves along to the next account and on down the line."

Agent Andrews resumed scribbling in his notepad. "That is quite a setup. And you are telling me that you—by yourself—broke into all these accounts? That you can prove what you're saying?"

At that moment, my printer spit out the final sheet of the dossier. I gathered the double-sided pages and put a heavy-duty staple at a precise forty-five-degree angle in the upper-left-hand corner. The fact that I owned a heavy-duty stapler and believed that there was a rhyme and reason to properly placed staples should come as no surprise at this point.

"This," I said, handing the document to Agent Andrews, "explains everything. All the money laundering. All the fraud. All the victims. All the account information, codes, and diagrams. You name it; it is all in there."

"Everything?"

"Everything."

Agent Andrews handed the dossier to Agent Smith, who slowly flipped through its pages.

"You said that you were able to track payments made from Mr. Wimby's accounts to other entities. What have you been able to discover about those recipients?"

I sighed. I'd spent days digging through the corporate registration databases in the Cayman Islands, Isle of Man, Monaco, and so on. The documents existed, but they contained no useful information. "Not that much, I'm afraid," I said. "All the recipients are limited liability corporations headquartered in notorious tax havens. I could track a few layers deep, but I never got to a person's name. It usually ended up as a private company owned by a bunch of other private companies, and the only person signing the forms was a lawyer. Pretty much a dead end."

"Pretty much a dead end," Agent Andrews repeated, looking at his partner more than me. "So, you were not able to identify the individual accomplices to Mr. Wimby's fraud?"

"No," I said.

Agent Smith looked up from his page flipping of my dossier and nodded at Agent Andrews.

"That's unfortunate," Agent Andrews said. "But it looks like you've got poor Mr. Wimby nailed to the cross."

"I think so," I said, flinching at the imagery.

Agent Andrews nodded to himself as his eyes flitted around my gar-office. I imagined him deploying this pregnant pause strategy on nervous criminals under hot interrogation lights. "Let's go back to something you said earlier," he said, breaking his silence. "You said you knew where Mr. Wimby had the money hidden. Is that correct?"

"Yes."

"So, where is it?" he asked. "Secret safe? Treasure map?"

I smiled. "No. He has it all in a bank account in Zurich, Switzerland."

His eyes narrowed. "Can you show me?"

I turned back to my computer and logged into my Crypto-Wallet account. With a few keystrokes, I updated all eight of Cyrus's secret accounts and consolidated the transaction history. "As you can see here," I said, pointing to my screen, "seven of the bank accounts have zero balances, but this one"—I tapped the transactions coded for the Zurich account—"has two hundred seventeen million dollars in it."

Once again, Agent Andrews's DVD hit pause as he stared expressionless.

"That's where he has it hidden," I said, trying to break him from his trance.

Agent Andrews cleared his throat. "Did you say two hundred seventeen million dollars?"

"Yes."

Agent Andrews's eyes searched the ceiling of my gar-office as if he needed help and his next question was hiding in my rafters. "Is that...? Did he take two hundred seventeen million from his ExOh investors?"

"Victims," I corrected.

"Right. Yes. My mistake," he said. "Is that the tally of his ExOh fraud?"

"No," I said. "He only raised sixty-five million through ExOh. The Zurich bank account seems to have been getting money from other sources outside ExOh. Cyrus must have other things going on. He is a try-hard thief, it would appear." I laughed, but Agent Andrews did not join in on the fun. Instead, he cocked his head and said nothing. I couldn't be certain, but his expression indicated that he might have been listening to whoever was speaking through his earpiece.

"Interesting," he finally mumbled. "And you're telling me that all this information is in here?" He pointed to my dissertation in Agent Smith's meaty paw.

"Yes."

"The account numbers, the history, the log-in information. All of it?"

"All of it. Well..." I paused, wanting to be more precise. "I should say: all the information you would need to track the money and verify the balances. If you wanted to *transact* in those accounts, you'd need a little more information from Cyrus himself, or a little assistance from the bank."

Agent Andrews pursed his lips. "Well then. I guess we'll find out how cooperative Mr. Wimby chooses to be, won't we?"

We sat in silence for a few seconds as the light outside the gar-office slowly faded.

"So, what happens now?" I asked.

Agent Andrews again turned to his mute partner, receiving the slightest of affirmative head nods. "We'll take care of the rest," Agent Andrews said.

"So...will you just go and arrest him?" I asked.

"It doesn't work quite like that," Agent Andrews said as Agent Smith stood to leave. "We will take your research back to headquarters and discuss the matter with the higher-ups. It will take a few days to come up with an action plan for getting Mr. Wimby off the streets."

"So, what should I do in the meantime?" I asked.

He wagged a finger at me. "Nothing out of the ordinary. You are to behave exactly as you've always behaved, Mr. Crawford. It is imperative that Cyrus Wimby remain in the dark. Imperative. You perform your duties just as you always have; do absolutely nothing to raise his suspicions. Am I clear?"

I shook my head, struggling to imagine how I could go on working with Cyrus while Agent Andrews and the FBI's *higher-ups* chewed the fat. "Give me an idea," I said. "Just a ballpark. Are we talking days? Are we talking weeks? Please don't tell me we're talking months?"

"Don't worry," Agent Andrews said as Agent Smith exited the gar-office without a goodbye. "I suspect we'll have the situation under control in a week."

Agent Andrews stood abruptly and followed his partner down the driveway. I stumbled behind them, contemplating how I could manage to avoid Cyrus for the next seven days.

"How will I know when you've taken action, Agent Andrews?" I asked as Agent Smith opened the Sprinter's sliding back door and climbed inside. "Are you going to give me a heads-up?"

Agent Andrews put one foot high on the van's floorboards and turned his head to me. For the first time that visit, he smiled. "Don't you worry about that, Mr. Crawford. You won't need a heads-up. You'll know."

## CHAPTER FORTY-THREE

"What was that all about?" Cricket asked when I came back inside. "Did you just convert to Jehovah's Witness?"

I laughed; it was good to be home.

Trip had just woken from his nap, and he and his massive wheelchair were now at the dining table playing a game of Qwirkle with Isabel while Cricket made dinner. I told her all was well, promised to explain later, gave her a kiss on the forehead, and went to the sink to begin cleaning as she cooked. When we first married, she found this habit of mine annoying—I was perpetually washing something that was still in use. But over time she had come to appreciate it. Like a surgeon whose instruments were available on call—scalpel, suture—I made sure everything she required to cook a wonderful meal was clean and at the ready.

In the immediate aftermath of Agent Daniel Andrews and crew's unannounced visit, I was euphoric. It was over; I had done it. With the mission complete and a rock-solid case delivered to the hands of the FBI, I realized how heavy this load had become. Colors were brighter, tunes were prettier, jokes were funnier. The dinner Cricket was cooking—chicken enchiladas, Trip's favorite—made my stomach grumble excitedly instead of turtling. True, I had been eating from a hospital cafeteria for nearly a month, so anything would have been an improvement, but it was notable how positively my body suddenly responded to the thought of food. It seemed I had finally turned the metaphorical corner.

Seeing my family back together under one roof—the kids smiling, Cricket laughing, all of us preparing to eat a meal that I did not expect to send me into gastrointestinal shock—gave me a sense that the universe was telling me I had finally done something right. I got no joy from ratting out Cyrus Wimby, but it did seem just. And by discovering the buried treasure where Cyrus kept his grift, I had every hope this story would have a happy ending for all of ExOh's investors not named Wimby.

Don't get me wrong. I didn't think of myself as a hero. But I did believe that the final telling of this story would show I had acted bravely and, in that bravery, had helped a lot of people avoid massive losses. Maybe this was the *greatness* I had wanted to believe I was destined for.

After dinner, we resumed a version of our typical nighttime routine. I gave Trip his sponge bath, since I was now the expert, and Isabel was reinstalled as Trip's bedtime reader. She was disappointed to learn that we had progressed all the way from *Percy Jackson: The Lightning Thief* to *Percy Jackson and the Last Olympian*.

"How am I supposed to know what happened in between?" she argued.

"In summary, Percy and Annabeth slayed a lot of bad guys," I said, and then sent her off to read.

Trip passed out quickly, and after Isabel came back into our room for multiple final, final, *final* hugs, Cricket and I were blessedly alone.

"So," she said, climbing under the covers, "what's new with you?"

Again, I laughed. There was so much to tell, and I was so very exhausted. I rubbed my eyes. "I invite you to accept the Lord Jesus Christ as your sav—"

"Okay, funny man," she interrupted, slapping me on the

chest. "Did that guy read you your Miranda rights or did you take the Fifth?"

"I sang like a canary," I said, laughing. "It was crazy, right? The world works in mysterious ways, I guess. I was planning to drive down to Los Angeles on Monday and talk to the FBI there, but they beat me to the punch."

"So, it *was* the FBI?" she said. "Holy cow, Hollis. How did they know to come looking for you?"

"Good question," I said. "Agent Andrews began by saying that he was just doing field work and pretended to know almost nothing. And honestly, I believed him, so I started from square one. Then he flipped the script on me and said he knew all about ExOh's *purported* business plan but wanted me to give him the inside skinny. The straight dope. The 411. The—"

"Easy there," Cricket interrupted. "Sounds like he good cop and bad copped you in one interview. You got the deluxe interrogation experience. Well done."

"Yeah." I laughed. "They must have been on Cyrus's trail for some time. Agent Andrews has an excellent—and surprisingly attractive—poker face."

We kept on like this for more than an hour, revisiting parts of the story in more detail and debating Cyrus's state of mind.

"Do you still think Genevieve is in the dark?" I asked.

Cricket nodded. "Poor girl. Priscilla too. They deserve our sympathy, Hollis, not our suspicion."

When we could barely talk anymore, Cricket broached another interesting question: "Why do you think Cyrus picked Montecito of all places?"

"Are you kidding?" I said. "I can't imagine a better place to launch a scam than Montecito."

"Why?"

"Think about all the attributes that we piled onto Cyrus Wimby without question," I said. "I mean, he told a story about Saudi Arabia and royal families and oil and we all just nodded our heads and accepted it. *Obviously,* he was successful. *Obviously,* he was smart. *Obviously,* he was rich. Is he a Saudi royal? *Obviously.* And then, when he goes on to talk about his latest business venture, it just seems so *obvious* that this rich, smart, successful man of royal lineage would be starting a new global trading business that no one really understood."

Cricket shook her head. "But maybe he was all those things?"

"He was most definitely *some* of them," I said, "but not all of them. Regardless, the point is that we granted him those attributes based solely on perceptions. We were not skeptical; we were not on guard. That is the way things are here in Montecito. It's like, if your zip code is 93108, then you must have done something right. How else would you be here?"

Cricket eyed *me* skeptically.

I tried a different approach. "You're the room mother for Isabel's and Trip's classes, right?"

"Duh."

"And you know all the other parents, right?"

"Two for two."

"What do you really know about how all those people came to reside in a place where the median home price is more than two and a half million dollars?"

"That's not..." she objected. "I'm not going digging around in people's personal business. That is rude."

"I totally agree," I said. "It's none of our business. But in the absence of actual knowledge, we default to filling in the gaps with assumptions. They must be smart, we think. They must be accomplished. They must be rich. How else would they be here?"

She nodded, not convinced but no longer defiant. "What does everyone think of us, then?"

I smiled. "We're on scholarship."

She slapped me in the chest with the back of her hand and laughed. Our conversation dwindled to phrases and grunts. Finally, Cricket picked up her book, professing that she needed to read just a few pages to fall asleep.

I turned off my light and rolled over, grateful for the feel of my own pillow. The last thing I heard was Cricket say, "I'm very proud of you, Hollis."

# Chapter Forty-Four

After Friday evening's euphoria came the weekend's reality check. At some point in the next five days, I would again be unemployed. Was I even employ*able*? With a Swiss cheese résumé that included a stop as the CEO of a company soon to be known as a massive fraud, it was a fair question.

The more I considered my future, the more I wondered if maybe I was not suited for the corporate game. I seemed hardwired to zig when I was supposed to zag and to speak up when I was supposed to shut up. Maybe my future was not in the bowels of a *new* employer but in *no* employer. I had demonstrable computer skills, I was self-motivated, I did not need a boss riding roughshod to keep me on task, and I kind-of-sort-of hated working in teams. Wasn't I the perfect candidate to hang out my own shingle as an independent contractor?

As the old saying goes, the downside to being self-employed is that your boss is an asshole. While true, it seemed to me that I might be the only person on the planet who could enjoy working for me. And while being an independent contractor meant giving up the comfort of a corporate safety net, who was I kidding? I was about to be unemployed for the fourth time in almost nine years, and I had drained my retirement savings account to a pittance. I was a razor blade to safety nets.

Thinking about being my own boss helped offset the anxiety I felt waiting for the FBI to bust Cyrus. Agent Daniel Andrews had said it would happen within a week, but that I would not have advance knowledge. The waiting reminded me of the feeling back in high school when I stalked the mailman for nearly three weeks, anxiously anticipating my SAT results.

I decided to leave my *out of office* email notification intact even though Trip and I were home from the hospital and my gar-office was fully accessible. What was the point in getting caught up on all my emails for a job that was about to go poof in a few days? I figured.

The problem was, I was the only ExOh team member who knew that the company's death was imminent. BatSignal was still alive with communication from Noah, Kai, Umed, Reuben, and Cyrus. There were new press releases to write, chock-full of fresh, creative lies about ExOh's clients and revenues. There were hints that yet another fresh round of investment capital was on its way. And there was tremendous concern for yours truly, as expressed in Umed's recent query: *Where the fuck is Hollis?*

Cyrus phoned me on my mobile as well. I didn't return the calls in the hopes that I would never have to. Surely the FBI would act soon, right?

But by Wednesday morning, the FBI had done nothing, and I was going stir crazy in anticipation. Cricket suggested I walk Isabel to school, if only to subtract my nervous energy from our home's aura. Normally reluctant, Isabel seemed excited by the prospect of strolling to Montecito Union Elementary as we used to. Embracing the rare opportunity to make both of the women in my life happy at the same time, I said yes, even though the excursion risked a face-to-face encounter with Cyrus.

Uncharacteristically, Isabel held my hand the whole walk to school and did not disavow knowledge of me two hundred yards from the school's entrance (though she did let go of my hand).

She allowed me to escort her all the way to her classroom door without protest. As I said goodbye—wanting a hug but settling for a wave—it struck me that this could be the last time she would ever allow me to make such an intrusion on her *real* life. The thought was a stark reminder of our family's increasing rate of change. Our deck of cards had been tossed in the air; the next hand was utterly unpredictable.

It was a poignant moment, and I turned from the door of Isabel's classroom grateful that I had risked leaving home. Naturally, on the way back down the school's breezeway, I paid for that gratefulness when I ran smack-dab into Cyrus, lurking at the head of the valet line like a bully in search of lunch money.

"My friend," he said. "You are one hard man to track down."

I nodded.

"Come," he said, placing an arm around my shoulder, "we have much to discuss."

"I've got to get home to Trip," I protested, my stomach seizing up for the first time in days.

Cyrus's smile faded. "We have some pressing business, Hollis. When can you make yourself available?"

I shook my head. "I don't know, Cyrus. I've got to coordinate with Cricket. It's com—"

"I'll come to you, then," he interrupted.

I wasn't prepared for this. Cyrus had never been to my home; I wasn't even sure he knew where I lived. But in that moment, on the fly, I was hard-pressed to come up with a reason why he couldn't come to our house. "I don't really have a great place for us to meet," I lied.

"We'll make do," he said. "Ten o'clock." He patted me on the shoulder and walked away.

All the way home, my gastrointestinal pain raged like Omaha Beach. It struck me as comical that I once thought these health issues were driven by diet or drink; it was nothing but good old-fashioned anxiety, albeit on steroids.

I arrived home just as Cricket and Trip triumphantly finished their puzzle and told Cricket of our pending visitor. "I am a horrible liar, Cricket," I groaned. "He's going to see right through me."

"Come on, Hollis," she consoled. "You can do this. It is probably the last time you'll ever see him out of stripes. Have some fun with it."

I opened the gar-office's sectional door, booted my computer, did one final scan of the room for any materials related to my secret sleuthing operation, and dusted off my guest folding chair. How fitting that Cyrus would sit in the same seat Agent Daniel Andrews of the FBI had sat in. Cricket was right. I needed to embrace the irony; it might be the only way I could get through it without blowing my cover.

At twenty-five after ten, I heard the crunch of Cyrus's leather-soled shoes on our pea-gravel driveway. Considering my stoner-level paranoia, it was a good sign that he was tardy as usual.

"Quite the setup you have here," he said, trying to hide the disgust on his face. He pointed to the folding chair hesitantly; I nodded and smiled. He pulled the silk handkerchief from the breast pocket of his jacket and thoroughly wiped the chair. Of course I was insulted, but I enjoyed his discomfort. When he could clean no more, he shook out his handkerchief, stuffed it in his pocket, and gingerly took his seat.

As usual, he held in his hands a stack of papers, many of which would no doubt require my signature. One of the most painful conclusions of all my research into Cyrus Wimby's lies was that this—my signature—was the essence of my role at ExOh Holdings. I was the United States citizen stooge. Cyrus could not have cared less about my actual capabilities. He simply needed an upstanding citizen with a clean background check who could open a bank account, pose as a member of the board, and raise absolutely zero eyebrows. I was the fool who volunteered for the job, but it could have been anyone.

"So," Cyrus began, "before I forget, how is Trip doing?"

I grimaced. *Before I forget?* Did he say that? Cyrus was not dumb, and he certainly was not naive. There could be no doubt that the *man* in the woods had intended to grab Priscilla and that Trip was unfortunate collateral damage from a botched job. Cyrus was directly and irrefutably responsible for the near death of my son, and he knew it. How could he sit there and pretend that what happened to Trip was a simple accident that he had the luxury to casually inquire about as if he were curious about the weather? I have never punched a man in my life, and I probably would have lost a fistfight with Cyrus, but in that moment I didn't care. I wanted to see him feel real pain, a small sample of what Trip had experienced.

"Doing better," I finally said when my sanity returned.

"Very good, my friend. A blessing indeed."

I gritted my teeth and nodded.

"Well then." He thumbed off a subset of his papers. "I have decided that Entre Nous does not really fit with the overarching ExOh business plan. I discussed the matter with John Colton, and he agrees..."

I bobble-headed along, reminding myself that none of this mattered.

"To facilitate an orderly transfer of Entre Nous, I have negotiated a deal to sell the label and its assets to a foreign buyer for one dollar."

My eyes bugged. "Wow. One whole dollar? You must have negotiated hard."

Cyrus smirked. "Yes, well. Entre Nous continues to lose money. I felt it best to cut our losses."

"Who is the new owner?" I asked, vaguely curious.

"You don't know them," he said.

"What does that matter?"

He smiled. "Fine," he said. "A group of wealthy individuals acting through a special purpose vehicle incorporated in the British Virgin Islands. The entity is called La Revanche." He handed me the papers. "Your signature is required."

I flipped to the final page, where, once again, John Colton's signature was electronic. I wondered if John had ever been consulted on any of the issues to which his virtual John Hancock was attached. Nevertheless, I signed. Who cares, right?

"Fantastic. Thank you, Hollis," he said as I passed the signed copy back to him. "Huff Monroe reached out to me yesterday to inquire about the move to the NASDAQ exchange. Do you have any update for me on that front?"

Talk about rearranging deck chairs on the *Titanic*. I shook my head. "No."

"Very well. I will relay to him that you are continuing to work on it for the benefit of all of ExOh's shareholders."

I leaned back, rubbing my eyebrows. Huff Monroe had more money than I could count; he probably wasn't someone who deserved a mountain of my sympathy. But how would I feel when I bumped into the Montecito citizens who had been duped during Cyrus's dinner parties? It would happen eventually at the Country Mart, Honor Bar, or farmer's market. No matter how much I aided the authorities in the recovery effort, I would always be recognized as that nitwit who helped Cyrus Wimby deflower Montecito.

"We have a few important new customer announcements," Cyrus continued. "You should have received the details from Noah on BatSignal. Can you whip up a press release for me?"

"Okay," I said.

"Today?" Cyrus clarified.

There was no way I would write another press release for ExOh. "You got it," I lied.

"Fantastic." He smiled, setting his ream of papers below him on the dirty outdoor rug I was using as gar-office decor. "You know, Hollis. You have done a terrific job for ExOh Holdings in your brief tenure. I hope you know how much I appreciate it."

"Thank you," I said cautiously.

"I literally could not have done all of this without you..."

What does it say about me as a human being that his gratitude inspired some perverse feeling of pride in me? After all, the *this* which I had helped him *do* was nothing but a fraud. But for reasons I cannot explain, I am fairly certain that I blushed when he thanked me.

"And as a token of my gratefulness," he continued, "I would like to do something special for you."

The only special thing I wanted was for him to depart and never return. "That's not necessary, Cyrus."

"I insist," he said. He pulled his phone from the interior pocket of his suit jacket and swiped a few times. "As we sit this glorious morning, ExOh's stock is at $64.28." He raised his eyes from the screen. "Congratulations."

I nodded, lost for an appropriate verbal response.

"The deal we struck when you joined on as chief executive officer of ExOh was for you to be compensated with one hundred thousand shares priced at ten dollars per share—one million dollars—fully vested in a year's time."

Again, I nodded, remembering the deal, how it once made me so excited and now felt a giant cream pie flattened against my face.

"As you and I are both well aware," Cyrus continued, "it has not yet been a year since that contract was written, thus you are not yet technically a shareholder and have not personally bene-fited from the meteoric rise in our stock price."

"That's...that's correct," I said. A second pie in the face; I had agreed to a dumb deal and then agreed to have it held out in front of me like a rabbit at the greyhound track.

"Let's fix that," Cyrus said.

My forehead wrinkled. "Okay."

Cyrus reached back down into his pile of papers and pulled a single page off the top. "This is a resolution signed by John Colton and me, expediting the vesting date of your ExOh shares to"—he handed me the document—"today." I looked at the one-page letter; as always, John Colton's signature was electronic.

"Uh, wow...uh, thank you," I said, though my inflection almost certainly made it sound like a question instead of a declaration. There was no other possible answer, at least as far as I could conceive in that split second. If someone offers to put millions of dollars within reach, you say *thank you* even if you know you will never touch it.

"Oh, you're quite welcome," Cyrus said, smiling proudly. "At a price of $64.28, your net worth just increased by six million, four hundred twenty-eight thousand dollars in the matter of a few seconds. How does that feel?"

It would have felt fantastic had it been real. Instead, it made me feel nauseous. From the day I justified cashing in my retirement savings, this was what I dreamed of. Now it was just a hoax —paper money, soon to be torched. "It feels...terrific, Cyrus. Again, thank you."

"Oh, there's more," he said. "I've gone to the extra trouble of readying those shares for trade." He lifted his cell phone. "I have the broker at Humphrey Brothers on speed dial. With your shares now vested, you can sell them. Why don't you take some money off the table and give yourself a *real* payday?"

My nausea reverted back to paranoia. Was Cyrus testing me? Had he been tipped off about my conversation with the FBI? Or was he blind to my sabotage and only trying—in his twisted, sociopathic way—to do something he considered nice?

The potential gamesmanship sent my if-then decision loops into overdrive. If Cyrus was simply trying to be nice, then my refusing to sell shares might tip him off that I was onto him. On the other hand, if Cyrus was suspicious and was using the offer to sell shares as a test, then refusing would confirm his suspicions, while accepting would refute them.

There was another option too. Perhaps Cyrus was neither suspicious nor trying to be nice but was, instead, trying to drag me into his cesspool of illegal deeds. He had to know that I was the very definition of a *corporate insider*; I could not sell shares on a whim unless I wanted to bunk up with him in prison.

Call it a test or a trap or combination of both, there was no way I could accept Cyrus's offer to sell any of my shares. If I blew my cover, so be it. I would rather that than jail.

"It would feel great, Cyrus," I said, calculating an eye-of-the needle answer. "And thank you for going to the trouble of getting it all arranged. But I'm not ready to sell any of my ExOh shares. I think the stock will double from here, and I'm a long-term investor."

He smiled, rolling his earlobe between his thumb and forefinger. "That's good to hear," he mumbled.

I waited for the next item on his agenda, but he sat quietly, his face scrunched in contemplation. After thirty seconds, he gathered the rest of his documents and stood.

"Is that everything?" I asked, standing as well.

"It would appear so," he said. He rolled the documents into a baton and patted them against his leg.

"Okay, well," I said, anxious for him to leave. "I'll get back to work, then."

"Yes," he said, but he didn't move to exit.

"I'll get you that press release," I blurted, instantly chastising myself. One of my *in-the-fog* strengths had always been remaining at ease with the awkward silence that discomforted others. But just then, I had leapt to fill the void, reminding Cyrus of work I had no intention of doing.

"Take your time," he said, his eyes drooping pensively.

"Okay, then," I said, placing a hand on the small of his back to usher him out. Touching was another out-of-character move for me; what was next, a man hug? But I needed to get Cyrus out of my gar-office fast or else I was going to do something I would really regret. "I should go check on Trip," I offered, trying to speed him up.

"Of course," he said, finally beginning the short walk from my gar-office to his Porsche.

I walked with him till I was parallel with our front door, then stopped. Unfortunately, he stopped too. We both stood there silently, my discomfort growing by the second. Finally, Cyrus turned to face me again and stuck out his hand.

Reflexively, I did the same. When we shook, my hand looked like an anchovy in the tentacles of an octopus.

He pumped my hand twice, eyeing me as if he could see through my pupils. I was no expert in reading emotions, but Cyrus's eyes were heavy with something. It wasn't the bravado, confidence, or even anger that I had recently grown accustomed to. If I had to guess, it was sadness.

I nodded uncomfortably, then wrestled my anchovy from his octopus.

He dropped his eyes to the gravel drive, turned, and was gone.

# Chapter Forty-Five

The next morning, we woke to crisp, fog-free skies. Sometimes paradise makes it hard not to smile.

I confessed to Cricket that I couldn't take another run-in with Cyrus. She called me a wimp but agreed to let me stay home with Trip while she escorted Isabel to school. As penance, I would be Trip's stand-in teacher for the day—a penalty I secretly enjoyed.

One of my sidelines of study during Trip's hospital convalescence was researching how to teach reading and spelling to kids with dyslexia. I was sure to begin as a below-average tutor, but my hourly fee was excellent. Already, Trip and I were developing a solid teacher-pupil relationship in math. Trip loved to talk and hated worksheets. So I worked up a curriculum to make math a conversation about the things that interested him; needless to say, Legos featured heavily in these lesson plans.

Of course, I couldn't pretend to be Trip's teacher forever. Both of us would eventually have to grow up. Trip would have a second of many surgeries the following week to begin the repair of nerve damage in his quadricep; his physical therapy would begin shortly thereafter. But already Montecito Union Elementary had made gracious arrangements to accommodate his massive wheelchair and—barring further setbacks—the plan was to have him back on campus by the beginning of November.

My growing up was harder to schedule. Technically, I was still the chief executive officer of ExOh Holdings, but the clock on that experiment was nearly zero. I spoke hypothetically with Paul about my independent contractor idea, and he thought it was perfect. He suggested that CryptoWallet had several delayed projects in need of someone with skills just like mine. This made me smile as I thought of all the boreholes I had dug in CryptoWallet's supposed security. If Paul was right, and I landed CryptoWallet as an initial client, my new business would be off and running. Paul and I even brainstormed before coming up with the perfect name for my new shop: Fogbank Consulting.

As exciting as that was, it couldn't begin until the current chapter in my life was closed. And so, I waited.

Just after lunch—a meal I was beginning to enjoy again for the first time in months—my phone rang. It was naptime at the Storyteller Children's Center, and if I was going to hear from Cricket during her workday, this was the moment when those calls would ring through.

"Would you kindly tell your FBI friends that if they want to talk to me, they can just walk up and say hello?" she asked.

"What in the world are you talking about, Cricket?"

"Your pals in the Sprinter van?" she clarified. "They're parked across the street from Storytellers like they're on a stakeout."

I shook my head incredulously. The FBI was dotting i's and crossing t's to take down Cyrus Wimby. They weren't staking out my wife. "Santa Barbara is filled with Sprinter vans," I challenged. "You're con—"

"No," she interrupted. "I am not confused. I have a pirate's monocular from the dress-up bin trained on them as I speak. This town might have more than its share of Sprinters, but absolutely none of them are driven by dudes wearing suits."

She had me there. "Just go out and ask them what they are

doing," I suggested. "Agent Andrews, Agent Smith, and Agent Green. I'm sure it's—"

"No," she again interrupted. I heard the rustle of her hair; she was shaking her head. "I'm not going out there, Hollis. Something isn't right."

Cricket—whose intuition was the airbag in my careening car—was warning me of a feeling in her gut, and in true tin-eared fashion, I was set to dismiss it. Thankfully—before I could say something patronizing like *don't be silly*—the doorbell rang.

Though I didn't recognize the faces, I spied navy blue suits and serious expressions through the front door's sidelight windows: more FBI agents. I wanted to throw the door open and scream hallelujah. Instead, I put the phone back to my ear and relayed the news to Cricket. "It looks like the FBI is watching over both of us, dear. They just rang our doorbell."

"Ask them why they've got agents outside the Storyteller Children's Center, okay?" she pleaded. "I do not have a good feeling."

"Of course." I chuckled, moving to greet my visitors. "I'll let you know."

Two new agents stood outside my door that afternoon, a man and a woman. As with Agents Andrews, Smith, and Green, they flashed their bifold wallet credentials and introduced themselves.

The first to speak was Agent Quinton: brown eyes, a putting green of brown hair, and a brown tie. Lean and angular, he looked like a cross-country runner. His suit was navy but not nearly as tailored as the ones worn by Agent Andrews and crew. He looked nice. He looked professional. He looked somewhat like me.

Agent Quinton introduced his colleague, Agent Randall, who remained mute. Agent Randall was a five-foot-two African American woman with piercing obsidian eyes and a magnificent explosion of curly hair. She offered no smile; her arms were already folded over her chest as if she anticipated being underwhelmed. Physically, she was the polar opposite of Agent Smith from my last batch of FBI visitors, but she was no less intimidating.

I said hello, shook the only hand offered—Agent Quinton's—

and led the two agents around the house to the gar-office. Now a veteran of FBI visits, I scanned the street as we walked, noticing the all black Chevrolet Suburban parked across the street and yet another agent standing outside the vehicle. I thought back to Agent Andrews and crew, with their P90X muscles, natty suits, and Mercedes Benz Sprinter now parked outside Cricket's place of work. That must have been the advance guard, I reasoned; this was the cavalry. Though, what did I know? Other than what I had seen on the silver screen, the answer was not much.

As before, I made the gar-office as hospitable as possible, finding and dusting off a second folding chair for my two visitors. We all took our seats; I smiled, waiting for my update.

"Appreciate you talking with us, Mr. Crawford," Agent Quinton said.

"Of course." I assumed there would be many more meetings to come until the Cyrus Wimby affair could be filed away.

"We just have a few questions," Agent Quinton said, flipping through a manila folder until he found what he was looking for and holding it up for my viewing pleasure. "Have you seen this man before?"

I cocked my head slightly, examining the black-and-white photo. My mouth went slack.

"Maybe this picture will jog your memory," Agent Quinton said, holding up a second photo of the man, this time taken in front of my home with yours truly standing next to him.

The photographed man was Vlad: menacing, didn't-know-where-Cyrus-lived Vlad.

"How did...?" I started, then stopped.

"Do you know this man?" Agent Quinton repeated.

"Yes," I said. "Well, I mean, I have met him," I clarified. "Obviously, right. There I am in a picture with him." I chuckled uncomfortably as my mouth went sandpaper dry.

"*How* do you know this man?" Agent Quinton said, filing away his photos.

"Well," I stammered. "He approached me in front of my

house one day. It was a few months ago. I had never seen him before. He told me that his name was Vlad and that he was looking for my boss. And then I told him that I was on my way to see my boss, so he told me to get in his car and he would drive us both over there." My nervous recollections sounded like the sort of sloppy story my children would tell. *Stay calm, Hollis*, I told myself. *These guys are on your team.*

Agent Quinton turned to Agent Randall and nodded.

"Who is your boss?" Agent Randall asked, speaking for the first time. Unfortunately for me, her voice was as piercing as her eyes.

"Are you kidding me?" I said with a nervous laugh. Surely Agent Andrews had given the rest of the FBI team the backstory along with my dossier on Cyrus, right? Why were we repeating things? Did they just need to hear me validate prior information? What a waste of time. "Look, I appreciate the need to be thorough," I said. "But I think if you'll go back and read—"

"It's actually a really easy question," Agent Randall interrupted. "But if you'd rather be cute about it, we can move on. I really don't care."

I raised my hands in surrender. "I am sorry. I wasn't meaning to—"

"How does your boss know Vladimir Petronovski?" Agent Randall again interrupted.

I flinched. Not that Vlad's full name meant anything to me, but the full ring of it was ominous. "Well, I'm not certain, but Cyrus—Cyrus Wimby, that's my boss's name—Cyrus made it sound like he and Vlad had been business partners before," I said. "Vlad was in town to get an update on the business I was involved in: ExOh Holdings."

"I see," Agent Quinton said. "So, were you present during their meeting?"

"I was only there for the beginning," I said. "I was dismissed; Cyrus sent me home."

"Is this you exiting that meeting, approximately ten minutes after you arrived?" Agent Randall said, flashing yet another eight-by-ten black-and-white photo.

My forehead wrinkled. "Yes," I said. "Where did you get these photos?"

Agent Randall filed the photo away without answer. "What do you know about Vladimir Petronovski, Mr. Crawford?"

Why were they asking about Vlad? He certainly seemed like a shady character, but shouldn't they be asking me about Cyrus? A creeping fusion of anxiety, fear, and bewilderment weighed on me like a stone. "I really don't know him at all," I protested. "Somehow you guys have found photographs that bookend the only time I ever met him; what are the chances of that?" Another nervous laugh. "We have never communicated other than that brief ten-minute period, and Cyrus didn't tell me anything about their meeting other than what I've already relayed. That's it; that's all I know."

The agents again looked at each other, communicating in silent head nods and subtle twitches just as Agents Andrews and Smith had. They must teach this code at FBI school, I thought. Agent Quinton went back to his manila folder and pulled out four more photos. "Do you recognize any of these men?"

I examined the photos one at a time. Three of the four were hard-looking men, reminiscent of Vlad. Thankfully, I had never seen any of them before. The fourth sent a shiver down my spine.

"This one," I finally said when my voice returned. "I don't know his full name. I only know him as Landon. He was introduced to me as Cyrus's longtime friend and was set to be the chief executive officer of ExOh." I paused. "But he died in a surfing accident, and then Cyrus asked me to take that job."

Agent Randall snorted and shook her head. "Surfing accident?"

"Yes," I asserted weakly. "I was one of the people who found his body on the beach."

"Sure, sure," Agent Randall said. "One hundred percent accident." She stood and moved to examine my gar-office in more detail. Not that there was anything to hide, but the naked exposure of a stranger rifling through my things made me uncomfortable. Even if my things were flat-tired bicycles and old garden equipment.

"What is your relationship with Cyrus...Wimby, was it?" Agent Quinton asked.

*Wimby, was it?* Was this guy joking? Was I supposed to believe that the last name of the chief bad guy had escaped his memory? I swallowed my frustration and smiled. "I work for Cyrus Wimby. I'm the chief executive officer of ExOh Holdings," I said. "At least for a little while."

Agent Quinton cocked his head. "You expect your employment to terminate?"

"I don't see how that can be avoided," I said with another nervous laugh. "Do you?"

The agents looked at each other quizzically; Agent Randall retook her seat.

"How long have you worked for Cyrus Wimby?" Agent Quinton asked.

At this question, I likely rolled my eyes. Granted, rolling your eyes at a pair of FBI agents is unlikely to be well received, but it happened reflexively. As before, I had already answered this question with Agent Andrews. Replowing old fields was a waste of all our time. I hoped we could jump through this validation exercise quickly and get on to new material. "Six months," I said.

"And tell me about your company," Agent Quinton continued. "What does ExOh Holdings do?"

I sighed. Dumb move.

"Do you have a problem?" Agent Randall asked as much with her eyes as her voice.

I shook my head. "I'm sorry. It's just—with all due respect—we've been over this already."

Agent Quinton looked at his partner; Agent Randall shrugged. "We have?"

"Well," I backtracked, "not me and *you*, we. But with Agent Daniel Andrews and his partner Agent Smith."

Agent Randall reclined, crossing her arms over her chest. Agent Quinton, meanwhile, leaned forward, elbows on knees, his hands clasped in prayer. My heart began to gallop.

"Tell me about Agent Daniel Andrews," Agent Quinton said.

My eyes darted pleadingly from one agent to the other. "Agent Daniel Andrews?" I repeated as if the problem was that they had not heard me correctly. "Of the FBI? He's the head of the Global Trade Surveillance unit, has a master's degree from Cornell...is a guest lecturer at Harvard. He's kind of short. Very handsome. He looks like...like...like one of you, only a little better..." I heard my voice squeak, my confidence disappearing like water circling a bathtub drain.

Again, the agents consulted each other in their indecipherable, wordless language. Agent Quinton turned from his partner back to me and rested his chin on top of his clasped hands. "Here's the thing, Mr. Crawford. The FBI doesn't have a Global Trade Surveillance unit."

"And," Agent Randall added, "there is no Agent Daniel Andrews."

# Chapter Forty-Six

As I stared back at Agent Randall, her words—*there is no Agent Daniel Andrews*—ricocheted around my cranium. I decided that I needed clarification. "What do you mean?"

"I mean," Agent Randall said slowly, as if she were talking to a child, "that no one by the name of Daniel Andrews is an agent with the Federal Bureau of Investigation."

That was indeed clearer, I thought. "Then who was I talking with?" I asked the two agents.

Agent Randall shook her head pityingly.

"Your guess is as good as ours at this point," Agent Quinton said. "What did this Mr. Andrews want to speak with you about?"

I stared into my lap, trying to recall the shattered mirror of that meeting. "He was..." I jumped to my feet as my memory caught up with my newly augmented reality. "Call the police!" I yelled. "Call them right now! Agent Andrews—or whoever the hell he is—is stalking my wife as we speak!"

Agents Quinton and Randall eyed each other skeptically.

"I am not kidding!" I screamed. "She's in danger. She knew it, and I dismissed it. She called me like five minutes ago and said they were right outside her work. Please, PLEASE! Call the police now!"

Agent Quinton stood, whipped out his cell, and had the Santa Barbara police department on the other end of the line before I could reach full hyperventilation. He paced my gar-office, speaking with police dispatch while I trailed him, gushing names, addresses, and descriptions into his free ear.

"Mr. Crawford?" Agent Randall said, tugging me by the shoulder. "Let Agent Quinton take care of this, okay?" She beckoned me to retake my seat. "I know you're in a bit of shock, but the more you can tell us the better. So, again, what did this Mr. Andrews want to speak to you about?"

I sat, my hands shaking like I was operating a jackhammer. "He, uh," I began. "He...he wanted to talk about Cyrus Wimby. At first he said he was doing fieldwork, filling out the file."

"Filling out the file?" Agent Randall repeated.

"That's what he said," I pleaded. "But then he told me he knew all about Cyrus and the company and just needed my help filling in the missing details."

"Mm-hmm," Agent Randall said, unimpressed.

"He had a partner with him. Two, or maybe it was three guys," I continued. "There was an Agent Smith. Much bigger than Andrews but not as good-looking. He sat in on our meeting, but he never spoke. And then there was another one Andrews called Agent Green. He also looked like he was capable of squashing me. He never spoke either. Andrews sent him to the car. And I think..." I paused, remembering the shadow of a fourth person in the front passenger seat, "I think there was another person waiting for them in the Sprinter van. Someone who—just judging by their outline—seemed kind of small."

"Sprinter van?" Agent Randall asked.

"Yes."

"A Mercedes?" Agent Randall sighed, shaking her head. "That was your first clue, Mr. Crawford."

I dropped my head, feeling myself shrink under the growing realization that there was no end to my colossal mistakes.

"Cruiser is on its way, lights flashing, sirens blaring, Mr. Crawford," Agent Quinton said, returning to our makeshift huddle.

"Mr. Crawford was filling us in on his visit with the Village People," Agent Randall offered. "So, what did this Mr. Andrews want to know about your Cyrus Wimby?" she asked.

"He..." My voice cracked. "He was asking me about the work Cyrus was doing. About ExOh Holdings. And, I mean..." I swallowed hard, praying that I already knew the answer to my next question. "Cyrus Wimby is why you are here, right?"

Agent Randall shook her head and pushed out of her chair, returning to rummage through my things as if bored by my pathetic story.

"No," Agent Quinton said. "We're here because of Vladimir Petronovski. He is a—"

"A very bad guy," Agent Randall interjected from over her shoulder.

"Indeed," Agent Quinton confirmed. "We've been following up on various leads to re-create Petronovski's movements over the last five months, when he first entered, then fled, the United States. Relative to many of the bad guys we track, he is a bit of a mystery."

"We only know of you," Agent Randall added, "and the man you call Cyrus Wimby, through our reconnaissance efforts on Petronovski. You and Wimby are simply *persons of interest.*"

I must be misunderstanding them, I thought. *Ask again,* the densest part of my brain requested. *Maybe they will answer differently this time.* As if the FBI agents were Magic 8 Balls that just needed a good shake. "But...but you are here to arrest Cyrus Wimby, right?"

"Not yet," Agent Quinton said. "Should we?"

I buried my forehead in the palms of my hands. What had I done? Were fake Agent Andrews and his pals—if any of those names were real—good guys or bad guys? I had revealed all my double-crossing work to them. Work that minutes ago had been the crowning achievement of my life. Was Cyrus working for Petronovski, or was it the other way around? I was confused and simultaneously terrified.

"What did you share with Mr. Andrews?" Agent Quinton asked.

"I shared...everything," I admitted.

Agent Randall guffawed. "You shared *everything*, did you, Mr. Crawford? Let me guess. Did your boss create a hostile work environment? Does he tell off-color jokes within earshot of the ladies? Does he refuse to recycle?" She picked up my garden hoe. "Does he eat genetically modified vegetables?"

"Sarah," Agent Quinton said, "cut him some slack."

"Sure, no problem," Agent Randall said, setting the hoe back down. "I mean, Mr. Crawford here claims he had no idea that he is riding around town with a fugitive on Interpol's Red Notice list, but I'm sure he's got the goods on Cyrus Wimby." She turned her folding chair backward, then sat, crisscrossing her arms over the chair's back. "So, tell us, Mr. Crawford. Tell us all about your big, bad boss, Cyrus Wimby. Tell us *everything*."

The good news was that my initial intuition that Agent Randall and her piercing eyes would not be the most understanding of interrogators had proven correct. From my vantage *in the fog*, this was an astute observation; score plus one for me. Unfortunately, Agent Randall was now sitting three feet away from me and seething like a recently branded bull; minus one for me. My hands resumed their jackhammer shake as I turned from her glare to my computer and sent my dossier on Cyrus to the printer. "Cyrus Wimby is a con man," I began, forcing my voice to rise from shell-shocked whisper to something approaching confidence. "He is the mastermind of a global fraud that has bilked US investors of more than sixty-five million dollars. Through a network of thieving partners, he has stockpiled more than two hundred seventeen million dollars in a bank account in

Switzerland. I've tracked it all down and documented every counterparty, every transaction, and every account. That document"—I pointed to my wheezing printer—"spells out all the details."

Agent Quinton cocked his head and turned to his partner. "Don't know about you, Sarah, but that's a pretty good *everything* if you ask me."

Agent Randall grunted her approval just as Agent Quinton's mobile rang.

"Quinton," he answered, then listened. "Nothing?" He paused. "You checked inside?" Another pause, my heart pounding in my ear so loudly, I could barely hear him speak. "Thank you, Officer," he concluded, hanging up his phone.

My eyes opened to saucers.

"Whoever was watching your wife left the scene before the Santa Barbara police arrived," Agent Quinton said. "The officers checked inside and everyone—other than your wife—was blissfully unaware of the watchers. That is, right up until the cruisers screeched to a halt in front."

I exhaled and only then realized I'd been holding my breath since his phone rang. "So, everyone is safe; everyone's fine?" I asked, needing reconfirmation.

Agent Quinton nodded. "You wife reported that the Sprinter van hauled ass out of there seconds before she heard the police sirens."

I dropped my face into my palms. Once again, danger had been at my doorstep, and once again, I had smugly dismissed it. What might have happened had the *real* FBI not shown up at precisely this moment, alerting me to the unfounded lunacy of my assumptions? For a *smart* person, I was the dumbest man on planet Earth.

"I know you're reeling, Mr. Crawford, but stick with us, okay?" Agent Quinton said. "Time is of the essence."

I raised my head and nodded.

"You can prove this?" Agent Quinton asked. "The fraud, the millions, the bank accounts?"

"Yes," I said, turning back to my computer and launching CryptoWallet. My hands still shook, but seeing the FBI agents perk up at the prospect of evidence gave me some measure of hope that I could still redeem myself. "Once I infiltrated Cyrus Wimby's bank accounts," I began, pointing at my screen like a weatherman, "I linked them via this application so that they could be tracked more easily." With a few more keystrokes, my Crypto-Wallet began to repopulate. "There are eight bank accounts in total. He uses seven of the eight to distribute money, but this one"—I pointed to the Zurich account—"is where he keeps…"

My voice trailed to silence as I stared at the screen.

"What are we looking at here, Mr. Crawford?" Agent Quinton asked.

"There's a boatload of numbers on the screen," Agent Randall added, "but I don't see the honeypot."

I clicked refresh, hoping against hope that something would change. Again, the numbers filled the screen. The conclusion was the same.

"Speak, Mr. Crawford," Agent Randall said.

I tapped the screen, highlighting the Zurich account. "This account. As of last Friday, it had more than two hundred seventeen million dollars in it."

"And as of today?" Agent Quinton asked.

"It's…" I shook my head. "It's empty." The blood drained from my face as I slumped in my chair. *How can this be?*

Agents Quinton and Randall stood from their stooped positions. "That's a tad anticlimactic, don't you think?" Agent Randall said. Now it was Agent Quinton's turn to grunt in reply.

As I sat staring at my unchanging screen, I wondered how this situation could get any worse. I had enthusiastically linked up with a con man, I had burned through my retirement savings, my son had been gravely injured because of my association with said con man, I had naively turned over a trove of evidence to fake FBI agents, I had allowed my wife to be stalked by said fake FBI agents, and I had turned my back on the treasure chest long enough for the bad guys to steal it out from under me. It seemed like I had done all the damage I could do; the old trope *it is always darkest before the dawn* ran through my head just in time to give me a brief smile before I heard the crunch of gravel underfoot. The other FBI agent—the one that had been guarding the Chevrolet Suburban—was sprinting down my driveway, looking frantic.

"Agent Quinton," the new guy said. "The stakeout on Riven Rock."

*Riven Rock?* I thought. *Cyrus's house?*

"What about it?" Agent Quinton asked, still staring at my computer screen.

"I just received a message that four Santa Barbara County Sheriff's cruisers pulled through the gates."

That's the thing about the old *always darkest before the dawn* nonsense. It's misleading on two fronts. First, it's incorrect, at least as it pertains to the colloquial meaning of the word *dawn*. Setting aside the effects of moonlight, the moment during a given night when a particular point on planet Earth is at its darkest is when the sun is aligned one-hundred-eighty degrees from that point; the point's antemeridian. As the earth rotates and sunrise approaches, the sky gets lighter, not darker, even if imperceptibly so. Second, while the saying was coined to provide a ray of hope to those in despair, it naively suggests that humans can accurately distinguish degrees of darkness. For the most part, we cannot. Therefore, while present conditions may appear very *dark*, that observation is meaningless. It can always get much, much darker.

"Hell's bells," Agent Randall said, shaking her head. "Mr. Crawford? You're coming with us."

# Chapter Forty-Seven

Agents Quinton and Randall assigned their partner to babysit Trip—which he thought was incredibly cool—and loaded me into the back of the FBI's Chevy Suburban for a high-speed ascent through Montecito to the mansions of Riven Rock. Just before pulling away from my house, Agent Quinton flipped the in-dash switches activating the Suburban's lights and sirens. I pictured my neighbors rushing to their windows, iPhones in hand, sharing photos on the Nextdoor app captioned *what's going on at the Crawfords' house???* and *I always thought there was something strange about that Hollis. His poor wife and kids!*

As the Suburban blazed through town, Agent Randall shook her head, staring out her window at the diorama of Montecito daily life. The dog walkers, bicyclists, and joggers alongside Olive Mill Road returned her gaze, eyeing our speeding, cacophonous Suburban suspiciously. Ambulances and the occasional fire truck: these Montecito residents were accustomed to seeing around town. But the Suburban suggested something far more ominous. *Turn that hullabaloo down,* the furrowed brows of the pedestrians implored. *You've got the wrong town. Those things don't happen here.*

I used to think that too.

While the Suburban screamed externally, no one spoke inside the car's cabin. I sensed that the agents had some idea of what awaited us, but if so, they did not clue me in. Having proven myself to be easily suckered, maybe they just didn't trust me.

In a few breathtaking minutes, we were out front of the Wimby estate, parking on the edge of the street where a sidewalk would have been if Montecito had sidewalks. Sheriff's cruisers blocked the road in both directions, and an ambulance waited at the end of the driveway.

Beside the ambulance's bumper, two EMTs chatted with their hands in their pockets, watching the scene with the urgency of garden snails. The back doors of the ambulance were closed. There was no gurney set to wheel someone to care; no defibrillator ready to shock a heart back to life. They weren't even sporting a first aid kit. The EMTs had already examined what lay beyond the hedges and determined that there was nothing for them to do.

My heart skipped a beat. The idle ambulance, the indifferent EMTs, the sense that fate had already played its hand and won—it was just like the time Landon's body washed ashore at Hammond's Beach.

In a daze, I followed Agents Quinton and Randall as instructed. We made it through the gates before we were stopped by a sheriff's department officer, and I was told to wait out of earshot. Eventually, the local cop made a call on his walkie-talkie, and suddenly I was being waved to the front lines. If my heart was beating fast before, now it was sledgehammering the inside of my rib cage.

All around the property, a squadron of officers were zigzagging like kids on an Easter egg hunt. Agents Randall and Quinton escorted me silently, their expressions grim. Fear coursed through my veins like I was a real-life character in a horror movie, and whatever was inside the house might hurt me. It was a curious emotion given that I was surrounded by officers of the law equipped with guns. There was no reason for me to be afraid, but if someone had given me the chance to leave, I would have turned on a dime and sprinted.

We made it to the front door just as another local officer stepped out to meet and stop us. "What do the Feds want with this?" he asked.

Agent Randall looked around the local officer into the home's rambling foyer. She stepped back and shook her head. "*Want* isn't really the word," she said. "We have reason to believe that this incident is tied to a case we are working. I'm not really looking to have a big dick contest at the moment, but I think if you'll let us through, we might be able to help."

The officer jutted his chin at me. "Who is this?"

It was an obvious question. I was wearing an old pair of khakis, Sperry Top-Siders, and an untucked button-down oxford —obscenely casual by the standards of my escorts.

"Hollis Crawford," Agent Quinton offered. "He's a local; you don't know him?"

The officer shook his head.

For reasons that make no sense in retrospect, I felt ashamed that the sheriff's office and I were not on a first name basis. I was about to defend myself when the officer thought better of his answer. "Wait. Crawford? Are you related to Cricket Crawford?"

"She's my wife," I said.

He nodded. "You're good," he said to the agents and stood aside.

Saved once again by my better half's tireless ability to make friends and ingratiate herself. Absent her, I was as connected to this town as a transient in a tent.

Whatever perverse thrill I had at passing the front-door entrance exam evaporated once I crossed the threshold. I recognized the Wimbys' foyer in the way one recognizes classmates at a reunion: in pieces and then all at once.

Agent Quinton handed me a pair of latex gloves just like the ones he was donning himself.

"I won't touch anything. I promise," I said, my hands raised high.

"Just put them on," Agent Randall insisted. "You're like talking to one of my kids. Not everything is a negotiation."

The foyer was the Wimby home's hub. The left spoke led to the sunken library, where Cyrus and I had our meetings. To the right was a formal living room. Straight ahead was a wide wooden staircase leading to the second story's bedrooms and offices. Behind the staircase was a wall of ten-foot-tall, glass-filled sliding pocket doors that led to the patio, pool, and beyond. To the left of the staircase was a hallway that led diagonally to the kitchen, dining room, informal family room, and garage. Diagonally to the right was a two-bedroom, two-bath guest suite.

The foyer itself was normally outfitted like a luxurious waiting room. But this day, the couch, chairs, coffee table, grandfather clock, and low-slung antique bureau had been pushed back against the walls to make more room in the center for what can only be described as an *arena*. In the arena, under the massive empire chandelier, sat a single chair on bare wood floor.

I recognized the chair instantly, though I had never sat in it. It was from the Wimbys' formal dining room; a captain's chair with six-inch-wide armrests. Two other dining chairs were positioned on the side, directly in front of the grandfather clock and facing the center of the arena. Something was missing from the room, but I couldn't immediately identify it.

As I moved from the abstract to the specific, my vision played tricks on me. I took one step forward to regain my focus. Dots and squiggles danced in front of me. Was this what they called eye floaters? I took another step forward. The dots and squiggles stopped moving but did not disappear. I began to take another step forward, when Agent Randall's arm caught me in the chest.

"Stay out of the blood," she said.

*Blood?* Following her eyes, I looked down. There, below my hovering right foot, was a half circle of maroon, the flat side of the circle indirectly illuminating what was missing: the foyer's rug.

I stepped back, planting my once hovering foot safely on dry wood, and saw the dots and squiggles for what they were: sprays of blood. The room looked as if someone had placed a spin art machine in the center, set it on high, and unleashed a torrent onto the turntable. The missing Oriental rug revealed clean wood flooring, but beyond its former borders, the couch was soaked, the clock was showered, the walls were peppered.

"Step over," Agent Randall advised, calling me to approach the chair at the center of the arena.

I followed her instructions in the exaggerated fashion of someone afraid of nicking a tripwire. The chair loomed, seeming larger now that I had crossed the rug's imaginary boundary. Below it sat a tangle of blood-smeared rope and wads of gray duct tape. On the chair's wide, flat armrest were several bloody tubes, each nearly three inches long. One of the tubes had a ridge around it that winked in the light from the chandelier.

"What's that?" I said, my voice a hair above a whisper.

Agent Randall pulled a pencil from the breast pocket of her jacket and rearranged the tubes until I saw clearly what they were: dismembered fingers.

I shuddered, my mind harkening back to Landon's nine-fingered corpse on Hammond's Beach. "Those are Cyrus Wimby's fingers," I said.

"How can you be sure they are his?" Agent Randall asked.

"Cyrus had really long fingers," I said.

Agent Randall chuckled morosely. "Indeed, he did. Some men would call that six inches." She continued to pick at the ridge on one segment of the finger, until a crust of blood flaked off, revealing what lay underneath. "Do you recognize that ring?" she asked.

I nodded, remembering how Cyrus used to spin the ring around his finger when he was lost in thought. "It's Cyrus's wedding band."

"Very good," Agent Randall said.

"There's more," I said. "Remember the photograph you showed me of the man I identified as Landon?"

"The surfing accident?" she said, one eye closed suspiciously.

I nodded. "When we found Landon on the beach, he was missing a finger too."

She shook her head. "No one thought that was strange?"

I returned the shake. "They thought he'd snagged his finger on the reef, and that's what held him under."

Agent Randall rolled her eyes. "Well, I think we can label that theory as debunked, don't you?"

I nodded.

"However, combining this here"—she continued, tapping the segmented digits with her pencil—"with your memory of Landon's quote unquote accident creates a meaningful piece of intel." She paused to smile. "The Petronovski clan has a finger fetish."

I clinched my fists as if my own fingers were at risk.

All around us, men and women scurried, looking for ports of entry, gathering suspicious objects, marking all areas where a drop of blood appeared beyond the devastating spray pattern in the foyer. The two other chairs—positioned as a macabre audience—had slashed lengths of rope and duct tape below them as well, but far fewer splashes of blood.

"Why do you think these chairs are cleaner?" I asked.

Agent Randall looked up from a squat position by the center chair and answered with the confidence of someone who had seen it all before. "Because people were sitting there," she said. "The blood landed on the witnesses instead of the chairs."

I closed my eyes again. Was this where Genevieve and Priscilla sat? Were they tied up here? Were they sprayed with his blood? Were they forced to watch as Cyrus was tortured to death?

Agent Quinton appeared from one of the back hallways. "Sarah," he hollered. "This way."

I followed as well, afraid to be left alone with the now empty chairs.

"The drag pattern is through here," Agent Quinton said, pointing to the kitchen tile. I couldn't see what he saw until I was at the far end of the room with the sunlight striking the tile from the opposite direction. Even on clean floors, the smudge of something heavy being dragged across the floor was evident.

"Through the garage," I heard Agent Quinton say from the garage. This drag pattern was easier to spot; the garage had a layer of light brown dirt with a swept path through it.

"Through the drive," Agent Quinton continued, walking farther ahead on the driveway gravel, now trenched under the weight of the dragged object. "To a car waiting here," he said, stopping at the end of the trench.

"No blood trail though," Agent Randall said. "Mr. Crawford? Did there used to be a rug back there at the foot of the stairs?"

The missing rug. I nodded.

"So, this is definitely a murder scene," Agent Randall said. "You don't roll a living man into a rug and drag him through the house."

Agent Quinton nodded in agreement. "So, the working theory is that they rolled the victim's body into the rug, dragged it to here, loaded it into their escape vehicle, then departed." He tapped his chin with an index finger.

"What about Genevieve and Priscilla?" I interjected.

"Wimby's family?" Agent Randall asked.

"Yes," I said. "His wife and daughter. Do you...?" I didn't want to finish the question, but I had to. "Do you think they were the ones sitting in those other chairs?"

She nodded. "Stands to reason. Those chairs were positioned to force someone to watch what was happening."

Even though I had feared this, hearing Agent Randall voice it made me shudder.

"No evidence of them thus far," Agent Quinton said. "Perhaps they were taken separately?"

My eyes gravitated toward the gravel trench, imagining the

Oriental rug holding Cyrus's lifeless, bloody body, dragged and then heaved into the back of some windowless van. I thought of Genevieve and Priscilla: Were they bound and gagged? Were they watching? Were they loaded into the van as well, forced to sit alongside their dead husband and father? The surrounding gravel glinted a rainbow of sparkles back at me, but something larger caught my eye. I bent to examine it. "Agent Quinton," I called. "I, uh…I think this is your evidence."

Agent Randall joined me, using her pencil to lift what I had found: a baby-blue and red Rainbow Loom friendship bracelet with white Perler beads. "You recognize this?" she asked.

"It was Priscilla's," I said. "She made one just like it for my son."

Agent Randall nodded—noting my ashen color—and patted my shoulder.

"Okay," Agent Quinton said. "So, it looks like our escape vehicle likely contained the entire Wimby family. The father—presumed dead—and the mother and daughter—possible kidnapping victims."

Agent Randall turned to me: "Do you know if Mr. Wimby had security cameras?"

I nodded. "He put them in a few months ago, right after Vlad showed up the first time." I ran down the driveway to the gate with its entry keypad and hidden camera. "It's right…here." I pointed to what was once a security camera and was now a scattering of broken plastic and wires on the ground.

"Any more cameras?" Agent Randall asked.

I led them to the camera in Cyrus's office; it, too, was in pieces.

"I assume he kept his computer here, right?" Agent Randall said, pointing to the empty desk.

I nodded.

"We'll get the techies involved and see if we can track down any online footage," Agent Randall said before heading back downstairs.

I stayed behind. The last time I'd been in this office was the day I discovered the RemoteToken fobs. Had they been returned to their original resting place when Cyrus came back from Fiji? Against any reasonable logic, I wanted to believe that the scene one floor below was a random act of horrific violence, unrelated to my divulgences to fake FBI agent Daniel Andrews. I slid my latex-covered pinkie under the drawer handle, praying it would be locked, its RemoteTokens safely inside. For an instant, I felt the drawer resist, sending my selfish hopes soaring. Then the resistance gave way and the door glided open revealing its vast emptiness. The fobs were gone.

I exited Cyrus's office just as two other officers exited the Wimbys' master bedroom. For whatever reason—perhaps the latex gloves—they breezed by me without acknowledgment. In their wake, I could smell Genevieve's star jasmine perfume, a scent cloud stirred by the passage of bodies. Across the stairway landing lay Priscilla's room, an explosion of pink paint and a large, framed photo of her horse, Rosaland.

A fresh burst of nausea blossomed in my stomach. Maybe Cyrus had earned some degree of retribution through his treachery, but not this. And maybe Genevieve had turned a blind eye when she shouldn't have, but I didn't see her as complicit. But Priscilla? She deserved none of this. And who did the Wimbys have to thank for the turning tide that brought this fresh hell to their doorstep? It was hard for me to feel anything other than directly responsible.

I made my way back down the wide stairs on gimpy knees. Not thirty minutes earlier, I was gut punched at the thought that my tipping off the fake FBI agent had led to yet another theft. If only it had just been money. Now, standing in the home of my former boss, it was impossible not to see a direct line between my mistake, the torture and death of Cyrus Wimby, and the abduction of his wife and child. Even when I tried to do the right thing, I screwed it up.

Agents Quinton and Randall called me into an initial Q and

A with the Santa Barbara County Sheriff's office. The sheriffs were stumped. They suspected robbery but found no evidence of missing property.

"The cars, the jewelry, the artwork, it's all here. I found five hundred dollars at the top of a sock drawer," one of the sheriff's deputies quipped. "If this is a robbery, it's the sloppiest robbery I've ever seen."

"It *is* a robbery," Agent Quinton said, "but not the kind you were expecting."

"Mr. Crawford?" Agent Randall said. "Can you fill these guys in on the two hundred seventeen million reasons why someone would want to torture and kill Cyrus Wimby?"

So, for the second time that day I presented the abridged story of Cyrus Wimby's con operation to a panel of law enforcement officials.

"Why did they need to kill him?" one of the officers asked, looking pained. There weren't many murders in Santa Barbara County and certainly not gruesome scenes like this one.

"Well, um..." I cleared my throat. "They needed Cyrus's cooperation to get the money out of the Zurich account." Yes, I said *cooperation*. I cannot recall a less accurate euphemism.

"Given what we know, it's also likely that there was some double-crossing and misleading between Mr. Wimby and his assailants," Agent Randall added. "These people do not let that sort of behavior slide."

When I finished, the officer from the sheriff's department who had greeted our crew at the front door and challenged our right to be on premises turned to Agent Quinton and said, "We look forward to handing this case over to the Feds as soon as you guys are ready."

I passed around my contact information to the sheriff's crew in case they had follow-up questions, and the FBI agents agreed to take me home.

Agent Quinton sat with me in the back seat, he on the phone and me in silence. When we pulled up in front of my house, he put away his phone and turned to me. "Tomorrow morning, my best forensic accountant will be here from DC," he said. "We are going to take that report of yours apart, paragraph by paragraph, and begin the hunt."

This was my moment to exit the Suburban, but instead I sat, burying my head in my hands. I wanted to get as far away from this day as possible, yet I didn't want to enter my house and face my family.

"Hey," Agent Randall said from the front seat. "That was messed up back there, but it wasn't your fault."

I lifted my head and nodded reluctantly.

"Agent Randall is correct," Agent Quinton said. "It's foolish to blame the spark for the explosion."

I nodded again. "Thank you," I whispered.

"Bright and early tomorrow, Mr. Crawford," Agent Randall said just before I shut the Suburban's door. "Try to get some sleep."

# Chapter Forty-Eight

By the grace of the Almighty, Isabel and Trip were asleep when I walked in our front door. I didn't have the mental strength to explain what I'd witnessed to my children; I was still struggling to explain it to myself. I knew that my reprieve would be counted in mere hours, but that was better than seconds.

Cricket was, of course, waiting for me and answering texts from roughly a thousand friends who had heard *something* and were concerned; Montecito is a small town, after all. I threw myself at her, hugging her so hard she asked me to let go. But I couldn't let go, and I couldn't stop apologizing for dismissing her warning about the Sprinter van stakeout.

She held my head between her hands. "Honey? I swear: It's okay."

This only made me hug her harder.

She wanted the complete download, but before I could begin, I begged to stand in a scalding shower for ten minutes. I have never needed to scrub my skin clean quite so badly. If only I could have scrubbed my eyes, too.

Pink from the shower, I climbed into bed. "What have you heard?" I asked.

"No one knows anything," she said, "other than that something really bad must have happened."

*Something really bad*, was a good CliffsNotes summary, but I wasn't going to get away with brevity. "Remember the FBI agent who you joked was a Jehovah's Witness?" I asked.

"Yeah?"

"Well, he wasn't either of those things."

She cocked her head and squinted.

"Exactly," I said.

From that perplexed expression, I began my story, rewinding to Landon and his missing finger all the way through Cyrus and his summarily detached ones. Even the most exotic fantasies from the Montecito rumor mill had paled in comparison to the truth. Cricket's facial expressions ranged from wide-eyed shock to sour-lemon disgust. She knew far more truth about the Wimbys than the rest of Montecito, but even for her, the events of the day were impossible to process. The incongruity of it challenged the brain to construct alternate hypotheses, each one wilder than the next.

*But maybe...*

*Do you think...?*

*What if...?*

Unfortunately, these were impossible wishes; I had seen, and nearly stepped in, the blood of truth.

"What happens now?" she asked as midnight came and went.

"The FBI will be back here tomorrow morning to go through everything," I said.

She shook her head. "I'm so sorry, Hollis."

I kissed her forehead. "What in the world do you have to be sorry for?"

She laughed sweetly. "I have no idea," she admitted, "but I certainly *feel* sorry."

"You and me both," I said.

"Hey," she said, sitting up and pulling my chin to face her directly. "This isn't your fault either, Hollis."

"Okay," I mumbled.

"What are we going to tell..." she began, pausing for a tonsil-viewing yawn, "...the kids?"

"I don't know," I admitted. "I mean, I can't lie to them. Then again, I don't think I need to burden them with the gruesome details. This will be hard for Trip to understand, especially considering all he's been through and his friendship with Priscilla. But I don't want to be one of those parents who assume their kids can't handle the realities of the world. I'm thinking that maybe—"

Cricket's first slight snore interrupted my stream-of-consciousness rambling. I nodded to myself; even this unbelievable story had a time limit. Whatever the right answer, hopefully it would occur to me in the morning.

# Chapter Forty-Nine

I WAS unable to heed Agent Randall's warning to get some sleep. In fact, as I lay in the dark, staring at the ceiling, it occurred to me that I might never sleep again. A disaster had occurred, but given that the fake FBI agents had also been stalking Cricket, it could have been so much worse: It could have been *my* disaster. Suffering something between a cocaine high and a tainted trip, I tossed and turned until the first crack of sunlight freed me from the burden of further pretending.

I was in the kitchen making coffee when Isabel and Trip cornered me for an explanation of the previous day's events.

"The police don't really know what happened," I began, choosing my words carefully. "It looks like Mr. Wimby was hurt."

"Badly?" Isabel asked.

I cleared my throat. "Yes," I said, holding fast to honesty as long as I could.

"What about Priscilla?" Trip asked.

*Keep to the script,* I reminded myself. "We don't know, Trip. Priscilla wasn't there. Her mom was not there either." This response was technically true, even if it was woefully inadequate.

"Where did they go?" Isabel asked.

"We don't know that either," I began before breaking my

string of technical truths and embracing a lie. "I think they may have just decided to leave Montecito." I counted this as a white lie that did more good than harm. My kids feared the prospect of kidnapping more than death, and I didn't want to inspire nightmares of mothers and children being snatched from gated homes.

"Is Priscilla okay?" Trip asked, his eyes moist.

I bent over his chair and palmed the back of his head. I wanted so badly to assure him that she was fine. That Priscilla and her mom were on some great adventure, having fun, eating cotton candy, seeing the world. But I couldn't make the words come out. "I hope so, Trip."

A knock at the front door signaled that my family time was over. It was 7:15 a.m.; these guys were not joking about bright and early.

"Who are they?" Trip asked.

"They are the guys who will find Priscilla and her mom," I said. "And I'm going to help them." Trip broke into a wide smile: his dad the hero! Unfortunately, this only made me feel worse.

I greeted Agents Quinton and Randall plus two fresh faces on the front porch and led them back to my gar-office. No one batted an eye at the conditions, which made me far less self-conscious. Agents Quinton and Randall brought a folding table from the back of the Suburban and a few extra chairs. Suit jackets came off, sleeves were rolled up, and everyone got to the grim task of chasing murderers and thieves.

The work began with a whiteboard: Who were the players? I organized them into insiders—a group that included Cyrus and the quartet of Umed, Kai, Noah, and Reuben—agents—principally ExOh's stockbrokers, CPA, and rubber-stamp lawyer—and outsiders: the company's investors.

"Have Larry, Curly, and Moe heard the news?" Agent Randall asked, referring to Umed, Kai, Noah, and Reuben.

"I...I don't know," I admitted.

"We're not off to a good start here, Mr. Crawford," Agent Randall said.

"How did you communicate with them?" Agent Quinton asked, trying a different approach.

"By..." I cleared my throat, instinctively embarrassed at what I would say next. "By BatSignal."

Agent Randall tossed her pencil in the air and dropped her head, defeated.

To prove that I was not referring to the actual-yet-fictional Batman, I whipped out my phone, opened the BatSignal app, and typed out a message to the team: *Have you heard the news?*

BatSignal promptly informed me that the accounts of everyone except Cyrus and me had been deleted.

"Interesting," Agent Randall said. "We'll put a pin in that and revisit later."

Agent Quinton shook his head. "This is all well and good, but the most important name is not on your whiteboard, Mr. Crawford. Where does VIP fit into this?"

"*VIP?*" I asked, the distant chime of familiarity echoing in my head.

"Vladimir Ignat Petronovski," Agent Randall said. "The worst of your bad guys."

"VIP," I repeated, my eyes fixed to the floor. "There was a..." I began, turning from the table to rifle through my trusty manila folders for the slip of paper that suddenly seemed like a smoking gun. "Back in June," I continued, "Cyrus came up with this crazy transaction where he had ExOh purchase a controlling stake in his wine business. The price was one million dollars, and I was the one who wired the money." I found the piece of paper I was looking for and waved it like a flag. "Cyrus told me to wire the money to this bank account in Bermuda: an account for VIP Partners LLC. He said it was his personal account, but now I'm thinking...maybe not." I handed the paper to Agent Randall. She examined it, then passed it to Agent Quinton; they shared a knowing nod.

"Your friend Cyrus must have been in very deep, Mr. Crawford," Agent Randall said. "One million dollars typically buys a man a pretty long leash. But in this case, it bought Cyrus Wimby less than three months."

I shook my head, recalling the moment when Cyrus handed me the slip of paper instructing me to wire the $1 million dollars. It happened on the day of our first meeting post Vlad's ominous visit—the visit that included my riding shotgun in Vlad's Mercedes. Cyrus had seemed so calm when discussing Vlad, dismissing my obvious skittishness like a parent who laughs away a claim of monsters under the bed. Damn, Cyrus was good, or—at least—he had been good. He had redirected my legitimate questions of him into my own self-reproach and personal doubt. It was textbook gaslighting, and I was Cyrus's rube.

"Well," Agent Quinton said, "now we've confirmed what we already believed." He stood from his folding chair and began ripping chunks of pages from my heavy-duty-stapled dossier on Cyrus. "Let's go get these guys."

He passed the subsections of my report around the gar-office, assigning me to work principally with the forensic accountant, Agent Willows, a forty-nine-year-old former CPA who had worked with Irving Picard, recovering the money stolen in Bernie Madoff's Ponzi scheme.

"Let's start by inventorying the known financial assets," Agent Willows suggested. "Is there anything beyond the bank accounts?"

I nodded. "Well, their home here in Montecito is worth at least ten million. On top of that, you've got the furniture, artwork and the three Porsches—"

"Hold it right there," Agent Willows interrupted. "I've already been down that path. None of that is real."

My forehead accordioned. "Well, of course it's real. I mean—"

"Sorry," he interrupted again. "I mean, none of those assets are real assets of Cyrus Wimby. The house was rented fully furnished. The cars are leased."

My mouth hit the floor. *Rented? Leased?* Not that there was anything wrong with being a renter—I was one! But Cyrus had once specifically told me, *I bought a little home in your country*, and I was sure I wasn't the only one to hear this tale. Besides, like everyone else, I had looked it up on Zillow. "I think you're mistaken," I argued. "The house was sold just a few months before I first met Cyrus, and it was never listed for rent."

"True," Agent Willows acknowledged. "But I spoke with the real owners—a Chicago man and his wife. They purchased the home as a winter getaway, then received an unsolicited offer for a one-year lease at an astronomical rate. Wimby graciously offered to keep the deal private so that the owner wouldn't have to pay any taxes. That's why it never showed up in the public record."

Among all the other more meaningful lies, there's no reason this one should stand out, but it did. I had complimented his pizza oven—*we modeled it on one we saw in Venice*—his tapestries —*found them at a fantastic bazaar in Morocco*—his putting green —*I had it shaped like the fourteenth at Pinehurst*—and his pool —*it was designed to match my family home on the outskirts of Riyadh*—and he accepted my flattery as if earned. The success of these lies was made possible by Montecito's tall-hedge obsession with privacy. Cyrus had approached a completed masterpiece and made up his own backstory, and we all believed it because we had no evidence to the contrary and no reason to look askance. "You're kidding me," I finally choked out.

"Cyrus Wimby's only interest in those assets is the security deposit," Agent Willows said, "and I think it's safe to say he's going to forfeit that."

"Okay, well," I restarted. "Cyrus has a house in Fiji. I sent a package there this summer. I have the address—"

He shook his head before I finished. "That was a VRBO."

"Uh..." I searched my memory for more. "They moved here from Paris. Cyrus told me they have a house in the 16th arrondissement."

Agent Willows pursed her lips.

I stared blankly in my own lap. Cyrus Wimby's flaunted hard assets were all fakes. Just like his business. Just like his life.

"Let's focus on the bank accounts, then," Agent Willows said. "Walk me through how you gained access."

I shook my head to clear it, refocusing on the only assets that remained. As soon as I explained how I used the RemoteToken serial numbers, Agent Willows jumped through five derivatives of questions and explanations to the punchline: "Wait a minute! You hacked their server? That thing is like Fort Knox, and I know because I've been to Fort Knox." For the first time in my life, I felt like a rock star, albeit a very gullible one.

Agent Willows and I started from the top of the funnel, picking apart each transaction and payee, beginning with the Miramar account controlled by me. As the money moved from the US to Hong Kong, we examined each side transaction and the curiously named private corporations receiving payment. The research I'd done identifying the owners of the accounts was "helpful," Willows said—a verbal pat on the head—but he assured me that the FBI could tap resources that would peel the onion all the way back to its bulb.

With each bank—the limbs of a tree—Agent Willows unpacked the nuances for my benefit. It was like listening to the New York Philharmonic live instead of on cheap iPhone earbuds. I was taking a crash course in the art of money laundering and finally understanding why Cyrus and friends had arranged their labyrinth this way. Agent Willows emphasized two rules in his explanation. First, a bank account with no money in it raises no suspicion. Second, banks and regulators move like sloths: If you move the money fast enough, they don't even see it.

Under that rubric, Cyrus's setup was perfect. His seven feeder accounts almost never carried balances overnight: check. And when money moved, it sprinted: check. The Zurich account—based in secretive Switzerland, where billionaires the world over stored their pocket change—was the perfect place to hide in plain sight. That is, until I found it.

After pruning all the branches of the tree, we finally reached the trunk: the Zurich account. The last time I viewed this account through my CryptoWallet, I was so stunned to see the zero balance that I had not registered *where* the money had gone. But now, with Agent Willows by my side, the rest of the picture became clear. On the morning Agents Quinton and Randall appeared at my doorstep, all $217 million and change had been wired to an account at Bank Sepah.

"Bank Sepah?" I asked.

Agent Willows nodded. "Iran," he said, then grabbed his phone to start making calls.

*Iran?* Before this moment, I would have failed to accurately identify Iran on a globe. Now the name was being thrown around my gar-office as casually as the agents were throwing back coffee. It is embarrassing to admit this, but I felt like I had finally been invited to have lunch at the cool kids' table.

With Agent Willows calling in global favors, I sat down with Agent Quinton for a full debrief of my meeting with the man I now knew to be Vladimir Petronovski. I managed to keep it a secret that I almost peed myself that day, but I don't think my limited observations shed much light on the FBI's principal target.

With the FBI's prodding, we pored over my documents and memories for two days, teasing out the mundane and the potentially significant. My gar-office had never been more alive than in digging into the death of Cyrus Wimby.

Eventually, I had given them everything I had to offer; the remaining gaps would be filled with elbow grease and, more importantly, time. I can't believe I am saying this, but I didn't want them to leave. With the FBI camped out in my gar-office, I could pretend I, too, was a crimefighter and not an unemployed, ex-CEO of a bankrupt company who—according to the gossip around Montecito—may have played a part in ripping off Montecito's finest and then murdered my coconspirator.

Hours before the team packed up for good, Agent Willows got the call he had been waiting for regarding Bank Sepah.

"Is the money still there?" I asked when he hung up.

"Of course not," he said. "The account was liquidated three days ago."

"What country?" Agent Randall asked.

"Iran," I said, in my best *duh* accent, trying desperately to be part of the team.

"Wrong," Agent Willows said.

"But you said—" I argued.

"I said it was an Iranian bank, but that doesn't mean all the bank's branches are in Iran." He turned to Agent Randall. "Moscow," he said. "Liquidated in gold. Bank Sepah had to call in their reserves at the Bank of Russia."

My heart sank. The killers were lost to the winds.

"Specie!" Agent Randall said, excited. "Now we're cooking!"

My head swiveled back and forth between Agents Randall and Willows. "What?" I asked. "Why is converting the money to gold and removing it from the bank a good thing? Haven't we"— yes, I said *we*, so shoot me—"lost the ability to track the money now? They've gone underground."

"Fill your student in, Agent Willows," Agent Randall said.

Agent Willows smiled. "You are correct, Hollis. Now that the money has been withdrawn, we cannot track it anymore. But you need to remember that electronic currency is global—simultaneously everywhere and nowhere. Knowing the name of the bank the money resides in might help you get the money, but it probably won't help you get the bad guys."

"And don't be mistaken, Mr. Crawford," Agent Randall said. "I could give two bits about the money. I want the hombres. And now that they have cashed out—in gold, no less—they are anchored. Do you think they are carrying two hundred seventeen million in gold in their carry-on luggage?"

I shook my head.

"You're a fast learner, Mr. Crawford," Agent Randall said. "Indeed, they are not. So, the game just changed. No longer are we tracking bits and bytes; now we are tracking skin and bones. They just left your world, and they entered mine."

Like I said, I was at the cool kids' table.

The FBI agents continued packing their things while I made a few thumb drives of everything for them to take on the road to their next horror show. This was not the end, of course, but this was the end of the first phase. And, unfortunately, it was the end of my role. The bell had rung; lunch at the cool kids' table was over.

I walked the group to the Suburban and said my goodbyes, thanking them for all they had taught me and the patience they had shown.

"What's next for you, Mr. Crawford?" Agent Quinton said from the driver's-side window.

"I'm starting my own consulting shop," I said, proud that I had a plan and was voicing it.

"Agent Willows?" Agent Randall said. "You think you could use the services of Mr. Crawford here on an ad hoc basis?"

"From time to time," Agent Willows acknowledged.

"Sounds like we'll be in touch," Agent Quinton said, then pulled away.

# Chapter Fifty

When there is an oh-my-god, you-won't-believe-this story, I am not the guy folks normally think to run to for the inside scoop. And even in this bizarro moment—where I was actually the only Montecito citizen who both knew the Wimbys and had witnessed the scene on Riven Rock—it seemed that the town's elite gossips preferred to manufacture their own stories instead of speaking to me.

The *Santa Barbara Independent*, *Noozhawk*, and local ABC affiliate KEYT reported the few details provided by the Santa Barbara County Sheriff's Department: three family members missing from a "grisly" scene. This information void created a fascinating social science petri dish as alternate versions of the story competed for the public's ear:

The Wimbys were abducted by the Saudi royal family.

Cyrus murdered Genevieve over a suspected affair.

Genevieve killed Cyrus in self-defense after years of abuse.

Cyrus was bipolar; it was a murder-suicide.

Cyrus was in financial distress; he murdered his family, then killed himself.

Cyrus was in financial distress; he faked his own death.

A Chinese/Turkish/Russian assassin murdered them all.

For a family the Montecito community seemed to love and embrace, the Wimbys certainly didn't come out of these imagined stories sounding like innocent victims. I wondered what this said about the petri dish. Had there been a layer of latent suspicion from the beginning, or did people just enjoy sordid tales?

Within days, the story graduated from local news to national news. With the increased attention, the Santa Barbara County Sheriff's office warmed to providing more details on an unnamed source basis.

"Mysterious Cyrus Wimby Presumed Dead; Fortune Missing," read the headline in the *Los Angeles Times*.

"ExOh Holdings' Founder Murdered," read the *Wall Street Journal*. Within the article, the *Journal* softened their stance on the declaration of murder, but still managed to quote a loose-lipped sheriff's deputy, who said, "Given the volume of blood found on the scene, it is safe to say that Cyrus Wimby was tortured to death."

The cherry on top was a multipage article in the Sunday edition of the *New York Times* titled: "The Curious Case of Cyrus Wimby: Fraudster and Victim."

While the sheriff's office and FBI had yet to discover a body, common wisdom held that Cyrus Wimby was indeed dead. Genevieve and Priscilla were officially declared kidnapping victims, but with each passing day, hope that they were alive dwindled. The staff of Montecito Union Elementary made the on-campus counselor available for students who knew Priscilla and were struggling with processing her disappearance. On the subsequent Friday Flag day, the school had a special "memory moment" to honor Priscilla. Trip did not want to attend, but Isabel told us that it was beautiful.

Shocking as it was, this tragedy had a time limit on the psyche of Montecito. With the national news articles written and digested and no new leads from the sheriff's office or the FBI, the *Curious Case of Cyrus Wimby* slowly faded from conversation. At least, for those with the luxury of moving on.

# CHAPTER FIFTY-ONE

ExOh stock's final day of trading was the day Cyrus and family disappeared. I should have called the OTC and paused trading as soon as I discovered the scene on Riven Rock, but in the midst of everything else, I forgot. It was far from my largest sin. Ironically, not a single share traded on that final day—the stock opened and closed at $65.05. This lack of activity only went to underscore the smoke-and-mirrors role that the entities in the Caymans and Hong Kong had played manipulating ExOh's stock price. The rest of the investors had been passively enjoying the show from the comfort of their seats. Unfortunately, the light-hearted, rom-com movie they'd been watching was about to turn apocalyptic.

As erstwhile CEO of a soon-to-be bankrupt company with no other identifiable employees, I was the only sucker who could be tasked with nailing ExOh's coffin. I wrote the most anticlimactic, depressing press release in the history of press releases and filed the paperwork to officially delist ExOh's stock. The stock had already dropped to a single penny, but once it was delisted, it was no longer salable, even at that nostalgic price.

Cricket had warned her parents that their faith-based investment in me was gone. Nevertheless, I called them as well to explain. They were gracious in the face of their loss and assured me that they were okay. In that moment, I wished they would get angry, asking me things like *Why didn't you tell us?* and *How could you?* But they asked no questions other than inquiring about me and my health.

The answer to their unasked question was that I couldn't tell them without binding them in a catch-22. If they knew of my suspicions and sold their stock, they would have been guilty of insider trading, subject to financial penalties and criminal charges. In the battle of the rock and the hard place, losing money was the far better outcome.

If I were wishing for anger, though, I would soon get all of it I could handle. The first lawsuit arrived at my front door the following morning, filed by none other than John Colton. This irony was a hoot. I drove to Miramar Bank and Trust, and I showed John that he had been a signatory to every board resolution of ExOh Holdings. After screaming of hacks, scams, and forgeries—all truths, I was sure—he calmed down and informed me that he would be withdrawing his lawsuit provided that I move my personal bank account from Miramar Bank and Trust. I laughed; my current balance of $18,761 and change was happy to find a new home.

The next lawsuit came from Huff Monroe and included the investors he introduced to Cyrus. This one refused to go away quietly. The depositions were excruciating. In the absence of any evidence that I had profited from the admitted fraud, the lawyers attacked me personally.

*How could you not have known about...?*

*Why didn't you...?*

*Don't you think...?*

I felt like a sacrificial lamb before a congressional hearing.

At some bleary-eyed point in the process, stuck in the interior conference room of a Los Angeles law firm, I returned from the restroom to overhear Huff consulting with his lead attorney.

"Huff, the FBI has already declined to press criminal charges.

We can beat this idiot up all day long, but it's pretty clear he didn't orchestrate this fraud," Mr. Lead Attorney said.

"Can we sue him for being an idiot, then?" Huff asked.

"Unfortunately, no," Mr. Lead Attorney answered. "If stupidity were grounds for financial penalty, the poverty rate would be through the roof."

Truer words have never been spoken.

The lawsuits were over, but there were still indignities to be suffered. ExOh's rubber-stamp lawyer was suspended from writing any more *opinion* letters for publicly traded companies for a single year. He had been paid $50,000 for five minutes of work; I suspected that he greeted the suspension with a shrug and a grin.

ExOh's CPA was exonerated by the Securities and Exchange Commission based on the affidavit I had signed at Cyrus's begging. He had not received nearly as much compensation as the lawyer, so this felt karmically just.

Unfortunately, based on that affidavit and my position as both chief executive officer and a member of the board, I received the brunt of the Securities and Exchange Commission's ire. For the role I played, I received a permanent ban from serving on the board of directors of any publicly traded company. This ruling stung, even though the practical effect on my future career path was as impactful as the National Football League permanently banning me from playing quarterback.

As to my career path, I did not upgrade to LinkedIn Premium and apply to every job in Santa Barbara County. Instead, I followed my heart and formed Fogbank Consulting. It was easy enough to pay the $800 to the state of California and receive my brand-new taxpayer ID, but could I generate income? Could I build a business? Could I finally do right by my family?

We were all about to find out.

# Chapter Fifty-Two

In between my planning for Fogbank Consulting's launch, Trip and I would study reading, writing, and vowel sounds for one hour a day. It was hard, tedious work; Trip had to force his brain to memorize things that nondyslexic children internalized without thought. It was as if he had to dedicate part of his mental capacity to conscious inhaling and exhaling.

But with weeks of persistent practice under our belts—devoid of my foolish old mantra that we just needed to *work harder* —Trip made tremendous progress. It was clear he still hated the way reading aloud made him feel, occasionally getting frustrated to the point of an *I am so stupid* outburst, but he refused to let that feeling stop his progress.

A return to the second grade at MUS was around the corner, and with it, a less coddling audience. Again, I felt the sorrow of a parent who could not save his child from pain. For Trip to understand how far he had progressed—and return to school with the necessary confidence to fend off the devils of doubt—he needed to practice his ever-improving reading skills in front of anyone other than me. Thankfully, Cricket had just the group: the children of Storytellers.

As I parked in front of the modest one-story home on De La

Vina where Storyteller Children's Center was located and Cricket dedicated her days to children in need, my nerves tingled. Kids can be cruel, I knew. Even disadvantaged ones.

I unloaded Trip's wheelchair and helped him scoot from one seat to the next. Trip brought with him three of his favorite kids' books—books he had only recently mastered—and a plan to entertain for half an hour. Over my shoulder was a duffel bag stuffed full of toys that Trip wanted to donate to Storytellers. The apple does not fall far from the tree.

We entered the old home's white picket fence, wheeled up the ramp, and found Cricket in the living room, squatting beside a table of seven children and a pile of crayons. To the children of Storyteller's, she was Ms. Cricket. She wore a once-white apron stained with colorful paint and chalk and dye and food remnants. In the deep front pockets, she was known to carry small lollipops for children having particularly tough days.

Despite the inhospitable world confronting these children, their smiles were electric. They didn't behave as if the deck had been stacked against them. Instead, they seemed to understand that spending their days at Storytellers was a gift; a sign that perhaps good fortune had found them after all.

When I wheeled Trip into the Storytellers living room, his chair and half-body cast became instant attractions. The kids *ooh*ed and *aah*ed, wanting to examine the workings of the wheels and the brakes; asking if they could draw on Trip's cast. I saw relief and camaraderie spread across Trip's face; my nervousness melted away as well.

His first book was *There Is a Bird on Your Head!* After a few early stumbles, he hit his stride. The kids moved from crisscross applesauce to sitting on their knees to get a better look at the pictures.

His second book was *How I Became a Pirate.* He read this one flawlessly, adding his pirate accents to the appropriate parts. Unbeknownst to me, he had an eye patch in the front pocket of his shorts, and read the book wearing the eye patch; already, he was showing off.

His third book, his favorite when he was a kindergartner, was *The Book with No Pictures*. There is magic in the words *Blork, Bluurf,* and *Glug.* Trip hammed it up like a stage actor, and the children howled.

As Trip read, my eyes were drawn to Cricket, sitting with the other Storyteller teachers in a row of mini school chairs. As happy as I was for Trip—and I was beaming—it was Cricket for whom my heart felt the greatest joy. This day represented a union of her worlds: home and work, a synthesis of everything she loved most. I had promised to give her this and inadvertently done my best to snatch it away. For this failure, I was most grateful.

# Chapter Fifty-Three

Clyde Bostich, founder and CEO of CryptoWallet, had me wait in the company's glass-walled corner conference room for twenty-eight minutes. The old me would have steamed at the indignity; the new me was happy to be there. This *make 'em wait so they know who's important* schtick was as old as Abraham, but it was much harder to pull off in the tech world's standard office decor of limitless transparency. CryptoWallet's new digs, an upgrade to commemorate the $30 million equity raise, were an open play pit. The only walls were the clear glass ones separating the conference rooms. So, while Clyde made me wait, I watched him clear as day as he frittered away the twenty-eight minutes from his wall-less desk. He picked up his phone, typed on his computer, fiddled with a pencil, and—knowing that I was watching him—generally looked far more uncomfortable than I felt. Besides, Paul was sitting right there with me; Clyde could take all day as far as I was concerned.

When Clyde finally ventured into the conference room, he greeted me smugly. Again, I didn't care.

"Sorry to hear that *thing* you were doing didn't work out," Clyde said. "Messy ending there, eh?"

I flinched.

"Sorry," he said. "Poor choice of words."

"It's okay," I said.

"So..." He leaned over the conference room table as if we were going to share a secret. "What happened?"

"Well..." I began, pausing for effect, "I would love to tell you, but I am working closely with the FBI to help them wrap up the case. They've *requested,*" I said with air quotes, "that I not discuss the case publicly, so..." I pantomimed locking my lips shut and throwing away the key. This had become my new approach when asked about the Wimbys and the scene on Riven Rock. The canned answer served two purposes. First, it allowed me to avoid discussing it, and I really didn't want to discuss it. Second, it gave the impression that I was playing an integral part in an FBI investigation, immediately boosting my cachet. I would love to brag that the line and its logic were my inventions, but I would be lying. They were pure Cricket.

"Understood," Clyde said. He leaned back in his chair, crossed his legs, and laced fingers over one knee. "So, what can I help you with, Hollis?"

I could feel Paul nod encouragingly as the meeting had finally reached its launching point. "Honestly, Clyde. I don't think it's what you can do for me but what I can do for you."

Clyde uncrossed his legs and rolled his eyes. "Hollis. I appreciate that—"

"Hear me out," I interrupted. "If you're not persuaded, I'll promise to leave you alone."

He cocked his head.

"What have you got to lose, Clyde?" Paul offered.

Like a Roman emperor sparing the life of a gladiator, Clyde shrugged and gave me a thumbs-up.

From that moment forward, I scared the ever-loving feces out of smug Mr. Bostich. I explained how I used a CryptoWallet account to hack into the RemoteToken server and eight bank accounts I did not own. I showed him my FBI dossier—redacted, of course—and illustrated how I could have used the portal to steal money if I had wanted to. By the time I was done, it was Clyde who looked to be suffering from gastrointestinal issues.

"How long did all that take you?" he asked.

"A week," I said. "I was going slow to make sure you guys didn't notice."

He shook his head. "Can you fix these issues?"

"Yes, I can."

"How much will it cost me?"

Per usual, I had not thoughtfully considered the business aspects of my proposal before this moment. My goal was to validate the *concept* of Fogbank Consulting—to prove that someone would hire me. But Clyde was now ready to discuss the dollars. "Well, I—"

"I've proposed a three-year consulting agreement," Paul interrupted.

I froze. This was news to me.

"Go on," Clyde said.

"We pay Hollis at the same rate we were paying him before he was fired, plus the thirty percent salary bump we all got after the capital raise," Paul continued.

My eyes bugged. Paul was completely ad hoc, off script, and on the fly! And thank God, because I would have asked for a fraction of his suggestion and said *thank you* if I got it.

"He's not an employee; he's a contractor," Paul added. "I'll manage his work. It will be project based with specific deliverables."

"And this?" Clyde said, waving my redacted dossier like a flag. "What becomes of this?"

"He's agreed to sign a nondisclosure agreement," Paul said. "The only people who will ever see that document are the FBI."

Clyde smiled; that was precisely what he wanted to hear. "Terrific—"

"But," Paul interrupted, "to sign the NDA, Hollis demands that the three-year consulting agreement be fully guaranteed. I explained to him that this was a big ask, but he informed me that this term was nonnegotiable."

Clyde unsmiled and drummed his fingers.

I kept my face expressionless. Paul didn't need my help, and if I spoke, I was likely to ruin his fantastic improvisation routine. *Go along to get along*—Cricket's long-ago advice rang in my head like a trumpet. All this time, I'd been looking for a way to appropriately deploy this wisdom, and now I finally understood how. I smiled and kept my mouth shut.

"You think this is a good deal, Paul?" Clyde finally asked.

Paul nodded. "I think these holes need fixing, and if anyone found out about this, we would get murdered."

Again, I flinched.

"Sorry," Paul said. "Poor choice of words."

Clyde swiveled a full three-hundred-sixty-degree circle in his chair. "Fine," he said, slapping the table and standing. "Paper it."

He walked around the table to me and offered his hand. "It's good to have you back, Hollis."

# Chapter Fifty-Four

As with her first visit, Agent Randall showed up at my front door unannounced. She was alone this time, dressed in jeans and a hoodie and driving her own bright red Mini Cooper, not the Bureau's black Chevy Suburban. I froze, instinctively afraid I had done something wrong.

"At ease, Mr. Crawford," Agent Randall said. "It's a Saturday; I'm in jeans. How many more disarming signals can I send?"

"Call me Hollis," I said, breaking into a smile.

Cricket came to the front door to greet our visitor and invited her inside. Isabel said a sheepish hello; Trip asked her to scribble an FBI badge on his cast.

"Do you have a few minutes to talk?" Agent Randall asked.

"Sure," I said, recognizing that this would not be a family conversation. "Would you like to go to my office?"

"God no," she said, shaking her head at the thought of my grungy gar-office. "I'm hungry, and I'm buying. Just tell me where we should go."

Cricket gave wide-eyed Agent Randall a goodbye hug, and the two of us climbed into her Mini. I directed her to Santa Barbara's Funk Zone and my favorite food in town: Mony's Tacos.

"You're telling me that the best Mexican food in Santa

Barbara is next to a strip club?" Agent Randall asked, perplexed by Mony's proximity to Santa Barbara's Spearmint Rhino *Gentlemen's Club.*

"Just wait," I said.

We ordered at the counter, took our complimentary, fresh-from-the-fryer tortilla chips, and ventured to the eclectic buffet of salsas, where Agent Randall got her first hint that Mony's was not your average taqueria.

"Pistachio salsa?" she said.

"Just wait," I repeated.

We pounced on one of the rare open tables and set upon the chips like a couple of vultures. "Officially," Agent Randall said, licking her fingers, "I am not here."

"Okay."

"We haven't spoken," she continued. "You haven't seen me."

"Okay," I repeated. "It's nice not to see or speak to you."

"With that out of the way," she said, sliding an eight-by-ten photo across the table, "tell me what you see here."

The scene was the base of an unnamed ski resort in the fall. Such resorts all look the same to me, so initially I had no idea where the photo had been taken. But in the background, I noticed a tower in the center of a plaza. On the tower was a large clock surrounded by advertisements written in a language I didn't know. While I couldn't read the words, the clock was digital, displaying date and time down to the hundredths of a second. I didn't need such specificity to grasp the important takeaway. The clock's date revealed that the picture was recent, taken only two weeks prior.

Atop the tower was a symbol that needed no translation: the Olympic rings. I thought back to the day the FBI told me that the $217 million that had once been in Zurich, Switzerland, before journeying to Iran had been cashed out in gold at a bank in Moscow.

Thanks to that memory, I knew where this picture had been

taken. Sochi, Russia: the only Russian city to ever host the winter Olympic Games.

"Sochi, Russia," I declared, looking for my gold star.

"Very good, Hollis, but this isn't the geography bee. What else do you see?"

Reluctantly, I turned to the part of the photo I had been frightened to acknowledge: the people. It didn't take long for me to answer. "Vlad and Agent Daniel Andrews," I said.

"I think we've established that he's not an FBI agent," she said. "That's partial credit. Now look closer. Examine the faces. Tell me what you *see*."

My brow furrowed. I was failing a test I did not understand. Again, I turned to the photo. Of course, I had known for a long time that *Agent Daniel Andrews* was just a placeholding identifier for a man whose name I did not know. But when I saw his Hollywood-leading-man face, it was hard for me to think of him by any other possible name. Here he was yet again, seemingly caught midsentence, his hands gesticulating in the air. Short, muscular, aviator sunglasses, dangerously attractive; I saw Agent Andrews every time my doorbell rang.

I retrained my eyes on Vlad, pictured listening to his photo mate with his hands in his pockets. As I remembered from my prior encounter, Vlad was wearing a trench coat, his white-blond hair was slicked back, and his handsome features were clouded by a perpetual scowl. To complete the ensemble, a cigarette once again dangled from the corner of his mouth.

What more was I supposed to see? What bound them other than greed and sociopathy? My eyes scanned their faces left to right; right to left. Again. Again. Again.

And then I saw it.

They were short of stature. They were extremely attractive. They had the same large, wide-set eyes in various combinations of stone and emerald. The shape of their mouths, the crinkles at the corners of their eyes, their snub noses: all the same.

They were family.

I looked up, my eyes wide, but said nothing. Agent Randall recognized my expression. "Indeed. The man you knew as Agent Daniel Andrews has been identified as Pavel Petronovski, Vladimir's son."

I shook my head. "How did you get this picture? Are you working with the KGB?"

Agent Randall choked on a tortilla chip. "Please, Hollis," she said when she finally recovered. "The KGB will work with the FBI on the day Satan buys a snowmobile. These pictures are courtesy of some good old-fashioned spy work. Back when the Russians hosted the Olympics, they put up cameras everywhere for the television broadcasts. Some special operatives masquerading as giant slalom aficionados bugged them and—so far—they've been undiscovered. We got lucky this time. Facial recognition software identified Vladimir and—thanks to some serious elbow grease—we discovered Pavel."

"Discovered?"

Agent Randall sighed. "The sad truth, Hollis, is that we know very little about Vladimir Petronovski. Family members, associates, spouses, mistresses, lovers, children: normally we would be able to tell you how he likes his eggs cooked. But, to date, Vladimir Petronovski has stymied those attempts. Pavel here is a breakthrough. We are hoping it leads to more."

The air rushed out of my balloon. I had naively assumed the FBI was something akin to all-knowing. They might not nab all the bad guys, but they certainly knew who they were. That Vladimir Petronovski had been so clever as to keep them in the dark about information as elemental as his family members scared me.

At the same time, I couldn't help but tip my hat to the Petronovski clan. If there was one person guaranteed not to pick up on their genetic tie in time to make that information useful, it was me. If Cricket had been with me on the fateful days when I met Vladimir and Pavel, she would have seen the resemblance, but I didn't. From my perspective, the study of people's faces has always been a fruitless venture. I don't notice the subtle shifts in expression and manner that others perceive as informative, so I miss the opportunity to store away details about how their noses wrinkle when they laugh or how their eyebrows twitch when they are irritated. Within the *fog,* all of that is white noise.

I returned to the photograph, seeing the two men again with fresh eyes. Now that I perceived their familial relation, I could not unsee it; it was so plain I felt foolish. But something else gnawed at me about these two blood relatives. With their rhyming images on display, I was struck by the sensation that the faces of these two men were not my only memory of these features; I had seen them in someone else.

Our burritos arrived, and I set the photograph aside, still unsettled by the feeling that I was once again missing an important detail thanks to my *fog.* Agent Randall had followed my lead and ordered adobada with rice, beans, onions, cilantro, and a sprinkle of cheese wrapped in a large flour tortilla and then grilled. She availed herself of a fork and knife for the first bite. "Holy strip club!" she said.

"I know."

She put the knife and fork down and picked up the burrito with her hands. "The whole time we were hanging out in your spider cave, we could have been eating this?"

"Sorry," I said with a smile.

"You should be," she mumbled with her mouth full.

We sat in relative silence for several minutes, enjoying our food as the line outside Mony's swelled with the weekend tourist crowd. With three-quarters of her burrito inhaled, Agent Randall finally set it down and caught her breath. "Well," she said, "since I am not here and not speaking with you, I'd like to unofficially ask for your help on something."

"Yes!" I said a little too enthusiastically. As morbid as it sounded, I missed my time at the cool kids' table, working with Agent Randall and her colleagues.

"Since you're a software guy, you can appreciate what we are up against. The breakthrough with Pavel Petronovski was huge. Before, we were searching digital footprints using Vladimir as the only common link. The addition of Pavel's image and profile exponentially increases our reach. But if we're going to finish filing out Vladimir's extended family tree, we're going to need more."

"More is indeed better," I said.

"That's brilliant," Agent Randall said, rolling her eyes. "Can I write that down?"

"Sorry." I raised my hands in surrender.

"When you recounted the day Pavel Petronovski and team showed up at your house," she continued, "you told us that you saw the outline of a fourth person sitting in the Sprinter van."

"Yes," I agreed. "Someone kind of small, someone who made the outline of the seat itself look big. It had to be Vlad, right?"

"At the time, we believed so," Agent Randall said. "But after scouring our sources and utilizing our best intelligence, that theory has been ruled out. On the day Pavel Petronovski visited you, Vladimir was captured on video at a café in Istanbul. Someone else was in the front seat that day."

I put my hand over my mouth.

"With Vladimir eliminated from the sweepstakes," she said, "we are looking for other candidates. Is there anyone—*anyone*— you can think of who could have been in the Sprinter that day?"

I was shaking my head before I had a chance to speak. The events of those days had been on replay in my head ad infinitum, and no one outside the usual suspects had popped onto the screen. I rummaged through my mental inventory: dead, missing, tall—no one fit the bill. "I'm sorry," I said. "I can't think of anyone."

She nodded as if she already knew my answer but had to ask. "What about photographs? We've likely collected every digital image of Vladimir and Pavel Petronovski that has ever existed, but the more we add to the collection, the greater our knowledge. We've added every image of Cyrus Wimby from press clippings, your corporate website, and Cyrus's prodigious social media accounts to the catalog, and our computers are crunching those now, but still, we need more."

I squinted, trying to think of how I could help. "Those are all the places I would look as well," I said. "I'm not sure what more I can—"

"Did you take any photos of the Wimbys? Any shots of their dinner parties? Any pics with ExOh investors?" she interrupted.

I shook my head. "I'm not really a photograph guy."

"Shocker," Agent Randall said. "But there are loads and loads of such pictures online. Who was taking all these photos?"

I rewound the tape in my head. As Agent Randall said, I recalled photos of Cyrus giving his speech at the Central California Economic Summit, him with investors, him at the Entre Nous opening, him, him, him. And, of course, there was a group photo from every dinner party the Wimbys hosted, including plenty of photos of the Epicurean delights themselves. All the business photos went on ExOh's website, and all the entertainment ones went on Cyrus's social media.

I frowned. "Genevieve took the photos," I said. "She was like Cyrus's handler. She was always trying to help him promote himself and ExOh. And she loved posting photos of his wine and her desserts."

Agent Randall pursed her lips. "What about your wife? We've already gone through everything she's posted online, but I'm wondering if she has anything private that she would be willing to share?"

"I can go through her iCloud," I said. "What specifically am I looking for?"

"Anything," Agent Randall said. "Anything at all. But specifically, we have zero digital images of Genevieve and Priscilla Wimby. Cyrus was a regular bon vivant, and we're mining that data now, but adding Genevieve or Priscilla could be a boon. Genevieve might have socialized with Vladimir's wife or mistresses. Priscilla might have had a playdate with the child of another foot soldier in Petronovski's army. Hell, Petronovski might sponsor a book club. Who knows. But adding either of their faces to our database might help."

My eyes drifted skyward as I tried to find the memory of a two-dimensional photograph of Genevieve or Priscilla. Had I seen one anywhere? Surely Cricket had snapped a photo at some point. Sadly, I felt like Genevieve's and Priscilla's faces had already faded to the recesses of my brain, even as I struggled to keep hold of them. "I'll look," I finally said. "We've got to have something."

"Thank you," Agent Randall said, rubbing her face and sighing. "I know it's an invasion of your privacy, but it's in your best interest."

"What do you mean?"

She closed her eyes. "Look, Hollis. I've got to be straight with you. Despite my early optimism, we haven't made the progress I'd hoped for. Petronovski's guys are good. They have not yet stumbled..."

My heart rate anxiously ticked up.

"The truth is, you should be dead already."

The uptick double-timed. I placed my remaining burrito back on its plate; I was no longer hungry.

"The good news," she said, "is that they appear to be long gone at this point. And now that we have digital intel on them, Vladimir and Pavel Petronovski will never safely enter the United States again."

My heart rate slowed from chased-by-a-tiger to running-the-forty-yard-dash.

"But it's the ones we don't know and can't track," she continued. "Those are the ones that have me worried."

Back to being chased by a tiger, I managed to nod as if death threats were an everyday occurrence for me. "Do we need surveillance? The witness protection program? Should we move, or—"

She raised her hand. "Not yet, Hollis. There has been no threat. In the eyes of the FBI, you are not in danger. I am only relaying this message because you're a smart guy who might notice something that the rest of the world misses. I'm asking you to keep that radar tuned and sharp. While I think it's surprising that you're still alive, I also think that the fact that you *are* still alive makes it unlikely that the bad guys will bother reaching out to you again. You are yesterday's news; they don't need you anymore."

The fact that the bad guys didn't need me anymore was hardly reassuring from the perspective of me wanting to live a long, torture-free life.

Agent Randall finished her burrito and the remaining chips, running a finger around the pistachio salsa container to siphon out the final drips, the news of my potential demise having no effect on her appetite. I folded my napkin and placed it on the table; I, on the other hand, had not eaten a bite since Agent Randall told me to watch out.

"You going to finish that?" she asked, pointing to my half-eaten burrito.

I shook my head.

"Let me get a to-go box," she said. "I'll lop off the end and share it with Agent Quinton. He's a taco man, but I think this might swing his vote."

I couldn't help but smile.

# Chapter Fifty-Five

In time, my mind no longer fixated on Cyrus, the blood, his disembodied fingers, or the fact that everyone involved with his murder was still roaming free. Instead, when my thoughts wandered back to Riven Rock, I thought only of Genevieve and Priscilla. Were they still alive? Were they being treated well?

I also no longer thought of myself as the cause of the fall of the house of Wimby. Cyrus had brought that on his family. But I wished I could have stopped him without inadvertently causing bloodshed. I wondered at the eerie timing that brought Pavel Petronovski—aka Agent Daniel Andrews—to my doorstep at precisely the moment when I was most vulnerable to being fooled. How many pieces had to fall in place for those events to occur in such a narrow, precise window? The odds were staggering, yet it happened.

As I promised Agent Randall I would, I scoured Cricket's iCloud account for photos of Genevieve or Priscilla, but I found none. I pressed Cricket as to why she had no photos of them, and she told me I was crazy; of course she had photos. But when she took her own tour through iCloud, she also found none. Dumbfounded, she retraced her memory and concluded that Genevieve had always been so quick to whip out her phone, snap photos, and share them, Cricket never felt the need to take her own photos. It was a disappointing outcome; both because I couldn't help the FBI and because, without the benefit of a photo, we would all eventually forget what Genevieve and Priscilla had looked like during the brief time in which our lives were intertwined.

Most days, I didn't think about the Wimbys at all, returning my mental energies to productive endeavors. With Fogbank Consulting now a legitimate business, thanks to Paul, I was busy doing work I loved and collecting actual cash compensation: two revolutionary changes in my life.

One of my most pleasant discoveries was that being an independent contractor instead of an employee was like running a marathon at 60 percent of my actual weight. Without the tedious team meetings, lunches with colleagues, coffee breaks, and annoying office mates—see previous discussion of my residence *in the fog*—my efficiency was off the charts. I was getting paid more and working less. I was happier. This efficiency opened the door for Fogbank Consulting to add new clients. Why not shoot for the moon? I thought, as I targeted Agent Willows and the FBI. True to his word, Agent Willows and I had a meeting scheduled for just after the New Year.

As the calendar rolled to November, Trip was ready to return to Montecito Union Elementary. On his first day back, in what was now our family tradition, we traversed the short distance to MUS on foot, with me pushing the wheelchair. As Isabel, Cricket, Trip, and I scooted up San Ysidro toward the campus, other parents honked in approval.

When we reached campus, I turned to wheel Trip toward his classroom as always, but Cricket pulled my sleeve, directing us toward the school's central courtyard. I froze. The courtyard was home of the Flag Day ceremony where I'd first met Cyrus and Genevieve. I didn't want to go back there. I pulled; Cricket pulled harder. I reluctantly gave in.

As we spilled from the breezeway into the courtyard, we were met with a sudden chorus of cheers. *Welcome back, Trip!* signs hung from the exterior of the school's auditorium. A three-deep throng of parents cheered and hooted. Students, led by the principal and superintendent, leapt to their feet for a foot-stomping rendition of Queen's "We Will Rock You."

*Wait a second,* I thought naively. I knew Trip loved that song, but how did they know? Apparently, while I had been busy feeling sorry for myself and judging everyone else, Trip had been making friends.

Isabel took over as Trip's chauffeur and wheeled him into the mass of clapping, stomping students; soon, he was mobbed.

I'm not sure when I began to cry, but by the time I realized that Cricket was squeezing me breathless, I could feel the droplets slaloming down my cheeks to splash on her shoulder. Trip was not the only one to receive a hero's welcome that day. While students surrounded his wheelchair, parents surrounded Cricket and me, joining in our hug.

The great irony was that I'd always believed it was an accomplishment that would give me the necessary sense of worthiness to feel at home in Montecito. How could I have been more wrong? I had accomplished nothing; I had been a party to more destruction than creation, and some of the people in this crowd were themselves victims of that destruction. Yet, on that day—surrounded by those who barely knew me and couldn't care less about my professional qualifications or net worth—I finally felt the connection. It had been there all along.

# Chapter Fifty-Six

In winter, those who inhabit gar-offices earn their stripes. Of course, there are plush garage offices in Montecito, those with track lighting, automatic doors, and insulation. But they don't really count. Those deluxe imposters are to gar-offices as glamping is to camping.

That year, Montecito's winter came early and lingered long. Yes, I recognize that forty-five degrees is hardly winter by most US standards, but when you're working in an uninsulated shed that retains only the air temperature you are trying to avoid—heat in the summer and cold in the winter—forty-five degrees makes for very uncomfortable typing.

Cricket bought me some fingerless gloves, and I dug through the attic to find an old wool hat, a scarf, and a space heater. My computer was particularly upset by the frosty conditions, often stalling inexplicably and whining at high volume. Nevertheless, I pressed onward, boosting my internal temperature with coffee, tea, and hot water with lemon, until my bladder burst and/or the air warmed sufficiently to strip off the layers.

As Christmas approached, my first project for CryptoWallet was nearly complete. Working with Clyde through Paul was an absolute joy, and the work showed it. Already the scope of my assignment was expanding. If only we had learned of this professional arrangement sooner. Then again, I'm not so sure the old me would have appreciated what the new me knows. Perhaps this painful, devastating journey was a necessary prerequisite.

The first semester at Montecito Union Elementary would be over in a few days. After the holiday break, Isabel would begin her final semester of elementary school. After that, junior high, high school, college, marriage, motherhood, and retirement; God, I was getting old.

Trip continued to recover swiftly. He graduated to a walker ahead of schedule, and in the spring, he would have plastic surgery on his partially missing ear. In the meantime, he had begun wearing the costume ears of Spock. Where I would have grown my hair longer and hidden the injury, he chose to magnify it, purposely diffusing any silly second-grade meanness. His proud ownership of this setback was yet another example of Cricket's resilience in his DNA.

Holiday cards were rolling in daily, and thanks to Cricket, we had hundreds to look forward to. Our family card had been mailed out just after Thanksgiving. I had proposed a photo taken on the day of Cricket's pier-to-pier triumph, but Trip wanted the cover shot to record this as the year of his shattered leg. At his request, we staged a hospital room and dressed as doctors and nurses; we made light just as everyone seemed to desire.

Between Christmas and New Year, we would have our annual Holiday Card Oscars dinner party with Paul and Jenny's family. This family tradition predated our children, but now they were active participants. Of course, there was an Oscar for *best card*, but there were also ones for *best photo* and *best inscription*. Conversely, there were awards for *worst card*, *worst photo*, and *worst inscription*, the latter usually being awarded to a braggadocious, multiple-page letter written in third person. Even from the vantage of the *fog*, I knew better.

On this particular day, I was working away in the gar-office when Cricket walked in to drop off the day's mail delivery for my initial review. Her day at the Storytellers was complete; soon she would pick up the kids and be Mom again. She kissed me on the cheek as I typed, then dropped the mail beside my computer.

"Do you know anyone getting married?" she asked.

I waited for the punch line of the joke.

She pointed to the stack of mail and raised her eyebrows. "There's a card in there addressed to you. It's thick. Feels like a wedding invitation."

"Both of my friends are already married," I replied.

She patted me on the head and laughed.

I went back to work, trying to solve a nettlesome coding problem that had vexed me all morning. After several failed iterations, I took a pee break that had been calling for at least an hour, then turned to the mail.

The bills were all in my name, unfortunately, so mail-opening was often a gloomy process of tallying the looming account debits. But on this mid-December day I also received my paycheck, delivered in the form of an actual paper check, since I was a consultant and not an employee. I was grateful for this trivial inconvenience; at least there was something to make the account balance go up.

Last in my stack of mail was the card Cricket had highlighted. There was no return address, and the postage was foreign, in an alphabet I didn't know. Greek? Polish? I took a second to admire the weight of the card. If this was a wedding invitation, it was going to be a gala event. I slid my pointer finger under the lip of the envelope and ripped. Immediately, a faint aroma sent my mind reeling. I knew that scent, didn't I? But from where, and why? Then it hit me.

It was star jasmine.

My shaking hands rattled the envelope's jagged lip. With each shake, more wafts of star jasmine emerged. Carefully, I reached into the envelope—as if I were afraid something inside might bite —and pulled a cream-colored, handwritten card.

Other than the star jasmine scent, the thick stock was

elegantly simple—no monogram or return address, just an embossed navy border. Crisp print handwriting covered both sides, pulling my eyes toward the line that began with my name.

> Dear Hollis,
>
> You cost me someone I loved. Yes, he was arrogant and sloppy and—to his demise—greedy, but still, I loved him.
>
> My father is grateful for your discovery and finds it comical that my husband's hand-chosen stooge was the one to unearth his treachery. I, however, find no humor in your meddling. While my daughter and I have accepted our sacrifice as an offering at the altar of family, acceptance does not equal forgiveness. Rest uneasy, Hollis Crawford. I will collect your debt.
>
> On the back of this card, you will find the key lime pie recipe you hounded me for so many times. But try as you may, you will never replicate my pie. Like several other men you and I used to know, you lack an ingredient essential to both key lime pies and a long lifespan: loyalty.
>
> Until we meet again ...

# Chapter Fifty-Seven

When I finished reading the note for the fifth time, I fell backward into my chair, panting as if I'd run a race. How could I have been so wrong?

While I stared at the rafters of my gar-office, a scene stolen from a movie played out in my head. In it, I was a detective standing before a corkboard filled with suspect and victim photographs connected by threads of yarn. One by one, I disconnected the yarns that labeled Genevieve a victim and took a fresh look at my many mistaken assumptions.

Central to my failure: I miscast Genevieve Wimby. She was omnipresent at every turn in our winding journey, but I mistakenly viewed her as the supporting wife, not the kingpin. I applied the stereotype that women are less vicious, less conniving, less manipulative, less evil, less *bad* than their hairy, lumpy, XY chromosome counterparts. When I discovered a crime, I jumped to the conclusion that the man had perpetrated it without giving the woman her due. Shame on me.

*No one is eating steak until someone slits that cow's throat,* Genevieve once told me. A wiser man would have understood at that moment who was really in charge. But I missed it.

I missed that it was Genevieve, not Cyrus, who organized the dinner parties and cultivated the invite list. She cased the networks at Lotusland, the Montecito Club, the Polo Club, the Valley Club —wherever the wealthy comfortably congregated—found her marks, and lured them to innocent gatherings, where Cyrus would work his magical schtick.

I missed that it was Genevieve who wrote Cyrus's Central California Economic Summit speech, and thus, it was she who invented the fictitious ExOh Global Relief Charities. That evil masterstroke alone tipped more than $20 million into her pocket.

I missed the implications of the frantic call from Fiji when it was Genevieve, not Cyrus, who knew which of the RemoteToken fobs was needed to access the bank account—the one with the yellow fingernail polish, not the one with red tape.

I missed the meaning of Genevieve's mocking rhetorical question of Cyrus: *You want to man the helm?* As in, *You want to be in charge, Cyrus?* Perhaps Genevieve had decided that this particular confidence scam demanded a man front and center. Or perhaps it was simply Cyrus's turn to quarterback their evil enterprise. Either way, Genevieve had the gumption to question Cyrus's facility to lead, and thus, presumably, she had the ability to take it away.

And with Genevieve's reference to her *father* and *family*, I now realized what was gnawing at my subconscious on the day Agent Randall showed me the photograph of Vlad and Pavel Petronovski in Sochi, Russia. I had indeed seen Vlad's and Pavel's features on another person: Genevieve. They were *all* family, and as Genevieve made clear in no uncertain terms, Cyrus had been sacrificed in an offering to that family.

Like a puzzle nearing completion, missing pieces fell faster into place. The lack of photographs of Genevieve and Priscilla? This was not an accident. Vladimir Petronovski had successfully hidden the reaches of his evil enterprise from US law enforcement for many decades, and he had taught his children to do likewise. Genevieve had always jumped at the offer to take up a position *behind* the camera to avoid being *in front* of it. For the rest of us, the distinction was unnoticed. Pictures were taken and shared—no one spent time analyzing who wasn't in them. Meanwhile, as if setting up Cyrus for the fall from the beginning, Genevieve plastered his image everywhere. Given the size of Cyrus's ego, I doubt he even noticed.

With Genevieve's loyalties fully revealed, I once again revisited my metaphorical detective's corkboard and unwound more yarn of previous assumptions.

The *real* FBI and I had assumed that the person in the front seat of the Sprinter van on the day of the *fake* FBI's visit to my home had been Vladimir Petronovski. But—thanks to a video feed from Istanbul—we had since learned otherwise.

Now I knew the truth: The shadowy figure swallowed by the Sprinter van's front seat that day was Genevieve Wimby.

Vladimir had not needed to come back to the United States to find out what Cyrus was doing with his money. He had his son and daughter to do it for him. With Pavel playing FBI agent and Genevieve in the Sprinter whispering into his earpiece, they talked me into revealing everything I knew about Cyrus's money movements.

What tipped Genevieve off that something was amiss and that I might have the answers? To understand that, I carefully unwound the yarn connecting Priscilla's would-be kidnapper— the man in the woods—to Vladimir. Vlad had no problem offing his son-in-law, but he would not have hurt his flesh-and-blood granddaughter. No, whoever was behind the man in the woods was not a Petronovski. No doubt, it was someone involved in Cyrus's secret side hustles—someone who felt they had not received an adequate slice of Cyrus's illicit pie.

Even as I grieved in the hospital with Trip, Genevieve was connecting the dots. Who would be so bold as to attack her family? As she wrote in her note to me, Cyrus was arrogant and sloppy; she instinctively knew that he was the root cause. So, Genevieve graciously allowed me a whole five hours after Trip had been released from the hospital before she and her brother descended upon me in disguise to learn what I knew.

My mind flashed back to the moment I revealed to Pavel—posing as Agent Daniel Andrews—that Cyrus had stashed $217 million in the bank account in Zurich. I pictured Pavel sitting across from me, his head cocked, contemplating that news. I recall thinking at the time that his expression looked like that of a man listening, and now I know I was correct. In his ear was the voice of his sister relaying that—to put it kindly—Cyrus had been less than forthcoming about the size of his treasure chest. Double-crossing the Petronovski family? What was Cyrus thinking?

With my evidence gathered and my dossier written, Pavel and Genevieve knew that time was running out. At some point, I would have followed up with the *real* FBI, and all the money would have disappeared. They had to act quickly, and they needed Cyrus's assistance.

I could only imagine what came next. Was Cyrus given an option of cooperation? Did Genevieve participate in his torture? Did Cyrus die thinking that—despite all he had done—Genevieve's love was enough to save him?

I shuddered.

As the story crystallized in my head, I found it harder to believe that the Petronovski family had let me live. Judging by Genevieve's note, it was not a unanimous decision. I guess my old pal Vladimir felt he owed me—the hand-chosen stooge—a favor for having discovered and revealed the treachery of his son-in-law. In a twisted way, I guess I also owed Cyrus a thank-you. Had I only discovered that ExOh itself was a scam, I probably would have died in a surfing accident like Landon. But since I inadvertently discovered the much larger scam victimizing innocents *and* Vladimir, I was allowed to live.

For now.

I wondered why Genevieve bothered writing to me and outing herself as a member of the Petronovski family when the working assumption was that she was unrelated and dead. Wasn't hers the perfect cover story to continue a life of crime outside the spotlight? I would never know the answer to that for certain, but I suspected she felt so invincible inside Mother Russia, with the loyalties of her family intact, that the risk was worth the reward. As Agent Randall of the FBI made clear, there would be no cooperation from the Russian government; Genevieve was untouchable. Further, Genevieve knew she had no digital footprint, obfuscating the FBI's attempts to track her should she leave the comforts of home. And last, but definitely not least, how could Genevieve set up shop inside my head and ruin every good night's sleep for the remainder of my life if she didn't reach out and let me know she was alive and in a vengeful mood? Well done, Genevieve. Mission accomplished.

With a pile of yarn at my internal detective's feet, I began to reconnect the nodes on my corkboard. Vladimir Petronovski was the executive chairman of this fraud and murder enterprise. Genevieve Wimby was its chief executive officer. Her brother, Pavel Petronovski, was its chief operating officer. Cyrus had been only the vice president of sales. Important but disposable.

There was more to discover for sure, but for the first time since the bloody scene on Riven Rock, I understood enough to appreciate how close I had been to pure evil. The Petronovski clan was as cold-blooded as they came. Certainly, Cyrus had been a fool to cross them, but for Genevieve to sanction, and perhaps even participate in, the torture and execution of the father of her child took some serious dedication to the cause. That's CEO material if I've ever seen it.

Cyrus was dead; Priscilla was alive. The $217 million in stolen money was safely in the Petronovski coffers. Everything else was just noise. As soon as my heart rate settled back below 150, I would call Agent Randall to see if she thought that the witness protection program was starting to sound like a good idea.

In the meantime, I would not be making any key lime pies.

Cricket knocked on the jamb of the open gar-office door, interrupting my trance. "Why don't you walk with me to pick up the kids?" she asked, waving a hand in front of her nose. "I think you need some fresh air. Smells like you have a rodent for an officemate."

I nodded, standing to stretch my back. "New candle," I groaned. "Rose petals, cedarwood, lavender, and mouse droppings."

She laughed as I innocently placed Genevieve's card back in its envelope and the envelope on the top of the teetering stack of notes and materials that compiled my Wimby files. I would tell Cricket about it, of course, but not right now. I wanted one more carefree walk with my wonderful wife, through our beautiful neighborhood, to our amazing community school; one more chance to take it all in before a whirlwind of uncertainty descended on us all.

"Shall we?" I said, offering Cricket my arm.

She took it, and together we walked from my gar-office into the crisp blue Montecito sun.

Until we meet again, Genevieve. Until we meet again.

# Acknowledgments

Montecito, California, is indeed the paradise presented in this story. As such, the town has a long history of attracting con artists, grifters, and scoundrels to its sun-drenched shores. A dozen such stories inspired *Montecito*, including that of a Montecito man I knew all too well. The Securities and Exchange Commission won judgment against him for fraud, even as he fled the US for safety overseas. While it was easy to delete the sordid experience from my resume, I doubt I will ever fully expunge it from my head.

*Montecito* would not exist without the love and support of my wife, Maggie, and son, Thatcher, who encouraged me through thin and thinner. My sister, Jenny Cordell, gave me more pep talks than a Hall of Fame football coach. And Mariano and Eileen Catbagan were my heroes at every step of the journey—it is one of the great blessings of my life to have married into their family. None of us knew what I was getting into when I started this topsy-turvy joyride, but I am forever grateful that the word *quit* never crossed my family's lips.

I am indebted to Gwyn Lurie, Tim Buckley, and Zach Rosen of the *Montecito Journal* for serializing this story in the pages of their newspaper and on their website from July 2022 to February 2023. The popularity of the story and the positive feedback from readers was a fresh log on my waning campfire.

In that same vein, it was my friend Jen Hulford who read a draft of *Montecito,* loved the story, and introduced me to Gwyn, suggesting that *Montecito Journal* readers would love it, too. I know Jen will claim that her effort on my behalf was *nothing*, but oh what a nothing it was.

I can't imagine this story without the deft editorial skills of Kristen Weber. Kristen possesses that rare ability to encourage even as she raises the bar. In addition to helping me turn my manuscript into a worthy novel, Kristen has a deep appreciation for the many, many ways in which the journey from writing a manuscript to becoming a published author is a soul-sucking, confidence-obliterating nightmare. As such, she has lifted me from the pits of despair on many occasions. If you're a writer in search of a multi-skilled developmental editor, I can't think of anyone better.

Karen Folsom's astute illustration of a suited, wine-swilling shark atop the Montecito Union schoolhouse adorned the first installment of the *Montecito Journal's* serialization of this story and instantly became its mascot. I am grateful to her for illustrating the cover of this book as well.

This book was blessed by a talented team of experts who found and corrected my grammar and logic mistakes and then beautified the final product. Thank you to Penina Lopez for her copyediting brilliance, Elaini Caruso for her eagle-eyed proofreading, and Angie McCauley for her interior formatting prowess. All three are pros through and through.

I also owe a special thank you to Chris and Brian Wolf. I wrote the first drafts of this novel in the attic of their home on Humphrey Road, a place my family and I will always cherish.

It is heartening how relationships are rekindled when you announce to the world that you've written a book and need readers. Pat Findley provided me with more than ten thousand words of critique, correction, and praise. In the end, she gifted me something more valuable than all her feedback combined. Berta Nance and Judy Martin rallied a tribe of teachers from my hometown high school to provide me with more love and support than I deserve. And University of Alabama luminary Cathy Randall revived her role of angel on my shoulder, just as she had from long before I knew that I needed an angel.

Since I took the long way from manuscript draft to published novel, the number of people who provided words of encouragement during the journey are legion, and all of them deserve a thank-you paragraph of gratitude. Unfortunately, that is impossible, so I hope listing their names will suffice to document my unending appreciation. Daniela Matson, Courtney Ellett, Kelly Moler, Kay Findley, Emily Boon Cardwell, Pat Albee, Martha Kerekes, Cheryl Harris, Susan McCoy, Pearl Bloom, Carol Dailey, Gerry Sinzdak, Ben Wiener, Dana Seltzer, Rick Hulford, Patrick MacMichael, Jeff Becker, Dawn Fitzgerald, Candy Hedrick, Shelley Van Zant, Chris and Emily Johnson, Michelle Fivel, Stacy and Erik Smith, Misha Cooper, Macy McGinness, Mary Firestone, Lucy Firestone, Jenn Paul, Erin Hollander, Jill Smith, Lorraine and Hugo Gerstl, Chuck Genuardi, John Marr, James Brandon, John Elliott, Margot Heiligman, Bill Williams, Angie Billon, Jen and Warren Rissier, Jennifer Rameson, Jud Easterwood, Kevin McCall, Sean Shirley, Jay Cashmere, Marla Griffith, Tara and Jason Schaeffer, Leslie Hunt, Becky Brooks, Tara Tucker, Brandon Hess, Scott and Jane Whitman, Laura Davis, Landon Lack, Elizabeth Rao, Tamah Halfacre, Ryan Siemens, Mark Silverberg, Cliff Wyatt, Molly Weiner, Ron Graves, David Taylor, Betsy Friedl, Tal Avitzur, Kristen Salontay, Eric Crabtree, Jin and Jennifer Lee, Brad Singer, Heather and Philip Dracht, Susan Akins, Judy Alban, Casey Miller, Annette Robson, C. Lee Kirch, Deborah Ward, Katey O'Neill, Sasha Leiterman, Lindsey Berrett, Michael Hamilton, Jeanette Nadeau, Kim Holmquist, Chris Cochrane, Pam McIllwain, Dave Sims, David Krouse, Phil Myers, Steve Calk, Kenan and Betsy Siegel, Nina Merzbach, Matt Farrah, Hamish Davidson, Tim Smith, Simon Rees, Greg Cooper, Trip Thomas, Greg Hutton, James Lewis, and Andrew Banks.

That this book exists in any published format seems a miracle to me. Eleven years ago, I left the world of steady paychecks to pursue the dream of becoming a novelist. Full of ego and delusion, I dove in, certain I could elbow grease my way to success.

Failure after failure ensued. I began again. And again. And again.

A few times, my breakthrough was so close I felt the breeze on my face as it brushed by me. Many more times—embarrassed, heartbroken, and disillusioned—I was ready to give up.

But each time my hope reservoir drained to its dregs and logic begged me to throw in the towel, an uncanny gust of wind arose and pitched me forward. Looking back at those tipping points, it is clear they were not the result of happenstance, irony, or luck. They were a divine hand carrying me through my weakest moments, leading me to this ultimate one. So with my last acknowledgment, I want to thank God for gracing me with the strength I did not have, the endurance I could not summon, and the favor I did not deserve. For years, I bushwhacked through the publishing industry jungle mistakenly believing I was in search of an outcome, when my soul only yearned for the journey. And with the journey at its end—and my eyes open wide to the blessings of its trials—I am humbled to offer this work as my gift to Him.

If you are reading these final words, you are one of the dedicated few who strive to squeeze every penny's worth out of your purchases. Bravo and thank you. It has been my honor to share this story with you. I hope it made you laugh, shake your head, and, at least once, surprised you.

# ABOUT THE AUTHOR

A native of Tennessee and a graduate of the University of Alabama and the Stanford University Graduate School of Business, Michael lives in California with his wife, Maggie, and son, Thatcher. *Montecito* is his first published novel. You can read about the inspiration for *Montecito*, download the book club guide, learn about his forthcoming work, or just say hello at www.bymichaelcox.com or with the QR code below: